Praise for
Beneath a Marble Sky

"[A] spirited debut novel. . . . With infectious enthusiasm and just enough careful attention to detail, Shors gives a real sense of the times, bringing the world of imperial Hindustan and its royal inhabitants to vivid life."   —*Publishers Weekly*

"Jahanara is a beguiling heroine whom readers will come to love; none of today's chick lit heroines can match her dignity, fortitude, and cunning. . . . Elegant, often lyrical, writing distinguishes this literary fiction from the genre known as historical romance. It is truly a work of art, rare in a debut novel."
—*The Des Moines Register*

"Agreeably colorful . . . [with] lively period detail and a surfeit of villains."
—*Kirkus Reviews*

"An exceptional work of fiction . . . a gripping account."   —*India Post*

"Highly recommended . . . a thrilling tale [that] will appeal to a wide audience."
—*Library Journal*

"The story traces the construction of the mausoleum against the background of war, rebellion, and religious fundamentalism, and it contrasts the opulence of the court with the severe poverty of the citizens."   —*Daily Variety*

"*Beneath a Marble Sky* is a passionate, lush, and dramatic novel, rich with a sense of place. John Shors is an author of sweeping imaginative force."
—Sandra Gulland, author of the Josephine B. Trilogy

"[A] story of romance and passion . . . a wonderful book if you want to escape to a foreign land while relaxing on your porch swing."   —*St. Petersburg Times*

continued . . .

Beneath a Marble Sky

A LOVE STORY

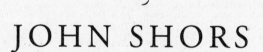

JOHN SHORS

NEW AMERICAN LIBRARY

New American Library
Published by New American Library, a division of
Penguin Group (USA) Inc., 375 Hudson Street,
New York, New York 10014, USA
Penguin Group (Canada), 90 Eglinton Avenue East, Suite 700, Toronto,
Ontario M4P 2Y3, Canada (a division of Pearson Penguin Canada Inc.)
Penguin Books Ltd., 80 Strand, London WC2R 0RL, England
Penguin Ireland, 25 St. Stephen's Green, Dublin 2,
Ireland (a division of Penguin Books Ltd.)
Penguin Group (Australia), 250 Camberwell Road, Camberwell, Victoria 3124,
Australia (a division of Pearson Australia Group Pty. Ltd.)
Penguin Books India Pvt. Ltd., 11 Community Centre, Panchsheel Park,
New Delhi - 110 017, India
Penguin Group (NZ), cnr Airborne and Rosedale Roads, Albany,
Auckland 1310, New Zealand (a division of Pearson New Zealand Ltd.)
Penguin Books (South Africa) (Pty.) Ltd., 24 Sturdee Avenue,
Rosebank, Johannesburg 2196, South Africa

Penguin Books Ltd., Registered Offices:
80 Strand, London WC2R 0RL, England

Published by New American Library, a division of Penguin Group (USA) Inc. This is an authorized reprint of a
hardcover edition published by McPherson & Company. For information address McPherson & Company,
P.O. Box 1126, Kingston, New York 12402.

First New American Library Printing, June 2006
10   9

Copyright © John Shors, 2004
Readers Guide copyright © Penguin Group (USA) Inc., 2006
All rights reserved

The quotation from *The Essential Rumi* is reproduced courtesy of the translator, Coleman Barks. The quotation of
the Upanishads is from *Ancient Wisdom and Folly*, translated by Sanderson Beck and reprinted by his permission.

REGISTERED TRADEMARK—MARCA REGISTRADA

New American Library Trade Paperback ISBN: 0-451-21846-9

The Library of Congress has cataloged the hardcover edition of this title as follows:

Shors, John, 1969–
Beneath a marble sky : a novel of the Taj Mahal / John Shors.
p. cm.
ISBN 0-929701-71-2
1. Mumtaz Mahal, Empress, consort of Shahjahan, Emperor of India, d. 1631—Fiction.   2. Shahjahan,
Emperor of India, ca. 1592–1666—Fiction.   3. Memorials—Design and construction—Fiction.   4. Jahanara,
Begum, 1614–1680—Fiction.   5. India—History—1526–1765—Fiction.   6. Taj Mahal (Agra, India)—
Fiction.
I. Title.
PS3619.H668B46 2004
813'.6—dc22   2004001374

Set in Adobe Garamond
Designed by Ginger Legato

Printed in the United States of America

PUBLISHER'S NOTE

This is a work of fiction. Names, characters, places, and incidents either are the product of the author's imagination or are used fictitiously, and any resemblance to actual persons, living or dead, business establishments, events,
or locales is entirely coincidental.
   The publisher does not have any control over and does not assume any responsibility for author or third-party
Web sites or their content.

for Allison

There is considerable evidence that the Mughal emperor, Shah Jahan, built the Taj Mahal in memory of his beloved wife, Mumtaz Mahal, and that not long after its completion a power struggle ensued among their sons. Scholars disagree on numerous matters, however, including the construction methods of the Taj Mahal, the identity of the principal architect, and even how long the mausoleum took to build. Answers to these questions are obscured by rumors, politics, and the sands of time. Insofar as is possible, then, the larger story surrounding *Beneath a Marble Sky* is historically accurate; to dramatize these epic events I have taken necessary liberties with events, customs, and the actions of characters drawn from history. It is, therefore, a work of fiction.

PART 1

The minute I heard my first love story,
I started looking for you, not knowing
how blind that was.
Lovers don't finally meet somewhere,
they're in each other all along.

RUMI

*I*n the early days, when I was still an innocent girl, my father believed in perfection.

Once, musing over his empire, contemplating the splendor he had created, he composed a poem. On the vaulted ceiling above his Peacock Throne he had an artist inscribe in gold, "If there is a paradise on the face of the Earth, it is this, it is this, it is this." Simple words from a simple man. But how true they were.

Sunrise over the Yamuna River has often prompted me to think of Paradise. From the broad shoulders of the waterway I have cherished the sights before me as I might cherish the face of my lover. This morning's views are as inspiring as ever, especially after having been away in hiding for so long. To my right sprawls the magnificent Red Fort. Opposite, awash in the sun's blood, stands the Taj Mahal, neither soaring as a falcon might, nor cresting like the sea. Rather, the mausoleum arches upward, strong and noble, a gateway to the heavens. Knowing that the Taj Mahal was built for my mother is among my greatest joys, and my most profound sorrows.

Today, I am not alone. My guardian, Nizam, patiently rows our boat across the Yamuna. Behind our craft's bow sit my two granddaughters, Gulbadan and Rurayya. No longer girls, each is a wondrous incarnation of my daughter. Looking at them, I think that time has moved too swiftly, that just yesterday I was stroking the soles of their diminutive, untested feet. My love for my granddaughters is even stronger now than it was then. When I see them I feel as if I'm moving forward into places harboring no regrets, no memories to remind me of my scars, those thick welts upon my mind and body.

Gulbadan and Rurayya giggle, whispering as young women do—of the men who strut before them, of the dreams they encounter. When I was their age my emotions were more closely guarded. On the surface I acted much the same, but within the thick shields of my defenses dwelt more troubled thoughts, thoughts often dominated by a yearning for acceptance, a need to feel worthy.

One of the few people ever to glimpse my insecurities was Nizam, who now propels us to the far bank, away from the prying ears about the Taj Mahal. A banyan tree perches at the river's edge, its tendrils kissing the water. To me, banyan trees resemble giant spiders, their branches falling straight to the ground like legs. Nizam ties our boat to a limb that plunges below the ripples, then nods to me. This confirms what I'm thinking—that we're isolated and quite safe here, safe enough for Gulbadan and Rurayya to hear the story of how they came into being.

The tale has never been told.

"My darlings," I begin, loosening the sash that bites into my stomach. "Your parents brought you to Agra, and asked me to travel here, because they believe you're old enough to entrust with a story." I pause, my eyes seeking theirs. My will at this moment is stronger than my emotions, and I force my voice to harden. "Are they mistaken?"

Gulbadan, the eldest, toys with a silver ring, which is as gouged as the planks of this decrepit boat. "What do you mean, Jaha?"

"I mean, can you keep a secret? Or are you like magpies on a water buffalo's back, chatting away when hawks are about?"

"But why must we be so careful?"

"Because, child, like any woman who has defied men, I have enemies. And such foes would pay dearly for this knowledge. With it, they would see to your undoing, as would the Emperor."

"The Emperor?" Gulbadan asks, her ring forgotten. "Surely we can't concern him."

"Emperor Alamgir," I say, "may Allah forgive his crimes, would wrong you if he heard these words."

"But he doesn't even know us. He—"

"He knows much, much more than you realize, Gulbadan. And just because he hasn't met you hardly means he's incapable of hurting you."

"Hurting us? But why?"

My sigh lingers and is beset with regret. "You must understand that we . . . that we kept secrets from you. Secrets I'll share today but that would have been perilous in your possession if you had been too young to safeguard them."

Neither granddaughter stirs, hardly seeming to breathe as a temperate breeze tugs at their brown robes. Simple garments also house my aged flesh, though I'm disguised as a Persian woman, shrouded in black shapeless cloth and wearing a veil that covers my face. When we met this morning, Gulbadan and Rurayya asked why I was in disguise. My lie about avoiding a greedy moneylender came easily, and as with all the other lies, my granddaughters believed me instinctively. But I'll no longer deceive them. Not after today.

"What do you know of the Emperor?" I ask.

Gulbadan glances at the Red Fort. "People seem to . . . well, either they worship or detest him. Though most detest him."

I start to speak, but Rurayya interrupts me. "Why is he so cruel, Jaha?"

How many times have I pondered this question? A hundred? A thousand? "The Emperor," I reply, still somewhat unsure of the answer, "always felt unloved. He was mistaken, but that didn't matter, for when you deem yourself unloved your world is quite cold. At first there's jealousy, then bitterness, then hate. And hatred soured Alamgir's heart."

"But how do you know anything about his heart?" Gulbadan wonders.

I hesitate, for Gulbadan and Rurayya have been misled all their lives. How would I react, I ask myself, if our places were switched? Can a young woman cope with the idea that she isn't a commoner, as she's been raised, but in fact, an emperor's descendant? Will my precious granddaughters understand the need for our deceit? "Alamgir was once called Aurangzeb," I respond finally, meeting their stares. "And I was once his sister."

Nizam nods at these words, the shadow cast by his turban bobbing upon Rurayya's lap. "His sister?" Gulbadan repeats in disbelief.

I lean toward my girls. "We had to protect you. If we hadn't—"

"But how can you be his sister?"

"Because my blood, your blood, Gulbadan, is as royal as his."

"Royal? Your father was a fisherman like mine. He died in a storm!"

"My father was the Emperor. Emperor Shah Jahan."

"Impossible!"

"But true."

Gulbadan's mouth opens, but no words spring forth. Her brow tightens. Her hands drop. "Then why do you live so far from Agra? And why . . . why have you lied to us? Why have we never known?"

"When you hear my story you'll understand."

"But why are you telling us now?"

"Because of your little brother."

"Because of Mirza? You make no sense!"

I have rarely seen Gulbadan so upset. Rurayya acts as if she's awakened to find a sky with two suns. "Please, please listen, Gulbadan. If you listen, I'll explain."

My granddaughter stifles an angry reply. I close my eyes for a moment. Silence descends and I question the prudence of our decision. They are certainly old and wise enough to keep my terrible secrets. But will events ever unfold that might warrant such knowledge?

"I must tell you of our family's history, and of the beliefs of those long since dead," I say. "I can't predict the future, but in these troubled times the throne may someday be empty. If it becomes so, and if Mirza is willing, he might try to claim it. He's far too young to hear of these tidings today, but you are not. Mirza will need your guidance if he wishes to follow the path his great-grandfather so carefully laid—a path that led to peace and compassion, not the war and mistrust surrounding us today."

"But Mirza's just a boy," Rurayya replies.

"Yes, but someday he will be a man, just like your father. And his blood is royal. Such blood could reunite the Empire again. It could save thousands of lives. That is why I ask that you listen well. You'll tell this story to your brother when he's ready. You will all need to know it if Mirza ever seeks the throne."

Gulbadan glances in the direction of her distant home. "And until he's ready we will deceive him, just as Mother deceived us?"

"She only deceived you, child, because she loves you."

"But Mother never lies," Rurayya says.

"You'd lie, Rurayya, to protect your children. And so would you, Gulbadan. You'd tell a thousand lies, tell them each and every day for however long you needed to. And then, one morning, a morning much like this, you would tell the truth."

"What is the truth?" Gulbadan demands.

I point across the river to the Taj Mahal. "Do you know why it was built?"

Heads turn toward the marble teardrop. "Emperor Shah Jahan," my youngest granddaughter replies, "created it in memory of his wife."

"In memory of our great-grandmother?" Gulbadan asks.

"Your great-grandparents lived extraordinary lives," I answer. "Nizam knows their tale. Your parents know it. But we're old, and the story must not wither with us."

Rurayya looks at Nizam, who confirms my words with another nod. My friend is as honest as a mirror, and Rurayya's lips part in wonder. "How did it begin?"

Though I am no teller of tales, my words rise swiftly, as I hope my story will temper their misgivings. I explain that before my father ever knelt on the Peacock Throne he was called Khurram, and that as the Emperor's favorite son he was expected one day to rule the Empire.

"When Khurram was fifteen," I continue, "he visited a silk and beads shop. Inside, sitting atop a cushion, was my mother, Arjumand. Her beauty, the poets claimed, could make rainbows weep with envy. And so Khurram was drawn to her. He asked the price of a bead and she curtly replied that it wasn't a bead, but a diamond. When she told him it cost ten thousand rupees, a sum she believed he could never afford, my father quickly produced the money.

"The next day, Khurram went to his father, begging for Arjumand's hand in marriage. The Emperor himself had encountered the madness of love and could hardly deny it to his son. Yet he decreed that five years must pass before Khurram could wed Arjumand. Meanwhile, in a marriage of political convenience, my father was wed to Quandari Begum, a Persian princess."

"Why do we never hear of her?" Gulbadan asks, her anger ebbing.

"Because my father's other wives were as important to him as camels," I answer, subduing a smile, pleased that Father placed Mother far above her predecessors. "He supported them in the harem but rarely saw them."

"And after five years," Rurayya wonders, "what happened?"

"Khurram and Arjumand were married under a full moon, within a ring of golden torches. Afterward, the air was so thick with Chinese rockets that night became day."

Gulbadan's gaze swings from the sky to me. "But, Jaha, where's the danger in this?"

"The seeds of danger were sown soon afterward, when I and my brothers and sisters were born. We caused the Empire to plunge into war, a war pitting brother against sister, father against son."

"You?"

"I was a part of it," I reply slowly. "I tried to do what was best, but one can win only so many fights."

"What fights? What did you do?"

"Hear me out, Gulbadan, and soon you will know everything."

CHAPTER I

My Awakening

W iping yogurt from my lips, I stared about the imperial harem. The living quarters for select women of the Red Fort, the harem was a collection of apartments, gardens, alleys, retreats, terraces and grottoes. No man—except the Emperor, his sons, guests and eunuchs—was allowed into this world.

The Red Fort itself was like a lacquered box seeming to contain an infinite number of compartments. Inside the perimeter of the citadel lay the common grounds, mostly bazaars, mosques, temples and courtyards. The fort's interior, segmented by stout sandstone walls, was comprised of more private spaces consisting of apartments and halls and stables. And within the very heart of this dizzying network stretched the imperial harem.

Thousands of women, supported by the Emperor, lived here. His wives, the most powerful of the harem's residents, had their own palaces within its walls. My grandfather, Emperor Jahangir, had seventeen wives—a small number compared to his ancestors' spouses. Though Grandfather was dead, his wives, being much younger, still remained with their scores of servants. Most of the harem's women were concubines, who excelled in the arts of dance and music and were always available for the Emperor's delight.

The royal children also lived within this realm. I didn't like it much, for the harem was a house governed by strict rules. My brothers could do almost anything, but girls enjoyed little freedom. In Grandfather's day, female guards from the Amazon enforced the rules. Father had long since sent them away, but dozens of other guards were forever eager to keep me in check.

The harem's rooms were equal parts magnificence and comfort. Floors were strewn with cashmere carpets and silk cushions, walls with paintings and mirrors. Alleys were lined with manicured trees, thick enough to discourage the gaze of outsiders, but not a gentle breeze. Everywhere fountains spouted from square pools brimming with untroubled koi.

I now sat in an immense room along with servants and concubines, as well as my brothers and sisters, who were swathed in silk and precious gems. A pair of wet nurses fed my twin sisters, who were only a few months old. Behind them stood my mother, Arjumand. Like most noblewomen, she was dressed in a short-sleeved shirt tight enough to seem a second skin and tucked into a loose skirt that fell to her ankles. Over her shoulders draped a cashmere shawl.

Everyone in the room, save eunuchs, servants and lesser concubines, wore jewelry. Strands of pearls adorned necks while precious stones dangled from each ear. Fingers and toes bore coveted treasures—gold and silver rings inset with sapphires and emeralds. Ladies' nails gleamed in a variety of colors, though usually scarlet.

Beauty was revered within the harem, and most women competed to invent new clothing trends. The most fashionable ladies wore sections of peacock feathers or garlands of flowers in their hair. Others preferred colorful veils pinned atop their heads and falling back upon their shoulders. These veils were typically silk, though in cooler months women might wear pashmina, woven from the purest and most refined of cashmere fibers.

Eunuchs and servants dressed in simple tunics and robes. Standing next to Mother was her slave, Nizam. Though he'd been her attendant for almost a hundred moons, I had only recently learned his tale, which belied his gentle disposition. For when Nizam was only five, a Persian warlord slew his parents and seized him. Boys taken as slaves were usually castrated, but the warlord wanted his underlings someday to fight and was unwilling to stunt their growth with the gelding knife. Nonetheless, he ensured Nizam never pursued women by removing a portion of his manhood that Mother wouldn't describe to me.

For several years thereafter Nizam had lived in a sprawling tent, serving the warlord's women. When he pleased them, he was fed. When he failed to accede to their demands, he was beaten. His fate might have been forever unchanged, but praise Allah, our forces had overrun the Persians. Glimpsing Nizam's bruised face, Father plucked him from the captured slaves. And though he became Mother's slave, she cared for his wounds and treated him kindly.

Nizam had seen fifteen summers. Two years his junior, I was wise enough only to realize what little I knew of the world. I understood some things, such as my love for my parents, and their adoration for each other. The latter was easy, as Mother was often at Father's side, regardless of whether at war abroad or at court conducting the Empire's affairs. Whenever possible, my brothers and I accompanied her, for Mother wanted us to witness our father's kingship.

Of my four brothers, Dara had always been kindest to me. He was just a year older and we were closer than many women in the harem thought appropriate. Setting my yogurt aside, I moved nearer to him. "Can you help me?" I asked, handing him an intricate bamboo cage the size of Father's fist.

He looked up, pausing from his calligraphy. "You distract me too much, Jahanara," he said. "Father will be unhappy with my work."

"Unhappy with you? That I've never seen."

Dara shrugged my words aside, taking the cage. Inside perched a trio of crickets, which often sang to me at night. Some bamboo at the top of the cage had cracked, and I feared that my crickets would escape.

"How did it break?" he asked.

"It's old."

He winked, a seemingly effortless action I wished I could duplicate. "You'd better be more careful with your pets. I wouldn't like to step on them." I started to speak, but Dara continued, "After all, Hindus believe we can be reincarnated into such creatures."

I failed to see how I might become a cricket, but stayed silent. Dara knew much more about such subjects. Mesmerized by the dexterity of his hands, I watched him wind a silk thread about the splintered bamboo. In the time it would have taken me to draft a brief letter, he finished.

"Would you like to be a cricket?" he wondered.

Dara took such thoughts seriously, so I didn't comment on the boredom a cricket must endure. "Perhaps if I lived in a banyan tree, where I might explore."

"What about in your cage? Would the views be as interesting?"

"You think I should free them?"

"Do whatever you want," he replied, and then tugged affectionately at my hair. "Which I know you will."

As much as I enjoyed the crickets' music, I realized Dara was right. For I lived in a cage of sorts, and few vistas existed indeed. "Would they prefer trees to grass?" I asked.

"Trees, I believe," he said, returning to his studies.

I'll leave them on a high branch, I thought, where no cats or lizards can vex them. While I debated which tree in the harem might make the best home, I noticed Aurangzeb had been watching us. The third of my four brothers, Aurangzeb was often sullen and remote. When our eyes met, he looked away. After hanging my cage from a teak post, I walked over and knelt on the carpet next to him. "Want to play a game?" I asked, for I was weary of books.

Aurangzeb snickered. "Games are for girls."

"You could teach me polo."

His laugh was high-pitched, reminding me of a squealing pig. "Polo?" he echoed scornfully, his delicate face tightening.

"I'd like to learn—"

"Only men play polo."

Though Aurangzeb was merely eleven, I held my tongue. For a moment, at least. "Then why do you play?" I asked innocently.

His lips clamped shut and he pounced on me, digging his knees into my chest. I knew he wanted me to whimper and plead, so I struggled to remain silent, scratching at his legs. Barely stronger than he, I succeeded in knocking him backward. Aurangzeb flung himself at me again.

"Dara!" I cried, suddenly fearful of Aurangzeb's temper.

My older brother moved swiftly to intervene, but before he could reach us, Nizam, who despite his youth seemed infinitely stronger, grabbed us each by the neck.

"Cease your foolishness!" Mother commanded tersely. She stood behind Nizam, arms clasped. "The harem is a place for study and relaxation, and is hardly fit for a brawl. If fighting is what you crave, find yourself a pile of mud outside."

"But she—"

Mother's glare silenced Aurangzeb. "Obviously, you both need a little sun. Shall we surprise your father?"

Before we could utter a word, she motioned for Nizam to free us. As he did so, she exchanged her shawl for a copper-colored robe, gathering it about her shirt and skirt with a purple sash. Bidding farewell to her friends, Mother led us from the room and proceeded down an adjacent alley. Her anger with me was apparent, for I had let Aurangzeb untether my emotions, a break of etiquette. To be truthful, Mother scorned such rules more than I did, but by wrestling Aurangzeb I'd flaunted them openly, giving no thought to my actions. Mother, on the contrary, disregarded rules only to serve a higher purpose.

A pair of guards opened the harem gates as we approached. Behind Mother and Nizam were my other brothers, Shah and Murad; Dara, Aurangzeb and I followed separately. Beyond the harem, the Red Fort fell into a riot of activity. We shared the cobbled streets with hordes of traders, administrators, warriors and priests. Almost everyone seemed in a hurry, darting into shops and mosques, stables and barracks. Far above us on the upper level, pavilions teemed with nobles and their servants.

The Red Fort nestles on the Yamuna. Encircled by sandstone walls fifty paces high and six paces thick, the fortress was the seat of my father's empire. Upon its flagstones strode nobles and slaves alike. Formations of soldiers drilled incessantly in its courtyards, while several hundred warriors stood atop the citadel's parapets. Cannons projected from the crenelated walls.

Hindus and Muslims bustled about, for under Father's rule the Red Fort sheltered both sets of people. Though we Muslims ruled Hindustan, we comprised a minority of the populace. Our position was thus somewhat precarious. As Father often maintained, only by treating Hindus with respect could we retain control.

I observed those of the other faith as we hurried past. Their women wore saris—single lengths of cotton or silk wrapped about the body until only hands and face remained unconcealed. Muslim women's robes were stitched and our outfits consisted of multiple pieces.

All of us wore sandals, and mine clopped my heels ceaselessly as I followed Mother. Piles of elephant and camel dung littered the way, and I had to eye the flagstones carefully. Normally, Nizam walked near me, but today, probably because of my fight, he remained by Mother. Though Nizam was often the victim of Aurangzeb's cruel tricks and might secretly agree with me about my brother's skills in polo, he was wise enough to guard his feelings.

Trudging through the Red Fort was like being a mouse on a ship. There were endless places to venture, accessed by twisting walkways and far-reaching stairs. Sandstone walls, clad with glazed tile, were often so high that I was unable to see what lay beyond them. Occasionally I would catch glimpses of towers and ramparts which shouldered warriors and rippling red banners.

I might have become lost, if not for the footsteps of Mother. Despite her purposeful gait, she exchanged greetings with many she passed. People often acted surprised when the Empress returned their compliments. But they shouldn't have—Mother was known throughout the land as one who dropped pearls into the tins of crippled beggars, or found homes for orphans. It seemed to me that much of Mother's happiness stemmed from helping those whom even commoners passed with disdain. A few times in the harem I had sipped from this cup of happiness when I was able to aid someone. The smiles of those I assisted warmed me.

Nodding to a pair of imperial guards, Mother paused as they opened a teak door leading into a massive structure, a sprawling room called the Diwan-i Am, the Hall of Public Audience. This chamber was much like our harem in its comforts and décor but even more splendid. The room's ceiling was covered with beaten silver, and its decorated walls enclosed a crowd of well-dressed nobles and warriors.

In the Diwan-i Am's center, atop his Peacock Throne, was Father. The throne was a raised dais bearing a cashmere carpet and a sizable red cushion embroidered with golden stars. Father always knelt on the cushion. Around him, twelve pillars supported the canopy. The pillars were inlaid with perfect pearls and the canopy was topped by a golden peacock. Sapphires coated its tail.

Gathered immediately below and in front of the Peacock Throne were high-ranking nobles. These mustached or bearded men wore silk tunics and strings of pearls. Several nobles carried muskets, while others boasted swords encased in jeweled scabbards. On either side of this assembly, servants used long poles topped with tear-shaped fans to cool Father and his audience.

More removed from the Peacock Throne, separated from the nobles by a gilded balustrade, stood officers of the army. A further balustrade, this one silver, divided these figures from several score of foot soldiers and servants, relegated to positions most distant from Father. Nobles, officers and soldiers wore tunics that fell below their knees and covered loose-fitting trousers. The jamas and paijamas were of brightly colored cotton or silk, the latter tightened about the waist by a sash.

As we entered the room, heads turned to regard Mother and shoulders straightened at her sight. I smiled at the reaction. Though emeralds, rubies and diamonds graced every spot of Father's throne, in Mother's presence men forgot such unimaginable wealth.

Quite simply, she was an orchid placed within a bouquet of poppies. She wore her robe tight enough to boast of the slightness of her body, which lacked none of a larger woman's curves. Rubies were pinned to her raven locks; her ears were contoured with pearls, and the lobes beneath carried emeralds set in silver. A golden hoop graced her nose. A delicate diamond necklace fell to just above her navel, and sapphire bracelets adorned her wrists. Like many noblewomen, she wore a miniature mirror on her forefinger so she could keep herself in order.

Mother's face never ceased to capture people despite its familiarity. Her bronze skin was soft and flawless, her lips sculpted. Her walnut-colored eyes were rounder than most of our people's, and her nose seemed somehow more tapered. If compared to her I knew I'd never be beautiful. My teeth were less straight, my eyes closer together. Yet we had the same skin and the bodies of the same ancestors. My brothers mixed her traits with those of our more average-looking father. The boys were slightly small for their ages, with thick hair and wiry muscles.

"You honor us with your presence," Father announced, rising. Broad in the shoulders as well as the waist, Father stepped down from the dais looking extremely pleased to see us. He wore a yellow tunic, a black sash and a crimson turban. His jewels were as plentiful as Mother's, though excepting a pearl necklace and a few rings, they were fastened to his garments.

Father said nothing of his children's arrival but smiled at each of us. I found comfort in his bearded face, which was round and fleshy. His nose had been broken long ago, and his chin was rather expansive. "You remind me, Arjumand, that this morning's business should end, for don't even leopards rest every now and then?"

From our left emerged a low voice. "Forgive my impertinence, my lord, but one matter can't idle."

"And what is that, Lord Babur?"

"A serious subject, with serious consequences."

I'd heard of Lord Babur from Mother and recalled him to be a powerful noble, though held in little esteem by my parents. A squat man, Babur was dressed in a silk tunic with lime and ivory stripes. A sword hung from his side. As was customary when seeking an audience with the Emperor, Babur touched his right hand to the ground. He then produced a gift that was proportional in value to his rank, as protocol dictated. I was close enough to Babur to see him hand one of Father's servants a decorative quill designed to compliment a turban. Jade and lapis beset the piece. The ritual complete, Babur nodded to his servants, who then pulled an old man to his feet. He was bound in chains, and his face was a mask of dried blood.

"What has been done to this man?" Father demanded.

"It's not what has been done to him, my lord, but what has been done to me." When Father kept silent, Babur continued, "This criminal owns a petty piece of land next to my fields. As petty as a fly on a wall. When his crops failed, he turned to what came most naturally to him. Thievery, that is. My guards caught him pilfering our storehouse, a capital crime."

I glanced toward the corner of the room, where two muscle-bound executioners stood motionlessly. A pair of waist-high wood blocks rested between them on a colossal slab of granite. The stone was grooved so that blood would drain into awaiting ewers. The blocks were stained and gouged from numerous sword strokes. Though Father was always reluctant to order a man's death, sometimes he had no recourse. Today he must have been fortunate, for the executioners' blades were bright and clean.

Father moved toward the accused, regarding him for a moment before asking, "Your name?"

The man, who must have seen many, many seasons in his field, lowered his head. "Ismail, my lord."

"A Persian name, isn't it?"

"Yes, my lord."

"Well, Ismail, what do you have to say for your crime, if indeed, you committed one?"

The man swayed, licking his lips nervously. "My lord, my sons had the honor of warring for you. My boys were proud to fight under your banner. They served you well, and they . . . my lord, I hear they died as men."

"Then the honor is mine."

"Thank you, my lord, thank you."

"But now, Ismail, you must speak against the charge."

"My lord, they were my only sons." The farmer waved a fly from his bloody nose. Sweat or perhaps tears glistened upon his cheeks. "Without them, I couldn't harvest my crops. My rice rotted to pulp. It still stands in my fields—"

"Laziness doesn't justify thievery."

"Be patient, Lord Babur," Father said. "Our laws entitle him to speak."

When the Emperor pointed at him, the old man cleared his throat. "My wife and I were starving, my lord. Starving night and day. I asked Lord Babur for food, but when he refused, I stole a sack of rice."

"So his words are true?"

"Yes, my lord."

Father returned to his Peacock Throne. He seemed to wander in thought as he stared at the underside of its canopy, which was inlaid with jewels arranged to resemble orchids. "The law calls for your death," he finally said. "But I've no desire to see a man executed who gave fine sons to the Empire. How can such a man be killed for a sack of rice?"

"He broke—"

"I'd rather, Lord Babur, pose the question to my wife, than to one so involved with the matter."

Around the room, nobles whispered excitedly. Though almost all believed women had no minds for such issues, each was aware that the Emperor often asked his wife for advice. Despite being unversed in politics, I understood that Mother stood in a difficult position. She'd never seek the farmer's execution but could hardly offend a noble such as Babur.

Mother walked over to the farmer, beckoning me to follow, surprising me with her request. He bowed deeply to us. "Take his hands, Jahanara," she said. "What do they feel like?"

The nobles' whispers increased at her question. Yet I didn't look to our audience, but to the old man. When he raised his hands before me, I held them in my own, tracing his palms with my jeweled fingers. "They're hard, Mother," I replied, my heart pounding mightily. "As hard as teak."

"The hands of a thief or a laborer?"

"A farmer, surely."

Babur bristled but didn't dare interfere. Mother smiled at me before turning to her husband. "My recommendation is simple, my lord. Ismail shall forfeit his land but not his life. He'll sign a deed ceding his farm to Lord Babur." The accused slumped, for by relinquishing his farm he'd ensure himself a life of destitution and beggary. However, Mother was not finished. "But, my gardens wilt these days, and I need someone with experience in such matters to rescue them. Could you be that someone, Ismail?"

The farmer fell to his knees. "Truly I am, my lady. Truly."

"Then I've found my gardener."

"And my wife?"

Mother laughed unreservedly, as if only I were present. "She'll join you in the Red Fort, of course, for what man could think straight without his wife's advice?" When she winked at the Emperor, a few nobles, despite their feelings, smiled.

Father chuckled, for an instant looking like an ordinary husband and not the Emperor of Hindustan. "Is this decision acceptable to everyone involved?" he asked, spreading out his hands.

Babur, who must have been thrilled by the prospect of obtaining more land, nodded. "Indeed, my lord. As always, the Empress finds the best solution."

"Then the matter is put to rest, as are these tedious affairs."

At his announcement the room emptied of nobles, servants and warriors. Ismail was released by Babur's men and hurried forward to kneel before Mother. Beaming, she grasped his raised hands, then asked Nizam to find the man quarters near her gardens. After they departed, she whispered to Father, "Babur may be a worm, but I could think of no other way to quench his anger."

Father slipped on his jeweled sandals. "Thank you, my love. You've saved me once again." His eyes dropped to me. "And you were perfect, my flower! Perfect! Were you nervous, like a horse standing above a cobra?"

"Yes, Father. Though I'm but a mouse."

He laughed, turning to his sons. "A pity your mother wasn't born a boy. She'd be a splendid emperor. Better, by far, than I."

Three of my four brothers grinned. Aurangzeb, however, tugged on Father's tunic. "But the law says to execute criminals. Now he may steal from us." Aurangzeb, as usual, spoke loudly. To me, it seemed he was forever afraid of not being heard.

Father's smile vanished, as it often did when Aurangzeb said something he didn't approve of. "Perhaps, but he has earned the right to prove his worth."

"How?"

"He sacrificed his sons to the Empire. Had I done the same, I might expect my emperor to show me gratitude, not the executioner's sword."

"But he broke the law."

"Is a sack of rice worth a man's life?" Dara probed, for he almost always held the opposite view to Aurangzeb's.

"The law is the law."

"And it spoke," Father said, fondly patting Dara's shoulder. "He lost his farm, which went to his accuser, thanks to my brilliant girls." Father took Mother's hand and stepped away from his throne. "Come, we've talked enough of this. And as we've talked, my stomach's done nothing but growl like a wounded lion."

When I turned to follow them, I noticed Aurangzeb glaring at me. His eyes made me feel uneasy, and I wondered what I had done wrong.

LATER THAT EVENING, I rested on a tiger's pelt and gazed at the Yamuna. Above me rustled the heavy flaps of the canvas pavilion our servants had pitched near the riverbank. The scarlet structure possessed no sides, though stout bamboo poles supported its roof. An immensely broad and thick carpet, depicting marvelous arrays of roses, ensured the comfort of whoever lounged within the pavilion. Furs, cushions and gossamer silk blankets covered parts of the carpet.

As I rubbed my hand on the tiger's intricate fur, I wondered how a beast could be so beautiful and so frightening. Beside me sat Mother and Father, each clad in dusky garments. My baby sisters slept next to them under pashmina blankets. Much as I loved my sisters, I could rarely enjoy their company, for their nursemaids saw to every need. These women were quite protective of their duties and certainly did not want my help.

On the opposite side of the pavilion, a troop of dancers and musicians amused us. Versed in the Kathak art of storytelling, these entertainers recreated the famous account of my great-great-grandfather, Humayun, escaping from hordes of Afghan warriors. The tale was harrowing, for after defeating our forces the Afghans began slaughtering all our people— be they child, woman or man. Legend said that as the enemy overran our imperial guards, an attendant gave the Emperor a water sack. Inflated, the animal gut allowed him to swim safely across the Ganges. Thus, my great-great-grandfather was able to return years later and drive out the invaders.

Five men—with blood-spattered faces and naked chests—represented the Afghans. Another performer wore a pearl necklace, and clutched the inflated and leather-bound stomach of a horse to his chest. While musicians plucked upon sitars and beat against drums, the Afghan warriors chased the Emperor onto a wide bolt of blue velvet.

As the music quickened the dancers became caught in the river's currents and spun madly, flailing their arms about, while Humayun swam toward the opposite shore. When he finally stepped upon land, his pursuers fell, writhing atop the velvet, pulling it over themselves, disappearing beneath the river's blue waves.

We applauded the scene's conclusion vigorously. Though the Kathak was a popular art, which we witnessed almost every week, these men were among Agra's best performers. Father did them enormous honor by rising to give their leader, who had played the Emperor, several silver coins. Compliments were exchanged and then the sweating men folded their bolt of velvet and quietly left the pavilion.

Though I'd enjoyed the display, I glanced somewhat enviously toward the distant figures of my brothers, wishing that I could also be unaccompanied. Dara lounged near the river, his back against a magnificent cypress tree. He held an open Qur'an. On such nights Dara often read, though he studied the Hindu gods as much as the Holy Book of Islam, or any other matter. Father, an advocate of the arts, took pride in Dara's interests. In fact, they often shared sweets as they mused over architecture, poetry or music.

Happy cries caused me to lift my gaze. Shah and Murad, who seemed to find pleasure in each other and no one else, hunted carp at the water's edge with bows and arrows. Farther away, barely within hailing distance, Aurangzeb rode his gray stallion in circles. I might have ridiculed his polo skills, but Aurangzeb was a better rider than anyone his age. His mount was well behaved, as it should be, for not three moons ago I saw Aurangzeb beat it mercilessly with a bamboo rod.

Beyond Aurangzeb, who now drove his mount in twisting turns, were multitudes of our people. On the river, men returned from the muddied currents with boatloads of dying fish. Upon the shore, women mended nets or added colorful dyes to fabrics. Some families, much like ours, simply relaxed in the cool stillness of this autumn night.

"You were quite brave today," Father said softly to me.

"But I told the truth," I replied. "His hands were hard and he had to steal." Despite having last sat on Father's lap several years before, I felt an urge to do so. But my body was now too awkward, and so I dropped beside him. Around the pavilion servants lit torches to push aside the encroaching darkness.

Mother moved closer to us, leaning against the long, circular cushion supporting our backs. She reached over to reposition an emerald turtle pinned atop my veil. "Your beauty becomes you, Jahanara," she said. "But more important, so does your mind."

Though poets would never write of my face, as they did Mother's, I hoped to inherit a drop of her wisdom. "Truly?"

"I wouldn't say so if it were untrue."

Father leaned toward Mother to refill her wine goblet. I'd seen him do such tasks a thousand times, when even minor nobles had servants attend to these duties. Father, however, preferred to please Mother himself. And while most lords surrounded themselves with young concubines, Father chose to be alone with Mother. He was kind to his other wives but seldom visited them. Even at such a young age, I was keenly aware of the rare quality of my parents' love for each other, and often wondered if it was a blessing that I was destined ever to experience. It seemed impossible that I'd ever know such bliss, impossible that I might become worthy enough to merit a man like my father.

Weary, I closed my eyes. I leaned against Father, found the rise and fall of his chest comforting. He stroked my brow until the crickets' songs were loud and unbroken. Then he eased me onto a rug at his feet, placing a cushion beneath my head. When he kissed my forehead, I sighed and feigned sleep.

"Allah has blessed us with children," Father whispered. "So much pleasure in the making, so much joy in watching them blossom."

I'd heard of this pleasure before and fought my inclination to dream. Silence lingered, followed by the sound of a kiss. I opened my eyes a fraction and saw that their faces had separated but were only a finger's width apart.

"How is it," Father asked, "that my love for you does not lessen? My body stiffens with the years, my hands ache with the monsoon. Yet now, as I see you before me, I am struck only by joy."

"You married well," Mother replied mischievously. "If you hadn't found me, you'd be much older today. And I might still be selling beads to nobles, to greedy men only intent on pleasing their mistresses. To men who think with the wrong organ."

Father chuckled, his rumblings comforting to me. "The fools jest that I envy them, that I long for the women they hoard," he said, sipping his wine. "Do you think they could even fathom how I'd give up my empire for you, how without you by my side I'd be like a falcon with no wings?"

"You should have been a poet," she replied, smiling playfully, for Father delighted in words. "We'd starve, most assuredly."

"But, Arjumand, most poets write of pain, of misery, of want. I could only give verse to love, which most readers find a tedious subject. How could I write of hate, when I harbor none? Or of jealousy? Or of sorrow? No, it's better that the poets and philosophers debate these creations. They are not of my world."

"Nor mine."

"Then let them write, my love, while we live."

In the ensuing silence my heart beat strongly. And when they kissed again, I opened my eyes wider.

CHAPTER II

First Betrayal

Though Father may not have fully understood hatred or jealousy, one of his sons did. Yet it wasn't until four months later, slightly before the spring solstice, that I became fully aware of feelings Aurangzeb harbored, and of his capacity for treachery. Earlier, I had sensed his hostility mounting toward all of us: Aurangzeb wore his discontent as blatantly as the sword he'd started to carry. One day Dara would be the victim of his wrath, then I the next. We rarely deserved his scorn, but his outbursts came without warning.

I wasn't sure how to measure his moodiness, and once I told Dara that Aurangzeb reminded me of a bee. For how often had I been stung for no particular reason? Perhaps these troublesome insects believed me to be threatening, but I much preferred to watch them suckle nectar than incur their ire. Aurangzeb, in many respects, had a similar disposition. He drifted in his own world most days, but when he felt slighted whoever was near might get stung.

I experienced my first real wound on a warm afternoon.

My brothers and I had been studying intently in the harem. Mother surveyed Father's notes from a recent court session, while Nizam's hands fluttered rhythmically against a rosewood and deerskin tabla. The other women present gossiped quietly, drank wine, or plucked fruits from silver platters. Green and scarlet finches sang from gilded cages. The scent of opium lingered in the air.

I was expected to read widely, and a thick book rested on my thighs. The text was written in Persian, the official language of the court. Though we were now enemies with the Persians, they had profoundly influenced Hindustan. This inspiration began when my grandfather married a remarkable Persian princess, Nur Jahan, who thereafter fostered Persian culture within Agra's court. In all but title, Nur Jahan had, in fact, ruled the Empire.

Of course, I also spoke Hindi. I liked this unassuming tongue and used it when dealing with servants or the local population. Not many commoners could speak Persian, and most who could preferred Hindi.

Persian is certainly pleasing to the eye, often inscribed in graceful calligraphy that takes a lifetime to master. The text I was reading was one such masterpiece and concerned the history of our empire, boasting of the deeds of the emperors preceding my father. I memorized what each ruler had accomplished and the troubles he faced. Mother would test me later this evening, as she always did.

I was reading of my grandfather when I heard a distant muezzin's cries. I imagined him on a mosque's tower, filling the sky with his calls to prayer. As I set aside my book, many of the harem's inhabitants unrolled exquisite prayer carpets to stand upon. We prayed while standing, turned westward toward Mecca, with our palms facing the heavens. At certain times of prayer, we reverently bowed, touching our carpets with our foreheads. When the prayers ceased, we rolled up our carpets and continued with our activities.

I returned to my history, not closing my book until I knew the assigned pages like the patterns of my favorite robes. I then turned to Mother, asking her with my expression if she'd join me for a walk outside. She nodded and, accompanied by Nizam, followed me through the door.

"Who wrote the *Akbarnama*?" she asked abruptly.

The *Akbarnama* chronicled the life of my great-grandfather, Akbar, the most revered of our former emperors. "A writer, I think."

"Jahanara!"

"A writer named Abu'l Fazl."

Mother straightened my veil. "A simple answer would have been sufficient."

"Have you ever given such an answer?"

Her hands dropped and her face softened. She smiled, affectionately nudging me. "Only to please your father."

Our walk soon took us through a bazaar. Under its tents and canopies lounged dozens of vendors, tired men sitting behind iron scales, their tables brimming with dried fish, bolts of silk, sandalwood statues, incense and, above all, reed baskets heavy with spices. Hindustanis have always loved spices. If goat cheese or spinach wasn't drenched in curry or saffron, it would hardly be worth eating.

The scents of these seasonings mingled with smells lingering about each stall. Fragrances to savor abounded, fresh naan, roasting mutton, flowers, oiled leather, perfume. Less pleasant scents sometimes overpowered these wares, for within the towering walls no breeze removed the stench of sweat, of burning dung, of gunpowder, urine and caged animals.

Mother was polite enough to look at many goods, though she purchased only a pair of sandals for Nizam. As we left the bazaar she said, "You seem restless, Jahanara. Instead of acting so distracted you should simply ask your question."

How she could so easily read me was disconcerting. "Yes, Mother," I replied haltingly. "It's just that . . . well, we've done little but study these past days."

"And you propose?"

"My friend Ladli—"

"The child who helps in the kitchen?"

"She's going to the river later and asked if I'd join her."

"Today?" When I nodded, she paused, dust settling about her feet. "Only if you take your brothers. You should do these things together."

"But Aurangzeb is cruel to her."

"You won't have to swim with your brothers," Mother replied. "After all, it would be unseemly for girls and boys to bathe together." The sarcasm in Mother's voice was uncloaked. I was accustomed to such remarks, for she despised the confining customs of our society. While men pursued whatever game they desired, women were forced to act as shadows, hiding from the light, following only the movements of their husbands.

And how Mother abhorred shadows!

The Empress was one of the few women in Hindustan who could do almost anything she wanted. She didn't dress like a man, of course, but she spoke like one, unafraid to voice her true thoughts. Father indulged her behavior, and thus it usually went unchecked. I sought to be bold like her but worried more than she about offending my elders.

"We women must be cautious," she advised, stopping at a stand of lemons. She squeezed a few. "Dealing with men is like juggling hot coals. They're fairly harmless if you take precautions, but by Allah, they can burn you if you don't pay attention."

"Have you ever juggled coals?"

"No, but I juggle men every day. And I'm sure coals would be much less frightening."

We shared a laugh as we turned back to the harem, Nizam taking his usual place behind Mother. His hair was black, coarse and curly, while his face and nose were flat. Oddly, his right eye was somewhat bigger than his left. Still a young man, Nizam was already taller than many of Father's soldiers.

Whenever I looked at Nizam, he glanced away. Yet I often felt his gaze on my back. In many ways he was like an older brother, protecting me from dangers I was too young to discover. Though Nizam was her slave, Mother treated him sometimes as if he were my sibling. She abhorred that he had been maimed and made her thoughts well-known on the more common practice of castration. It was an ancient custom, however, for lords are leery of ungelded servants among their women. Her pleas for abolishment were ignored.

Mother was hardly one to retrace her steps, and she returned to the harem via the imperial workshops, known as the Karkhanas. An oversized courtyard housed hundreds of studios, which sheltered thousands of craftsmen, some of whom were Europeans and Persians. The complex reminded me of a honeycomb, as it was replete with narrow alleyways and circular structures. Artists and workers created weapons of every sort, colorful fabrics, silver drinking vessels, and jewelry for seemingly each part of the body. The most prestigious workshops contained bookmakers. Among these craftsmen were translators, painters, calligraphers, paper makers and gold leaf experts. They produced thousands of books each year, some even written in Portuguese, English and Chinese.

Mother wove through artisans, camels and bare-chested Hindu priests with equal ease. When at last we were beyond the Karkhanas, the alley widened so that we could stroll arm in arm. "We rarely take such walks anymore," she said suddenly. "I do miss them."

"As do I."

"Soon your father shall find you a husband, and then, I suppose, these walks will cease altogether."

A trace of sadness lingered in her voice. Her tone was infectious, for I replied gloomily, "But how am I to find love, as you did, if Father weds me to a stranger?"

She adjusted a diamond brooch in my hair. "Remember that many marriages of love begin as marriages of politics. Yours may be no different."

"And yet it could be."

Almost imperceptibly she dropped her head, which was Mother's way of nodding. "Sometimes, Jahanara, I wish that duty weren't such a sacred word," she admitted, slowing her pace. "But few words are more revered. Even if it is a weaker feeling than a mother's love for her daughter, men die for duty, and women . . . we women suffer for duty in more insidious ways. Our duty, just as those leading the Empire, is to follow whatever path is best for our people. And while marrying a silversmith might make you happiest, it wouldn't be best for Hindustan. For how could you help your people if you were to wield no influence?"

"I could live among them," I offered, trying to impress her with my insight, "and become their friend."

"As you should. But being a friend means sacrificing yourself. And as a woman of high rank, your opportunity to help others—one of your strongest opportunities, in fact—is to marry for political reasons. In doing so you strengthen your father's authority. You give power to his name and laws. And his laws, as you know, are good for our people."

"But don't we have a duty to ourselves?"

"We do. And I pray that you'll find love, as does your father. We found it and I wouldn't think to deny you such joy."

"Just the same—"

"Believe me, Jahanara, your husband shall be chosen with care. He won't be a lout, though he'll be important to the Empire's fate. As his wife, you'll have power. Substantial power. And, I hope, between all that duty and power you can come to love each other."

"But how can one love a stranger?"

To my surprise, she smiled. "And what of me?"

"You?"

"Certainly. Your father might have loved me from first sight, but do you think I cared a jot for him? He was but a spoiled prince, no more familiar to me than white hairs upon my head. Why would I want to marry him, when I dreamed of kissing Ranjit?"

"Ranjit? But I've heard nothing of him."

"Hush," she whispered conspiratorially. "Another tale for another time. But do you hear my message, Jahanara? If your father and I were thus introduced, and are now so inseparable, then why must your fate be any different?"

I had no answer and told her so. My mood brightened. I shoved my thoughts of marriage into a closet, bolting it shut. Then I asked of Ranjit, and listened intently to her whispers, reveling in the knowledge that she trusted me with such a story. When we finally arrived home, Mother kissed my cheek. "Now go. Play at the river."

I hurried inside the harem and collected my brothers. When I told them that we were to escape our studies, they chattered excitedly. I walked as fast as I dared to my quarters nearby and removed my fine clothes, for I had learned long ago that my friends seemed happiest when I dressed as they did. I pulled on cotton garments and replaced my jewels with simple rings.

Ladli entered my room, giggling when she saw my attire. A year older than I, she was my dearest friend. Even though a Hindu and a servant, Ladli knew my every secret. Like Nizam, she bore a dark complexion. Where his face was flat, however, hers was finely shaped. She was quite beautiful and, had she been born from an empress and not a seamstress, would have made a wonderful princess.

We met my brothers outside the harem. Each was dressed in worn garments, except for Aurangzeb, who wore the yellow tunic of a horseman in Father's army. Shah and Murad, normally quiet, gabbed like a pair of old widows. Dara, inevitably our leader on such rare adventures, started toward the river. His strides were steady and we drifted past the Red Fort.

People failed to recognize us and only bowed when they spied Aurangzeb. He didn't return their greetings, though he nodded to several soldiers. One warrior laughed at Aurangzeb's outfit, for it was far too large, as was his sword, which nearly touched the ground. My brother's brow furrowed and his pace quickened.

As we eased past crowds, I noticed Nizam following us, weaving around traders and then disappearing behind some tethered camels. How he could be a slave and so loyal, with neither parents nor future, was a mystery to me. Surely, Mother's kindness had nurtured his disposition, but it was hard for me to imagine the tragedy of my parents' deaths.

I continued to think about Nizam while we walked through a fruit and vegetable bazaar, where women stood with wooden platters atop their heads. The platters bore melons, grapes, chilies, almonds. Much bartering was done as buyers moved about, with younger merchants chasing down reluctant customers.

Leaving the bazaar, we descended a spiral staircase. We then shared a cobbled alley with a Jesuit priest, passing him hurriedly as his velvet robes reeked of rotting mutton. To a blind beggar I handed coins, while giving a wide berth to a dead Hindu dressed in colorful ceremonial clothes and awaiting a funeral pyre.

Our feet soon found the vast sandstone ramp exiting the Red Fort. Below the ramp, fat koi swam in the encircling moat. The moat was wider than a street and quite deep. Outside the Red Fort, Agra became even more chaotic. We didn't have to walk far to the river, but still needed to navigate our way through congested passageways brimming with every race, and as many shades of flesh as coins in a merchant's purse. In the faces before me, the endless combinations of eyes, noses, mouths and colors, I beheld the history of invasion and conquest in our lands—Greek, Aryan, Hun, Afghan, Mongol, Persian and Turk.

As many animals as people frequented the cluttered streets of Agra.

Because cows are sacred to Hindus, these creatures wandered freely in the city. Hung with copper bells, they stood or slept in the most inconvenient of places. Scavenging rats and crows also darted about the streets. Servants shooed these pests away from their lords, who often held peacocks, monkeys and cheetahs on leashes.

Within Agra's alleys greater varieties of clothing were also visible. Depending on their stations, men wore loincloths or armor or tunics. Lords displayed the brightest of colors and the softest of fabrics; farmers and laborers often went shirtless. Though women rarely interacted with men publicly, groups of ladies gathered about stalls and vendors. As with the men, the poorer a woman was, the less her sari or robe shimmered.

Steep levees held the Yamuna River, and we descended one as we might the side of an Egyptian pyramid I'd read about. Herds of cattle and beached boats—their bows decorated with carved heads of snakes, elephants, tigers and monkeys—crowded the shoreline. A slip of land, however, remained unencumbered, where placid water was filled with women beating clothes against rocks. Hordes of children surrounded the women, some helping with the wash, others playing in the water. Most of the children were younger than we, for our peers labored in the fields, or baked bread in the Red Fort.

Ladli, still wearing her sari, was the first to stride into a pool at the water's edge. Her body was no longer that of a girl, and I looked enviously at her jostling breasts. Embarrassed by the flatness of my own chest, I stepped, fully clad, into the river. I followed Ladli until the water rose to my ribs.

Suddenly sharp claws bit into my leg and I screamed, certain a crocodile had attacked me. My shrieks had barely diminished when Dara broke through the surface. He grinned, innocently asking, "What troubles you, sister? Did you step on something?"

Though I could receive a scolding for playing with him, I dove forward, surprising him with my quickness. He had his mouth open when we went under, locked together like two serpents. I held him tightly, and we rolled in ankle-deep mud until he finally broke from my grasp. My eyes widened in time to see him spit out a mouthful of brown water. Now I laughed.

Ladli swam over to us and held my hand, giving me a devious look. Dara's gaze, I noticed, lingered on my friend.

"I think my brother's taken with you, Ladli," I said sweetly. "You'll have to rescue him next time."

Dara, rarely at a loss for words, looked aghast. "I . . ."

Our laughter seemed to echo off the riverbanks. Dara threw a handful of mud at us, which spattered against our backs. He then dove into the water and swam back to shore.

"He'll be a fine emperor," Ladli said, switching to Hindi. "Much like your father."

"You always please his eye, Ladli."

It was my friend's turn to be speechless, a rare moment indeed, as her tongue was coarse enough to make any soldier proud. "No," she sputtered, "he doesn't see me that way. I'm a servant. Nothing more."

I wiped mud from her back. "Dara sees people for who they are, not as servants or nobles."

Her face wrinkled, as if she'd bitten into a lime. "You live in a house of mirrors, my little friend. It sparkles now, but when it shatters you'll see only fields of dung."

"Ladli!"

"However Dara may view us still doesn't make us equal."

"But it's true in his eyes," I replied, somewhat defensively. Looking toward the shore, I saw that Dara had climbed a boulder. His gaze might have been on us, or possibly on some elephants across the river. The ponderous beasts appeared content in the water, spraying themselves and each other. "Go to him," I said, glancing about to ensure that we were mostly alone. After all, strangers would frown upon an encounter between them. "He'd like your company." Her mouth formed a protest and I kissed her cheek. "He's fond of you, Ladli. He always has been."

"But why, why would a stallion want a camel?"

"You're no camel, but a . . ." I paused, wondering how he might see her, "but a snow leopard."

"A snow leopard! Really, Jahanara!"

"You are exotic to him. You're Hindu. You see things differently than we. And there's no one more clever or beautiful."

"Have you been gulping your father's wine?"

"Go to him."

She hesitated, then hugged me. "What if he spurns my company?"

"He'd be a fool to do so. And he is no fool."

Ladli turned, wiping mud from her arms as she waded toward Dara. She soon passed Aurangzeb, who stomped upon fish in the shallows. He said something to her, but she avoided his stare. When she approached the boulder, Dara rose. I smiled at his chivalry, proud that he was my brother. They sat an arm's length from each other and started to talk.

Floating on my back, with my feet touching the mud, I closed my eyes and reflected. I wished that I were talking to a boy, wished that there were someone who made me smile. If such a boy existed, I wondered what he was doing now. Perhaps he was the son of a nobleman and lived nearby in the Red Fort. Or he could be a carpenter, or even a soldier. Maybe he was born in a distant land and would someday visit Agra. Would I meet him here? Or would we grow old alone and apart? I suspected that my heart had an echo somewhere in the world, but I feared never discovering it.

Father once told me that would-be lovers were similar to mountains. Two peaks, wonderfully akin and compatible in every way, may rise to the clouds but never witness each other's majesty because of the space between them. Like a man and a woman from different cities, they would never find each other. Or, if the peaks were blessed, as my parents had been, they might be two mountains of the same range and could bask in each other's company forever.

Please, Allah, I prayed, let me be so deserving. Let my destiny be so grand. And please let it unfold soon. I dreaded what would happen once I came of age to marry and Father paired me with some stranger. I might never know love, never feel what Mother did as Father put his arm around her.

I was still dreaming of love when a shadow loomed above me and suddenly I was thrust underwater. An immense force crushed against my chest, forcing me down into the mud. Confused, I struggled frantically. I opened my eyes, but saw no more than if a brown blanket had been thrown atop me. I tried mightily to rise up from under it, kicking and clawing and biting, fighting the urge to scream.

When the weight on my chest abruptly lessened, I sprang to the surface. My nose burned and my lungs heaved as I spat out foul water. Recovering, I realized that Aurangzeb stood next to me. His face bore a wicked smile and he laughed. "What ugly beetles," he said, pointing at my chest. Baffled, I looked down. To my horror I saw that my robe had fallen aside and that only my thin cotton shirt enclosed my chest. My nipples, dark and hard, were plain to see. "I'd like to squash them," he added.

Shrieking in rage, I swung my fist as I'd seen fighting men do. I aimed for his nose, but he twisted quickly and I managed only to strike the side of his cheek. A copper ring on my thumb opened a cut under his eye. When a drop of blood tumbled down his face and fell into the water, he slapped me. The blow was loud and a few women looked at us from the shore.

Aurangzeb's lips drew back to reveal his teeth. "You'll regret that," he promised, quoting a verse from the Qur'an that spoke of vengeance.

"I hate you!" I snapped, though it was untrue. "And I hate your foolish verses!"

"You would," he retorted before wading back to the shallows. When he was near the shoreline, he sat down and placed some mud against his cheek. I wanted to cry, but such a display would only be a victory for him, so I bit my lip and rearranged my robe. I then dropped into the water until it came up to my neck. I kept Aurangzeb in my vision, however, as his revenge would be cruel. He glared at me, and his glare was enough to make me wish Dara was closer.

I had decided to return to the harem when I heard a muffled shriek. Thinking that it must have been some ploy of Aurangzeb's, I turned cautiously, gazing about the river's muddied waters. At first I saw only elephants and floating debris. But then, farther out in the Yamuna, I glimpsed a small arm waving frantically. I heard another cry. It was a child's voice and my heart dropped like a stone as strong currents swept the child downstream toward me. I looked for an adult to shout to, but no one was near.

I hesitated, then pulled off my robe and swam from shore, hoping to reach him. Kicking hard, I pulled at the water with my hands. The child seemed to hold something. As I neared him I spied the submerged log but could hardly protect myself as it hammered into my side. Though my breath was smitten from me, I grabbed a branch with one arm and the boy with the other. He must have been only six or seven.

I tried to scream as we were pulled swiftly downstream, but my lungs ached, and my pitiful cry didn't carry far. Aurangzeb, who was the closest to us, looked up. I assumed he'd rush to our aid, but instead he watched us silently. He might have even grinned. Soon we'd wash past anyone who could help us and I shrieked again in terror. Praise Allah, a pair of fishermen heard my call and pointed to me. Their boat was beached and they urgently pushed it into the water.

The current intensified around a bend. My grip on the tree was firm, as were my fingers as they grasped the child's clothing. One of his arms had a frightful gash and he was bleeding badly, his face was without color. He began to slip deeper into the river, dragging me with him. The water seemed horribly cold.

I was desperate when I saw the boat churning after us. The two fishermen pulled upon oars, while two other figures stood at the bow. I realized Nizam was present, as was Aurangzeb, who held a rope. The child started to go under and I thrust him up with the last strength I possessed. My arms had turned leaden.

Just when I thought I'd go under, the rope splashed beside me. I grabbed it with one hand and Aurangzeb hauled us toward the boat. We struck its planks and Nizam lifted the boy, then me from the water. I collapsed against Nizam and began to sob, tears of relief mingling with tears of sorrow. For I knew Aurangzeb had ignored my pleas and that he'd only come to help when the fishermen saw us.

I wanted to speak, but the world dimmed as I fell in and out of consciousness. I was barely aware of the oars pulling us to shore. Then I was carried somewhere, shadows falling across me. I saw images, dreams perhaps. A blanket finally embraced me, followed by my mother. She spoke to me and her words came as riddles. I drifted, then slowly, intolerably slowly, climbed. When the world seemed to finally brighten, I opened my eyes. My parents and siblings were present, crowding around the carpet, blankets and cushions comprising my bed. "Mother?" I mumbled.

When she heard me speak, Mother kissed my face, my lips. "Oh, Jahanara, we were so worried!"

Father bent over me. "Do you hurt, my child?"

"No . . . no, Father."

I saw his tears and I cried too. My parents held me as if I were still drowning, Mother squeezing my hands. Father, more prone to emotion than any man I knew, said, "Better I should lose my empire than you, Jahanara. How could the sky live without its stars?"

"It would be lonely," I said, for despite their touch I felt nothing but loneliness.

"You were very brave today," he replied, stroking my cheek.

"Indeed," Mother said quickly, and I recognized that her pride surpassed even Father's, because as women we weren't expected to do anything courageous. "You saved the child."

"I did?"

"Yes, bless you," Mother added. "And your brother saved you."

"But he—"

Aurangzeb stepped forward. "Repay me later," he interjected, the wound on his cheek oozing red.

I massaged my temples as if to rub away the day's memories. "I'm . . . I'm so tired." I was unable to look at Aurangzeb.

Father kissed me and then slowly walked out of the room. Mother and my brothers followed him. As Dara turned to leave, I motioned for him to stay. He shut the door behind him and came to my side. "Why are you crying?" he asked.

"Because he . . . because Aurangzeb saw me." My voice turned from a whisper to a whimper. "He wanted me dead."

Dara stiffened, scratching at his brow beneath his turban. "Wanted you dead?"

"Yes!"

"You make no sense, Jahanara."

"But I do! I do! He left me to die."

"He saved you, commandeered the boat. He said—"

"He lies!"

Dara stepped away. "I saw him rescue you. He pulled you from the water and even cut himself in the process."

"I cut him!"

"You need rest," he said, turning toward the door. "You're confused now, terribly confused. But after you rest, these nightmares shall disperse."

Yet rest would not temper my fears.

And I felt so alone that the room seemed to shrink, suffocating me.

Drowning me.

CHAPTER III

Childhood Lost

It is said that time mends any injury. Much as I disbelieve this notion, I confess that as the months passed I had fewer nightmares about Aurangzeb. A day came when I was able to look at him without shuddering in fear, without wondering why he would let me drown. Though I loathed him for stealing my youth, for turning me overnight from a girl into a young woman, this passage was inevitable. I was a princess, after all, and had been trained since childhood to understand that life was anything but simple. The sons and daughters of emperors were expected to become adults at an early age, and in truth I'd been shirking my responsibilities. But after Aurangzeb's treachery I said farewell to my childish ways, for I knew they were shackles in this world of adults.

In the months following, my routine changed dramatically. Instead of seeking entertainment, I sought knowledge. Rather than escape my duties, I faced the tasks before me. Each day I spent long hours in the harem, studying everything from architecture to dance to politics. While most girls arranged each other's hair and learned to cook exotic dishes, I practiced calligraphy or memorized geography. There were no summits to the mountains of books Mother lent me, no subjects too trite or trifling. Following her advice, I became more socially active in Agra's court. Success, she explained, has almost as much to do with your friends as it does yourself. She'd told me so since I could first reason, but only now did I listen.

Over the next year I sought more acquaintances. Whether at polo matches or hunting expeditions, I chatted with lesser nobles and merchants on Father's behalf. Although the lords often resented these conversations, on occasion I sensed their eyes drifting greedily about my body. At first, I was uneasy with such glances, but as time passed

I learned that lust is one of man's most glaring weaknesses. Mother, at my insistence, secretly taught me of these matters. She explained how a man's body worked. She told me of his needs and, most important, of his desires.

Mother embarrassed me immensely by making me practice social graces with Nizam. For instance, she dressed him like a lord and asked that I serve him wine. I then attempted to pry information from him with little more than idle chatter. Though Nizam tried his best to act the part, he often smiled at my blunders and halting sentences. But with time and much practice, his smiles lessened in frequency. I slyly tricked him into confessions. I asked questions that any vain man must answer, no matter how resolute his intentions.

Equipped with confidence, I was ready to speak with nobles who Mother claimed were attracted to me. Most men thought my youth and sex made me as threatening as a toothless cobra. They grew gallant when I pretended bashfulness, told me secrets when I prepared to walk away. As the Emperor, Father could have controlled these men in any manner he wished, but it seemed he'd rather sweeten them with honey than subdue them with his fist. And so I wooed them.

Father watched my progress vigilantly. Though Hindustan had prospered under his rule, that prosperity also reflected Mother's engagement. She despised war, and because of her influence upon Father, we no longer spent precious gold and lives trying to expand northward, deeper into the land of our enemy, the Persians. Instead, we fortified our borders. We built roads and bridges. We became rich through trade. Naturally, many men still wanted to war against our foes, but these were the sort I was sent to sweeten. I often found myself chatting with them, innocently feeding their egos, or those of their disregarded wives.

I'd have learned none of these skills if not for Mother. She counseled me on countless matters—about our laws, for instance, or which nobles were friends and which were foes. She could tell me the traits of anyone important—whether they were tolerant of Hindus, whether they preferred to bed girls or boys. With equal relish I learned of their fears and their desires. Both, I was trained, were of consequence.

My brothers also studied these things, though in a different manner. To my surprise, only Aurangzeb took such lessons seriously. While Shah and Murad chased skirts, and Dara devoured philosophers' works, Aurangzeb made his rounds in the court, befriending many of our leaders, especially the officers of our army. They liked him, for the taller he grew, the more he spoke of war's merits, of how it strengthened our empire.

Aurangzeb delighted in undoing much of my work. If I befriended someone significant, turned him into a column upon which we could build things, Aurangzeb acted like the wind, subtly pushing against the column, forcing the soil from beneath it. I rarely even knew it had collapsed until weeks after the fact.

Dara, to my dismay, cared little for statecraft. Though Father's favorite son, and therefore heir presumptive, his loves were the arts. And while Father adored poets, painters, architects and scholars, he also understood that they only enhanced the quality of our lives and were not the grain upon which our empire feasted.

The first time I ever spoke to Dara of his shortcomings he paid me as much heed as he might the dirt beneath his feet. It was late in the day, and after finishing our studies and prayers we'd retired to one of the largest gardens in the Red Fort.

The best of our gardens served to remind us what lay ahead, if we lived virtuously, that the Garden of Paradise was perpetually lush and infinitely enchanting. The sanctuary we sat in now was called Shalimar Bagh, the Abode of Love. Water flowed through narrow channels between the mango, date and lime trees, gathering in square pools and spurting in gentle fountains. Everything in the garden was decidedly geometric. The plantings and waterways formed octagons, cubes or even triangles.

At the far end of the garden, pruning a series of rose bushes, was Ismail, the old farmer my mother had rescued. The garden, beautiful already, had brighter hues after Ismail's arrival. He worked here from dawn until dusk, and no plant or tree lacked his signature.

Dara and I sat on a square mound of grass between several of the many waterways. It was pleasant here, abundant with shade and delightful smells of nectar. Dara was clad in a crimson tunic and a white turban. He was trying to develop a beard, and a few dark hairs hung from his chin. I wore a yellow skirt and shirt beneath a full-length robe of almost transparent blue silk. A turquoise veil painted exquisitely with white cranes was pinned atop my head. We wore our veils opposite the Persian manner, and thus mine fell back upon my neck, covering my hair but not my face.

Between us rested a plate of grapes. I plucked one from its stem, then said, "You never really told me what happened with Ladli."

"What?"

"When she went to you."

"Went to me?"

"At the river." My brother, who knew so much of books, sometimes tested my patience. While my mind ran, his sauntered.

"You waste even fewer words than Mother. Must you always be so direct?"

I shrugged before eating another grape. "I can be as sly as a cat."

"But hasn't she already told you everything?"

"Not everything."

"Well, what did she say?"

"That you asked her about her beliefs, about the caste system."

Dara started to make a sweeping gesture but, sighing, let his hands drop. To me, he seemed serious for his age. But then, so did I to my friends. "Hinduism," he said, "even if my view is unusual among Muslims, is a beautiful religion. I love its gods, its karma. But I don't agree with the Hindu belief in the caste system. Why should someone with lighter skin be held above the rest, or a merchant be worth more than a laborer?"

"I suppose it allows them some sort of order."

"Impartial laws, Jahanara, create order. Not discrimination."

"But are we so different? Are you and a boy working in the fields considered equals?"

"I know," he admitted, nodding slowly. "Just as I know that regardless of how much I care for Ladli, I could never marry her."

"You could ask Father for his consent. After all, he asked his father if he could marry Mother."

"True, but I can't do the same," he countered sadly. "Remember that Father was first wed to other wives. But Mother, being Mother, didn't worry about competing against them. Ladli would hardly want to be bothered by it all."

We were silent, and the chatter of birds surrounded us, drowning out Ismail as he scrubbed a marble walkway. I twisted a ruby on my thumb, watching how the sun gave life to the star inside. "Do you love her, Dara?"

"The philosophers say that love—"

"Do you love her?"

"Love has nothing to do with it. Because love her or not, I'll marry for political reasons, just as you will. And believe me, we'll marry soon. I've already heard Father talk of his plans for us."

I considered the squat man Father might choose for me, forcing an image of him away as I might discard a rotten apple. I focused again on my brother, wishing to talk about something that lately had often been on my mind. "Aurangzeb's certainly popular these days. He doesn't spend his time reading or writing but practices with his sword, or befriends our generals."

"So?"

"So, does it ever . . . has it occurred to you," I whispered, "that when Father dies, Aurangzeb will claim the Peacock Throne?"

Dara dropped a grape. "Really, Jahanara, since when did you start thinking about such things?"

"Mother wants me—"

"To speak of nonsense?"

"You think it's nonsense," I asked, "that Aurangzeb might want the throne? Sometimes, when Father speaks of giving it to you, I see how angry it makes him. He tries to hide it but can't. Aurangzeb has always known that you're Father's favorite, and that no matter how much he excelled, the throne would be yours. How do you think that makes him feel? How would you feel if Father loved you less than Aurangzeb, and everyone knew?"

"But I can't—"

"It would hurt, Dara. And I think it hurts Aurangzeb so dreadfully that he didn't mind watching me die. So dreadfully that he might fight you for the throne."

My brother swiped halfheartedly at a troublesome fly. "I've never tried to hurt him. And I never will." He paused, watching the fly settle on the trunk of a nearby pomegranate tree. "I want to be his friend as much as you do. But he knows the Emperor has the right to choose his successor. It's always been so."

"True. But just because Father intends that you take his place doesn't mean that you shall."

"Aurangzeb won't fight me."

As he reached for another grape, I leaned closer to him. "We are no longer children, Dara. Perhaps we should stop acting like them."

"You're not as old as you pretend."

"Perhaps not," I retorted, suddenly irritated by his single-mindedness. "But our great-grandfather was only thirteen when he inherited the throne. Was he pretending then? Would you be pretending if Father died?" Part of my vexation stemmed from the knowledge that Dara was right. I was too young to speak so. Yet Mother expected me to try and grasp such subtleties. After all, she had spent the last year training me in matters of the court. And I could never disappoint her. Nor did I wish Dara to ignore Aurangzeb. "How can you know so much about philosophy and gods," I asked, "while knowing nothing of your own blood? Do you realize how many wars have been fought over the throne? How many brothers have killed brothers?"

"Several wars. Almost a dozen brothers."

"Then is it so impossible to imagine that Aurangzeb might harm you to take Father's place?"

Dara was silent for the period it took Ismail to scrub the remainder of the walkway. I could tell he was disconcerted, for often he glanced skyward, as if seeking divine guidance. "I still don't believe your version of the river," he finally replied. "But if you're right, and Aurangzeb covets the throne, what should I do?"

I tried to picture myself as a trusted advisor. What would Mother say to Father if his brother were his rival? "Do what he does. Start making friends, alliances. Spend less time reading about religion and more time by Father's side. Let the nobles see him with you, instead of only with Mother and myself."

Dara removed his turban, then ran a hand through his raven locks. "Even if he cares for me little, I could never fight him. I don't even want to think about it."

His face harbored pain, a pain that reached out to touch me. I knew he had tried to make amends with Aurangzeb but was met with the same hostility as I. How is it, I asked Allah, that we can love our brother and yet still feel him slipping away? What am I doing wrong?

Dara's sister again, and no longer a fledgling advisor, I took his hand. "Believe me, I'd rather lay in the harem and gossip with my friends than talk about this. But we're unlike our friends. You are to be the Emperor, and I'm . . ." I paused, still unsure of my role. "And I am your sister. I love Aurangzeb and I want no fight with him either. But he frightens me, Dara. And I would think that he'd frighten you."

Dara nodded weakly, but said nothing. I realized then that he was too decent for such thoughts and that I'd have to protect him. But how could I, a girl of barely fifteen summers, protect one brother from another? How could I protect myself?

CHAPTER IV

Darkness

Fate soon showed me just how hard it is to look after anyone, especially myself, for I was wed during Nauroz, right before the dry season of my sixteenth year. Wed to a man I would come to despise.

The dry season in Agra is a time when the land itself appears to die. Grass withers and yellows from the heat and shortage of rain. Herds of cattle rest unmoving for days without end. Prior to our dreaded summer, praise Allah, Agra hosts a brief bout of springlike weather. We celebrate this respite as the Persian New Year.

Normally, my mood would have been buoyant, for Nauroz lasts two weeks and is embraced by all of our people, regardless of their religion. Moreover, Nauroz features extravagant and massive parties, Chinese rockets and exchanges of gifts. Yet entertaining feelings of joy was impossible with the rapid approach of my nuptials. Indeed, I watched fireworks and ate sweets without really seeing or tasting anything but the bitterness of my thoughts.

On the day of my wedding I rose early, though reluctantly. After a breakfast of melon, I bathed in waters laden with lavender and eucalyptus oils. Then servants rubbed lotus perfume into my skin as my hair was dried above a diminutive fire of rosewood. I was handed cloves, which I sucked until my breath smelled like cinnamon. Artists skilled in composition then addressed my flesh, wiping betel leaf against my lips, numbing and coloring them crimson simultaneously. A russet paste of henna, lemon juice and oil was used to decorate my hands and feet with ornate patterns. Finally, attendants sewed strands of diamonds into my hair.

My wedding unfolded in the Red Fort's grandest courtyard, a square more than three hundred paces from side to side. Its sandstone walls each boasted forty archways, through which one could walk to adjacent gardens, bazaars and residences. Atop the walls, red banners fluttered restlessly.

Hundreds of witnesses were gathered within the courtyard, mostly nobles who had arrived early to secure the most favorable positions. Surrounding the proceedings was a score of war elephants, some draped in English velvet, others in Chinese silk or Turkish gold cloth. The elephants' tusks were swathed in black fabric that made the tusks' tips even whiter. At the courtyard's corners, gilded pens contained cheetahs. These fleetest of creatures had silver collars and vests of embroidered linen.

Father had given me many jewels for the affair, and I glittered in rubies and emeralds. My clothes had never been worn before. An outer layer of silk was nearly invisible, except for a painter's renderings of indigo irises. Beneath this robe lay a turquoise dress. Its fabric moved with the skin of my torso, tight enough that one might see the rhythm of my stomach as I breathed. The dress was much looser about my legs.

The shell of my being must have looked grand, but inside I was suffering. Though Dara and I often spoke of duty, it seemed that duty now sought to smother me. All the dreams I'd harbored as a child were so distant. They were the dreams of another life, of a person I hardly recalled. She had yearned to find a lover, someone whose presence would quicken her pulse.

The man I desired, whoever he was, remained far from me today. In his place, grinning at my side, was Khondamir. A stout man, he hardly rose to my height and was more than twice my age. But he was a powerful silver merchant and had long opposed many of my father's policies. Our marriage, Father hoped, would help to change his views. Father also greatly wanted to use Khondamir's trading contacts in Persia to find friends north of our border. Father needed such friends to make peace with the Persians, which he had to make for the sake of the Empire. Though Khondamir seemed to take little interest in me, he was eager for our coupling, as the arrangement brought him within touching distance of the Peacock Throne.

During the ceremony Khondamir's eyes often wandered to my chest, which had swollen during the past months. I was painfully aware of his gaze and tried not to ponder my fate later that evening. Instead, I absently stared at my parents and siblings, who stood a step below me on a gilded platform. My two baby sisters, whom I last saw a moon ago, were swathed in gossamer silk and held by servants. Father wore his military casings, and the emerald-studded hilt of an ancient sword jutted from his hip. Mother might have been a rose. Draped in a thin green robe and a scarlet dress, she radiated beauty, somehow spreading it beyond my brothers, who filled indigo tunics and stood shoulder to shoulder between our parents. Dara seemed saddened by the day, whereas Aurangzeb grinned maliciously. Shah and Murad could have been asleep.

Our wedding, like all such tableaux, was long and dull. Prayers were offered to Allah and pleasantries exchanged. I'd wept after last night's festivities and today sprang no tears. I smiled and bowed. I stood beside my husband.

When the ceremony ended, servants assembled an enormous feast. A dozen lambs were roasted over open flames. On gold and silver platters skewers of beef and vegetables steamed. Vast piles of rice, nuts and fruits were everywhere, and mounds of kulfi—a dessert fashioned with sugar, mango, lemon juice, cream and roasted pistachios—were served in marble bowls. Before eating, we reassembled under the shade of hastily erected red tents. After servants placed fresh linen atop Persian carpets, we sat and sampled morsels endlessly. Throughout the meal, attendants fanned my family, the breezes drying sweat and keeping flies at bay.

Imperial dancing girls entertained us while we ate. Their torsos were covered with the thinnest of fabrics, leaving little to one's imagination. The girls moved like saplings amid wind and were accompanied by trumpets, drums and stringed instruments. Beyond our tent, jugglers and acrobats competed to further amuse us.

When the feasting concluded we left the courtyard and proceeded outside the Red Fort. Father had suggested that a polo match be held to entertain the nobles and the general population. Polo had been invented by tribal horsemen inhabiting the plains to the east of Agra, and was one of our favorite spectacles. For my wedding day an immense stretch of open ground near the river had been groomed of weeds, and goals were erected at either end of the playing field. Surrounding it rose tents of the nobles, filled with more food, as well as wives and concubines. The largest tent shielded my family from the sun. We sat on wool carpets and watched the players prepare their mounts.

My brothers took to the field. Dara and Shah had changed into tunics and turbans of black, whereas Aurangzeb and Murad wore white. Father raised a water buffalo's horn to his lips and blew. A guttural cry emerged from the instrument and the teams gathered on their respective sides. Horses, their manes combed and tails braided, pranced and neighed. Gold and silver bells about the stallions' necks rung vigorously as the riders practiced swinging long poles. These were straight and true for more than the height of a man but curved at their bottom ends.

A rosewood ball was dropped upon the field and the game began. Khondamir, his bride suddenly forgotten, roared with the crowd. Mother tried to get my attention, but for the first time in my life I ignored her. Though my parents believed Khondamir would make a good husband, and I believed I was performing my duty, I felt betrayed nonetheless.

I prayed to Allah that Khondamir was honorable, and I watched the match with fleeting interest. However, I could hardly fail to notice that Aurangzeb was by far the best rider of my brothers. The ball seemed to always be against his stick. Once, when only Dara was between him and his goal, Aurangzeb sent his mount careening into Dara's stallion. Dara was flung from his saddle and Aurangzeb scored easily. When he raised his arm in triumph, many in the crowd cheered. Dara nodded to Aurangzeb before limping back to his horse.

Though Islam forbade alcohol, and many devout Muslims refrained from this vice, on my wedding day an abundance of wine flowed. I had my first taste of its sweetness sitting next to my husband, the only pleasant experience I was to know that afternoon. We drank from jewel-studded goblets and much liquor was consumed. Men and women normally bound by the strict rules of our society began to unravel. Khondamir actually smiled at me, a grin revealing yellowed teeth and swollen gums. I started to feel somewhat clumsy. My head seemed inordinately heavy, and my mind, usually so sharp, dulled. Yet I drank more, for I'd heard of men escaping in drink, and thoughts of escape occupied my mind. If wine could somehow save me, I'd sip it until no grapes remained in all of Hindustan.

I didn't even realize when the polo game had ended, but dusk was falling when strong arms lifted me atop a palki, a short couch mounted on twin poles. Four men then carried my litter toward Khondamir's home. A palace of sorts, the rambling structure stood far from the river. I'd only seen it from a distance and dimly recalled it to be a sandstone edifice encircled by palm trees.

Khondamir's servants lit torches as they walked, surrounding my litter. My husband rode beside me on a gray stallion with black spots. When he saw me looking at him, he grinned, then removed something from a saddlebag and began to eat. My thoughts moved like slugs and I moaned quietly, pulling flowers from my hair and pocketing uncomfortable jewelry. The world seemed to spin in frenzied arcs that threatened to make me ill.

I dared to close my eyes. When I finally opened them I was being carried down a candlelit corridor. A door opened and I was laid atop a sleeping carpet. I mumbled graciously to my bearers, staring at the revolving ceiling. Horns jutted from every wall, and somehow in my wicked state I deduced that Khondamir must have been a hunter.

When I saw him stagger drunkenly into the room, I pretended to sleep. At first I thought he might rest beside me, but then I felt his hands on my clothes. His fingers were greedy and ripped my precious robe. He peeled it from me with such strength that I was rolled to my side. Terrified, I continued to feign sleep, desperately hoping he would lose interest.

But when I sensed his breath on my bared chest I knew he wouldn't. Suddenly his mouth was upon a nipple and I fought the urge to gag. Mumbling to himself, he attacked it like a piglet might suckle a sow. Though repulsed, I felt it harden, which seemed to fuel his passion even more. My heart raced as he licked and tasted my flesh. I trembled at his teeth, for they weren't gentle. Nor were his fingers, which clawed and poked at my secret places.

I heard him spit, then sensed wetness between my legs. There came an unbearable weight as he pressed down upon me, his breath fouling my lungs, his belly slapping against mine. A sharp pain erupted when he thrust himself inside me. He was moving next, rising and falling, and suddenly I could no longer make any pretense of sleep and cried out. I thought my hurt might make him pause, but instead it served to motivate him further. His gyrations became more frenzied. His hands pinned my arms to the carpet, pushing down, holding me in place.

My body seemed to split apart. Mother had warned me of pain, but not such fire as this. I gritted my teeth as my husband licked my neck, cried as I tried to break free of his grasp. Though I knew nothing of lovemaking, I doubted it was meant to be so full of woe. I'd heard other women speak of it fondly, and believed Mother even enjoyed it. Yet here I lay, biting my lip until it bled, weeping as my husband battered away at me.

When I thought I'd surely die, he suddenly howled like a wild beast. I felt him grow even larger, drive himself deeper. He convulsed, then abruptly collapsed atop me. I inhaled his stench as he lay unmoving. Silence reigned now. Though my world still spun, I thanked Allah for the alcohol, because I sensed that without it, my suffering would have been even more horrific.

Soon Khondamir snored. Putting my forearms against his chest, I rolled him from me. Shedding silent tears, I hobbled to a corner, where I sat with my back against the wall. When I saw blood seeping from between my legs and a cut on my nipple, I cried harder. My tears seemed endless as I thought of all that had gone wrong, of the love I was sure to never find.

The night and I aged together.

THE FIRST DAYS with Khondamir were dreadful. In light of my duty, I did my best to forget my wedding night. I moved forward, as Mother had always taught me. The wine must have clouded his senses, I reasoned. Surely he didn't know he was hurting me.

Such thoughts consumed me as I sought to make Khondamir happy, sought to earn his affection. Alas, I quickly realized that he cared nothing for my feelings. I didn't seem to exist in his presence and might have been a gnat in the corner for all the attention he gave me. However much I tried to be helpful, he was disinterested, at best, in my efforts. His indifference was upsetting, as I was accustomed to being taken seriously. Even my father, the most important man in the Empire, often paused as I tried to offer advice. Yet Khondamir, a fool if ever one lived, thought he'd married a dull-witted camel.

It became obvious that he'd wed me hoping that I might bear him a son. Despite his reputation as a hornet that sipped nectar from many flowers, he had never sired a child. Why he believed I'd produce one when so many others had failed was unfathomable to me. And frankly, even though I hoped to have children, I couldn't imagine Khondamir as their father. I wanted no seed of his to take root within me, especially since I experienced too many nights like the first, nights when he stumbled home drunk and used me until he fell unconscious.

One evening he even hit me, a backhand slap that split my lip. Apparently, I had been unresponsive to his groping. While I trembled naked on a tiger's pelt, Khondamir yelled at a servant to ride to the Red Fort and return with a practiced courtesan. My husband forced me to watch their gyrations, demanding that I surpass the woman's wanton displays in the future.

He finished with me, and as he did I began to understand the concept of hate. Other emotions I grasped fully. I feared Aurangzeb. I loved Father and worshipped Mother. Beggars I pitied and children I envied. But hatred was a feeling I had never experienced, nor wanted to. Nevertheless, that night, as I bled and wept and hated, I contemplated fleeing this creature or, better still, slipping some poison into his rice. Surely the world would not lament his departure.

I missed my family terribly in those days. My parents sent me letters and gifts but were on a military campaign to the south accompanied by my brothers. Dara wrote of Aurangzeb's bravery in the field, how he had left the safety of Father's tent and joined our soldiers at the front line. There he killed his first man.

Though I possessed little interest in war, I'd have enjoyed being with them, exploring new lands and listening to officers argue. Such a fate was infinitely more desirable to wandering about Khondamir's home, which had precious few books and mostly sullen servants.

As days turned to weeks I feared that my fate would be forever unchanged. Steeling my emotions as steadfastly as I could, I let my misery surface only in the darkness of night. Mother had never let any man rule her feelings, and I knew she expected me to be as strong. And so I resisted my tears. I endured until Allah finally decided to set me loose.

My taste of freedom began with a morning like any other. Khondamir expected me to join him for breakfast, and we rested on his terrace, eating yogurt and peeling pathetic little oranges. The wool carpet beneath our knees was badly faded, and stained from multiple mishaps.

I felt bold that day and asked if I might ride one of his horses.

"You?" he scoffed, his voice high-pitched for a man of his girth. "On a horse?"

"I've always—"

"Would you ride naked?" The image must have amused him, for he smirked, chunks of orange dropping from his ponderous lips.

I was accustomed to his crude attempts at wit and ignored him. "My lord, I've not seen my friends for weeks."

"So? Weeks? Months? What does it matter? Why would I care for your friends?"

"Because I'm your wife."

Khondamir belched, the fat on his face rippling. "You're a whining child is what you are. Nothing more. Nothing less. Now why don't you scurry somewhere and make yourself useful?"

"Why don't you—" I stopped, suddenly afraid what he might do if I asked him to scurry off a cliff. "Why don't you give me something to do?"

"Fine. Cook my dinner."

I bit back an angry reply. Was this how husbands thought of wives, that they could do no more than boil rice? Eating the last of my yogurt, I sighed, looking about his estate. Though Khondamir was a rich man, made so by the silver mines he owned, obviously he spent little in the way of servants. The roof on his home needed repair, weeds choked his garden, his horses were thin, and the sandstone wall encircling his property bore innumerable cracks and gouges. I wondered where he hoarded his rupees and gold.

"Damn these oranges," my husband said, his beady eyes shrinking. "Must they be so small?" Glaring at me, he added, "Must all my fruits taste so bland?"

I knew he referred to my listlessness in bed but pretended not to catch his meaning. "Perhaps your fruits," I replied, "deserve more care."

"Are you, woman, an expert in such matters? Is your experience so vast?"

"What matters, lord? I know only that your trees are dying."

He turned in his chair to stare at his orchard. Many trees—mainly apple, orange, pear and cherry—dotted his land. Though summer was in full stride and each branch should yield a substantial harvest, all held sickly fruit and yellowed leaves.

"Do you have a gardener?" I asked, suspecting he was too tightfisted to employ one.

"What good are gardeners? How hard is it to water and pluck?" He belched again. "Too hard for you, I imagine."

I rose from the table, my heart hastening. I had spent countless afternoons in gardens and believed I understood why his trees ailed. "If I tell you how to save them, my lord, would that be worth something to you?"

"How dare—"

"Worth a simple ride on a horse?"

He swatted at a wasp. "On a nag."

"Then call your servants."

Unlike servants found in other palaces, the men my husband hailed didn't wear eye-pleasing tunics, but patched and moth-eaten garb. As they assembled by our table, I pointed to the smallest and sickest tree. "Please, pull it out." They looked to their master for confirmation and he cursed them, motioning that they do as I commanded. The servants moved to the tree, which was no taller than they, and carefully withdrew it from the soil. "Come here, my lord." I said, walking to the sapling. I knelt to the ground and inserted my finger into the wet soil. When I smelled my finger I was reminded of a decaying beast. "Do you smell that?" I asked, sticking my hand before his bulbous, vein-infested nose.

Khondamir grimaced, stepping back. "What does it mean?"

"It means, my lord, that you water the trees too much and that their roots rot."

"Well, woman, must I put words in your mouth? What can be done?"

Isn't it obvious, fool? I thought, savoring his ignorance. "Stop watering them. Stop for at least ten days. Then, if Allah smiles upon you, they should recover."

Khondamir grunted before yelling at his servants for their ignorance. He told one to prepare the stable's oldest horse. "Go," he said to me.

Thrilled to be rid of him, I hurried to my room and changed clothes, opting for a simple brown robe. I also removed my jewels. Not trusting Khondamir, I lifted a brick from the floor, dug a small hole in the dirt beneath, and set my ornaments there. The brick I replaced and the dirt I dropped into a potted plant.

Not bothering to tell my husband good-bye, I walked to the mount, a ragged creature far along in years. Once, it must have been a fine horse. Though malnourished, the large mare still stood proud. I caressed her brow, then noticed that the servant had placed an expensive saddle on her.

"He said an old horse, my lady, but not an old saddle," the man whispered.

I smiled, and climbed atop her. "Thank you. Thank you so much." I handed him a coin, which disappeared into his tattered tunic. "Dry the trees well," I added, "or I fear we'll both be in trouble."

He untied my mount and handed me the reins. "My lord always said to water them twice a day," he replied, not hiding his glee.

I grinned, bade him farewell, and spurred the mare forward. She didn't seem to mind my weight and sauntered down a well-beaten and dusty path that led to the Red Fort. Though my family was gone, I relished the notion of seeing Ladli. I had last spoken to her on the day of my wedding and I longed to hear of the happenings in her life, as well as in the Empire.

I passed many homes along the way. The most elaborate works were comprised of sandstone bricks. Poorer structures were bound with no more than mud, wood and thatch. The path itself was lined with palm trees and the occasional beggar. I dropped coins to several, though when too many ragged men followed me, I wished them well and urged my horse ahead.

The path turned into a road, which I soon shared with merchants, priests and soldiers. A column of warriors headed south, and I suspected they would rendezvous with Father's forces. The men wore leather armor studded with short iron spikes. A few carried muskets, though most bore bows and quivers of arrows. Elephants plodded behind them, pulling carts laden with shields, helmets and other supplies. Black cannons, as long and thick as a man, trailed several of the beasts.

The soldiers looked at me oddly as they passed, for rarely did one see a woman on horseback, especially without escort. Though these were hard men, with full beards and scarred faces, I heard only a few crude remarks. When I spied the battalion's leader, a young captain I had met before, I called to him. He shouted my name and steered his mount toward mine. After we exchanged pleasantries, I inquired about the fighting to the south. Apparently, it had started when a fierce Deccan raiding party crossed into our southern lands. For years they had sought independence from the Empire. On this occasion the Deccans had burnt down homes, stolen rice and taken children as slaves. Such events were so common that the captain hardly commented on them. Still, the fighting was bloody and Father had requested reinforcements.

After wishing the man good fortune, I navigated the cluttered streets. The closer I drew to the Red Fort, the more congealed my environs became. Normally, merchants hawked all sorts of wares to me, but now, in my plain robe, I inspired few propositions. A toothless butcher did point me toward a rack of hanging meats. Flies covered the haunches of beef, and I turned my gaze elsewhere.

My energy waning, I approached the citadel. Its sandstone ramp was being swept clear of dung and washed clean by a score of slaves. Most were Hindus, for when I was halfway up the ramp, and a muezzin's wails for prayer commenced, only a handful of workers and myself turned toward Mecca. I prayed for our soldiers and for the safety of my family.

I was tempted to ask Allah for help with my husband but decided that He had nobler projects to attend.

I left my tired mount with a stable boy and headed toward the royal apartments. It took little effort to find Ladli. She was busy peeling carrots in the imperial kitchen, where she so often toiled. When she saw me, she let out a squeal and dropped her knife. An older servant was about to admonish her when I cleared my throat and asked that Ladli be dismissed.

My friend came to me quickly. We hurried from all ears and before long found ourselves atop one of the fort's mighty ramparts, which had been designed to hold fighting men and offered a splendid view of Agra. Thousands of homes, mosques and bazaars stretched far into the distance before merging with the river or gentle hills. The mosques' minarets rose like giant brown needles into the sky, high enough so the muezzins could be heard far and wide, and high enough that these men could not look into windows of adjacent homes, where views of women might distract them.

Built alongside the river, Agra is shaped like a crescent moon. At the Yamuna's banks are mostly palaces, stone and brick with lush gardens. Farther from the river rose the homes of the commoners, as abundant as monsoon raindrops and growing more tightly packed together each year as our city swelled above five hundred thousand.

Most distant from the river and its breezes were Agra's slums. From our perch atop the Red Fort, the slums reminded me of a dirty carpet. A seemingly infinite number of hovels rested so close together that it was hard to discern the narrow paths separating them. Mother had taken us into this realm on several occasions, as she wanted us to see how those less fortunate lived. While she spoke to the poor of their needs, my eyes wandered about the foreign environs.

Rats, odors, filth and disease infested Agra's slums. Ragged children hunted the rats. The poorest of the poor ate these creatures, roasting them in wretched alleys above dung-fueled fires. It had been agonizing for me to look upon the homeless, for open sores covered faces and arms, and flies covered sores. I was told that thousands of these people slept outside on beds of festering hay. The more blessed of the slum's inhabitants dwelt in decrepit mud-brick homes. Many such shelters had collapsed and were long ago looted of timber and stone.

"Shiva's been busy," Ladli said, interrupting my thoughts.

Shiva was the Hindu god of destruction and creation, and yes, had been busy, for within the slums, the thatched roof of one hovel was ablaze. I turned toward Mecca and said a quick prayer. In part to spite my husband, in part to help the fire's victims, I promised Allah to send a servant into the slums with coins for those injured. I'd send a physician as well. Though Ladli was equally accustomed to such sights, I saw her lips quiver as she spoke to her gods. I squeezed her hand. "I've missed you."

"But why?" she asked, her russet-colored face tightening as she hugged me. "Doesn't a certain buzzard keep you happy?"

"Me, happy?" I shifted atop a sandstone block. "I'm just another scrap of meat for his gullet."

"Truly?"

I watched the smoke drift upward, diffusing into the pale Hindustani sky. "Not too many years ago, I came here with my parents. We picnicked. They fed each other cherries and spat the pits below." I picked up a pebble and tossed it off the side. "They're so in love, Ladli. I always prayed that I'd have the same."

"But you don't," she said, her voice interrupted by the faraway trumpeting of elephants. On a broad riverbank, a circle of men assembled. Even from this distance I could tell that they were nobles, for the colors of their tunics were bright and varied. All the men held long spears. Before them, in the center of their circle, stood two elephants.

Knowing that the beasts would be prodded until at last they charged each other and bloodied their tusks, I shifted my gaze to a tiny mirror on my finger. I found myself wishing I loved a man who cherished the imperfections of my face. Though Mother possessed no such flaws, I was certain that Father would have delighted in a stray mole, or a crooked tooth, had they been hers. "He struck me the other night," I confessed. "And then he made me . . ."

"Made you what?"

I hesitated, the memory too foul. "Nothing. But can you imagine my father striking my mother? He'd die a thousand deaths before doing so."

"The dog!" she stammered. "That worm-infested, bastard son of a whore."

Her tongue always made me smile, and today was no exception. "Really, Ladli, the things you say."

"Perhaps if you hadn't been raised in the harem—"

"I can curse if I want to."

"Show me."

"What?"

"Who, you say, did you marry?"

I grinned, suddenly feeling warm and uncaged. "A pox-ridden maggot of a man with a brick for a brain and a dung heap for a home."

Ladli fought the urge to laugh. "Not bad for one so highborn. But surely you can be more inventive. Practice sometimes in his presence, when he reminds you of certain creatures."

"Like a boar?"

"A boar is much too clever. He's more of a toad, for you won't find an uglier, nor a more witless creature." She tugged at her sari, loosening its embrace from her ample breasts. Though a garment that made her look magnificent, saris seemed always to torment her. "I'd like to whip whoever devised this," she said. "Or better yet, make men wear it for a day."

"Can you imagine Khondamir in one?"

Her jaw dropped at the thought. "I'll try not to, my little Muslim friend."

As we chuckled I tossed more pebbles off the rampart. Ladli continued to fuss with her sari. The fire had spread below and consumed several hovels. I said a second prayer for their inhabitants before turning to my companion. "Can I ask you something?"

"Only if you've a tongue."

"Did you and Dara . . . ever kiss?"

Her smile flickered, then vanished. "I'd have liked to, but since he married that ornament, it will never happen. Not with him wed and me beneath him."

I recalled his wedding, an affair just two months before mine. His wife seemed a kind woman and a part of me envied him. "Has there been anyone else?"

"One."

"Do I know him?" I asked, taken aback by her admission.

"Do I know who you know?" Before I could answer, she added, "But not likely. He's the son of a fisherman. He sneaks me away on his boat."

"It continues?"

"Why wouldn't it?"

"But what if someone discovers? No one would marry you."

Ladli was about to respond when she spied a ladybug at my feet. She carefully picked it up, and held her hand open so that the creature might fly to safety. The wind bore it away. "Could be my great-grandmother," she jested, though in truth she took such matters seriously.

"What of the boy?"

"Nobody will find out. And I see no reason to keep myself untouched so that some old lout can grope me."

I considered my experience. The pain, despite lessening considerably, was still a part of the exchange. "What's it like?"

"Sometimes, the world seems to shake. Others, it's as peaceful as the river."

"Does it hurt?"

"Only in a good way, the way sherbet makes you cringe because it tastes so sweet."

I recalled my husband's sweaty, reeking embraces and found it impossible to conjure up such images. Lovemaking with him was like being lain upon by a chamber pot. "Please be careful," I finally said.

"Don't worry, Jahanara. And don't worry over your future. One of these days you'll find someone who makes you shake."

"I doubt it," I replied sadly.

Ladli rose to save an enormous caterpillar. "Food for your husband, the toad," she said, setting it away from our feet.

"He would probably eat it, for he's always stuffing something into his mouth."

"Take it home for him. Mix it up in some curry and he'll be none the wiser."

I smiled at the thought. As much as I wanted to stay with my friend and continue such banter, I needed to return home. So we hugged again, and started back toward the kitchen.

Little did I know then of how right Ladli was—that indeed I would discover such a man. For the face I would come to cherish, the spirit who would capture my own, was laboring within the Red Fort's walls.

CHAPTER V

A Promise to Keep

Not until summer's end did I finally see my family. Our forces secured a major victory to the south, and columns of men and mounts returned to Agra amid great fanfare. While throngs of Hindustanis applauded from the sides of a dusty road leading to our city, cannons rumbled from atop the Red Fort. Hundreds of enemy soldiers had been captured, and these unfortunate men headed the procession, stumbling into our lair chained to one another. The Deccans had been stripped of their armor and wore nothing but loincloths. Most were muscular figures and would command high prices as slaves.

Khondamir watched the prisoners pass with interest from our spot near the road, for his silver mines demanded fresh men. He would arrive at the imperial stockade early tomorrow before the bidding commenced. I'd heard through the whisperings of a servant that my husband had an arrangement with someone in the army and hence was always able to buy the fittest men.

"Pathetic creatures, aren't they?" he asked, devouring handfuls of pistachios. His plump figure bestrode a stallion while I sat on my old mare. Still, I was pleased to be present, even if my husband was merely showing me off to those lining the road. He had insisted I wear my best robe and jewels to honor our returning victors.

"The prisoners look weary," I said, for though the Deccans were our foes, they were bloodied and sagging. In the oppressive midday heat their bodies glistened with sweat.

"Wait until they stay a month in my mines. The cowards should have died fighting."

Despite my husband having never seen a battlefield, I checked my tongue. "Perhaps they were taken by surprise," I offered.

"There's no surprise, woman, in war. Face an enemy. Gut him. Kill him. But you wouldn't know that. All you know is trees."

I wasted no further words on him. Instead, I scanned the vast procession for my family. Discerning faces among the throngs of warriors wasn't easy, as most men wore helmets over grimy features. An endless stream of foot soldiers trudged behind the prisoners. Then came war elephants, hundreds upon hundreds of them. The behemoths pulled cannons, as well as carts laden with plunder, wounded warriors and sacks of grain. A slight man, known as a mahout, sat on the neck of each elephant, guiding his beast by tugging at its leathery ears with a hooked pole.

For a moment I feared I'd missed my family but then spied the royal banners announcing the Emperor's presence. Drumming my fingers on my saddle, I waited impatiently as Father approached. Father returned from battle, as always, riding the largest of all the war elephants. Like most of our bigger elephants, in addition to carrying a mahout, this beast bore a platform atop its back. Father sat on a cushioned dais, seemingly comfortable beneath the shade of a richly decorated umbrella. A musket overlaid in gold leaned against his thigh.

Before and behind Father's elephant were several white stallions, which my brothers rode. These mounts wore decorative, though protective, coats of leather and steel. The leather armor resembled a blanket that had been draped over each steed, beneath its saddle. Such coverings were dyed in bright colors and inset with copper, silver or gold studs. The horses' faces were clad with painted iron masks.

I waved to my siblings and Dara broke rank, spurring his mount toward me. The crowds, mostly peasants in filthy garbs, ebbed before his massive stallion. Dara offered coins to a few beggars, removed his gilded helmet, and wiped sweat from his brow. He looked displaced in his chain mail, a layer of steel scales set upon iron mesh that would stop all but the fiercest of blows. Silver spikes protruded from the mail, sharp and unblemished.

As convention dictated, Dara exchanged pleasantries with my husband.

They spoke briefly of the battle. My brother must have wanted to show his affection for me, because he leaned in my direction. Yet with Khondamir looking on, he merely smiled. "It does my heart good to see you, Jahanara."

I yearned to touch him but remained motionless, for such a display would surely enrage Khondamir. "I missed you," I replied, still drumming my fingers, despising the fact that I couldn't reach out to him. "Where is Mother?"

"Somewhere in the rear guard. She wanted to ride but is big enough with child that Father demanded she rest on a litter." Dara winked slyly, for we both knew Father could never truly demand anything of his wife.

"Can I see her, and you?"

My brother grinned, and after Khondamir's stained mouth, Dara's teeth seemed unnaturally white. "Tomorrow, in honor of his victory, Father's hosting a qamargah. Meet us a half morning's march upriver and we'll pass the day in the tent."

"You won't join in the chase?" Khondamir asked incredulously, for a qamargah was the most popular of hunts.

Dara shrugged. "Striking down a terrified animal is something I'll gladly refrain from."

"Plenty of warriors," Khondamir countered, "will enjoy the kill. As will I."

"Please do. And while you hunt, I'll talk with your lovely wife."

Khondamir grunted at the remark, as if I were anything but lovely. Dara stiffened, but seemed unsure whether he'd heard an insult. I hoped he might rise to my defense, but instead he bid us farewell and hurried to resume his position at Father's side. The army was entering Agra, and Khondamir, noticing that most of the nobles were returning to their shops and homes, wheeled his mount about. I followed him, excited about the prospect of seeing those I loved.

At dinner I could hardly sit still, and at night, when my husband thrust his filth inside me, I was able to force him from my mind. I slept little afterward, awash with eagerness for the coming day. I longed to feel Mother's belly and hear of the Empire's health. There was so much I was missing.

When dawn emerged I prepared a meal for Khondamir. He rose early for the qamargah, ate my food grudgingly, and headed toward his mount. His servants would be on foot, while I was given a decent steed. Blankets and provisions were stowed in saddlebags, and we set out at a brisk pace. Khondamir brandished a stout longbow and sword but no musket. Guns were rarely used in such hunts, for they diminished the skill of the hunter by making the kill too easy.

The journey upriver was uneventful. My husband ate roasted duck and drank arrack from a goatskin bag as he rode. Arrack is a potent drink fashioned from fermented rice, molasses and palm sap. I had sipped it once and would have guessed it to be liquid fire if I hadn't known better. Khondamir, however, enjoyed it immensely. On occasion he consumed it all day, or at least until he cursed me, fouled himself, and fell unconscious.

My husband didn't offer conversation as we traveled, and I made no effort to initiate words. At one point he did turn to me and say irritably, "A wife worth a tin of salt would ask if her husband is well."

"And how are you, my lord, this fine day?" I inquired sweetly.

He tossed a half-eaten drumstick in my direction before spurring his horse ahead. I patted my stallion and began to hum. I knew many songs and whispered them as the land drifted beneath us. The indifferent sun climbed and the river grew narrower and faster. More trees rose here than in Agra, and they dotted the landscape like unruly hairs. Between them swayed thick prairie grass, which hid much wildlife, though I saw three hawks, high above, skipping along currents of air.

When we finally reached the royal camp, mid-morning was upon us. The first thing I noticed was a massive fence encircling the camp. The fence was made of bundled branches the height of a man. These bundles had been placed upright and were tied together, forming a vast circle. To walk from one side of the circle to the other side would have taken longer than was necessary to boil an egg. In the circle's center stood a sprawling tent. A thicker, but much smaller, circle of wood surrounded this embroidered enclosure.

As such hunts commenced, thousands of soldiers—spread in an immense loop throughout the countryside—beat drums and slowly walked toward one another. Frightened animals trapped ahead of the men were forced toward the wooden circle, which had large openings for the beasts to escape into. Once the animals had been corralled within the circle, its openings were shut, effectively ensnaring the animals. Hunting ensued.

I'd experienced several qamargahs and must confess that I took no pleasure in them. Men struck down spotted deer with arrows, while trained cheetahs chased slighter game. A hunt, depending on the size of the circle, could last for an afternoon or several days.

This structure appeared smaller than most, and I gathered that Father didn't want to spend too much time in the countryside. Certainly with our enemies pressing in the south and north, he had more urgent engagements. Besides, hunting was far from his favorite passion. He only pursued it to reward his nobles and the officers of his army. After all, most men reveled in the killing.

Dara, perhaps adhering to Hinduism's belief that all life was reborn, and hence a chased fox could be an ancestor, had never taken part in such sporting. I appreciated my brother's disdain for hunting and was unashamed that he would likely be the only man present in the tent. After bidding my husband good luck, I dismounted and hurried into the cool structure.

Indeed, Dara sat on a cushion, studying Sanskrit and eating fried balls of goat cheese. Very few Muslims could read Sanskrit, which was the ancient written language of Hinduism, and my brother was determined to master it. Mother rested next to him, her belly swollen to the size of a watermelon. I removed my sandals and, avoiding platters of food and drink, made my way to her. "You're so big," I said, placing my hand on her hard stomach.

She hugged me tight, and I smelled a trace of musk on her skin. "How I missed you, Jahanara."

My eyes teared, but I sought to remain composed. "Why did you leave for so long?" I asked, abruptly vulnerable to the memories of the past weeks, biting my lip so that I wouldn't cry. "Father isn't the only one who needs you." I felt childish to speak so, but my love for my mother was like a cub that constantly requires meat, and she had been gone when I longed for her most.

"What's happened?"

"Marriage, Mother. Marriage happened."

"So?" Dara interjected quietly, aware of the other noblewomen in the tent.

"So, some people, my dear brother, are less grand than you think," I whispered. "And we weren't all paired as fortunately as you." I adored Dara, but sometimes his naiveté emboldened me. "Perhaps if Allah hadn't blessed you as a man, you'd see things differently."

Dara set his book aside. "Khondamir treats you poorly? But yesterday he seemed decent. Is he—"

"Please stop," I said, unwilling to describe to Dara what should have been obvious.

Mother squeezed my hand. "We're home now, Jahanara. And I'm sorry, truly sorry that marriage has been hard for you. Allah knows we didn't intend it to be. What can we do to help?"

She had always been a woman of unending strength, and I sat up straighter at her response, suddenly afraid she might think me weak. Regardless of my resentment at being married to Khondamir, I couldn't lead her to believe that I placed my happiness above my duty. She had been wed in the same manner, and if I were ever to merit her approval I'd have to bear most of my pain in silence. "Tell me," I said, as servants brought us water sweetened with lemon, "of your time south." I touched her belly. "How is the child?"

"Leaping like a monkey." Mother smiled, then wiped a damp cloth across my forehead. She also repositioned a strand of pearls about my neck.

"Does it hurt?"

"No, but even now, after so many pregnancies, it feels distinctly odd."

I knew that she, despite her unusual liking of politics, enjoyed the process of becoming a mother as much as any woman. I wondered if I might be the same. Was my will so stout that I could be a loving mother and a woman whom men treated with respect? Was it even possible for a woman not wed to an emperor to obtain such standing?

"The fighting was grim," Mother pronounced, scattering my thoughts. "I saw much of it from a bluff." She glanced at Dara, and I sensed something pass between them.

"What happened?" I asked my brother.

His eyes, usually untroubled, blinked with emotion. He started to speak, then stopped. Mother dipped her head and he started again. "I . . . I killed. I killed my first man."

I was unsure what to say, for he coveted life much more than did his peers. "Oh, Dara," I muttered, feeling woefully inadequate.

"My musket blew a hole clean through him."

"I'm so, so terribly sorry."

"As am I. Sorry for him, sorry for what I saw."

"What did you see?"

"Our brother."

"Aurangzeb?"

Dara appeared to gather himself, and then his words spilled forth, as if he could contain them no longer. "He was on the front line, with all the troops. There was so much dust. So much noise. The elephants trumpeted in horror and the cannons . . . the cannons were like endless thunder." He paused, rubbing his brow. "I could hardly think, Jahanara. But I saw Aurangzeb lead men. They followed him to death, and die they did. But they opened a gap in the enemy line, and they poured through it, slipping in the blood, falling and not rising."

"You can speak of this later if—"

"You should have seen him," he interrupted. "One moment, he slew two men with a single sword stroke. But not ten heartbeats later, because it was time for prayer, he put down his blade and faced Mecca." Dara shook his head in disbelief. "Men were dying all around him, and elephants running wild. But he was calm. Inhumanely calm. He recited his prayers and then fought with renewed vengeance. When the enemy retreated, he had their dead beheaded and made a great pile of these . . . trophies."

"Severe, I know," Mother said. "But the men loved him for it and our enemies fled."

"Yes, they did love him," Dara added slowly, as if he found such reverence incomprehensible. "They chanted his name and thanked Allah for his presence. You see, he only fights with Muslims. Hindus he sends to me. And they come gladly."

"What does Father think of this split?" I asked, aware of the distant beat of drums.

"Father," Dara responded, "wants to continue the peace between us and our Hindu friends. But he's reluctant to curb Aurangzeb."

"As he should be," Mother said. "A father's strength is revealed in his sons. The artists and politicians adore you, whereas the soldiers flock to Aurangzeb. It's a sound combination."

I rarely disagreed with Mother, but I did now, for the power of our empire rested in its army. Yet my tongue made no move against her opinion. "You were right to kill that warrior, Dara," I said. "I'd rather have him dead than you."

My brother thanked me. He turned westward and his lips fluttered in prayer. The drums increased in zeal and I was suddenly transfixed by their pulsations. Standing, I looked outside our tent and saw beasts running into the wooden edifice. At first only a few gazelles appeared. But then came a tiger, a handful of antelope and some hares. Soon scores of animals darted wildly about the enclosure. They ran all in the same direction, circling to my left. Mounted men cheered as the gates closed behind them and the killing ensued. My husband, perhaps fearful of getting trampled, sat on his stallion at the periphery and feebly shot arrows at the frenzied beasts. I saw him strike nothing.

My brothers and Father were among the few on foot. Shah and Murad went after a boar together, firing arrows into its bloodied flanks. Father stood behind them. His bow was raised, but he seemed reluctant to kill. Aurangzeb, meanwhile, paced in the center of the boiling cauldron. His tunic was splattered with gore and his curved sword rose and fell in murderous arcs. Everything toppled before him. I saw a tiger charge his position, and suddenly Aurangzeb lunged forward as a cobra might strike. His blade opened the magnificent creature's throat and it died thrashing against him.

Sickened by the carnage, I sat down, leaning my head against Mother's belly. I thought I could hear the baby's heart, but the thumping might have been the huntsmen's drums. "Are you nervous?" I asked.

She reached over to fasten a golden brooch to my veil. "Even after having so many children, I am a bit. I want you with me, Jahanara."

I stopped toying with the hem of my robe. "Will you ask my husband?"

"I would, though by your earlier tone he'd likely ignore me. And then I would surely insult the fool." Mother grimaced, and I knew she'd enjoy nothing more than to inform Khondamir of his shortcomings. "Your father will deal with him," she concluded. "And no matter where I am, you'll be by my side."

"Truly?"

Mother kissed my cheek. "Your presence shall make the pain bearable."

I cherished my mother then. If I had known what pain awaited her, I'd have held her and not let go.

IT WAS THE SEASON of monsoon when the baby came. Mother had accompanied Father and his advisors to Burhanpur, a muddy locale in the upper region of the Deccan. Our enemy had sought revenge after its defeat, and so our army marched south to defend our interests. I had argued against Mother making the journey, but she insisted. My parents were rarely apart, and for her to stay in the Red Fort while he campaigned in the south—however sensible the notion—to them was incomprehensible.

Because the child was near, I'd also ventured to Burhanpur. My husband had been less opposed to the idea than I had thought; I suspect he was pleased to see me go. In my absence he could enjoy more of his fruits without having me spoil their moods. After all, Khondamir's girls often appeared uncomfortable with me nearby, as most were honorable young courtesans and had no wish to offend the Emperor's daughter.

Burhanpur was a wretched place. The city knew little but war and its inhabitants acted accordingly. We stayed outside its borders, camping amid immense fields of wheat. Father, like his predecessors, always spearheaded major war efforts from within a portable capital. This city of endless tents housed several hundred thousand men and women. It was an unimaginable complex of bazaars, armories, hospitals, mosques, temples and even a harem. Aside from the multitudes of warriors present, priests, concubines, merchants, blacksmiths, cooks, artists and administrators inundated the hay-covered streets. At the city's periphery, temporary stables held tens of thousands of elephants and camels and horses.

To walk from one end of this city to the other took half a morning. Remarkably, after the present engagement with the Deccans ended, the entire site would be packed into bullock carts and returned to Agra. And when the next key battle ensued—whether in the Thar Desert or the province of Bengal—the city would be transported, unpacked, and arranged in the exact manner as it had been in Burhanpur.

In the center sprawled the imperial tent. The largest such shelter in Hindustan, this tent could easily have been mistaken for a palace. Its red walls were the height of a rearing elephant and created a boxlike structure two hundred paces from side to side. The tent contained every conceivable luxury.

I was quartered here with my parents. While Father spent day after day scheming with his officers in an adjacent pavilion, Mother and I listened to the distant fighting from atop cashmere carpets and silk cushions. I'd have infinitely preferred to hear songbirds chattering as I knelt on jagged rocks, for the clamor of battle was far too unsettling. Unceasing cannons rumbled during daylight. At night the screams of the wounded kept us flinching in prayer until dawn once again spread its colors.

Servants burned sandalwood incense within the imperial tent to mask the smells of camp. They needn't have bothered. Whenever the tent's flaps were opened, foulness entered along with whomever was calling. Scents of damp hay, unwashed soldiers and cooking fires mingled with the stench of rotting flesh. Not only did hundreds of men decay in the hospitals surrounding us, but scores of ravaged elephants and horses were also attended to. The elephants were immeasurably valuable to our army, and no expense was spared to heal their wounds.

Considering the sights, sounds and smells, Burhanpur was a dreadful place to give birth. Yet Mother and I had done little but pray for an end to the killing since our arrival at the front. And while the killing remained unchecked, the life within Mother eased our sorrow.

The baby grew impatient during our second week in Burhanpur. After Mother's water broke, the royal physician who always accompanied Father on such ventures was immediately summoned. I was present, as was Father and three midwives. Though husbands rarely witnessed births, Father had never missed the rise of one of his children. He told me once that he knew no happier moments than during Mother's deliveries.

The night was auspicious for a birth, cool and full of wind. Beyond our canvas walls a storm raged. The rain was heavy and, for once, the roar of guns was only a memory.

Mother lay on blankets with her head and back propped against cushions. The physician felt her pulse before ordering clean linen. A silver bowl of water steamed beside him and spread upon cloth were instruments of steel. One resembled a pair of joined ladles. I'd been to several of Mother's birthings and wasn't unduly nervous. Though in pain, she seemed more radiant than ever. I thought she looked beautiful without all her jewels and told her so.

"Sometimes," she quietly confided in me, "I loathe the jewels. But diamonds mean power and without power I'm without worth."

I'll never equal her, I remember thinking then. Impossible that I should be as lovely or well loved.

I kissed her and held Father's hand. We knelt by her side, leaning toward her. When the first contraction came she whimpered. "It comes," she said, beads of sweat appearing on her forehead despite the night's coolness. The physician had counted to two hundred and ninety-five when the next contraction arrived. It seemed stronger than the first.

Candles flickered in the drafty room as the physician felt the contours of her belly. He was an old man, with a chest-long beard and a slight limp. He had delivered more babies than a water buffalo has ticks, yet the Emperor's child must have unsettled him, for he seemed ill at ease.

"What should we name him?" Father asked, brushing her hair aside.

"Him?"

"He kicks too hard to be a girl. And, my love, your belly's never been so swollen."

"We—" a contraction spawned within her and she bit her lip. She breathed deeply, collecting herself. "We could name him after an artist," she muttered. "Too many names of warriors and emperors float about this land."

The physician handed her a cup of tea. "Drink this, my lady. It will ease your discomfort."

She thanked him. The tea must have been bitter, for she grimaced. "Is it poison?" she asked, trying to smile.

"Only to the pain."

More contractions came as the night ebbed. They drew closer. Mother thrashed and her eyes teared. "I wish I could take your suffering," Father said softly. "Take it and bury it far within me."

I wiped her brow. "Does the first hurt the most?"

"If only that were true," she managed, then was overcome by pain. Father cringed when she moaned, and I suspected her agony had reached out and grabbed him as it rent her. She asked for something to bite on and I gave her the cloth. Her contractions were more frequent now. Her whimpers turned to moans and the moans turned to shrieks.

"Can you see him?" Father asked impatiently.

Thunder boomed. "A leg, yes," the physician replied. "It's a breech." Father's face quivered. I was uncertain what this meant and revealed my ignorance. "It means," the physician offered worriedly, "that the child fights to remain in the womb. He's not ready."

Mother screamed and I clutched her hand. "He comes, Mother, he comes." I prayed as I spoke, pleading with Allah to ease her misery.

"He does," Father echoed. "And when he's here, I'll hold you both all night."

She tried to reply yet could only moan. Her tears welled and I knew she suffered terribly. "Pl . . . please," she stammered.

"Can you give her nothing else?" Father asked suddenly, the ferocity in his voice frightening me.

The old physician paused. "Too much is dangerous, my lord. But I'll give her a bit more."

Drops of the tea fell into her mouth. I could see that her tongue bled from where she had bitten it. Her face, always so serene, was twisted in agony. I looked from her to the physician, who removed a bloody cloth from between her legs. "You must push harder, my lady," he said, somewhat urgently. "Truly you must."

"But the pain."

"Push, my lady. Push harder!"

She screamed and thrashed. Father and I held her down while the midwives brought fresh water. "Glorious Allah," Father prayed, "let it be over soon and I'll build You a beautiful mosque. I'll feed and clothe Your poor."

I also prayed. I turned to Mecca and begged Allah to deliver the child. Alas, only screams and thunder answered me. The physician asked her again to push, desperation clear in his voice. Blood pooled on the floor and the fresh bowl of water was already crimson. The old man had his fingers inside her and was trying to reposition the child. I hoped desperately to hear him wail but heard only Mother's tortured moans.

"What happens?" Father exclaimed, hurrying to the physician's side.

"The child is twisted, and too large for the birthing canal. He tears her and she bleeds to death."

Father staggered. "Then shed her of him now," he wailed.

Mother's cries weakened. Her eyes started to wander. "Hurry, Father!" I shrieked. "You must do something!"

Father pushed the old man aside and knelt before her. "Tell me what to do." As the physician explained how to reposition the child, Father yanked off his rings and eased his fingers into her passage. He tried to be gentle, his face contorting with consternation. Father wasn't able to turn the baby, but suddenly the child dropped free, the cord tight around his neck. He was bloody and beautiful and lifeless. Father carefully set him aside. "Make the bleeding stop," he beseeched the physician, who applied clean linen to the opening. The cloth quickly reddened.

"I'm sorry, my lord. She has little time left."

"No!" Father wailed. "You must do something!"

"She is in Allah's hands. Not mine."

Father fell beside her, weeping, and called her name. "Please, no!"

Her eyes flickered, and then a spasm of hurt encompassed her. "Hush, love," she mumbled.

"Please, Allah," he pleaded. "Please, please, please let her live. Take me instead. Please take me."

My tears mingled with his upon her face. "You must . . . you must stay with us, Mother."

Her head wobbled and she tried to smile. "I . . . fall asleep."

The physician and his midwives left the tent. I kissed her brow fiercely, clinging to her as I had to that log in the river. "Please don't go," I begged, my world dying with her.

"Come closer," she said, her lips scarcely moving.

I leaned forward until my face was a hand's breadth from hers. "Stay."

"I . . . need you."

"Me?" I asked.

She tried to raise her head, and I bent even lower. Mother twisted so that her mouth was against my ear. "Watch over him," she whispered faintly.

"But, Moth—"

"You are strong enough . . . more than strong enough."

"No, I want you here. You should be here."

"Please."

"You can't leave!"

"Please, Jahanara."

Her eyes were unguarded, and despite my overwhelming grief, I recognized her distress. I looked to Father, who knelt with his head upon her feet. "I'll try," I promised, my voice choked with tears.

"I love you. And I'm proud, so very, very proud of you." She motioned for me to kiss her. Holding her tightly, I touched her lips with my own, feeling the warmth of her, not wanting to let go. I finally withdrew for Father. He kissed her more gently than I, and when he eased away, she smiled. "My love?"

"Yes?"

"Will you . . ." She seemed to fade and return much weaker. "Will you grant me favors?" He could only nod. The power of speech seemed to have left him. "First," she continued, "always . . . care for our children. And second, fall in love again."

"No, my love is with you."

She feebly shook her head. "Then build me something . . . something beautiful. And visit my tomb . . . on the anniversary of my death."

"I shall," he said, weeping like a child.

She seemed to gulp for air. "Let me die . . . feeling you . . . touching you."

He leaned down. Cradling her, he whispered, "I'll always be with you, my love of all loves." Her lips quivered, but no sound came forth. "Always, my love," he whimpered. "Always."

Then he kissed her. He held her long and soon she did not stir.

We cried together.

And the sky wept with us.

PART 2

Those who believe in the Qur'an,
And those who follow the
Jewish scriptures,
And the Christians and the Sabians,
And who believe in God, and the
Last Day
And work righteousness
Shall have their reward.
They shall have nothing to fear,
nor will they sorrow.

THE QUR'AN

A cup of chai cools in my hands. A breeze gathers in the distance, unsettling tranquil waters. Though I am a hard woman with a barbed tongue, I'm still sentimental and prone to the welling of emotion. And breezes, especially those rising from beyond the Taj Mahal, can make tears bloom within me. For breezes remind me of kisses.

And kisses can be eternal.

"What happened, Jaha," Gulbadan asks quietly, "after she died?"

I force a memory aside. "My father," I say, "locked himself in a small room and wouldn't show himself to anyone. Not even me." I pause, recalling how profoundly I had wanted to comfort him. Of course, I needed him also, for my sorrow was unyielding. I longed to sense his love for me, even if it were nothing compared to his feelings for Mother. "We heard him weeping and praying without end," I add distantly, setting down my cup. "When he finally emerged after two weeks, his eyes were so red and damaged from weeping that from then on he had to wear spectacles."

"Truly?" Rurayya asks, her young voice cracking, her hand reaching out for mine.

"Indeed, child. Father emerged from that room a changed man. Part of him was broken, and he would never love again." I squeeze Rurayya's fingers, stroking them with my thumb. As a young woman, I couldn't have grasped the totality of Father's loss. But I do now. For I feel that grief is the most potent of all emotions, save love.

"But then he began to build," Gulbadan offers.

"Yes," I reply, and my mind sweetens. "To build a monument fit for his love, he called upon the Empire's greatest architect, a young man who could transform jade into flowers, marble into paradise."

"And who was he?"

"Isa. Isa was everything."

CHAPTER VI

The Truth of Dreams

·:·

The Peacock Throne still glittered, but the man atop it did not.
Sunlight slanted into the Diwan-i Am through its many windows.
Yet dimness prevailed here, for no candles burned. The room was empty
aside from Father, Dara and myself. Since Mother's death, Aurangzeb
had been given partial control of the military and now probed north into
enemy territory, a masterless land that always encroached upon ours.

We had so many enemies in those days. Northward flourished the
dreaded Persians, who sought to expand their empire. Southward lay the
Deccan, a part of Hindustan but governed by an iron-fisted sultan who
fought for independence. Other foes nipped at our flanks—fierce Rajput
clans to the west and Christians from beyond our shores.

Aurangzeb fought them all.

Father, meanwhile, was a shadow of the man I once knew. His white
tunic, the color of mourning, was stained and his hair was unkempt. In
the moon since Mother had died, the only thing he had done was to buy
a colossal parcel of land near the river. Upon this land his wife would rest
eternally.

I still found it nearly impossible to imagine Mother as dead. I awoke
each morning expecting to see her and, after recalling that she was gone,
met the day reluctantly. I opened books but couldn't read. I ate delicacies
but didn't taste. Each thought of her provoked a longing—an empty,
lifeless ache that I'd never known. Her death seemed immensely unjust
and I struggled to find meaning in her absence. But without her to guide
me, I saw it in nothing.

She had asked me to be strong, and so I endeavored to help Father,
spending as much time as possible with him. We prayed together. We

grieved together. And when our mood was right, we whispered of memories.

"Father," Dara said, disrupting my thoughts, "you must hold your sessions in court again. The Empire can endure your absence no longer." In the empty Diwan-i Am, his words reverberated eerily. "Besides, I need your help."

Father seemed unwilling to hear him. When he finally spoke I was somewhat surprised. "The nobles," he predicated, "shall do as you say. They know you stand to inherit the throne, and they'll flock to curry your favor."

"But my influence will swell with you behind me."

"And behind you I'll be," he replied forlornly. He adjusted his silver-rimmed spectacles before rubbing his nose. "Even a swan, though I'm told they mate for life, can't mourn forever."

"The nobles—"

"For now, Dara, I leave you to your own devices. You attend to their squabbles. You deal with your brother's reports on the wars."

"But he tells me nothing."

"Jahanara," Father said, "will help me with the mausoleum. Once it is under construction, she'll oversee the project while I return to my duties."

Though sorrow still assailed me, I sought to brighten for his sake, and I was eager to help. "Where do we begin, Father?"

A faint smile, so at odds with his demeanor, appeared. "Patience, my child." He called out and a royal guard entered the room. "Bring in Ustad Isa."

Ustad means "master" in Persian, and I knew the man would be some kind of builder, perhaps a sculptor or a calligrapher. I expected a wrinkled figure to enter slowly, but when the doors opened a different apparition strode forward. My first impression was that of a hawk. The man's face was narrow—but keen and not cruel. His eyebrows were arched, his eyes bold, and his nose slightly hooked. He had high, defined cheekbones that were obscured partially by a well-kept beard. A tall man, unusually so, he possessed a thin, tapered frame taut with muscles. He was not dressed in brilliant attire, as men of rank came before the Emperor, but wore the simple tunic of a laborer.

"Welcome, Ustad Isa," Father said, rising from his throne.

The young man bowed. "I am honored, my lord."

Father waved dismissively. He slipped on his sandals and stepped toward our visitor. "The honor is mine. Your works grace my land and your fame precedes you."

"My fame, my lord, is fleeting," the stranger replied softly. "Only the stones shall remember me."

Father shook his head so vigorously that for a moment I forgot about his sorrow. "This man, my children, is remembered by more than his stones. He creates mosques and forts that aren't buildings, but tapestries of rock. And if my sources are correct, he's been contracted to build the palaces of enough nobles to last him a lifetime."

"I'm blessed, my lord."

"Are you? Are you, indeed?" Father placed his arm around the man's shoulders, an act I had never seen him commit. "But is a poet blessed if he owns no ink, or a musician blessed if he grasps no instrument?" The stranger started to speak, but Father continued. "Would you like, Isa, to build something grand, something that shall remain when your bones are but dust?"

The architect turned to Father. "Might I ask . . ." He paused. Though he appeared confident, his voice was subdued, seeming to disagree with his disposition. "What might this something be, my lord?"

"The Rauza-i Munavvara."

"The . . . Tomb of Light?"

"I want you to build a mausoleum for my wife," Father said, clasping his hands as he mentioned Mother. For a heartbeat I feared he might cry, but he straightened, overpowering his emotions. "When you finish, I expect it to be the most beautiful structure in the world, for she was certainly the most beautiful woman."

A silence rose. Pigeons cooed outside the room's windows, which were an intricate stone lattice. I noticed that the stranger sweated. "Such a thing, my lord," he replied, "would take years, perhaps decades, to create. It would demand thousands of men and—"

"You'll have your years and your men."

"And how would it look?" he asked quickly, and I sensed his budding excitement.

"Most of Agra is red, but I'm weary of sandstone, for it's the color of blood. No, this building shall be white, the brilliant white of marble. White and only white. And it should resemble a woman, capturing her grace, her splendor—the majesty of Allah's finest creation."

"But what, my lord, of my contracts?"

Father pretended to tear imaginary paper. "Nothing to me. I'll buy them all."

"And where might this mausoleum rest?"

"Here. On the old polo grounds."

Ustad Isa hurried past Dara to a nearby window. On the opposite end of our crescent-shaped city, directly upon the river, stretched a vast tract of land where until recently only polo matches occurred. Our visitor tugged at his beard and I could almost hear him thinking. "I'd require twenty thousand men, my lord. Within three months."

"Can you build so soon?"

"I'll need a foundation, my lord. A structure to bear an immense load." The architect eagerly whispered something before twisting again at his beard. I wondered if he had forgotten that the Empress was dead. He seemed far too pleased, considering that he had been summoned to build a mausoleum. "Before I can start," he said softly, yet suddenly, "I require one more thing."

"And that is?"

"A painting of your wife, when her beauty was the fullest."

Father's smile was somewhat forced. "I can offer more. For my daughter, Jahanara, shall assist you on this project. And her face is a mirror of her mother's."

While this compliment wasn't quite true, I blushed nonetheless. Ustad Isa did me further honor by replying, "Then it will be a wondrous sight, for surely your wife must have made poets smile."

"Good," Father proclaimed. "Jahanara will be the link between us, as unfortunately, I've an empire to govern. But listen to her counsel wisely, Isa, for she is as clever as a crocodile in a waterhole." Most men would bristle at being told to listen to a woman, but the stranger only nodded. Father turned to me. "You'll live closer to the site in the Red Fort until the mausoleum is complete. Naturally, you're to visit your husband whenever possible."

It took me a moment to digest his words. As much as I rejoiced at the thought of escaping Khondamir, I was afraid of making my father an enemy of my husband. "Perhaps," I said, "you should pay my husband for my services. A bag of gold should keep him pleased."

When Father next spoke, his eyes unexpectedly swelled with tears. "You see, Isa, how my wife lives in her?" Ustad Isa said something in reply, but I watched Father. "Oh, sweet Mumtaz Mahal," he whispered, "how I miss you."

I had never heard him call her this before. It meant "Chosen of the Palace," and I realized it must have been a secret term between them. As Father turned away and moved toward a window, Dara had the decency to signal us to follow him. Ustad Isa and I left the Emperor alone with his grief.

Dara hurried to attend the nobles' needs. The architect bade me farewell, and then, perhaps trying to memorize my face, stared at me until I grew painfully self-conscious. "It will be beautiful, my lady," he promised. "As beautiful a sight as the world has ever seen."

I watched him stride down a crowded street, noting how tall he looked amid his countrymen. He started to twist around but must have thought better of it, for he turned instead into an alley and vanished.

In the ensuing days my life gradually improved.

As I expected, Khondamir was enraged when I told him I was to live in the Red Fort. He slapped me before I was able to withdraw a heavy gold necklace from my robe and drop it at his feet. I also tossed him a pair of rubies and an emerald-encrusted dagger.

"He vastly overvalues your wisdom," Khondamir said, picking up the items, unable to restrain his glee.

"He is the Emperor," I mumbled, my cheek already throbbing. "Perhaps his judgment is keener than yours."

That remark earned me another cuff, but his vexation was worth the pain. He came to my bed with more violence than usual that night, but having guessed his intentions, I'd smeared goat's blood between my legs. While he cursed my timing and ranted about his disgust, I smiled surreptitiously. How little such fools knew of women's bodies, I thought.

The following morning I wished him farewell. I was given an apartment high in the Red Fort, a sanctuary boasting a magnificent view of the river and much of Agra. The room was small, but its dimensions were somehow reassuring. I made it as comfortable as possible over the next few days.

The second time I met Ustad Isa was near the river, upon the large swath of land Father had purchased. It was an ideal place to build the mausoleum. Palaces of the nobility bordered it to the east, west and south. To the north coursed the Yamuna River. Farther northwest sprawled Agra and then the Red Fort.

Alone I made the long walk to the site, retracing countless steps I had taken with Mother. After passing beyond the Red Fort's walls I entered a network of crowded streets. Single-story buildings bordered these passages, the buildings being the only objects present that didn't walk, trot or hop. Aside from the usual sights, I witnessed a trio of Chinese traders heatedly arguing with the proprietor of a silk shop. Though the dark-skinned local towered over the Chinese and shouted so quickly that they had no possibility of understanding him, his hostility seemed to embolden the foreigners. Wearing yellow tunics and hats resembling overturned goblets, they pointed to bolts of fabric and spoke in broken and accented sentences.

I turned left onto a much wider street, skirting around a moaning camel. The beast was trying to mount a female. A man gripped its distended organ and sought to place it within the miserable female, which was held immobile by several more men. Camels were often reluctant to mate, and this spectacle was quite common. Still, I was reminded of my husband and found myself pitying the slighter animal.

The farther I walked from the Red Fort, the less chaos prevailed. The street I followed soon paralleled the Yamuna. I passed an enormous rice field bustling with water buffalo and farmers, then wandered by several grand palaces perched alongside the river. A sandstone bridge carried me over a stream, depositing me on the western edge of the land Father had purchased for the mausoleum.

At first Ustad Isa didn't see me. He held oversized leaves of paper and took notes as he strode about the area. As before, he wore the garb of a laborer. His gray turban was soaked in sweat and he appeared in a hurry. I noticed, however, that he ensured that each of his strides was the same distance as its predecessors. He walked in this awkward manner from the northern end of the parcel to its southern border. He then marched east to west and finally strolled about the entire perimeter. This process was time-consuming and so I rested, shielding my face from the hot sun.

The young architect finally noticed me and approached where I knelt on a diminutive blanket. In some ways he lacked the grace of my brothers, not holding himself upright and hardly strutting as a warrior might, yet his gait possessed a certain dignity and purpose. And he was strong, for I could see his muscles pushing at the seams of his tunic. They were the thick muscles of one who lifts stones and chisels marble.

"Good morning, my lady."

"The same to you, Ustad Isa."

A thought of Mother bloomed, as her mausoleum, after all, was the cause for this meeting. Yet today, unlike so many others before it, I didn't dwell on my loss. She would not have wanted me to, and though I'd been too weak to heed what would have been her advice, since leaving Khondamir's home I was able to ponder notions beyond her death.

I rose, nodding to Ustad Isa. The architect looked more hawklike than ever, with the sun behind him casting shadows across his angular face. "My lady," he said, "please call me Isa." His smile was slightly askew, as if one side of his mouth outweighed the other.

"Only if I'm Jahanara."

"You look lovely today, Jahanara."

I had purposely left most of my jewelry in my room and wore a simple robe and shawl. Even if he built treasures, I had sensed that Isa was at odds with everyday trinkets. Still, I was uncertain what to make of his compliment. "What, may I ask, were you just doing?"

He showed me his notes. "Ensuring that the dimensions of the parcel are as listed in the contract."

"Are they?"

"Nearly." He rolled his papers up and placed them in a basket with many others.

"Have you started on your plans yet? May I see them?"

He chuckled, and I was struck by what a happy man he seemed. "Your father told me to beware of your impatience."

"My impatience?"

"He said you were like a young swallow as it prepared to fly, forever leaping from the nest too quickly."

"He did? What else did he say?"

His crooked smile came again, though his teeth were long and true. "Only that he loved you, and that I was fortunate to have you as an assistant."

"And do you think, that I'm this . . . swallow?"

"I think, my lady, that you'd be more woman than most men could manage."

A presumptuous comment it might have been, but the corners of my mouth rose at his boldness. Normally, I was guarded with such displays around men, for smiles spoke not of wisdom, but of gaiety. And I needed to be known as someone wise. Yet today it felt good to relax, and my insides warmed.

"Let's walk the grounds," he said, motioning for me to lead. "Because if I'm to design something wonderful, I must commit this land to memory."

And so we walked. The first sight to catch my attention was a group of men building a boat. The vessel was mostly completed and the laborers caulked its seams with pitch. One withered man carved a tiger's head into the bow.

"A gifted craftsman," Isa said. "We'll have to hire him."

"How will you gather them all?"

"The artists? When the time is right, I'll send out messengers. I hope to find calligraphers from Persia, masons from Egypt, and even craftsmen from Europe."

Perhaps fifty Europeans dwelt in Agra. Though Father occasionally spoke with them about trade, I could hardly imagine them working on Mother's mausoleum. "You want Europeans working on this?"

"We need the world's best, Jahanara. I don't care where they call home."

I dropped my gaze, embarrassed that I'd so openly revealed my surprise. Mother would have been displeased. "Can you tell me," I asked, "of how it shall appear?"

"The mausoleum will sit near the river, while the grounds to the south are to be gardens."

"And the structure?"

"Think of what . . . imagine how a tear from Allah might look," he replied eagerly. His passion startled me, for soft voices usually hint of indecision, not the fire I now discerned. "That tear will be the dome. And the dome will be supported by a square structure full of great arches. Four minarets, placed beyond each corner of the mausoleum, will rise almost as high as the dome. And everything, from the courtyard to the tomb to the tear, shall be white marble."

I tried to envision such a sight but didn't possess the mind for it. "Do you have a sketch?"

"For the present it resides in my head."

I noticed then that Isa had forgotten his basket of papers. Pointing behind us, I replied, "But is your head the best place for it?"

His eyes widened when he saw his precious documents sitting unguarded. "The problem with artists, Jahanara, is that we often forget the more common things in life. Our heads are so high in the clouds that we don't see the world beneath."

"Then I'll just have to remind you where to plant your feet."

He smiled at my words, which pleased me in a strange way. I hadn't been pleased with anything since Mother's death. We returned to the spot bearing his papers. Once there, I folded up my blanket. "May I ask, Isa, your age?"

"Twenty-two autumns. And you?"

"Six less, though soon to be five." I caught his eyes then and held them, something few women would dare. Even for our people they were dark, and I found myself trapped within their depths. "Why," I muttered, forcing my lips to move, "did you become an architect?"

"I was born in Persia," he responded, answering my thoughts regarding his distinct features. "There my father designed things. Wells mostly, but once an aqueduct. After my mother died and illness struck him down, he gave what little coin he owned to a visiting architect so that I might become his apprentice."

"But what happened to your father?"

"He fought, fought like a bull elephant, but didn't last long. And so I lived with my master, a good, kind man if ever there was one. When his project ended we returned to his home in Delhi."

I thought of the pain of my loss and instinctively desired to comfort him. But I knew him far less well than was needed to do so. "How old were you?"

"Seven."

"And you never returned to Persia?"

"There's nothing to return to. The war makes it impossible at any rate, as I'd likely be beheaded as a traitor. No, Hindustan is my land. I feel hardly a tug from the north."

He smiled again, surprising me on account of his story. It seemed that he should have been more acquainted with sorrow than bliss, but he acted the contrary. Why, I wondered, did he so freely share his musings with me? Was he always so forward? Did he always feel so at ease with himself? Captivated by his voice, I asked, "You enjoy your work?"

"I'm fortunate, Jahanara. Truly blessed. For I can show my parents what I've done with their gifts." His eyes darted between my face and the land encircling us. "I could never be closer to them than when building."

Despite my desire for such a connection to Mother, his passion was infectious enough that I was not envious. "I look forward to . . . seeing you build," I said, trying to subdue my budding emotions. "For now I'll leave you to your duties."

"Your company is most pleasant. Would you return this evening? The moon shall be ripe and I hope to show you something."

"Then perhaps I shall come," I replied, suppressing a grin when his face tightened in consternation. I bade him farewell and headed back toward the Red Fort. As I walked Isa kept popping back into my mind. I saw his face, recalled his words. I wished that my husband were so gentle. Why did I receive him when men such as Isa graced the world? Perhaps I was mistaken, but I struggled to envision the young architect ever striking me.

Too much time had passed since I spoke to Ladli, so, dust-coated from my long walk, I sought her out in the royal kitchen. She was covered in beet juice, her hands stained purple from peeling. The head cook glared at me, as usual, when I stole Ladli from her services. Once outside, my friend squinted in the bright light, shielding her eyes from the sun. I heard soldiers practicing their warfare in a nearby courtyard and I walked in that direction.

We climbed a series of stairwells and were suddenly on a rampart high above the men. Several dozen were present, tough-looking warriors in shining helmets and leather armor. To my surprise, I saw that Aurangzeb led them. Though almost all the soldiers were older than he, they listened to him attentively. He held a musket and in short order showed his men how to load and discharge the weapon. There was a sharp crack as he fired, and a watermelon perched a stone's throw away shattered from the blast. The warriors cheered at his accuracy. As he handed his gun to a huge warrior, I wondered if Aurangzeb had shed a single tear for Mother.

"Who's the giant?" I asked my friend, for she harbored all the fort's gossip.

"A murderous half-wit, if you believe the rumors," Ladli replied, spitting to show her disdain. "They call him Balkhi."

"What do you hear of him?"

"That your brother freed him from prison so the lout could be his bodyguard."

"Why was he in prison?"

"Rape. He raped and mutilated a servant girl after returning from battle. She was Hindu and so your brother—may Shiva boil him in piss—forgave the creature."

I shuddered at the thought. "And what do the people say of my father condoning the pardon?"

My friend looked about us, ensuring our privacy. A guard was posted next to a rippling red banner but stood at least thirty paces away. "That his grief has blinded him to the matter."

A splattering of guns erupted below and more melons toppled. Aurangzeb cuffed a man who'd missed. The soldier stood immobile and my brother shoved a fresh gun into his hands. Fire belched from the weapon and a melon exploded.

"Why can't they use wooden targets," I asked angrily, "when so many of our people lack such food?"

"Surely you don't expect men to think? Least of all your brother." Ladli fingered a silver nose ring, the only piece of jewelry she wore. "Sometimes, Jahanara, I see him watching me. And his eyes . . . his eyes are wicked."

I wished then that my friend was not so physically stunning. I knew Aurangzeb had bribed the fathers of girls in the past, girls he had ravaged. "Then you must be careful, Ladli," I advised, "for Aurangzeb takes what he wants."

"What should I do?"

"Never show him any fear, because if he sees it, his head will swell with his power over you."

"What else?"

I imagined myself as Aurangzeb. Mother had taught me this trick, and I had learned to place myself within another's skin with little effort. People, after all, were never as private as they believed. "Go out of your way to be kind to him," I replied, tapping my foot as I thought, wishing I could confer with Mother, wishing she sat at my side. "Flatter him the way all the other girls do. He tires of them quickly and you'll soon bore him." An inspiration suddenly struck and I paused.

"What?"

I wondered if it was right to ask a friend to do something dangerous, something that wouldn't aid her, but me. "I'm unsure if—"

"Do speak, Jahanara. I grow older by the moment."

"Perhaps, if you desired, you could even earn his trust."

"His trust? But why?"

"You know so many secrets. Someday you'll learn information he can use. Give it to him. Let him kill an enemy or stop a crime. He'll gain face before the court and you'll become his confidante."

"I'd rather scrub a leper's boils."

"And so would I," I whispered, "under normal circumstances." I studied my brother as he ordered his men about. "Come to me long before you tell him anything. We'll decide together if he should know. And meanwhile, act unafraid around him. Completely unafraid. Give him some sweets, and try to catch his eye. But when you see him and you know that you'll talk, chew garlic cloves and make sure to breathe into his face."

Ladli looked at me oddly. "I didn't realize, Jahanara, that you were so . . . versed in such matters."

"I have a husband, don't I?"

"And what kind of fool is he?"

I pondered my choice of words as muskets roared and the stench of gunpowder drifted about us. "A man who could be outthought by a new-born, who makes love as if he were a goat."

She giggled at my effort. "You improve. But, truly, like a goat?"

"When it suits him."

"Then may Shiva be kind to you and let his manhood rot and fall off. Let it become a plaything for my dogs."

"Really, Ladli!" I exclaimed. "The notions you have. I could never best you in these contests." Ladli, my closest friend, seemed always to improve my mood. "I met a man today," I said quietly. "He's to be the mausoleum's architect."

"So? I met a cockroach. Is there a difference?"

"He appears to be everything that my husband isn't."

"Men deceive. They charm you at first, then once they've bedded you, their gifts disappear and their gallantry becomes as rare as their compliments."

I took her hand. "We need to find you a good husband, Ladli."

"Why? You think I'm so bored as to want to spend a lifetime taking care of some scoundrel?"

Despite her words I sensed that behind her feigned indifference she was as interested in finding love as was I. But she would never admit it. Because the afternoon was late, and I'd still much to do, we parted and I hurried to the Diwan-i Am, where Father and Dara stood before the Peacock Throne and oversaw the squabbles of nobles. I moved to the back of the proceedings, careful not to announce my presence.

With interest I watched Dara spearhead efforts to settle disputes. My sibling was becoming skilled at negotiation, and as I listened to his compromises I savored a sense of pride. If ever a just man dwelt in this world, more just than even my father, that man was certainly Dara. He truly believed Muslims and Hindus were equal and that it would be upon this equality that the Empire would flourish. While Father supported laws suppressing discrimination, I suspected his feelings were sometimes less noble than his actions. Dara, meanwhile, assumed that all men should be of the same rank, regardless of religious orientation. In fact, to prove himself true to this conviction, my brother had started translating the *Upanishads*—the fundamental mystical texts of Hinduism—from Sanskrit into Persian. No one had ever undertaken this arduous task, which Dara pursued quite seriously, as he was determined to give Muslims access to these famous works.

We dined together that evening, just Father, Dara and myself. Like Dara, Father often found solace in books, and I'd arranged that we eat in the imperial library, as we had occasionally done the past few years. Amidst this grand room we were served chicken fried in butter, replete with rice, raisins, cardamom powder, cloves and almonds. Rice wine filled our goblets.

The library was a vast refuge—half an arrow's flight from front to back. Much of its floor was covered in black carpets woven with ivory-colored quotations from famous texts. These included the *Qur'an*, biographies of our emperors, and the great Hindu epics. Sandstone shelves contained multiple copies of such works, the most renowned of which boasted hundreds of paintings. In all, more than forty thousand volumes were housed here. Fire was a dreaded specter within this priceless room, and a servant stood beside a bucket every five or six paces beneath the books. Several marble pools ensured a constant supply of water. A burning torch rose from the center of each pool, providing the room's only light.

The imperial library had always relaxed Father, and tonight was no exception. Despite our painful awareness of Mother's absence, we spoke of better times and reminisced about our lives with her. We savored wine. We smiled. It was a fulfilling evening, and ended when Father bowed to Dara and kissed me. I recognized then, more than ever, that we were his favorite children, and that only we brought happiness to his heart.

Darkness had fallen when I returned on horseback to the site of the future mausoleum. The night was cloudless and the moon full, its muted light falling on the Earth like a spell of enchantment. Some men claimed to see faces on the moon, whereas others spied everything from maps to mountains to mosquitoes on its surface. I thought it looked like a hole punched through the black fabric of night. Beyond it shined a light, a power surpassing my understanding.

When I reached the site's periphery, I tethered my mount to a cypress tree. Isa was already in the field. He stood before an easel bearing a large piece of canvas that had been painted black. Isa had his back to me and didn't witness my approach. His hand gripped a piece of white chalk that appeared to dance over the canvas. I had assumed Isa would have artists render his visions, and what I saw now nearly stole my breath. For his hand was truly like a dancer. It glided and it soared. It spun in tight arcs. It gave life to something wondrous, something he'd called a tear of Allah. To me, the mausoleum became a jewel surpassing even Mother's beauty. Its arches and towers and façades were not of this world.

Isa stopped drawing and thrust his fist in the air. He let out a sudden bellow then, a cry of joy so profound that I trembled. I'd never heard such ecstasy and doubted that I would listen to such a shout again. His cry echoed off palaces; it traveled across the river and died in faraway places.

"Thank you, Allah," he said. "Thank you for this gift." He looked skyward. "You'll enjoy it, Mother. And Father, please . . . please help me raise it."

I didn't dare go forward. I started to turn, but he must have somehow sensed me. When his gaze swung around and fell on my face, I shuddered, expecting him to be angry. Quite the opposite, however, was true. He merely set down his chalk and smiled. "What do you think, Swallow, of what we'll create?"

My tongue twisted awkwardly. "Better to ask a poet."

"But I ask you."

His gaze was so piercing that I almost turned away. Gathering my strength, I questioned, "Can you build such a thing? I've never, never seen—"

"It can be built," he interrupted quietly. "But I might be an old man when it's finished."

"But you would die content."

I thought he might hug me then, for his face was eclipsed by nothing save ecstasy. "You understand, Jahanara. You know me so little, yet you see me so well." He stepped closer. "Will you help me?"

"Of course."

"Good, because I'll need your help. Enemies will attack my plans, my methods and my costs. Nothing will happen without a friend I can trust."

"I can be that friend."

He bowed to me then, a bow of humbleness and gratitude. "Do you see the moon, Jahanara? Imagine how it will illuminate your mother's tomb. It shall never, truly, be night here when the moon is full. No, it will be something amid night and day. And if a place exists on Earth that Paradise does touch, surely this will be it."

When I saw him next he was crying. I'd never seen another man, except my father, cry. Yet Isa was unashamed and made no effort to hide his tears. He wasn't unmanly but seemed more a man than any I'd encountered, for his embrace of emotions made him appear quite powerful.

I thought of my mother, of my father, of what we were to build. Suddenly I bellowed into the night, as loud as my lungs could empty. And even if my bellow was a sapling next to his tree, the cry emboldened me and I no longer felt alone.

CHAPTER VII

Pain and Longing

The next few years were peaceful, quiet in the way Allah intended. Infants learned to crawl while our elderly journeyed to Paradise. Crops were sown and reaped, then sown again. Certainly battles were fought, but battles had always been a constant in our lives. At least we suffered through no famine, plague or shaking of the ground. Our homes rarely caught fire, and our prayers mostly seemed answered.

Once Isa perfected the dimensions of the mausoleum, work on the foundation began. Thousands of men labored that first summer to dig a vast pit that reached down until it struck water at the same level as the nearby river. Massive slabs of sandstone and granite were laid upon this muddy soil. The gaps between them were sealed with limestone plaster. After these behemoth stones filled the pit, smaller bricks were used to add another layer of strength at ground level. Isa also designed wells that ran down through the foundation, far, far into the earth. These were packed with granite to act as pilings on which the foundation rested.

Barges carried stones to Agra from quarries all over the Empire. Elephants then hauled the rocks to their final positions. The oldest men in the city told us the height of the fiercest flood and we raised our foundation a good two paces above that mark. The blocks that fell and shattered we used to line the river bank. We packed it deep with granite and sandstone, for Isa worried about time's ability to erode and make mayhem.

The field surrounding the foundation became a quagmire of men and mud. The men were of all races, sizes and ages. The mud was knee-deep after a rain and was often used to staunch bleeding wounds. A simple bazaar sprang up beyond the site's western edge, and merchants hawked endless varieties of food and drink, as well as tools, clothes, medicine, crafts and animals.

In those days—and for years that followed—Isa worked tirelessly from dawn to dusk. While others rested on their elephants or by the river, he built models and oversaw masons. I was almost always at his side and quickly we became companions, then confidants, then something more.

I don't know why we were initially drawn together. Perhaps it was a simple need for companionship. After all, we'd both lost loved ones. Though Isa was accepting of his fate, I sensed that his desire to create beauty stemmed from an old need to heal wounds. By building he constantly reminded himself of the love he felt for his parents. He believed they could see what he built, believed that his palaces and mosques made them smile. This conviction was the source of his happiness.

Alas, I was much less accepting of Mother's death. Indeed, I sometimes felt wronged by her departure. But in Isa's presence I felt less slighted, for a sense of warmth seemed to emanate from him, a gentle understanding that made me feel at home. Isa was so different than anyone I'd encountered, yet full of the same romantic yearning as Father, the same vigor as Mother. What he saw in me I couldn't be certain, but he did see something.

On occasion, after sunset, after the workers and merchants had departed, we'd sit on the unimaginably vast foundation and I'd discover him staring at me. His stare expressed what he never gave utterance— that he cared for me as a lover might, and if not for my marriage he'd have given himself to me then.

On such nights our thoughts were akin. We memorized each other's faces yet never touched. We whispered secrets yet never revealed our true desires. Isa honored my marriage, and as much as I despised my husband, I knew that by betraying him I'd betray Father, for if it were ever known that his daughter was unfaithful, he would lose tremendous face.

And so I resisted the urge to kiss Isa, even if I did in my dreams. In my dreams, at least, I could pursue fantasies. And pursue them I did. I kissed and held and adored him many nights. We made love. Our children followed.

I spent perhaps one night in three at Khondamir's home. My husband tried fiercely to sire a son, but his seed never took root. He blamed me, needless to say, and I visited every doctor and took every herb known to Allah. Khondamir often cursed my barren womb, though I knew it was as fertile as the Yamuna. After all, Mother had birthed many children. Could I have been so different?

To my delight, Father partly emerged from his sorrow and managed to rule the kingdom as he once did—despite his increased reliance on my brothers. Dara dealt with the nobles, while Aurangzeb climbed ranks of the military. Shah and Murad were sent to the far corners of the Empire to improve relations with our neighbors. My brothers were men now, broad in the shoulders and slim in the waist. Each was married and had fathered at least one child, all of whom I adored.

Except for my twin sisters—who were now being raised in Delhi by Mother's sister—I was the only sibling lacking children. To compensate for this shortcoming I surrounded myself with those closest to me. I asked Father, for instance, if Nizam could become my attendant. My wish was granted and he was soon like my shadow. Though he was not a man of words, I could trust Nizam with my very life. He was always where I wanted and needed him.

I also saw much of Ladli. At my urging she became another of my helpers with the mausoleum. Her fiery personality made her a favorite of the workers and they eagerly followed her orders. Bricklayers and master masons alike sought to catch her eye, for every man knew she was unwed, and her beauty reached new heights with each passing month.

Isa placed an extreme amount of responsibility on me. He'd explain what he wanted done, and I ensured that the builders followed his plans exactly. Furthermore, Isa had neither the time nor the interest to manage the inevitable conflicts that arose with such an undertaking. Fortunately, Mother had raised me to understand politics and I found that settling the squabble of a quarryman and an elephant owner was no different from solving a row between one lord and another. Even though I was less adored than Ladli, the men seemed to trust and respect me. They were aware that my father had commanded me to this post and realized that I whispered to him each night of our successes and failures.

My first significant failure, or at least a failure of sorts, didn't occur until the third year of construction. The affair was none of my making but quickly swept me up in its currents. A greedy merchant was the initial culprit. The rogue was caught using a scale with false ballast to weigh his customers' grain. In consequence, those wronged demanded his execution for the offense. Thus the merchant, and everyone aware of the plot, including his twelve-year-old son, was sentenced to death.

The execution took place in one of the Red Fort's immense courtyards with nobles and commoners ringing the square. Inside this circle of angry faces stood three war elephants. These beasts were clad in ceremonial silks and shuffled their enormous feet nervously. Despite being specially trained to maim and kill, the elephants were unsettled by the boisterous crowd. Kneeling before the giants were the six criminals. The merchant begged for their lives while deerskin drums rattled and people edged forward. The boy was terrified, weeping horribly.

Father, Dara and I sat on a raised pavilion, where we had an unobstructed view of the proceedings. Aurangzeb rode one of the elephants. My brother had been warring for several years now and had the appearance of a hardened fighter. He wore leather armor and his chin bore the scar of an explosion that had killed many of his soldiers. He was proud of his wound and made no attempt to cloak it with a beard.

Aurangzeb had taken up the habit of eating raw onions, and as he sat atop his favorite beast he munched one. The onions, I knew from personal experience, irritated the eyes of those near him. He liked causing discomfort and chewed the foul things whenever someone he didn't approve of was present, which seemed all the Empire save a few people. Somehow, the onions didn't affect him.

Aurangzeb's bodyguard, Balkhi, also sat on an elephant. By now we had all heard stories of Balkhi's mayhem, and even those of us in power did our best to avoid him. The man was a brute, and a brute given boundless rein by Aurangzeb was dangerous indeed.

Father, who hated such affairs but recognized their value in governing, called for the episode to commence. Many executions were carried out in this manner, for the extreme horror to those involved was thought a good deterrent to anyone considering a major crime. The crowd knew what to expect. Some cursed the merchant and his men, while others showered them with rotten vegetables.

Sickened by what was about to happen, but present at Father's request, I watched Aurangzeb closely. He sat on his elephant's neck and held a pole topped with a hooked blade. He used the blade, just sharp enough to draw blood, to tug the vast ears before him. When Aurangzeb pulled viciously on the creature's left ear, it bellowed and wheeled in that direction. The merchant before the beast wailed, his groin darkening as he soiled himself. The elephant knocked him down with a tusk, then used its powerful trunk to lift him up. Beating at its trunk, he cried for mercy, his voice rising to a shriek when Aurangzeb hooked an ear and pulled back. The elephant roared and, rising on its rear legs, threw the merchant high into the air. He landed awkwardly, his arm snapping like a twig underfoot.

Blood fell from beneath the elephant's ears, and I realized that Aurangzeb was further maddening the beast. It speared the man's leg with a tusk and tossed him again. He tried to limp away, but the monster knocked him down. The crowd cheered as a huge foot was placed atop the merchant's chest, causing him to scream in mortal fear as tremendous weight pressed down upon him. The elephant shifted its girth forward and suddenly the man's chest collapsed.

The other elephants' kills were equally grisly, leaving only three criminals unscathed. The beasts attacked two, while the boy put his head against his chest and scratched madly at his temples. Aurangzeb taunted him before urging his steed forward. Springing to his feet, the boy tried to run into the crowd, but men threw him back into the circle. He sought refuge again and was struck down.

I was ashamed of my countrymen then, a shame that profoundly saddened my heart. These intelligent, skilled people should have been anywhere but here, doing anything but shouting and pleading for a child's agonizing death. Suddenly I could no longer tolerate the barbarity of it all. I turned to Father, whose face trembled with disgust. "Show the child mercy!"

"I'm sorry, my child, but it's too late."

"Too late? What would Mother think?" I shrieked.

The question shook him. He paused for an instant, as if awaking from a long slumber. Then he rose from his cushion and loudly announced, "Mercy for the child!"

Aurangzeb, clearly overflowing with bloodlust, managed to halt his beast, then spun on its neck and stared at me. I realized that he had heard my outburst. Though fearful of his wrath, I was so disgusted to be his sister that for the first time in my life I spat—a pathetic flicker of spit that flew in his direction. For a man it was a harmless thing. But I was a woman, and upon that day many nobles witnessed the deed, and thereby knew my opinion of Aurangzeb. Some jeered me, whereas others spat to show their support.

Aurangzeb straightened in rage. "The criminal is guilty of—"

"Nothing!" Father interrupted.

"Nothing?"

"By Allah, that's enough! He's only a child!"

It had been years since Father had shouted so, and no one had ever seen him reprimand a son in public. Aurangzeb wavered for a moment, as if he still considered killing the boy. Then he nodded slightly. "Very well, my lord."

Father wordlessly left our pavilion, signaling that the proceeding was over. The elephants were led away and the crowd dissipated. Stunned by all that had transpired, I leaned against a tent post unsteadily. Dara approached from behind and placed his hand on my shoulder. He said nothing, yet stood quite close.

"It wasn't right," I mumbled.

"But you were, my sister."

I slumped despondently. "Why would Aurangzeb want to kill a child? Did we not love him enough? Did we—"

"We did nothing amiss."

I could never agree, for the cruelty my brother displayed must have stemmed from some bulb of discontent. But how to cut that stem was a riddle I couldn't fathom. We stood motionless as slaves dragged away the five disemboweled corpses and rinsed the bloodied flagstones. Clouds of burning sandlewood incense drifted by, unceremoniously dispersing the odors of dung and urine as the murderous place was restored.

I was about to leave when Balkhi entered the courtyard. A massive man with bushy eyebrows that merged together, he headed directly toward us. The longest sword I'd ever seen hung from his side, and fresh blood stained the hem of his tunic. Though Dara was an ample-sized man, Balkhi towered over him.

Aurangzeb's bodyguard, however, didn't gaze at Dara, but at me. "I speak for your brother," he growled, his thick beard covering his mouth so completely that I hardly saw it move. "The criminal was castrated by my lord." Balkhi might have grinned, though such movement was hard to discern, for my head spun at his words. "If he lives, keep him as your slave."

"The boy?" I stammered, my knees weakening. I found it hard to hear and a ringing emerged from within my ears. I swayed unsteadily and would have fallen, but Dara reached across to support me.

Balkhi laughed at my frailty. "Unwise, so unwise to spit at him. He——"

"Hold your tongue," Dara demanded, his voice lacking vigor.

Balkhi fingered the hilt of his sword. "The weakling on the throne won't live forever. And when he dies, I'll use the gelding blade on you both. I'll use it slowly." The warrior spat at my feet and walked away.

If my brother were a warrior, he might have killed Balkhi then. If I were a man, I'd have tried, for I understood the peril I faced. Aurangzeb's honor was slighted today, and he would not rest until I suffered. Alas, Dara remained still. And I was no man.

"You should kill that brute," I finally said, long after Balkhi had disappeared and my knees had ceased trembling. "Poison him; pay a soldier to slay him in battle. I don't care how you do it, but do something."

"One can't murder, Jahanara, and be righteous. I'm not of that make. Nor will I live in that world." Dara grimaced, pausing to massage his brow. "You want more killing, after what we saw today? More death?"

"He did the killing! And he's not finished!"

"I'll consider his threats but will do nothing more."

"Then you're a fool," I replied, wishing I'd been born as Dara and Dara as I. For surely he was too feeble to stand against Aurangzeb. "When Father departs this life," I said, "whether in two years or twenty, Aurangzeb shall kill us. We'll die and our children will die and his claim to the throne will be complete."

"He is our brother."

"So?" I exclaimed. "He may have our blood, but not our hearts. Did you see him on the elephant? He reveled in the killing! He castrated that poor boy for the sheer joy of it!"

"I don't—"

"He defied Father! And yet you think that because he's your brother he'll cede you the throne? Are you mad?"

"To fight him goes against every principle I hold dear!"

"The Prophet Muhammad, the founder of Islam, fought his foes!"

"But he was persecuted! I'm not!"

"But you shall be! And Aurangzeb's more dangerous than any of the jackals Muhammad encountered!"

Dara's face, which had always given me comfort, flashed with anger. "I'm not Muhammad, Jahanara! And if you wish to fight Aurangzeb, you had better do so yourself!"

I hurried from him. Though I loved Dara immensely, he also enraged me, for I feared his weakness would be our undoing. To stop from crying I bit my tongue, forcing myself to scheme as I stumbled forward. There must be a way out of this wretched mess, I thought, a road appeasing Aurangzeb's need for revenge. If I could satiate this revenge, I might remain safe.

As I debated what to do, I rushed to the royal physician's quarters, seeking the boy. When I saw the old man's face I knew his patient had died. "They brought him too late," he whispered, "and the cuts were too . . . much too profound."

Weeping, I left the physician and ran to the closest mosque. It happened to be the newly finished Moti Masjid, the Pearl Mosque. The site, entirely of white marble, boasted a sprawling courtyard and a façade segmented by seven identical archways. Above the archways, three large domes rose skyward.

In a corner of the courtyard I faced Mecca, praying that the child was in Paradise and that he would be content for all eternity. I also prayed for a way to quench Aurangzeb's thirst for revenge. I forced myself to scheme, and scheme relentlessly, for I understood that I must act with haste. Aurangzeb was deadly now and would strike without pause. I debated going to Father but decided that by involving him, I'd put the throne at even greater risk. After all, it wasn't unthinkable to have a son plot against a father.

The day lengthened as I prayed. When Allah finally graced me with an answer, I thanked Him until my cheeks dried of tears. His answer would bring me pain and humiliation, but I hoped it would spare me a worse fate. My plan depended on Ladli, and so I sought her in the royal kitchen, where she still worked on occasion. I pretended to be angry at her, demanding that she follow me. I must have been an adept actress, for Ladli's masters smiled as she shuffled past.

As soon as we were within a long unused storeroom, I hugged her. I told her that I loved her and that she would always be my friend. I also whispered of what had transpired, and of how I was in danger. She, unlike Dara, didn't question my words.

"What are we to do?" she asked.

"I have a plan," I answered softly. "But it involves you and is dangerous."

"Tell me."

"The only way Aurangzeb will leave me in peace is if he has his revenge. I hurt him today, and he needs to hurt me back."

"Like the child he is."

I ignored her remark, my mind still churning. "Does he consider you a friend?"

"Perhaps . . . yes, maybe he does. I cook sweets for his men or, better said, his snakes. And I fawn over him, even if he tells his snakes in that overwrought voice of his that he's bedded me. He lies to them and they cheer him for it."

My disgust with my brother deepened. "Good. Because I want you to betray me."

"Betray you?"

"Tell him that last week I stole from my husband." She started to protest, but I tightened my grip on her hand. "Tomorrow morning, whisper to Aurangzeb that I took a golden ring from Khondamir's chest. Tell him that I buried it under a brick in my room."

"It's true?"

"It shall be. Because Aurangzeb will inform my husband of the crime, and when Khondamir discovers the ring gone, I'll be beaten." I paused, wishing some other path existed. "I'll be humiliated in my own home."

"But he'll hurt you! There must be another way!"

"This way I can control the hurt. A beating from my husband will be better than a drop of poison from Aurangzeb, or the knife of one of his butchers. And yet, I think a beating will still my brother's need for revenge." I squeezed her fingers. "He'd rather disgrace me than anything else."

"But better to give the dog a lesser weapon! You'll lose face in court. The nobles will laugh—"

"My humiliation will never become public. I know my brother. Though he may be what you say, he'll realize that if Father discovered he betrayed me, he'd suffer." Because, I thought sadly, he recognizes that Father loves me more than him.

"But the pain."

"Frightens me. Yet . . ." I hesitated, wishing today was but a dream. "Yet I'm more fearful of what shall happen to us."

"Us?"

"After this," I whispered, "we can never be seen as friends again. For if Aurangzeb thinks that you deceived him, you'll die. So always we must appear as enemies. Only in secret can we be friends." My voice quivered and I bit my lip. "This pains me, Ladli. More, much more than you'll ever know. But it also saves me. And it may help me in the future. For as surely as the monsoon brings life, Aurangzeb will vie for the throne once my father dies. It cannot be given to him. Years from now, perhaps, if he trusts you, we can use this trust to our advantage. We can mislead him, or help Dara in some way."

"But is it worth so great a price, our friendship?"

I didn't know how to reply. The girl in me said no, but the woman said yes. "A time will come when any friend of mine shall be in danger," I forced myself to say. "And when that time arrives, I'd rather have you as Aurangzeb's ally than mine."

Ladli, always so strong, blinked away a tear. "Are we truly finished?"

"Not truly," I replied, gripping her hands in mine, struggling to contain my misery. "We'll meet secretly, and perhaps someday we may be seen together again."

Silence arose in the storeroom as Ladli contemplated our future, no sounds present save her quick breaths. When she trembled, I closed my eyes, despising myself for hurting her. "May Shiva forgive me, I'll do what you ask," she agreed reluctantly.

I held her, feeling the heavy toll of years, years short in number but becoming long with demands. I was tired of being strong, so weary of duty and scheming that at that moment I'd have traded my station with any serving girl in Agra. "Thank you, Ladli," I said, willing myself to disregard such thoughts. "It's a dreadful step, I know. But believe me, you do not want to be viewed as my friend when Father dies."

She shrugged, as if suddenly resigned to whatever future lay ahead. "When Aurangzeb is reborn as a slug you can step on him. Maybe even I will."

"If you're right about karma, he will be," I said, absently adjusting her sari, feeling the firmness of her stomach. "Tomorrow, seek out Aurangzeb and ask him to pay you for information about me. Demand a great deal, or he'll be wary. If he offers nothing, or even half of what you ask, walk away. But if he gives much, pursue our plan. And then, months from now, return to me quietly and we'll talk."

"More likely whisper," she foretold, then added a curse. "I do love you, Jahanara."

"And I you, my sister." I hugged her again, hiding my fear. For Khondamir loathed me, and the theft would give him cause to beat me senseless. I had never tasted the sting of a whip, and the thought of it against my flesh terrified me. "Be careful, Ladli," I said. "Be careful and be strong."

At these words we started to cry. Though she was like fire and I sought to be like steel, we weren't immune to swells of emotion. I did think of her as a sister, and losing her so soon after Mother's passing was more pain than I wished to bear. And I had to bear it alone.

I left her sniffling in the storeroom and returned to my home. I found Khondamir's ring, which was as thick as he. After hiding it beneath my secret brick, I lay on my sleeping carpet and blanket, trying to harden myself for what lay ahead. Feelings of helplessness and despondency bedeviled my sleep, and I drifted somewhere between the worlds of dreams and reality.

The next morning I tried to act naturally but had to excuse myself from breakfast to take a lengthy walk away from the river. I didn't want to look at the mausoleum, for its site was where I longed to be. I yearned to tell Isa of my woes, to let him protect me, but I could never ask him to do so. I'd be selfishly endangering him, as I had already done with Ladli.

After spending the afternoon at a mosque, I returned home just before dusk. When I neared Khondamir's grounds, Aurangzeb approached from the opposite direction. He rode a fine mount and wore unadorned leather armor and a curved sword at his side. My feelings conflicted as I saw his wicked grin. My ruse must have worked, but now I'd endure its consequences.

"Are you well?" he asked, his voice unnaturally loud, as always.

"Fine, Aurangzeb," I replied, trying to sound interested. "And you? How are your lovely children?"

My brother looked skyward. "The Qur'an says, 'Vying for more and more diverts you, until you go to the tombs. Then you will be questioned about comfort on that day.'"

"Why do you quote—"

"Only a sinner . . ." he paused to spit at my feet, "would steal from her lord."

"Steal from her lord?"

"Save your lies, sinner, for Khondamir." A roar erupted from within the house, followed by breaking glass. "He's found the ring."

I managed to pretend outrage. "Ladli! I'll have her whipped, by Allah. I'll—"

"Do nothing of the sort!"

Because he'd love the sight, I fell to my knees. "Please, please help me, Aurangzeb. Please don't leave me to him. I'm sorry, so sorry for insulting you. Please!"

He laughed before spurring his horse away. Rising toward Mecca, I quickly begged Allah's forgiveness, for I had stolen. But then I asked that He might protect me. I was still asking when my name was shouted. Wanting to hide my shame from the servants, I strode directly into my room. Khondamir was present, shaking in rage. He held the ring in one hand and the brick in the other. The brick he hurled at me. I ducked under it and didn't need to pretend to be terrified. I had expected him to be angry, but he seemed enraged beyond reason.

"My lord," I began, but he waived me to silence.

"You defile me!" he shrieked.

"I'd have repaid—"

"Silence!"

He stuck the ring on his finger and grabbed a leather belt from a nearby table. I blanched at the sight. "It's a mistake!"

Khondamir grabbed and tossed me, bottom up, over a table. "Move from this spot, and emperor's daughter or not, I'll have you gutted!" Spittle flew from his lips as he raged, and veins pulsed at his temples. He yanked off my robe, shirt and skirt. Suddenly I was naked. A drop of his sweat fell on my buttocks, followed by the heavy leather. The belt bit into me like a wild boar might. It tore at my flesh and I yelped in pain.

"Good, you bitch," Khondamir hissed.

"Please no!"

The belt assaulted me and I moaned. He grunted as he swung and stabbing pain followed each grunt. I began to swim in agony. For all I knew, he had set my backside afire and I was burning alive.

"Steal from me!" he screamed. "From me!"

"Please don't—"

"You whore!"

The blows continued.

"Please!"

"Silence!"

I bit the wood of the table as the beating raged. The timber splintered in my mouth and I tasted blood. I tried to stay quiet but could sooner have checked the movement of my heart. I beseeched him to stop. I promised him anything. I pleaded and writhed and whimpered. He must have liked hearing me beg, for his temper ebbed. The blows came less frequently, lacking the strength of their predecessors.

"Get up," he finally demanded.

It took all my strength to do as commanded. My legs were bloody and I wept at the sight. Gingerly, I wrapped my robe about myself. "I'm so . . . so sorry, my lord," I whispered.

"No whore will sleep in this house tonight," he replied, breathing heavily.

"But—"

"Leave!" he shrieked, slapping me across the face.

I could never walk to town, so I shuffled to the stables. A servant, his face hinting of his pity for me, helped me straddle a horse. A moan escaped me as my weight pressed down upon my wounds. I thanked the man, then weakly spurred my mount. Within a few steps my saddle was slick with blood.

Where to go? Nizam would help me but likely kill Khondamir. A dead husband would end one problem but enrage Aurangzeb. No, it would be easier to deal with Aurangzeb if I lived in shame with my husband. I could also seek Father, but alas, he'd avenge me a thousandfold. And love Dara as I might, his comforting face would do little to ease my mind.

I went to Isa. However much I hesitated to involve him, I knew he'd shelter me and do as I asked. Dusk had surrendered to night when I finally found him. Thankfully, our workers had gone home and the site was silent. Isa had erected a bungalow near the foundation and usually slept within its sandstone walls. I called out his name as I approached. I wailed and fell from my horse into his arms.

He asked no questions but carried me within. When he saw my blood-soaked robe he paused before gently removing it. Though ashamed of my state, I cried at the lovingness of his touch. Isa lay me, facedown, on his sleeping carpet. He then ran from the room. He was gone for some time and I began to worry. At last he returned with an aloe plant and wet rags. Isa wiped my wounds clean. He then used a pair of bricks to smash the aloe, which he smeared upon my cuts before draping a silk sheet over me.

"Forgive me," I whispered.

"Hush, Swallow."

He knelt before me and stroked my brow. He wiped away my tears. His fingers touched my lips and I kissed them, causing him to be still. The kiss lingered between us. When the moment had passed, Isa placed a goatskin flask of wine to my mouth. I suckled from it like an infant at her mother's breast.

"Do you want to tell me what happened?" he asked softly.

I took a long breath and whispered to him the tale, describing my brothers, my fears and my husband. He never interrupted and, when I was finished, sat in silence. He sipped the wine, then I heard his breath catch.

"I'm sorry, Jahanara. What can I do?"

"Just hold me."

And so he did. His hands, the strong hands of a man who created beauty, cradled my head. He looked into my eyes and his tears glistened. How I wanted him to kiss me then, despite my pain and humiliation! One kiss would have made the suffering easy to bear. Though I sensed his adoration for me, he didn't turn my face and place his lips against mine. No, to do that, at least in his mind, would have been to dishonor me, for a kiss then might be construed as pity. And I yearned not for his pity, but his love.

Through a window I saw the stars thicken. The moon was but a sliver. "How shall it look," I whispered, "in such paltry light?"

"Not as lovely as you, my Swallow. For that, we need a full moon."

My tears fell then, despite my effort to contain them. I didn't weep because of my pain, but because I wanted this man. I hungered for him, for we seemed to speak without words. Yet I could not have him. Nor would I ever.

"He'll pay for this," he said.

"Please don't try and avenge me."

"He deserves to die for what he's done."

"Then he will. But at the hands of Allah and no one else."

"But why?"

"Because what we build is more important than what happened to-night. And because of what happened tonight Aurangzeb will leave me in peace. I'll pretend to be humiliated in his presence and hence I'll be safe. But if Khondamir were to die, I would surely be at risk."

"You are at risk."

"His rage is spent, Isa. And we can't jeopardize your project."

Outside, my horse neighed. "You're a clever and fearless woman," he said so quietly that I had to strain to hear him. "Perhaps I should call you a hawk and not a swallow."

"I like Swallow better."

"May I . . ." he paused, collecting himself. "I'd like to lay down beside you." The fact that he'd ask brought more tears to my eyes. I nodded and he spread himself next to me. His arm went around my back and he held me closely. "What a gift you are," he said. "What a wondrous gift."

Though my pain had only relented a little, his flesh was warm and soothing. I wanted to feel more of him, more of his joyous touch. For the first time I truly understood how my parents had felt for each other. I understood the taste, the insanity of love. Because as sure as the sun would rise tomorrow I loved him so.

CHAPTER VIII

Allah Smiles

The Qur'an is a book of many faces. As much as Aurangzeb liked to quote its passages concerning revenge, misdeeds and hellfire, it is also a text that speaks often of forgiveness, charity and goodwill. Unlike my brother, I always found these verses to be the most profound. They comforted me tremendously.

"For God loves those who do good," the Qur'an says.

In the wake of my beating, I'd never have named myself as a doer of good, but I liked to think that before I died, much decency would come of my life. And so I tried to offset my mistakes with notions of the good I'd create. Yes, I had endangered my friend for a selfish cause. And yes, the poor had benefited little from my presence.

But I'd endangered Ladli only by having tried to save the boy. I had always treated the poor kindly, and in the future I'd seek to find them work at the mausoleum. For surely a man who has labored for his bread shall sleep better than a man who has been given his. And surely any man having worked on the mausoleum would feel closer, whether Muslim or Hindu, to Allah or his gods.

I often explored such thoughts as I healed from Khondamir's blows. Following that first night with Isa, I returned to the Red Fort and withdrew to my room. It was a fortuitous time to rest, because not two days after my beating began Islam's Month of Blessing, known throughout the land as Ramadan.

Some ten centuries before, during the ninth month of the lunar year, a caravan trader named Muhammad wandered the desert near Mecca while pondering his faith. One night the angel Gabriel whispered to him that he had been chosen to receive the words of Allah. In the following

days, Muhammad found himself speaking the verses that were later tran-
scribed into the Qur'an.

Since the Prophet Muhammad's enlightenment, Muslims have always
celebrated Ramadan by forgoing any sort of indulgence. For instance, we
renounce food and drink from dawn until dusk for the entire month. Allah, we knew through Muhammad's words in the Qur'an, expected this
sacrifice. Fasting, He said, made us appreciate the poor's suffering, as well
as learn the peace that accompanies spiritual devotion.

And so I fasted and healed in my room. I recited one-thirtieth of the
Qur'an each day until I finished the scripture. By the end of Ramadan,
celebrated with the festival of Eid al-Fitr, I was fully recovered. While
Muslims throughout Agra hung lanterns and decorations from their
homes, and dressed in their finest clothes, I ate dates with Father and
watched our city sparkle through the night.

The very next day I revisited my duties. Despite the success of my ruse
with Aurangzeb, I was careful in the coming months, because Khondamir never forgave me and punished me whenever possible. His beat-
ings, praise Allah, were much less severe than what I'd endured that
awful afternoon. I think Khondamir realized—though he'd drink boiling wax before admitting it—that I could have gone to my father after
his assault and the Emperor would have made him disappear. Conse-
quently, my husband treated me more like a slave and less like a criminal.

As my scars faded into thin lines, the cool winds of fall transformed
into the hot air of summer and then the driving monsoon rains. Only
three seasons visit Agra. Each is sacred in its own way, though none more
than the season of the monsoon, for these rains usher life to our crops.
And it was during the monsoon of my twenty-first year that I found myself on a barge with Isa, Nizam, and a group of trusted craftsmen.

During the previous months I had been forced to see Isa only at the
site, as meeting elsewhere was simply too dangerous. Though Aurangzeb
was rarely in Agra due to the fighting at our borders, I was certain he had
spies among our workers. In fact, Ladli had told me so at a clandestine
meeting. She didn't know the names of our watchers but could say with

certainty that several existed. They were ordered to record my actions, as well as document the expenses we incurred.

It was no secret that Aurangzeb abhorred the amount of rupees spent on the mausoleum's construction. After all, he wanted money for his army, money to expand the Empire. Yet the treasury was being depleted by the staggering costs of our project. Apart from the vast amount of materials necessary, we employed twenty-two thousand laborers. Aurangzeb, and many nobles, wanted to levy additional taxes on the Hindu majority to help pay for the mausoleum, but Father, at Dara's insistence, rejected such a policy.

My life became more complicated. Though I thought often of Isa and our night together, I was careful never to reveal my affection for him. Indeed, we spent innumerable days together overseeing work on the gardens, the main gate, or the immense marble platform on which the mausoleum would sit. Thousands of men constantly buzzed around us, and we could never be certain which eyes endeavored to dislodge our secrets.

Fortunately, we did have a few craftsmen we could trust. These men— each a friend of Isa's—had accompanied us to Delhi, where we were to fill our barge with a load of white marble. Immense teams of oxen had pulled our vessel, and six similar barges, upriver on the long journey. Loading these awkward boats was an arduous and dangerous process, and Isa wanted to be present so that he could train his men to safely conduct such undertakings. Fourteen workers had already died building the mausoleum, and Isa felt accountable to each of their families. I'd given the grief-stricken widows enough gold to last a lifetime but knew all too well that some things were irreplaceable.

The trip was my first to Delhi, and I marveled at its sights. After visiting my sisters, I explored our northern city in earnest. A sprawling hub of commerce and religion, Delhi abounded with mosques and temples. The mosques housed enormous congregations and boasted vaulted ceilings, domes covered in turquoise tiles and stone lattice windows. The temples were smaller and much greater in number, akin to piles of painted earth, often pink and covered with bright renderings of Hindu gods. The temples' interiors were grotto-like environs where the sounds of bells and chants echoed eerily.

The bazaars of Delhi were highly impressive, especially the new Chandi Chowk, or Moonlit Square. Though laborers hadn't completely dressed the area with yellow sandstone, nor finished its decorative pool, Chandi Chowk already bustled with merchants, artisans and buyers. As the monsoon season was unpredictable, giant canvas awnings covered the square, sheltering its patrons from sudden cloudbursts. Beneath these restless canopies merchants hawked Chinese porcelain, sitars, bolts of velvet, cashmere carpets and weapons of all sorts. For the right price exotic animals could be purchased—monkeys and mynah birds, and even a baby white elephant.

Artisans were showcased at Chandi Chowk, and their wares rivaled anything found in Agra. Jewelers offered brilliant settings of every stone. Silversmiths polished candelabras, mirrors, vases and platters. Masters of marble, gold, cloth, clay and wood also displayed their creations. Most prominent were painters, as no more revered a craft existed. These weathered men stood before easels and brushed lifelike images onto canvas. While the men were of average make and mold, their images of cranes, flowers, emperors, battles, festivals and lovers were magnificent.

Unknown as a princess in Delhi, I walked through such squares like an ordinary woman. The experience was both exciting and illuminating. I haggled for the first time and bought fresh pineapple and wine for Isa's men. They loved me more for the wine.

It took seven days to load all the barges, seven days spent amid gentle rains and muddied skies. I was in charge of recording the amount of marble purchased and ensuring that we were never cheated. Isa showed me how to reject faulty pieces—marble that was cracked, marred with unsightly sediment, or weighed too little. I rejected perhaps one slab in five and the quarry's owner soon took a dislike to me. Suspicious of his schemes, I focused on measuring the cuts of stone and not my proximity to Isa.

At sunset each day Isa and I were able to dine alone. We wandered the streets of Delhi searching for new dishes. I liked few of the concoctions but found pleasure in sitting beneath marble pavilions with Isa at my side. Sometimes, after wine emboldened us, we flirted as a young couple might. We whispered and grinned and touched. We gazed. We longed.

I wanted our time in Delhi to last forever. Though Muslim women were condemned to lives of subservience, no one I feared resided here and thus I could act myself. Some nights I imagined Isa as my husband. I pretended that only this world existed, that Khondamir, duty and pain were but words without meanings. Alongside Isa, I could fool myself into believing such notions. He made doing so easy, for his presence fueled my mind with a fervent, buoyant energy that I hadn't known before we met.

What can I say other than he was one of those rare people who made everyone around him feel better? No, he rather made everyone feel important. If the most junior worker had a suggestion, Isa pondered its merits. If his most trusted mason had a complaint, Isa devised a resolution. Unlike almost all men of rank, Isa listened to those beneath him. He listened with immense care, as if your words carried weight, as if your thoughts were of consequence. And when he responded, his insight and sensitivity were sometimes startling.

While most of Isa's men embraced him for his utter lack of conceit, those with us in Delhi held him in even higher esteem. I did my best to befriend these men, these masons with their scarred arms and sharp eyes. Treating them as a mother might, I gently bound their wounds and cooked them hearty meals. I was next to worthless in the kitchen but overcame this shortcoming by serving ample amounts of wine before dinner. The workers sang and gambled, and I told them stories of life as a princess. By the third night they adored me, and I considered them friends.

Nizam, who had been surrounded by women most of his life, also took to these men. They didn't disrespect him the way the nobles he was accustomed to did. To his credit, he lent his considerable muscles to aid them whenever possible. Soon they joked with him about life in the harem and inquired as to which concubine might be burdened by its tedium. My childhood companion, always so guarded, lowered his defenses in their presence. Through these holes I caught glimpses of his true self.

One afternoon, in the middle of prayer, I saw him smile. Later,

I asked him why he'd grinned. He replied, "Because, my lady, I was thanking Allah for this trip."

"Thanking Him?"

His gaze rested on me for a heartbeat, then traveled about the river. "This morning, as it rained, I walked along the water's edge. I saw a pink lotus."

I imagined him studying the flower, savoring his freedom. "I'm glad, Nizam, to see you so happy. You deserve this much more than anyone." He shrugged, but his eyes, when they finally settled on mine, hinted of agreement. Though his right eye was slightly oversized for his face, I saw beauty in its design. "Nizam," I said quietly, thinking that I was undeserving of such a friend, "I'll grant you freedom, if that's what you want."

"Freedom?"

"Yes. You can leave me now."

"But I'm a—"

"Slave?" I interrupted. "No. You're a man, a good man. And you've served me enough." I paused, displeased with myself that I had waited so long to utter these words. What right had I to oversee a man like Nizam? "You should go," I said. "There's little for you here."

Nizam straightened, as if my suggestion had given him pride, an emotion he rarely experienced. "Thank you, my lady. But my place is by your side. There I have freedom."

"But not true freedom. For you may be free to come and go but many still treat you as a slave."

"Let them, my lady. I wasn't born a slave. And I won't die as one."

I suddenly wanted to hug him but knew he'd be embarrassed by the gesture. And so I bowed slightly. "But understand, my friend, that you can leave whenever you wish. I'll give you a pouch of gold and you can disappear."

"Perhaps I will someday."

I smiled and left him. He seemed at ease that evening, and as we departed for Agra he sang a song that Dara had written, sang it in a voice as deep as distant thunder. The song told the story of Shiva, and our workers, mostly Hindu, hummed with him. They stuck bamboo poles into the river's muddy bottom to his cadence, pushing our craft into the water's embrace.

The darkness thickened, despite the lanterns burning at our bow. Isa hadn't wanted to leave so late, but the journey would take a full night and day, and tonight was cloudless—such windows were rare during the monsoon. Two men were stationed at the bow, and they occasionally stopped humming to shout warnings to our captain. He was a veteran of the river and knew its contours as if they were the faces of his children. The captain, who refrained from drink that night, often put his own weight against a stout pole connected to the steering rudder. The barge responded grudgingly to his motions, sagging with the frightful amount of marble.

"Keep a good lookout, men!" Isa shouted over the length of the barge. "If we meet no snags you'll have an extra day's wages!"

Someone cheered at the notion of more rupees for his pocket. Then the night stilled. I stood next to Isa and wordlessly he led me up the stacked marble until we were atop the pile. Below us burnt eight lanterns which silhouetted the figures of our men. No one slept that night, for we had to stay alert. Fortunately, the Yamuna River boasted a wide and deep channel for most of its length. Barring a mistake, we should encounter no mishaps.

Isa unrolled a sleeping carpet and spread it on the marble. We sat, inhaling the fragrance of the air, which was fertile with fresh rain and damp leaves. A spattering of stars flickered above. Occasionally we passed a fisherman's fire, or the silhouette of a home. For the most part, however, the only life we glimpsed was that of nature. Birds cried and fish splashed. Somewhere a tiger bellowed.

I gazed at Isa, cherishing what I saw. He wore an unadorned yellow tunic, as well as a white sash and turban. He hadn't trimmed his beard in more than a week, and it was quite unruly, contrasting with his face's angular features. "Thank you for bringing me," I said quietly. I sensed that he wanted to reach out to me, but because we hadn't touched since that night in his bungalow, he held back. "What occupies your mind, Isa?"

A star fell across the heavens, and I wondered if it was a good omen.

"I was thinking," he whispered, "that it would be nice to stay with you in Delhi. If not for the mausoleum, I'd surely be tempted."

"We would have nothing."

"Nothing, Swallow, or everything?"

I edged toward him. "Tell me what we'd have."

He had never spoken of his yearning for me, though he had hinted of it many times. Even now, he hesitated, as if by revealing his feelings he might somehow dishonor me. "You'd have . . . my love. I could offer nothing more."

I shivered. I had longed to hear such words for so many months. I'd prayed to hear them but never expected to be so blessed. "Then let's turn around, leave Agra forever."

"Would you do that?"

I paused. "Truly? I don't know. My father and brother need me. How can I place my . . ." I was fearful of hurting him, fearful of speaking the wrong words. "How could I place my love for you, as noble as it is, above my duty to them? To the Empire? And how could you leave your work, a project that's far more important than I?"

Isa put his arm around my shoulder and held me tight. "I do love you."

"And I you."

My heart quickened when I thought he'd kiss me. Instead, he looked to the stars. "Do you know, Jahanara, what I think of when I design? I think of you. I hold your face in my mind and seek to mimic its loveliness. I remember the shape of your body and try to equal its brilliance."

"You do?" I asked, immensely surprised.

"I watch how the sun reflects off your cheek, and I build so that the sun will dance off the marble in the same manner. I survive your absence in my heart, not having you as the mother of my children, by shaping stone in your image."

"Not my mother's?"

"No," he whispered, then sighed. "I can't share my love with you as I'm supposed to, the way a man shares such love with his wife. And so I build. I build to honor you, because this is the only way that I can love you, by sharing my love with the world. The first stone I laid had your name chiseled into its underside and the last—please grant me this wish, Allah—shall carry both our names."

I kissed him. When our lips met he was so startled that he froze. But then, like the river around us, he swirled about me and I felt as if my world were spinning. His lips were soft against mine and his hands caressed my face. I muttered his name and he kissed my eyes, my forehead and my lips again.

He groaned slightly before breaking away. The scent of him—a sweetness that might have been lemon juice—was gone. "This can't be," he said. "We have too much . . . far too much to lose."

I set my head on his shoulder, though I desired above all else to kiss him again. "I love you. I love you and I long for you." I grew silent, wishing that thoughts of want didn't mingle with those of fear. "And yet . . ."

"What, Swallow?"

"And yet I worry. I worry what our love might bring. I worry that we're doomed."

CHAPTER IX

A Sense of Love

O n the day that would ultimately serve to change my life, I stood staring at our creation. We were well into our fourth year of construction and the parcel of land was beginning to resemble something of beauty. To the far south stood the recently finished main gate. The height of thirty men, it was composed completely of red sandstone.

Beyond the gate to the north stretched the ornamental gardens. Since the Qur'an described four rivers flowing within Paradise, Isa had decided to mimic Paradise's loveliness by using two intersecting channels of water to create four identical sections of land. In the center of the four squares sat a round pool, made of white marble and containing koi. The surrounding plots of land were planted thickly with saplings, which would stretch into cypress and fruit trees by the time we finished the main structure. Under their canopies, flowers would blossom.

Set between the gardens and the river, the mausoleum rose with the sluggishness of a crippled elephant. But rise it did. The platform, as high as a palm tree, was a massive rectangle of reinforced stone slabs. Though structurally intact, it would be later encased in white marble. Children tried to run from one end of its vastness to the other while holding their breath. Not surprisingly, only a few succeeded in the game.

The base of the mausoleum had been finished and stood atop the platform. Isa had designed the building to resemble the offspring of a square and an octagon. A square for the most part, its corners were angled. The eight sides of the mausoleum would be graced with magnificent arches, towering structures that would support the enormous weight of the tear-shaped dome.

The arches were scantly begun, and I struggled to envision them rising as in Isa's drawings. Bamboo scaffolding obscured much of the site, hindering my imagination. The scaffolding, intricate and stout, held thousands of men and looked like a colossal birdcage. Certain sections were reinforced with brick towers, and within the towers master builders had fixed pulleys and block tackle. Elephants below pulled ropes to hoist stone slabs upward where men used poles to push them into place. Masons secured the blocks with plaster, and used iron dowels to join them together.

The process was becoming more dangerous as the structure rose, and we were lucky to go a week without a death—a fact that weighed heavily upon Isa's conscience, as well as my own. The peril, surprisingly, deterred few. We had more workers than we could accommodate. Craftsmen journeyed here from distant lands, and Isa conferred with these artisans long into the night.

Isa wanted the entire mausoleum to be inlaid with intricate patterns of semi-precious stones. Hindustan's finest carvers showed him majestic works of jade flowers, while calligraphers brought marble slabs bearing lapis-filled inscriptions of poetry and scripture.

It seemed at times that the project might never cease. And yet on that morning, when coolness still prevailed and the sky carried sheltering clouds, my mood was elevated. A messenger had informed me that Father would inspect the mausoleum shortly, and I looked forward to seeing him. Architecture was a hobby of his, and Father often made helpful suggestions to me, as well as exchanged ideas with Isa.

I watched with pride as Father strode through the gardens with the gait of a much younger man. He was a noble ruler, and the workers sensed his kindness. He repaid their bows not with the curt nod of a superior, but with friendly greetings. Wonderful with names, Father honored many of the master builders by inquiring after their children or wives. He applauded their progress and praised their ingenuity. Father's armed escorts, trailing slightly behind him, stopped as he approached me. "Good morning, my child," he said.

I took his arm and we walked toward the platform, circumventing heaps of sandstone, dowels, rope and bamboo. The hot season was ending and the ground was dry. Dust rose as we walked beside hardened elephant footprints and mounds of dung. "We need more barges, Father," I said. "We're short on stone and long on men."

He nodded, and I knew the matter would be handled. One of Father's profoundest fears was that he'd die before we finished. "The gardens," he said, pointing to the four squares, "shall be beautiful. Does the river fill them properly?"

Isa had designed the gardens so that underground passages from the river would always keep their canals and fountains flowing. "Perfectly," I replied. "It would take a terrible drought for them to dry."

We arrived at the platform's central staircase and ascended wide steps. From atop the mammoth rectangle of stone Father motioned toward the tower at each corner. "The minarets rise quickly."

Indeed, they were halfway completed, and when finished would be only slightly lower than the dome. As with the rest of the structure, they hadn't been dressed yet in white marble. Immense stacks of the precious marble lay beyond the platform and would only be added once additional sandstone was in place.

Father, replete in a silk tunic and jewels, climbed the scaffolding surrounding the main edifice. I followed him up a ladder into the bamboo latticework. A wooden walkway connected the scaffolding to the mausoleum and we crossed the abyss below. Dust-covered workers stood, sat, or knelt at endless stations about the scaffolding. Some chiseled, some plastered, some shouted commands. Hundreds more pursued other tasks.

Suddenly we stood at the highest point of the unfinished site. If the mausoleum had truly been a woman—after all, Isa had designed it to mirror a woman's grace—we'd be only as high as her knees. Walking upon a makeshift path set on the rising structure, Father headed toward the center of the mausoleum. There he wiped the sweat from his brow and seemed to lose himself in thought. I left him in peace. Mother, as she often did, now consumed him. His grief for her, even if it had lessened slightly with time, was still acute.

I would never forget the first few years after her death, when he gave up every worldly pleasure to mourn her. He wore no fine tunics, and left his jewels in their chests. He attended no festivals or dances or plays. Music he forbade in his presence. He even renounced the lure of flesh during this time and never entertained women. Father had since returned to the life of an emperor, but his mood had only partially improved.

"She's right below us," he said softly, "my Mumtaz Mahal."

Mother's pearl-encrusted tomb was buried beneath the main structure, accessible only by an underground passageway. As he'd promised on her deathbed, Father always visited it on the anniversary of that terrible night.

"One day, Father, one day you'll rest beside her."

"May Allah be so kind."

"She'll adore you for the creation of this mausol—"

"Taj Mahal," he interrupted quietly. "Allah sent me a dream last night, and in that dream, as was true in life, I saw you born."

"And?"

"It was during your birth that, for the first time, I called your mother 'Taj Mahal.'"

An elephant trumpeted below. "The mausoleum should be named after her," I said, remembering that he'd called her Mumtaz Mahal in private. "But where does 'Taj' stem from?"

"Mumtaz turned to Taz as the years passed. Then she was simply Taj." A faint smile crossed his face. He took off his spectacles and closed his eyes. "When we were alone, she was always Taj to me."

I reached for his hand, saddened and honored by how much he still missed her. "Shall you ever marry again?"

"No. I await our reunion."

I nodded but don't think he saw me, for he drifted somewhere into the past. I wandered back through the years as well, envisioning the two of them walking along the Yamuna, oblivious to everything but each other.

"Father?"

"Yes?"

"If Mother had been married to another, and you were only friends, and could never be lovers, would you . . . could you have endured?"

He shook his head. "Would a bee be content to sip water all his life, when there's nectar before him? Would a stag live in a valley, when there's a mountain he could climb? No, my sweet child, I would never have known contentedness. Indeed, I'd be much sadder than I am today."

"What might you have done?"

A pause lingered between us, and his eyes found mine. I realized then that he knew I didn't speak of him, but of myself. Father, unlike most men, was keenly observant. He understood women, as his heart and ours were akin. "Love, Jahanara, is more precious than gold. It should above all things be pursued." He took my hand. "But let that pursuit be a quiet one, a chase other hunters won't hear. For love, especially the love you seek, with the man you seek, can be most dangerous."

Far from surprised by his perception, but pleased that he had discovered my secret, I leaned forward to kiss his cheek. "I adore you, Father."

He seemed to consider my words. "Never deny yourself love, my child. For to deny love is to deny God's greatest gift. And who are we to deny God?"

THROUGHOUT THE FOLLOWING week I pondered Father's advice. Concentrating on my duties was unduly taxing and I made uncharacteristic mistakes. At one point Isa snapped at me when I ordered iron dowels of the wrong size. Livid, I stormed out of his hut. How could I think of dowels when so much more was at stake?

I avoided Isa for the remainder of that day, as well as the next and the next. I lost my desire to share his company, for his smile was like lime juice on a cut lip. It hurt me to be with him but not be able to touch him, to talk with him but not through words of my choosing. No matter how feverishly I fretted over our quandary, I could derive no solution that brought us together. After all, my husband would kill me if he discovered my unfaithfulness, despite his nightly debaucheries. And Aurangzeb would surely use such information against me. The entire Taj Mahal, as it was now being called at Father's request, would be at risk. For surely if its chief architect were caught in a major misdeed, the project would stumble.

Isa misunderstood my sudden coldness. He often motioned to me from the distance and I pretended not to see him. He asked Nizam to seek my feelings, but I resisted my friend's awkward probes. How Isa could inter-pret my emotions so aptly, and yet be blind to this particular state, galled me. Father would sense such misery. Unfair as it might be, I expected Isa to reach the same conclusions. Alas, he didn't, and so we drifted apart. When he left for Delhi suddenly, I was relieved. And I hated myself for it.

I spent less time at the Taj Mahal and more with my worthless hus-band. He was still determined that I give him a son, and sensing that Isa and I would never be as one, I tried to fulfill his demand. One night I was so despondent that I even sought his affection, whispering kind words into his ear. Yet he laughed at me, his chuckles continuing as I cried myself to sleep. Days passed and my misery increased.

When a letter arrived from Father, requesting that I settle a dispute be-tween two important nobles with palaces to the east, I was quick to leave Agra. Occasionally I undertook such missions, and as much as I usually dreaded them, on that day I was pleased to escape. Nizam, as well as four of Father's most trusted warriors, accompanied me. We rode forth before dawn and traveled without rest.

After leaving Agra we followed a great road northward. English traders had named this fabled passage The Long Walk. It certainly was of no-table length, paralleling the Yamuna all the way to Delhi and then Lahore. Rows of shade trees spanned both sides of the road, as did nu-merous inns and shops. Beyond the trees to the west, rice fields, as well as plots of melons, grapes, mangos, onions and lettuce, sprawled into the distance. To the east, set close to the river, rose the gleaming palaces of nobles. I'd been in several as a girl and knew their grounds contained marble pools and channels filled with lotus flowers and fish. The sur-rounding gardens were home to peacocks and cranes, as well as pavilions topped by golden cupolas. Hordes of servants ensured the sanctity of such realms, while armed guards kept unwelcome visitors at bay.

The Long Walk was inundated with camel-driven caravans, war par-ties, pilgrims and the occasional Jesuit. These priests wore black robes of velvet and bestrode fine mounts. About their necks hung rosaries, quite similar to the prayer beads Muslims used to count invocations. The Jesuits often read Bibles as they rode. Beneath broad-rimmed hats these devout men whispered in strange tongues.

We followed innumerable travelers for the better part of the morning, then turned east and crossed the river on a sandstone bridge. Once we traveled beyond the Yamuna's influence, the land we passed became parched. No banyan trees towered above flower-choked meadows as in Agra. Nor did groves of bamboo groan as trunks rubbed against each other. Instead, sickly bushes hugged the trail. Our horses stepped on cracked earth and kicked up clouds of dust. The grit found its way into our ears, mouths, eyes and hair. We tried to spit, but our throats were so dry that it hurt to hack.

Gradually, the land began to undulate. The horizon changed from brown to green and our spirits improved. The sun fell behind us, the shadows we cast lengthening, then disappearing altogether. As we neared our destination, the four warriors dismounted on a grassy knoll. Here they would make camp. The men were under strict orders to go no farther and would await my return before departing to Agra.

Father had arranged that Nizam and I stay at an inn flanking the Ganges River. Hindus had named the vast stretch of water after their compassionate river goddess, Ganga, and believed that it poured from the heavens until striking Shiva's head. The god's brow stopped the water's fall, and with his encouragement, it ebbed southward. Hindus claimed that if they touched the Ganges they would be cleansed of sin.

I'd never seen the legendary Ganges, but when we finally arrived at the inn I was too weary to study its broad face. Nizam helped me dismount and we sought the innkeeper, an old woman who greeted us kindly and showed us to our rooms. Nizam preferred to sleep on the river's bank and asked for only a blanket. I bade him good night before heading to my quarters.

My room was a diminutive affair with only a table, sleeping blankets, a bucket of water and a lantern. About to unpack, I noticed a letter on the floor. It bore the Emperor's seal, and I wondered what advice Father would impart concerning the dispute.

The letter, crafted in his elegant hand, read:

Sweetest Jahanara,

How can a father tell a child some things? How can he say that he loves her above all his children? Are not all children equal? Allah would say yes, but, may He forgive me, I cannot. For it is you, and you alone, who give me my greatest joy. Surely Mumtaz Mahal, my love and the harborer of all things good, resides in you. Sometimes, when you laugh, or cleverly outthink my best advisors, I see her in your face, hear her in your words.

You asked me what to do if love struck you down, as it does to a lucky few. I said you should seek it. And I believe in those words, no matter that our culture defines such a search as contemptuous. Your mother often argued that women should be able to pursue love as men do, and now, in secret, I shall tell you that I agree.

But how, Jahanara, can you seek love when to do so could mean your death? Does an ant seek to cross the web of a spider? No, child, it does not. And nor should you. Instead, let love seek you. For tonight is my gift and shall commence that journey.

No conflict of nobles demands your attention. This inn is a safe place, its owner a trusted friend. Your secret will know silence here. Stay three days. Enjoy your time together and return on different paths on different eves. And when you return, all I ask is that you save one kiss for your father.

Your love I hold against my heart.

I trembled as I gripped the paper. Though I hated to destroy such beauty, I tore the note into shreds, fearful it might find the wrong hands. My chest tightened in marvelous excitement and I pulled a mirror from my bag. The legacy of a day in the saddle was inscribed on my face. I quickly undressed and, using cotton rags dipped in cool water, cleaned myself as best as I could. I then put on a robe painted with butterflies, drawing it tighter than usual to enhance my figure. A few drops of lotus perfume rubbed into my skin; an orchid stolen from the inn's garden to grace my hair.

As I started to tidy my belongings, I paused, aware of shuffling feet.

"Jahanara?"

I opened the door and found him there, dripping wet and quite confused. He still must have thought me upset with him, for his face contained none of its usual happiness. "I was taking . . . a bath in the river," he said haltingly, "and saw Nizam."

"Father brought me here," I replied, wanting to invite him in, but hesitating.

His uncertainty didn't waver. "He sent a letter asking me to meet an architect here immediately."

"I'm the architect!"

"You?"

"Father planned it all, Isa. He ordered us here so that we could be together."

"He knows?"

"Only that I love you."

"But this past week you've—"

"I've despised myself," I interrupted. "My love for you, and my fear of what that love would betray, made me so cold. But there's no fear here, no watchful eyes, no deceit. There is only us."

He took a step into my room, his hand sailing out to touch my chin. "But your father, he truly condones our love?" When I nodded, Isa's crooked smile, so long departed, returned. "A remarkable man."

I wanted him in my arms, yearned for him with a passion that quickened my pulse. I pulled him close and his damp hands were about me, drawing aside my hair, caressing my neck. He kissed me. I felt his urgency in that kiss, yet it was almost impossibly tender. I muttered his name and his fingers dropped to my robe. His eyes sought mine and when I nodded he untethered my clothes, letting them fall. He made no move to touch me but stepped back, as if to study a mosque of his design.

"So beautiful," he whispered. "How can you be so beautiful?"

I placed his hands on my breasts. He traced their soft contours, almost in awe. I'd always been ashamed of my nakedness, as if it somehow made me weak. But now I quivered with a strange power. As Mother had often said, being a woman is nothing to be ashamed of, and this man, unlike so many others, didn't seem to think of me as something to belittle, but to behold.

My skin responded to his touch, tingling beneath his fingers. My hands worked upon his clothes and soon he was naked as well. His body was lean and muscular. Unlike my husband, his chest and long legs were almost free of hair. Isa lifted me to the sleeping blankets. My mouth found his and our kisses grew frenzied. I wanted him inside me and, reaching down, guided him forward. I sensed a coolness at first, a breeze between my thighs that quickly warmed. Isa didn't move with the wild haste of my husband but eased forward and back like an oar upon water. I found myself, much to my surprise, moving with him.

"My Swallow," he said, somewhat breathlessly, "how I love you."

My hands delighted in the hard muscles of his back. I pawed at him, and a burning surged within me that I'd never known. It soared, higher and higher, so high I could endure it no more. Suddenly I shrieked, my body convulsing. At the same time his body stiffened, and, crying out, he collapsed on me.

"So this is love," I said finally, when he rested in my arms. He kissed me happily and I pulled him closer.

As we lay tangled as one, it seemed that only our world existed. Nothing else mattered. Not hate or fear. Not the past or future. There was only the space between us. And this space shrank as we touched again.

OUR THREE DAYS at the inn passed like an eclipse, wondrous and fleeting. Breakfasts we spent with Nizam. His happiness for us was chiseled into his face, and Isa and I felt honored to call him a friend. He was the one person beyond Father who knew everything about our rendezvous. I think he reveled in the knowledge, though I suspected he'd die before betraying us. Understanding our needs, Nizam left us each morning after we finished our fruit and yogurt, returning only at dusk.

Isa and I rarely spoke of the Taj Mahal, or of anything concerning life in Agra. Instead, we explored the Ganges River and the surrounding countryside. We packed picnics and rode far into the horizon. We saw much wildlife and were constantly stumbling across foxes, cheetahs, tigers, gazelles, eagles and cobras.

Only a handful of settlements dotted the riverbanks. The few we spied consisted of farmers and fishermen. Unaccustomed to seeing strangers, they stared at us as they harvested crops or gutted their catch. Welcoming no gossip, we waved but seldom offered other greetings.

For much of the time we acted like children. We ran our horses, and skipped stones across the river. We chased each other through fields of wheat. Sometimes, when certain that no one was near, we spread our blankets at a hidden spot and made love. At first, such blatant carousing troubled me, for I was a princess, after all, not a courtesan. But in the wilderness, with Isa to encourage me, I learned to trust my body, not the nagging of my conscience. Our lovemaking was as varied as the environs in which we enjoyed it, sometimes defined by urgency, other times by serenity. We followed no pattern but always found solace in each other's flesh. Afterward Isa often swam naked in the river while I bathed in the shallows.

At dusk we drank wine with Nizam and the old innkeeper. Her husband, it became known, had served Father faithfully for many years. After he perished fighting the Persians, Father gave his wife money to buy the inn. She was a sweet, toothless woman who cooked us splendid meals and was always eager to sit beside us.

Our time at the river provided me with unsurpassed moments. Isa and I never spoke about our approaching separation, however much it simmered within our minds. Even during our last day at the Ganges, we failed to mention it. Instead, we traveled farther northwest than we'd ever been.

Early in the afternoon we came across a man burning his wife's body next to the river. Hindus often burnt loved ones' corpses in this manner, since they believed that only once the body was ashes did the soul no longer feel an attachment to the body. Such an uncoupling was necessary for the soul's progress to be unhindered, a passage which began when the ashes were cast into the Ganges. Within its sacred waters the journey toward reincarnation continued—unless the deceased had amassed enough positive karma over numerous lifetimes so that the soul was finally released from the cycle of rebirth.

The man appeared to have no children and, as he added wood to the fire, I wondered how he could bear life on this lonely stretch of river with his wife gone. My mood turned melancholy as we rode through prairie grass back to the inn. When Isa asked what troubled me, I turned to him. "Our time here is done. Need I say more?"

"I know you shall," he replied, trying to smile.

Despite my sour thoughts, I was pleased his understanding of me continued to expand. "How, Isa, can I stand beside you day after day and pretend as if nothing exists between us?" I sought the answer as he contemplated, but it shunned me, for I was made of blood, and only one of stone could stand so resolute.

Isa spurred his horse closer to mine. "This was a gift, Swallow," he said softly. "Thank Allah when you pray next, and thank your father. We're blessed, truly blessed, to have had these days."

"But I want more."

He pushed his turban higher on his brow. "Of course you do. As do I. But until that wish is granted, console yourself with the knowledge that our love is a rare thing. For I've seen many kinds of love, and most are hollow, passionless. They're a matter of convenience, nothing more. We might not share the same house or sleep together each night, but we have something that most do not. And we must be content."

"Content? How can I be content only as your assistant? Am I expected to subdue all my emotions?"

He chuckled at my frustration, which he did on occasion, for his teasings usually brightened my mood. Normally, I welcomed his banter, as my world was often such a serious place that his smile reminded me how it felt to be young. Right now, however, I was suddenly irritated by his bottomless optimism.

"I wouldn't expect you, Swallow, to subdue anything," he added. "As your father might say, it would be like asking clouds not to rain." He slapped at a fly, then added, "No, don't subdue your love. And don't worry. We're young, and many, many years stretch before us. Only Allah knows what will happen."

"Yes," I replied uneasily. "But now I catch your eye. Shall you still love me when I'm old? Or will you seek someone younger and lovelier?"

He pretended to think. "Well, now that you suggest it, I'll likely—"

Though he only jested, I spurred my horse ahead and left him coughing in a swirling cloud of dust. I didn't see how he could make light of our situation, and it maddened me that he would do so. Ignoring his calls to stop, I galloped ahead. My horse was fleeter than his, and I arrived at the inn well before him. I hurried inside and removed my sweaty robe. I was about to wash myself when he entered.

"Jahanara," he said breathlessly, "surely you realize I only jest. I'll never leave you for another. It would be like abandoning my work on the Taj Mahal to go build a—"

"Latrine?"

He grinned. "Exactly. And why would I leave you for a latrine?"

"Perhaps you have loose stools. Or a fondness for flies. How should I know why men act as they do?"

His face finally turned serious. Though he enjoyed vexing me to a degree, he was prudent enough to understand that he'd crawled beneath an agitated elephant. "I love you, Jahanara. And that love won't vanish with time, but will strengthen."

"Shall it?"

"You know little, truly, of how much I think about you. When I work, you're always in my mind. I see your eyes in a pair of gems, or hear your laugh when you aren't near."

"But how then," I asked, exasperated, "are you able to ride so composed, when tomorrow I'll leave? Perhaps you can live within memories, but I'm not ready for their imprisonment."

He reached for me and I stepped back. "Do you believe in fate?" he asked, approaching until we touched. I stayed silent, and so he continued. "For if you do, you must know that we'll be brought together again." My lover ran his hand through my hair, skewing my veil. "Not long ago, I thought fate was only a word poets invented to give their prose meaning. But then your father sought me. And while it might seem that he sought me for the Taj Mahal, I think that somehow I was meant not only to build it, but to find you. And now that I've discovered you, Jahanara, would I so freely let you go?" He paused as I unwound his turban. "An impossibility, I think. For I'm most at peace with you. I'm most complete with you."

"Truly?"

He put a finger to my lips. "Truly."

I wanted him then and stepped into his embrace. He tried to be gentle, but I made love to him with a haste born of fear, for despite his words, I wondered if our love would endure. Even love has its limits, and fate can be a foe as much as a friend. Yes, fate had brought me him, but fate stole my mother. Would it steal Isa next?

When our lovemaking ended, I fixed my gaze at the ceiling. I didn't rest in bliss. Instead, I plotted, pondering how and why and where we could be together. And though no answers came, I prayed that a day would arrive when we might live as man and wife.

CHAPTER X

Brothers as Princes

⎯⎯·⎯⎯

Soon after my return to Agra a major crisis sprang itself upon me. A note bearing no signature was secretly passed to Nizam, who placed it in my hands. Though only a rough toad was drawn on the paper, I knew who had sent it and, late that night, hurried to a prearranged meeting place within one of the many passageways under the Taj Mahal.

I arrived early, unlocked the iron door leading beneath the structure, and left it ajar for Ladli. When she arrived, I secured the door behind us. We shuffled down a black corridor until I felt comfortable enough to light a lantern. Still we didn't speak, but twisted through the mausoleum's bowels until at last we came to a door. Once within that storage room I bolted the door shut. I gave Ladli a robust hug. Since her feigned betrayal, she had ceased working on the Taj Mahal. Thus, it had been more than a year since I held her, and I now found it hard to let go. We exchanged kisses, then embraced again.

"You look magnificent," I said in Hindi, for womanhood had treated her kindly.

"As do you, my little friend."

"Are you well?"

"As well as a mouse could be in a bed of vipers." Ladli coughed, for dust speckled the air. Then she said hurriedly, "Sorry, but we haven't time for pleasantries. If I'm gone too long the dung eater will start to suspect."

"Who?"

"Aurangzeb, of course." I started to speak but her frown stilled my voice. "Jahanara, listen for once. Aurangzeb plans to kill Dara in three days."

My flesh tingled. Though we were safe here, I glanced about nervously. "How?"

"Aurangzeb and Dara will ride north, at your father's insistence, to negotiate a truce with the Persians. Aurangzeb has arranged for outlaws, dressed as Persians, to attack his force. They'll kill Dara and a few others before retreating. With Dara gone, Aurangzeb sees a clear path to the throne. And in the meantime, the traitor can fight the Persians, as he wants, instead of signing treaties with them."

Though my skin continued to crawl, and my heart surged, I was surprisingly clear of mind as I pondered her words. I'd expected such treachery; I just hadn't thought it would come this soon. "But if he yearns for the throne so dearly, why not kill Father instead?"

Ladli spat. "He's no dullard, Jahanara, even if less clever than you. He knows he isn't strong enough yet to rule the kingdom. The nobles follow the Emperor and Dara. If your father died, they'd support Dara. Aurangzeb would have the army behind him, and it might secure him the throne. But he's not one to take chances. He'll wait for your father to die, and with Dara gone, will become the next emperor."

"What of my other brothers, Shah and Murad?"

"As timid as kittens. Stationed at outposts on our frontier, they boast neither the favor of the nobles, nor the power of the army." Ladli reached down to pick up a cricket, which she placed on a crate safely away from our feet. "Aurangzeb scoffs at their strength, Jahanara. He knows the only man standing in his path is Dara."

"Two days after tomorrow?"

"As I said."

I sat on a grimy barrel, for despite my clarity, my legs felt weak. "Then I must convince Dara . . . I must convince him not to leave, and arrange his excuse so that Aurangzeb doesn't suspect you." I paused, for something here seemed amiss. "But why, Ladli, why would Aurangzeb tell you such things? Surely he can't trust you so?"

My friend, whose tongue was like an unbridled stallion, fidgeted slightly. "Because . . . because I realized that if I were to give him . . . if I gave him my body, in time I'd pry all his secrets loose."

"No!" I cried, horrified by the notion.

"What other way existed? You couldn't have expected me to earn his trust by baking him sweets?"

"But I never asked—"

"You didn't ask," she interrupted angrily. "And I'm no fool so don't treat me as such!" Ladli stepped away from me. "It just happened one day. He came to me, and I let him . . . I let him do as he wished. Because I knew then, as I'd always known, that I could best serve your father, and you, if I were his mistress."

I reached out to her in the flickering light. She retreated again, but I closed the distance between us, taking her hand. "Does he mistreat you?"

"Is he a man?" she asked harshly, and I knew he had beaten her. "But it rarely happens," she added, "for the coward knows I'm strong enough to leave him."

"When did it start?"

"Four or five moons ago."

"Is it—"

"He often asks of you," she said. "And I tell him little things, things that could never truly help him. But he wouldn't mind seeing you dead also. He's certain I hate you, but when I told him the people loved you so much that they'd turn against him if he killed you, he believed me."

"It seems my brother—"

"Connives as much as he defecates," she concluded, adding a curse. "Be wary of him, Jahanara. His evil swells. Have you heard what he did to the Christians?"

"Not a word."

"The Portuguese dug a new den in Bengal, a province so distant from Agra that they thought themselves safe. There they killed our people, taking our children as slaves. Aurangzeb discovered their crimes and marched to the coast with his best men. He captured the Portuguese, placed them in a church they'd built and set it aflame."

"I might have done the same. After all, they murdered our people."

"Yes, but would you have placed our children within the church, so that they would burn with the killers? You see, Aurangzeb believed that the Portuguese infected their minds. And so they were destroyed."

I saw children screaming, their hair on fire, and I slumped. "I should kill him," I whispered sadly. "He'll destroy the Empire."

"I'd gladly feed him arsenic stew if it were possible, but how? His bodyguard, Balkhi, samples all his food. The half-wit even sleeps nearby. And during the day Aurangzeb's protected by the Empire's best men. He's grown paranoid, Jahanara, and thinks every stranger must be an assassin sent by Dara."

The room felt hot and I pulled at a violet veil pinned at my brow. "Dara would never murder him," I said with finality and regret. "Nor could I, in truth. But I'd like to banish him, send him to some rock in the sea."

"Make it a small rock. A snake-infested stone with no water or shade."

"I'll go to Dara," I decided. "Whatever I do, Aurangzeb will never suspect you betrayed him. But still, be careful, my friend. Act surprised when you hear what's happened."

"He's my puppet, Jahanara. The brains in your family ran out after you." Ladli adjusted her sari, cursing the garment, as I'd heard her do on many occasions.

"Do you have needs?" I asked.

"The beauty of being a prince's mistress, my scheming little friend, is that you're well looked after. I've enough coins to last a lifetime."

"Then leave him! Escape tonight and never return!"

"Most of the money I give to a Hindu monk, who builds a temple." She finished toying with her sari. "Someday, I'll leave him. But only when you're safe, and only when I can brag to the zealot of the temple he paid for with his precious rupees. Brag of all the Hindus he made happy."

"Don't provoke him."

"Stop worrying. While he spends his next life slithering through offal, we'll drink wine and live decadently."

How can I not worry? I wondered. How would Mother cope with such calamities? "Thank you, Ladli," I said, hugging her. "You're more a friend than I have any right to ask for."

She shrugged. "Outwit him, Jahanara. Outwit him and we'll be together again."

I squeezed her tightly, hating to think of what she'd sacrificed in order
to gain Aurangzeb's confidence, and what she would continue to suffer.
But she was determined to help, and so I tried to shove from my mind
any images of my brother defiling her.

We retraced our footsteps through the tunnels and parted. The night,
thick and moonless, cloaked us well. I rode my horse hard to the Red
Fort, leaving him at the imperial stable, and headed toward Dara's
chambers. No one I knew saw me, for I followed corridors used solely by
slaves. Such passageways were usually empty this time of night, though
I passed a cook and a harlot as they debated the value of wine against
pleasure.

Despite his marriage, Dara preferred to sleep alone, because he often
worked late into the night. I found him thus, an ancient manuscript
propped upon his lap and a candle guttering nearby. My eyes glimpsed
enough of the text to see that it was probably the *Upanishads*, though
like most everyone but Dara, I was unable to read Sanskrit. I knew that
he'd finished a draft of his translation, and I surmised that he now must
be proofing his words.

"Where are your wife and son?" I asked, blowing out the candle.

"Why do you extinguish—"

"Be quiet, Dara. The night has ears."

"But must we speak in darkness? Can the night also see?"

"Keenly."

He sighed, knowing my presence portended nothing good. "What
troubles you?" he asked, and I retold the plot to kill him, my voice urgent. He listened impassively before inquiring, "How do you know this?"

I trusted Dara but believed I'd endanger Ladli if I revealed her. "I
can't say. But the information is good."

"Who gave it to you?"

"Please, Dara, don't ask me that again."

"But how I can judge the tale's validity if I am ignorant of its source?"

I resisted my temper, though my response was curt. "Do you trust me?

Because if you do, you'll heed my words: Aurangzeb shall kill you on your journey."

He ran his hands through his hair. "I don't believe it."

"Did you hear of the Christians?" I asked. When he nodded, I said, "Can one who murders children be suspected of nothing less than evil?"

"Fine! I'll bring my own men. They won't know of the plot but will shelter me."

"Your men? Or Aurangzeb's? Who controls the army, Dara? And how can you rely on loyalty when so much is at stake?"

"I'm to be the next emperor," he replied testily. "They had better protect me."

"Why? Aurangzeb could also be the next—"

"Enough, Jahanara! I do love you, but by Allah, you can drive me mad." Dara set the book aside, marking his place with a peacock's feather. "I'll bring twenty men I trust and will be quite safe. Further theatrics are unnecessary."

"Theatrics? I'm trying to save you."

"And I thank you for that. But you needn't say anything more."

I nodded, already thinking of how I could cancel the trip without either of my brothers suspecting anything. "Fine," I agreed, my foot tapping determinedly. "Twenty men should be enough. Too many would arouse Aurangzeb's suspicions and too few would leave you vulnerable."

He reached out and touched my shoulder. "Thank you, Jahanara, for relenting."

I didn't move from his touch, but neither did I respond in kind. "You make a mistake," I said quietly, "in treating him like a brother."

"Possibly. But he is our brother and I can't treat him any other way. I won't hurt him, for enough pain already exists in this world without brothers hurting brothers." I rubbed my brow in frustration but remained silent. I had failed tonight, failed completely, for Dara should have been swayed by my arguments. "Thank you for seeking me," he said, striving now to be gracious. "I wouldn't barter you for any other sister in the world, rash as you may be."

"Perhaps a mute sister would be more to your liking."

"Mother was hardly mute, Jahanara. And you're little different than she."

Yet I am different, I thought. She was so strong, so certain of the paths before her. My strength, if it can be called that, is born of necessity. It's false, and therefore, I'm false. "Mother would have demanded more action," I finally replied. "I must not possess her will."

"But you do. You do. I simply disagree with your philosophy."

"You think I covet blood? That I somehow relish it?"

"No."

"Then stop talking as if I do." I picked up the heavy book as he apologized. Leafing through its pages in the darkness, I inhaled the paper's aged scent. Why was my brother studying when he should be plotting? And why was I plotting when I should be loving? "I miss the life of a child," I said tiredly. "Things were . . . uncomplicated. Shall they ever be so again?"

"The Hindus would say yes, for they believe we'll play as children again."

"I'd like that," I replied, but I wasn't sure I could believe it.

"As would I."

I kissed him good night, then quietly left his room. My mind embracing and discarding schemes, I struggled to free Dara from Aurangzeb's trap.

THE DAY BEFORE my brothers were to depart, I crafted a plan. The previous night I had almost gone to Father but resisted the urge because I sensed that somehow it would misfire. Father would demand to know of my source, or in his rush to protect Dara, might reveal to Aurangzeb that we were privy to his plans. As much faith as I placed in Father, he was much less conniving than Mother. If he hunted, she stalked. If he listened, she devoured innuendo. And so I kept my knowledge from Father, for I feared that ultimately Ladli would die from his involvement. If Father simply killed Aurangzeb the problem would be solved, but he would never murder his son.

I alone needed to deal with the matter. Though I worked as usual by Isa's side at the Taj Mahal, my thoughts were elsewhere. I did whisper to him of my predicament, and he gave me what advice he could. But such advice was as worthwhile as my insight on building minarets might be.

Isa worried, which was unusual, and I reassured him by promising that Aurangzeb would never order my death for the exact reason Ladli had mentioned. Still, Isa wanted to protect me. I loved him without pause then, for I saw in his eyes that he was unable to imagine life without me. He talked of another journey to the inn, and I swore to plan a second rendezvous after this crisis was resolved.

For once, Isa occupied only a small portion of my mind. It was Aurangzeb who I pondered, and it was Allah who received my prayers. After much contemplation, He graced me with a solution, albeit a dangerous one. For it to unfold properly, I had first to visit the physician who was present when Mother died. I went to him wearing tattered clothes and a heavy veil over my face so that no one would recognize me. Stooping like a weathered woman might, I shuffled to his door. Once inside his mud-brick home, I pulled his curtains shut and revealed myself. His leathery face tightened in surprise.

"How are you, old one?" I asked politely.

"I'm so sorry, child, about your mother."

"Please, please, still your tongue." Each time I saw him, whether on the street or at a bazaar, he apologized for his failure during Mother's labor. "You did your best. We could have asked for no more."

"She was, quite simply, the loveliest of women."

"Yes, yes, she was," I said, envisioning her face. "She always favored you, always wanted you by her side." He tried to smile and I saw that he possessed only two front teeth. Outside, a dog howled. "My father wanted you as well. His loyalty ran deep. Are you as loyal to him?" I asked, wanting to provoke a reaction.

His offense was real. "But of course! Why wouldn't I be?"

"Do you trust that I'm his instrument? Will you do as I say and never give me reason for concern?"

The old man nodded. His head was wrapped in such a heavy-looking turban that I wondered if he could bring it up again. "You haven't cause to ask me these questions, my lady. I'd cut my own hand off if you ordered me to."

"Keep your hand, my friend. And I pose no order but a favor."

"Which is?"

"In the middle of the night my dear brother, Dara, shall become quite ill. This illness is for his safety and the safety of the Empire."

"But only Allah can predict—"

"He'll be served rancid meat, cooked for only a moment. The meat's poisons will make him sick, terribly so. But he won't die." At this statement I looked to him for confirmation, and he nodded ponderously. "When summoned, examine him with care, and then say that he may have malaria, or perhaps a fever. Add that he could recover in a week, or could die tomorrow." I paused, leaning closer to him. "You see, old one, he must be kept in bed for several days. If his illness isn't acute enough, and he tries to rise, give him something to loosen his bowels. And scare him mercilessly in the process."

"But—" the physician stopped, perhaps thinking it better not to question me. "I can do these things," he finally said. "But I don't like them."

"Just know that by doing them, you'll save his life. For if he's well tomorrow, he will surely die."

"Then I'll do my best to protect him."

I reached into my robe and withdrew a pashmina scarf, one so fine that it could easily be pulled through a ring. "For your lady," I said, certain that he'd refuse money, but couldn't resist pleasing his mistress. Alas, his wife had died some years before.

"But I'm too old for a—"

"I know many secrets," I interrupted, teasing him, trying to buoy his spirits and my own. "And she'll enjoy it against her skin."

He bowed to me affectionately, for he had brought me into this world. "You add meaning to this tired life," he said.

"Nonsense. Your mistress gives you meaning, not I."

"She's—"

"Lucky," I said. "As I'll be with you at my side, if Allah is so kind as to bless me with a child."

"It would be an honor, my lady."

"For me," I replied, grasping his soft hands. "Until then, old one. And please, don't speak of this again."

"Allah Himself couldn't pry the secret from me."

I winked at him and pulled my veil back over my face. Once on the flagstones outside his home I hurried into a narrow alley, where I peeled off my worn robe and veil, revealing my true clothes. I then mounted one of Father's stallions and hunted for Nizam. I found him at the Taj Mahal supervising a score of men who pushed a stone block into place. Like all the workers, Nizam was dressed in a cotton shirt and short leggings. His hands were bloody, yet his face was untroubled.

Nodding at him to follow, I tethered my horse to some scaffolding and walked to an empty part of the garden. Beside the marble pool and its colorful fish I told him what I needed him to do, though I withheld information concerning Aurangzeb's plan. I required Nizam's help, since he sampled our meals each night, ensuring the absence of poison. While we ate on special porcelain plates that cracked if they bore poison, the plates were unreliable and hence Nizam tasted each morsel after it had been served. He never cooked but often spent time in the kitchen, overseeing our dinner's preparation. I told my friend that he was to secretly add rotten meat to Dara's dish and flavor it heavily with spices. As always, Nizam was quietly delighted to be a participant in the plan. I stressed to him its importance and knew he'd guard the secret closely.

After pointing about the Taj Mahal and pretending to give him instructions, I left for the harem. I hadn't been within its enshrouding walls for many days, but I suddenly felt an urge to relax, now that my plans were in place. Time's passage had changed little in the harem, even if the women who had always surrounded me looked older and fatter. How can they sit here, day after day, I wondered, and do nothing but gossip? I greeted these women, who did little to help our sex, with feigned respect. Though their mouths told me how much they'd missed me, their eyes reeked of jealousy and irritation.

I lay on a thick blanket and tried to sleep. The sounds of the harem were unchanged—children playing instruments, birds chirping, women chatting and laughing. Incense wafted upon the air, as well as the scents of opium and musk. Having no men present was agreeable, I admitted. Perhaps I was too harsh on these women, for if the harem were the only place I could escape my husband, I'd be here every morning. And while most of the harem's inhabitants had no husbands to escape from, they seemed happy to be free of men.

As I fell asleep I wondered if I'd done everything necessary to undertake my plan. Yes, I decided, but clearly the ruse was dangerous. Dara, Allah help me, could get sicker than I wanted. Or Aurangzeb could somehow sniff out the truth. I'd have to be an able actress, for everything depended on me.

After a long rest I moved to a different quarter of the harem to join Father, Dara and Aurangzeb. We gathered for dinner in an ample courtyard. Though we'd rarely been entertained since Mother's death, Father asked for dancing girls to amuse us this evening. As soon as we knelt on a cashmere carpet, the girls moved opposite us and began to sway. Their torsos were clad, as usual, in transparent silk. Attached to their ankles were silver bells, which sang rhythmically as the girls twisted and shook.

Normally I'd have enjoyed the soothing presence of the dancers but was far too preoccupied with anxious thoughts. We talked about the peace treaty with the Persians and I tried to offer advice. Aurangzeb, naturally, scoffed at my words. I was pleased to receive his scorn, however, for it showed that he suspected nothing. Why my brother wanted war, I could only guess, but clearly he was a man who needed blood.

Aurangzeb and Dara were of similar build, but how different they looked. While Dara's face was as full as a ripe melon, Aurangzeb's countenance was lean and hard. Aurangzeb, unlike Father and Dara, only grew a mustache, and his scar stood out plainly. He wore nothing more illustrious than a white tunic, a black sash and a red turban. Attached to his sash was a battered leather scabbard sheathing his scimitar. Typically for him, but uncommon among nobles of all ranks, Aurangzeb bore no jewelry. He seemed to slide into different postures as he spoke, his movements so subtle that I thought he was sitting motionless when, in fact, he was shifting.

On either side of Aurangzeb knelt Father and Dara. Father wore a lime-colored, full-length robe, while Dara's was black. Father's robe was embroidered with scores of elephants, and Dara's bore paintings of cypress trees. Both men, as was the fashion of nobles, wore long pearl necklaces.

Pinned to Father's turban was a walnut-sized ruby in a gold setting. Dara carried a sword with an emerald-studded hilt. He adjusted it often against his side, seeking comfort. I suspected its blade had never tasted blood.

Though I used to wear a profusion of jewels, I did so less and less frequently. They were troublesome when working on the Taj Mahal, and the laborers, who would never touch one such gem in their lives, had looked at me somewhat accusingly. Once I dressed plainly the workers warmed to me faster.

Aurangzeb, refusing a goblet of wine that Father offered, read my thoughts. "Buried all your gold, sister?" I started to speak, but he motioned for my silence. "The Sacred Text says, 'Surely God does not love the ungrateful who disbelieve.'"

Dara hurried to my defense. "The Qur'an says much. It also asks, 'Do you see the one who repudiates religion? He is the one who rebuffs the orphan and does not encourage feeding the poor. So woe to those who pray without paying attention to their prayers.'"

Aurangzeb's face tightened, for he was a zealot and, like all such followers, believed the Qur'an was his instrument alone. "Take care," he warned, "that you know of what you speak."

Father, aware of the mounting hostility between his sons, cleared his throat. "We all know the Qur'an well enough. If you both wish to recite its verses, you should stand and face Mecca." When neither son responded, Father pretended to swat their words away. He then turned to me. "How proceeds the building, Jahanara?"

I sipped my wine, licking my lips so Aurangzeb could tell I enjoyed the forbidden drink. "We finished the—"

"Our money," Aurangzeb interrupted, "should be spent killing Persians, Deccans, Rajputs and Christians. Not building mausoleums."

"Money is unlike an egg," Father retorted irritably. "It can be split many ways. Moreover, would you deny your mother a suitable resting place?"

Though Aurangzeb would feed her corpse to dogs if the mood struck, he replied, "Never. But your architect is overly ambitious."

"Overambitious? Was Allah overly ambitious when He created Hindustan?"

"Surely you don't compare that fool to Allah?"

Aurangzeb's devotion to Islam was like a fever. Worried he might take a disliking to Isa because of Father's comment, I said, "The architect, Father, is good, but trust me, quite mortal. He relies on the master builders much more than he lets you believe."

"Truly?" Father asked.

"He's clever, but lazy."

Aurangzeb, who I feared would someday claim that the Taj Mahal was Father's utmost blunder, added, "Worse, he has no vision. None."

I bit my tongue. If Isa had no vision, Aurangzeb was blind, deaf and dumb. "The vision," Dara countered, "of an artist can't be compared with that of a warrior. What vision does it take to kill, to rape, to plunder?"

"Your words tire me," Aurangzeb pronounced. "They always have."

Father was about to respond when Nizam, followed by a long-legged servant, entered the room. Each carried two silver trays. After another servant covered the precious carpet with fresh linen, Nizam placed a tray on the floor before Father. He then served Dara. The tall servant set Aurangzeb's meal in front of him. My tray, substantially smaller, came last. Aurangzeb recited a brief prayer before we ate, asking for strength.

Dinner consisted of raan—leg of lamb cooked in yogurt seasoned with chili powder, coconut milk, ginger and cinnamon. Cucumber slices and buttered squash complemented the meat. Father thanked Nizam, who bowed and turned away. I thought the lamb was spicier than usual, but no one else commented on it. Dara's meat looked normal, but I'd insisted it be two days old.

"We'll leave early," Aurangzeb said. He spoke to Dara but didn't look at him. "Can you rise, as a soldier does, well before dawn?"

"Roosters rise early, brother, but does a more dull-witted beast exist?"

Such insults were increasingly common between my siblings, and Father took fleeting interest in the exchange. However, my attention was gathered by their words. "We'll ride far and hard," Aurangzeb warned. "The poets will be left behind."

Dara, though as naïve as a virgin bride, was no coward. Nor was he physically weak. "But not I," he replied, turning from Aurangzeb.

We finished the meal in silence. I suspected Father would have preferred to dine alone with me, as we often did. On such nights we spoke of the Taj Mahal or rekindled memories of Mother. Tonight the tension between Dara and Aurangzeb seemed to taint the air.

After we were served dessert, and the servants had left, Father looked at my brothers. "My sons, who are like a mongoose and a cobra in the same pen, put aside your differences, just once, for this journey. The Persians seek peace, and peace they shall have. But only, Aurangzeb, if you go in good faith. And Dara, on military matters, you'll obey your younger brother."

Father proceeded to advise them on negotiations, and then they left silently. I noticed that both their plates were empty. I was about to ask Father of his day when he said, "I don't know what to do with them, my child. I fear there shall be more than words between them."

I eased closer to him, leaning against the circular cushion bordering the carpet. "But you're still young and healthy. We won't have to deal with that problem for many years."

"Let it be so, please Allah. For what does a father do with two such sons?" He took off his spectacles and, after sipping his wine, whispered, "I love Dara, but is he strong enough to be the Emperor? I have always trained him to take my place, but perhaps I was mistaken. Perhaps Aurangzeb, as . . . vexing as he may be, would prove to be a stronger leader. And with enemies pressing on all sides, we might need a warrior, not a scholar, as our next emperor."

Dimly aware of the dancing girls and the ringing bells about their feet, I wondered if Father was right. "Who did Mother think would be best?"

He toyed with a heavy ring of silver. "Dara."

"Then you weren't mistaken." I kissed him and said good night, heading for my room. Though I'd soon be awake, I changed into my sleeping gown and sought rest. To ease my mind, which raced and twisted my stomach, I recited my favorite verses of the Qur'an, whispering them until my pulse slowed.

Much later—for the candles in my room had burnt themselves out— an urgent knocking caused me to bolt upright. I hurried to the door.

Outside stood Nizam, his eyes bright with fear. "Your brother, my lady! He's very sick!"

I didn't bother to dress, nor put on my sandals, but hurried to Dara's room. His wife, whom I had last seen a moon before, knelt at his bed. So did Father. A chamber pot beside Dara reeked of decay and vomit. Drenched in sweat, he moaned incoherently, gripping his sides.

"What ails him?" I asked worriedly, just as Aurangzeb entered the room.

"I've sent for the physician," Father said, glancing toward the door. "May Allah give his legs strength."

Dara moaned again and promptly retched. He lacked the will to turn to the chamber pot and hence vomited upon himself. His wife shrieked as I fell to my knees beside him. "What hurts?" I questioned, my heart raging so fiercely that I was certain others could hear it. "Tell me!"

"My . . . stomach," he stammered, barely coherent. "It feels afire!"

Hurriedly the old man shuffled into the room, carrying a wool bag and wearing the same oversized turban as before. I moved aside and he wordlessly took my place. "Where . . . where, my prince, does it ache?" he asked, winded enough that he could hardly string together two words.

"My . . . my gut."

The physician looked carefully into the chamber pot. "Your fever, my prince, is it cold or hot?"

"Cold."

Nodding, the physician inspected his patient. He felt for the strength of his pulse, studied the movements of his eyes. He then pinched Dara's tongue. "Too dry," he muttered.

"What's happening?" Father asked, turning from Mecca to the physician.

The old man considered his prognosis. "Too early to tell, my lord. Perhaps malaria. Perhaps some other wretched fever." He paused, leaning to withdraw some herbs from his bag. "I require tea," he said to no one in particular.

Nizam left instantly. Aurangzeb stepped closer to his brother, his face seemingly compassionate. "What can be done?"

"The herbs will help with the fever, my prince. He may be fine in a few days. It may take a week." The physician wiped his brow in apparent concern. "But if the fever doesn't abate, he could . . . he may leave us."

Father groaned at this news and Dara's wife sobbed. I draped a blanket over my brother's writhing form. "Should he eat or drink?" I asked, genuinely concerned, guilt rising in my blood.

"No food, my lady. But much of my tea. He'll drink it all night, no matter if he throws it up or gulps it down." The old man rose. "But you should all leave. If it's a fever, the infected air could steal into your lungs. I'll stay with him."

"Please," I begged, "please let me help."

"Not tonight," Father replied, taking charge of the situation. "The physician shall stay. The rest of us will return to our rooms."

"I want to—"

"Go, child!"

"Please."

"Go!"

We cleared the room as one, and I promptly slammed my door shut. My plan, even if unfolding as it should, was all too real. I wanted Dara's pain, which far surpassed my intentions, to stop. Perhaps Nizam had given him too much meat! How could I, who knew nothing of medicine, have expected to poison him just right?

In the hall I heard Father and Aurangzeb talking. My younger brother, it became evident, would travel to Persia alone. That journey was too important to forfeit, even now. Aurangzeb didn't argue with Father. His voice, though he tried to cloak it, rang with jubilation. After all, Dara might die tonight, die without the risky intervention of swords and men. Furthermore, though Aurangzeb had grown less transparent than in his youth, I was almost certain he would attack the Persian envoy.

After I heard Father depart, Ladli's familiar voice rang forth. Why she was in the royal chambers I could hardly fathom, but despite my turbulent emotions, I was quick to realize that she presented me with an opportunity to further fool Aurangzeb. Perhaps her intention was thus.

As my brother and his mistress spoke, I stormed out of my room.

Ladli stood barely three paces from me, and when she saw the rage on my face, her fear was real enough. "Get out!" I demanded.

I tried to slap her, but Aurangzeb caught my wrist easily, his grip so strong that I yelped in pain. "She's no concern of yours, sinner," he hissed.

"Do you hear him, you plague-infested, treacherous rat?" Ladli added.

"Treacherous? You betrayed me!"

"Am I the thief?"

"You—"

Ladli spat at my feet. "Be glad you're the Emperor's daughter, Jahanara, or you'd be flogged like a common criminal, a sight I'd certainly like to see! I suspect your pretty little body wouldn't hold up well."

"At least I'm no whore!" I shrieked, trying to slap her as Aurangzeb, while denouncing my language, threw me into my room. I banged my shins against a low table and toppled to the ground. Suddenly I was overwhelmingly confused. Ladli, though only playing her role, seemed actually to hate me. How was it possible for best friends even to say such things to each other? Could she be lost to me forever, now that we'd always have to pretend to be foes? Amid sudden tears, I vowed to meet her secretly again.

A series of moans emerged from Dara's chambers. Thoughts of Ladli fled and my concern for him returned. However much I wanted to sneak back and comfort my brother, as well as to tell him the truth, I could never mention what had happened. He would lose face, and never trust me again, regardless of whether I'd saved his life.

Trying to ignore his cries, I paced my room like a caged lioness, paced until my feet ached and my legs turned to stone. The night vanished slowly, as if trying to torture me further. When dawn finally emerged, I was still sleepless, praying for Dara and begging Allah's forgiveness.

Just after the sun reached its zenith, long after Aurangzeb left to face the Persians, the exhausted physician came to us and said that Dara's fever had yielded. The old man believed, quite incredibly to us all, that he'd be well. I broke down then, and Dara's wife and I cried together.

Dara, still reeking of filth, smiled at our womanly emotion.

CHAPTER XI

Daybreak

Though I made many mistakes in my life for which I paid dearly, poisoning Dara was not one of them. My dear brother recovered quickly from his ordeal and we all marveled at the strength of his constitution. The physician said that men often died from fevers of this sort. Yet Dara was healed in a matter of days. I hadn't expected my co-conspirator to spend the entire night with my brother and secretly rewarded him with a bolt of gossamer silk and a spool of golden thread.

Aurangzeb, as I had predicted, went northwest, seeking trouble. He later reported to Father that Persians had ambushed his undersized force, but I believed the opposite was true. Aurangzeb fashioned a pile of Persian heads at our border, and Father worried about renewed attacks from our foe. Our warriors, however, prized my brother for his victory.

Not three weeks passed before our reviled neighbors to the south, the Deccans, were again hoping to carve Hindustan in two. The Deccans had been troublesome in earlier times, but not altogether threatening. Alas, more recently a powerful sultan had risen in Bijapur, a city we claimed as ours but which the Deccans declared otherwise. This sultan sent his troops northward to raid, and raid they did, burning our crops and stealing our livestock. Father ordered Aurangzeb, with forty thousand battle-hardened warriors, to quell the rebellion.

We soon learned that Aurangzeb, after enduring harsh losses, had laid siege to Bijapur and captured it within a week—a tremendous victory by all accounts. The outcome pleased Father, for now the Sultan of Bijapur would have to pay tribute to the Empire and sign a profitable treaty of vassalage. His fame as a warrior spreading, Aurangzeb was appointed Viceroy of the Deccan. Fortunately, he was ordered by Father to stay in the south for many months, ensuring that the conquered remained on a short leash.

. Life in Agra was far removed from such conflict. We watched the soldiers and war elephants train but had little else to do with the fighting. After all, we had twenty-two thousand men working feverishly on our mausoleum and it swelled slowly upward. When the first structural bricks were set in place for the splendid, tear-shaped dome, we celebrated the achievement with Chinese rockets.

Early one morning Isa sent a pair of messengers to Father and me at the Red Fort, who requested that we follow them to the Taj Mahal. Though we had not eaten breakfast, we complied with their wishes. As they neared the sprawling site, the messengers turned to us and asked if we'd dismount, adding that Isa wanted us blindfolded and then guided to a clandestine location. Father's royal guards bristled, their hands darting to their sword hilts. A carefree wave from the Emperor, however, eased their worries.

Thus blinded, we were led up a series of steps. I feared stumbling into something hard, but my guide took extreme care to usher me around obstacles. Despite the day's freshness, the air buzzed with activity. Elephants trumpeted, masons chiseled and men chanted as they worked. Such sounds seemed heightened by my blindness, and I resolved to close my eyes more often. Surely the voices of birds, or the drumbeat of rain, must be even more rewarding than what I heard now.

I knew we had gone inside something when the edges of my blindfold turned from yellow to black. "Please keep your eyes closed," Isa softly advised. Hands withdrew the fabric from our faces, yet all was still dark. "These walls," my secret lover said, "which temporarily lean against each other, will become the skin of the Taj Mahal. They'll cloak her interior and exterior. And, if I might be so bold, they'll steal your breath, my lord. Now, if you'd please open your eyes."

Our world blossomed. The first thing I noticed was that we were in a room, rather a box, of white marble. But the marble, despite its brilliance, did little to captivate me. What did were the hundreds, no, the thousands, of flowers adorning the walls—delicate forms of lily, iris, tulip and narcissus. The corollas of these creations were gracefully tapered, while the petals and leaves were perfectly configured. Flowing vines connected the flowers.

I had never seen such beauty, not even in Allah's best gardens. For these flowers weren't of water and light, but of semiprecious stones. They were infinitely more colorful than the rings of a rainbow, or the hues of a sunset.

"Our masters cut thin tendrils of stone, which they inset into the marble," Isa said animatedly. "They fit the tendrils perfectly into the marble, then bond and seal them." His voice, serene as always, gathered speed. "You gaze at lapis from Afghanistan, jade from China and Burmese amber. There are pearls and coral from our coast, as well as jasper, green beryl, onyx, agate, amethyst and quartz from our interior."

At some places the marble was free of semiprecious stones but had been carved away to reveal immense white bouquets. These sculptures were smooth to the touch and had been polished until they glistened. Even the room's floor was a godlike work of art, boasting geometric patterns of black marble set within the white. Each line was as straight as the horizon and each angle as sharp as a blade.

No one spoke for some time. Finally, Isa said, "Try to envision it, my lord. The dome, of course, shall be pure white marble, as will the minarets. But the arches, the kiosks, the walls and the ceilings will be draped with such images."

I tried to imagine the finished Taj Mahal, and the mere thought of its beauty made me tremble. Father traced the flowers with his fingers, his palms. "One shall step inside the Taj Mahal and think he has entered Paradise." He looked toward Mecca and I knew he was begging Allah to let him live long enough to see the sight. "So much beauty," he whispered.

"I can feel her," I said, "within these walls."

His eyes glistened. "Yes, my child."

Isa smiled at me, and I was entranced by his stare. How could one man conjure such magic? Though the best craftsmen in the world toiled for him, I sensed his hands everywhere. They were the hands of a poet, perhaps, a man who could make one weep by looking at a stone. Suddenly

I wanted his hands upon me. I yearned to kiss each finger. For they were hands too precious for this world, this place of suffering and woe.

Why would such a man love me? I wondered. And could our affection, as noble as it might be, inspire him to create such majesty?

Love. Such a simple feeling, yet such a force of creation. My parents' love, I was sure, would be written about until the end of time. Our own love, may it last forever, would be celebrated unknowingly for centuries through the dressings of the Taj Mahal. How fortunate we were, I realized. Men like Aurangzeb might know victory on a field of battle; they might earn titles and untold wealth. But could they ever reach such a height as this? When they were decrepit and dying, would they be content with their memories, or wallow in their lost opportunities? I suspected that their regrets would be many, and I pitied Aurangzeb, for his life would never be as complete as mine.

I gazed at my lover, thanking Allah for this man, this most precious of gifts.

"You honor the Empire, Isa, with your skill," Father said quietly.

"I've only a small role in this play, my lord."

Father nodded, then asked, "Would you leave us, please? Go from this room, and ensure that no one draws near."

"Certainly."

When Isa was gone, Father placed his hands on my shoulders. "I understand why you love him."

"But Father—"

"Your adoration for him, child, is as open for all to see as the wares of a greedy merchant."

"It is?"

"You are young in such matters. But others are not. I see your love when you smile at each other, when your eyes linger upon meeting." He ceased speaking long enough to slide his smallest ring onto my largest finger. "I'm delighted you've found love, my child. I was wrong about Khondamir. I thought him to be noble, but he deceived me. And I'm sorry, more sorry than you'll ever know, about my mistake. Please, please forgive me."

"Nothing needs forgiveness."

He kissed my finger, the one bearing my new ring. "You must be much more careful. Your love is dangerous. If Khondamir or one of my enemies should discover it, Isa's life would be in terrible jeopardy. I could protect you, but not him."

I massaged my temples, as my head ached from a sudden fear of discovery. "But what am I to do, Father? How can I love him, as Mother loved you, if I can't hold him?"

Father turned to the nearest wall, once again tracing its flowers with his fingers. "Truly beautiful work. The best I've seen in a lifetime spent gazing at such masterpieces."

"But," I persisted, "what shall—"

"Don't always move with such haste, Jahanara. I fear that impatience is your true weakness, for the tiger that springs too early often goes hungry." I stifled a response, smart enough to realize that my rashness was a fault. Father chuckled at my intake of breath. "Do you think that I, who loved so much, would leave you alone in this plight?"

"You have the Empire to run," I offered lamely.

"Yes, even if my sons run it more each day. Soon I'll be a decoration, much like that golden peacock straddling my throne." Though he'd hardly mind such a life, I stayed silent. "I think it's time for you to have better quarters," he said finally.

"My room is fine. More than adequate."

"Your mother's quarters, as you know, are next to mine." He laughed, as if recalling a fond memory. I'd last heard him laugh, truly laugh, the night before her death. "We always slept in one bed," he said, "but she did relish having her own room. I think it suited her independence. No, even as deeply as we were in love, sharing one room for everything would have been like asking fire to live with water."

"But why should I take her quarters?"

"Because, my child of haste, my grandfather designed that room." Father moved closer to me, and whispered. "When the Red Fort was raised, an escape route was built from the fortress in case we were ever besieged."

"I've heard such a thing."

"But you haven't heard of the locked closet in the rear of your mother's room. For it's not only a closet. Behind her clothes is a stairway. And that stairway leads to a tunnel underground, which dives beneath the Red Fort's eastern wall and finally rises into the basement of a simple home I own in the city. If we were ever besieged, I might flee to this home."

I could hardly have been more surprised at this revelation, as I'd thought I knew everything about Father's plans. How many other secrets did he harbor? "But the men, Father, who built it. Perhaps they revealed the secret. It would be easy for an assassin to enter the house and proceed into the Red Fort. He could kill you anytime."

"True, but impossible. You see, when the Red Fort was first being built, my grandfather—may he feast in Paradise—discovered a plot to kill him. A group of nobles, including a court architect, were the culprits. Like all traitors, they were sentenced to be tortured, and then they and their families would be put to death. But Grandfather gave the traitors a choice. And they chose to live in the unfinished royal chambers, under his personal guard, where they were to build him a secret tunnel. Upon its completion, they'd be executed with mercy, and their families would be spared."

"And it was so?"

"It took them almost a year to build it. When finished, they went to the executioner's block. And thus their secret died with them. Grandfather passed the secret to my father and he passed it to me." He smiled, chuckling. "I've told it to the two women in my life. First, Mumtaz Mahal, and now you."

"Not Dara?"

"Only when he proves worthy of the knowledge."

I'd seen the closet door many times but never thought for a moment that it led to a hidden passageway. "You honor me, Father, by trusting me. But I don't see how it will help."

"Reason, child, before you speak. Better to answer such a question yourself, than to show anyone, even a loved one, your ignorance."

I pondered the scenario, biting my unpainted nails, as I sometimes did when nervous. "You say you own the house?" When he nodded, I continued. "If Isa, may I be so bold as to suggest, were to buy this house from you, might I meet him occasionally within its walls?"

He acted surprised at the notion, but his eyes gleamed mischievously. "An intriguing idea. If you moved into your mother's room, thereby gaining the keys to her closets, you could, in theory, journey to his house."

I jumped to him, throwing my arms around his neck. I kissed his cheeks repeatedly, the gray bristles of his beard scratching my chin. "How soon?"

"Immediately," he said, chuckling at my enthusiasm. "But so as not to arouse suspicions, Isa should wait a few weeks to buy the house. Can you wait for your love to be reunited?"

"Of course! And in the meantime, we'll do much better at hiding it."

"You must, my child, because otherwise Khondamir will have Isa's head. Even an emperor can do little to subdue an avenging husband."

"I love you," I said earnestly. "I owe you so much, and yet I'll never be able to repay you."

"Does an iris," he asked, tracing such a flower on the wall, "seek to repay the sun which gave it life? No, the mere beauty of the iris is tenfold thanks enough, for each day the sun can see the wonder it created."

I smiled at his ongoing attempts at poetry. "You improve."

"Truly?"

I gave him one more kiss. "Let us leave, Father. There's so much to do."

"Indeed. But before we leave this oasis, cleanse your face of that smile and act as if I reproached you."

Biting the inside of my lip until my happiness was contained, I followed him from the room. Outside, amid the multitudes of men and beasts, Isa oversaw the rise of the dome. When I spied him, I was again reminded of a hawk. His sharp face was so intent on his work that I half-expected him to soar above the dome and inspect his progress.

As much as I wanted my gaze to rest on Isa, I swung my head forward. I followed my father with adoration, for surely few such men walked the Earth.

* * *

A WEEK LATER, after Father had a pouch of precious gems delivered to Khondamir, I moved into Mother's room with little fanfare. For a princess, I had surprisingly few possessions, but nonetheless Nizam carried my robes, scarves, jewelry and books into my new quarters and helped me to unpack. It was strange being within the red marble room and its stone-lattice windows, for most of Mother's clothes and other belongings were still present. A cashmere carpet with a rendering of dawn or dusk graced the floor. Silk pillows and folded pashmina blankets lay astride. Paintings within gilded frames were hung about the walls depicting Father upon his Peacock Throne, the Red Fort, bouquets of miniature roses. Mother's favorite perfume—though perhaps my imagination was overindulgent—lingered in the air. After Nizam left, I tried on several of her most prized robes and found that they fit me quite well. Despite still missing her terribly, it felt reassuring to wear her clothes and walk about her room.

Father had told me of a false bottom in a drawer of Mother's writing desk. After bolting my door, I easily located and opened the hidden compartment. I expected to find within a single key, but instead a handful of items revealed themselves. Foremost atop the orderly pile were several poems from Father, which I glanced at but left unviolated. Beneath the yellowed papers rested objects from our childhoods, including a boy's first slippers, drawings of elephants and a ribbon-bound lock of my hair. I smiled at these treasures, my grin widening when my fingers embraced a clay incense burner that I'd once crafted for Mother. As a child, and indeed, still today, I lacked any semblance of artistic ability. In consequence the burner was so misshapen that I was unsure whether it was a turtle or a toad.

Brushing aside a tear I whispered, "Thank you," adoring her for having placed such treasured memories in her safe. While I carefully rearranged the box's contents, I found an unmarked and rusty key. I left the key there and replaced the drawer's false bottom. Continuing to organize my room, I thought of Mother, hoping she could see my doings. If her eyes were somehow upon me, she was surely relishing my use of the secret tunnel to reach Isa.

I could scarcely wait, but forced myself to be patient as the days passed. I made certain to work on the opposite side of the Taj Mahal from Isa, for he had nearly jumped from his skin in excitement when I informed him of Father's plan. Isa was even less able to hide his love than I, and so I avoided him like a rabid dog thereafter. Only through Father did I hear of my lover's purchase of the home.

Though I pushed my men hard, they seemed to like me, for I treated them well and rewarded them justly. And Allah smiled at me, for only one of my workers died in the full cycle of the moon, the poor man crushed to a pulp when a stone block fell atop him. He was Hindu, and therefore we didn't bury his body as if he were Muslim, but burned it.

I never thought the night would arrive when I could finally steal forth to Isa. Only when we were relatively certain of our safety did we agree to a meeting. Edgy, I barred the door to my room and lit a fat candle. Unlocking the closet door, I pushed dusty robes apart and stepped between them. Piled boxes blocked my path and I quietly moved them aside.

As Father had foretold, a stairway cut of rough stone confronted me. Holding my candle with one hand and clutching at the wall with the other, I descended. The stairway was circular and fell straight downward. It reeked of inattention. Dead spiders and ancient mice droppings littered the steps. Names lay etched in a section of the wall and I envisioned the traitors pausing here to leave their marks. How must it have felt to build this passage, knowing that after its completion your head would be cleaved from your body? I wondered if ghosts inhabited this realm, but decided that the men had died honorably and that their souls tasted no such torment.

The stairs ended and a passageway loomed ahead. The corridor was narrow, so much so that a large man might have to turn his shoulders sideways to move through. My candle was feeble in this black womb, illuminating only a dozen paces before me. I was gripped by a sudden fear of what would happen if my flame were to die. Surely I should have brought a lantern! The path, fortunately, was straight and true. Father had said it was designed so that the Emperor, if he lacked the time to find and light a candle, could follow it directly to the home.

I imagined passing beneath sleeping families and vast courtyards. At one point I saw a pair of beady eyes ahead, yet when I moved forward, the eyes slipped into a crack and vanished. The air was stale and I hurried on. How far must I go? More carvings appeared on the walls. These were curses, damning to endless deaths those who ventured here. Shuddering, I wondered if the curses were meant for my grandfather, or were designed to put fear into his pursuers.

Father had forewarned me about a trap, and as I came to it I paused. A stone block, knee-high and equally wide, occupied the middle of the corridor. Stepping on the stone sprang the trap. The floor immediately beneath it would collapse, then the walls, then the ceiling, crushing whoever had touched the block.

I carefully stepped over the trap, avoiding all touch with it. Knowing the passageway's end must be near, I lengthened my strides. When I saw light ahead I let out a small cry. The faint glow brightened like the dawn. I came to another spiral staircase and I hurried up its steps. Isa must have heard me coming, for he called my name. Suddenly I was in his arms. We took the last steps together, emerging into an underground storage room.

"Follow me, Swallow."

He led me up another set of stairs and abruptly we were within his home, a simple affair boasting only one large room. A smoke-stained hearth and iron pots occupied the far corner. Isa's paintings of the Taj Mahal and his intricate designs hung about the walls. Present also were a drawing table and a chair. Otherwise the room was void of furniture, save carpets, blankets and plush cushions. Isa had closed the window shutters and locked the door.

He hugged and kissed me for a time. Finally withdrawing, he whispered, "Your great-grandfather, my love, built this home to resist flame and attack. Its stone walls are as thick as my chest."

"So?" I asked, wondering why he'd speak of such unromantic things.

"So, Swallow, no one shall ever hear us here. Ever."

My reflection smiled in his eyes. He kissed me and I found my body yearning for his. It had been far too long since the inn, since I touched him. Our clothes dropped and we explored each other, candles casting their light on us as we loved. His lips were in constant motion against my flesh, sampling me like he might a course of fine wines. My hands sought to draw us together, continuing to do so even as we descended upon blankets and pillows. Soon he was atop me. His weight was comforting, warming. I pulled him more tightly to me, watching as our shadows, flickering against the wall, mimicked our rhythmic motions, ultimately merging as one.

When our lovemaking was finished, I lay with my head on his thumping chest. He stroked my brow as I thought about the future, of what might be. "Isa," I asked, "do you wish to have a child?"

"Only with you."

I hugged him, as I longed for children more with each passing season. "It shall be perilous," I foretold. "My pregnancy could endanger the Taj Mahal."

He wrapped my hair about his fingers. "I don't know, Swallow, which will prove more everlasting—the monument we create, or the child who might bless us. Our stone, of course, will endure for centuries. But a child . . . a child shall let us live forever."

"How few men think such thoughts," I replied. "Women in the harem who know nothing of politics and history ponder them each day, yet men seem to deem them trite."

"But how can a child, in all his beauty, be trite?" he asked, tracing the curve of my hips.

My mouth froze, for to voice my thoughts might dampen his mood. Here was a man who any child would be lucky to call father. Yet Isa would never be known as such. "But, Isa," I said gently, "this child, were we to have one, wouldn't be yours publicly. You could never, never show your affection. You could be a father only here."

A momentary sadness fell over him, but Isa, as I was coming to know, wasn't a man to dwell on what he lacked. And so dawned his uneven smile. "A child . . . our child, my love, would be blessing enough. How could I ask anything more of Allah? Surely He's granted me enough wishes already."

I glanced toward Mecca and prayed that my womb, as Khondamir so often complained, wasn't barren. While I was a woman who needed more than motherhood in life, I also yearned to love a child. A child would be a gift to myself, to Isa and to my father. For as surely as the stars rose each night, Father would know that my child was Isa's. And this knowledge would please him. After all, he was the shepherd of our love.

"I'll have to think of a plan," I said. "Khondamir, who hasn't fathered a child in two decades of trying, must be convinced that I carry his seed."

"But why would he believe you?"

I smirked at him, my spirits rising as I thought of our daughter, then our son. "You may be a master of stone, Isa, and the most astounding man I've met, but you know nothing of the guile of women. How do you think we flourish in this world where men decide what we can and cannot do? Because of your rules?" I laughed at the notion, recalling how Mother and my great-grandmother had led Hindustan in all but title. "Khondamir, trust me, shall think himself the father. I am uncertain how I'll do it, but when my honeyed talk is done, he'll boast to anyone with an ear of his deed."

Isa chuckled. "Am I equally malleable?"

"Like butter."

He rolled on top of me, pinning my arms to the blankets. "And now?"

"Just like a man," I said, trying to push him off. "What you lack in cunning you compensate for in muscle."

I resisted none of his kisses, or his efforts to again make love. Afterward, he continued to stroke my skin, as if he had found a pelt and was experiencing his first sense of touch. Though he had the singing voice of an ox, he hummed contentedly. He aimed to sing me to sleep, but as the night aged, I pondered the road ahead. If Allah were to grace me with a child, then I must fool Khondamir as completely as I'd boasted.

"Good night, my love," I mumbled, pretending to dim. His humming quieted, which is what I wanted, for it interfered with my thinking.

"Good night, Swallow."

One by one the candles flickered out. It was as black as ink in that room, but I was never more comfortable. I was warm, content, and with the man I loved. Inhaling the scent of his sweat, listening to his calm breaths, I thought about how to best my husband. When a solution finally offered itself, I rose silently, kissed Isa's brow, and started the long journey back to my room in the Red Fort. It would soon be dawn, and I was always an early riser. Tongues might wag if a servant's knock on my door went unanswered.

As I stepped over the trap, and finally came to the staircase, I perfected my plan the way a chef might concoct delicacies for his lord. It was a simple ruse, one that would never fool Aurangzeb. Luckily, only Khondamir needed deceiving. Let him think himself the father, and the rest could debate the truth.

So many secrets, I thought. They encircle me like moths about a flame.

Were I to know how many more secrets awaited me, and how many deaths they'd produce, I might have returned to Isa and stolen away from Agra. But if I had, no one would have been present to oppose my brother. And devils like Aurangzeb needed enemies.

HOWEVER MUCH I LOATHED neglecting my duties at the Taj Mahal, it was essential to fool Khondamir as quickly as possible. I went to my husband's home the very next afternoon. Riding one of Father's stallions, I held the reins in my right hand and a cotton bag in my left. Inside the bag was a pair of bull's testicles wrapped within a palm leaf.

Khondamir's trading increasingly took him beyond Agra, and I'd become an infrequent visitor to his home. His servants therefore greeted me with equal parts surprise and kindness. Though still embarrassed before them, since they thought me a thief, I handed them smoked yams, for which they thanked me profusely.

Today, Khondamir worked at one of Agra's bazaars, overseeing the sale of his wares. Convinced his workers cheated him, he often spied on their activities. Sometimes he even hired a beautiful woman to toy with his men, hoping, for instance, that they would give her a bargain on a silver bracelet. After a few such underlings were whipped senseless, others rarely strayed from the approved prices.

Khondamir's quarters had withered in my absence. For a man with so many rupees, he spent precious little on decorations. To better his room, I gathered wildflowers from his orchard and propped them up in simple Chinese vases. After sprinkling perfume about his floor, I lit incense and piled cushions and blankets on his sleeping carpet. Then I met with the cook and handed him my bag. He was hardly surprised by what I asked, acceding to my wish.

The tiles in Khondamir's washing room needed replacing, but the floor and walls were clean. A servant girl brought me three buckets of warm water. She was a pretty child of less than fourteen and I considered whether Khondamir had bedded her. After all, men such as him never hired unattractive women as servants. And surely older and more versed servants could better meet household needs.

After soaking myself under a bucket of water, I scrubbed vigorously with a hemp cloth. How good it felt to clean the day's grime from me. I had heard that Europeans never bathed and was repulsed by the notion, certain that they must reek like animals. Before slipping into a sleeping robe, I rubbed ambergris, a perfume created from the oils of giant whales, against my body. I also chewed cloves to sweeten my breath.

Finally ready, I sat on his thick carpet. I asked for a goblet of wine, remembering how it had dulled my senses during my wedding night. That eve already seemed distant, as if but the dream of a terrified girl. I recalled surprisingly few details, except for the feeling of fire between my thighs.

Khondamir returned home well past dusk. He grunted when he eyed me. "Well, woman, what brings you here? Run out of gold?"

I smiled, praying that my plan would work. "I was with my astrologer, my lord, and he said that tonight would be auspicious." Though many Hindustanis were dependent upon astrology, Khondamir scoffed. He started to undress, carefully setting his jewels aside. I stepped closer to him. "Last night, my lord, I saw the lucky star of Canopus. My astronomer claimed it was a good omen."

"For you to grow younger? To sprout fuller breasts?"

"For becoming pregnant," I replied patiently, "because I was thinking about your son when I looked to the sky."

Khondamir might have despised me, but he couldn't easily dismiss the words of a court astronomer. "But you're as barren as the desert. The driest, most lifeless desert in all of Hindustan."

"True," I agreed, trying to hide my distaste. "But later, I went to my doctor. When I told him what my astronomer said, he offered a remedy."

"Am I to pour water on you?"

What a simple tadpole you are, I thought. "He told me that a meal of bull's testicles would give your seed the strength it needed."

Khondamir actually paused, his bloated face tightening with interest. "I've heard of this remedy. But could it work on such a dead womb?"

"He thinks so. And earlier today, I had the biggest bull in my father's herd butchered. He had already sired many a calf."

A glint of respect showed in my husband's eyes. Or perhaps my mind was playing tricks, for the wine toyed with my senses. "You brought its balls?" he asked.

"Yes."

"I'll have my cook prepare them in the old way," he said proudly, as if it were all his idea. "Then we'll see if this astronomer of yours is worth the rupees you wasted on him."

I sipped more wine as he disappeared. I tried to think of Isa but found that his memory was tainted by these doings. Knowing that I'd go to him tomorrow night and make love to him, I felt like a courtesan. Who but such an escort would bed two men in the space of a day? And how could Isa ever forgive my promiscuity?

These thoughts angered me, for men who warmed many beds were congratulated, while a husband could legally burn alive an unfaithful wife. Why had Allah, in all His wisdom, allowed this injustice? Did He truly create us as playthings for our mates? If not, how then had He allowed men to mold us, as if clay, into what they wanted?

Someday, I promised myself, Khondamir would respect me. Though I'd never be seen or treated as his equal, he would become an instrument of my design. While he slept with scores of young women, and treated me like dust, ultimately I'd control his house, his wealth and his mind.

Khondamir was quite drunk when he finally returned. "Pray, woman, that your astrologer was right," he stammered. "Or I'll leave you for more fertile grounds."

I knew this threat was a lie, for he would never discard the Emperor's daughter. "It shall work," I said simply.

His breath, when it fell on me, reeked of his meal. Let it soon be over, I thought, sickened by him. Moaning to increase his desire, I closed my eyes and imagined I was somewhere else. The sun rose, and Isa and I stood before the Taj Mahal. Its face reflected the crimson light, glowing like a magical ember. Isa had his hand on my shoulder and I held our infant to my chest.

Even if the image were a dream—for we could never stand openly in such a manner—it comforted me. I no longer thought of the sweating, stinking man atop me, but of my lover and the child we might soon create.

Such a child was worth most any price.

OVER THE NEXT MOON, I visited Isa almost every eve. Allaying my fears, he seemed to care little that I shared myself between two men. And, thankfully, encounters with my husband dwelt less in my mind as the days passed, for I rarely returned to his house. Though he remained in Agra longer than customary, he protested my absence with feigned vigor and I suspected that the servant girl pleased him well into the nights. Her young body was doubtless more responsive to his than mine.

I hoped I was still attractive, but men rarely looked at me at twenty-two years of age with the same lust as they'd exhibited when I was sixteen. Fortunately, Isa was another matter. He eagerly awaited my arrival each night and basked in my presence. We made love on many, but certainly not all, of our evenings together. Sometimes we simply spoke in the darkness, or worked by candlelight on his drawings. He explained architecture to me as if I were an equal, and I did my best to acquire his knowledge. I was always an apt pupil in mathematics and often surprised him with how fast I could calculate the weight a column might bear, or the amount of marble needed to dress an arch.

Those nights were precious.

We worried only slightly about the constant danger of discovery. Once, when I returned later than usual to Mother's room, a servant had knocked, and not hearing me answer, became worried. When I finally returned, she was pounding on the door. Pretending that too much wine was within me, I staggered from my quarters. She must have thought me a louse, for she never came so early again.

Because of our nights spent talking, I was often tired during the day. I completed the tasks Isa assigned me, but still my energy lagged. Isa finally noticed my lethargy and forbade me to visit him for several nights. In his absence, I slept as a growing girl might, a dreamless slumber as thick as yogurt.

While the Taj Mahal continued to flow upward, I became somewhat less mindful of what transpired in the Empire. I did know that Aurangzeb and his bodyguard, Balkhi, continued to stir up trouble in the Deccan. Though my brother had successfully quelled the rebellion, he ruled the region with increasing belligerence. Stories abounded of Hindu temples being burned if taxes went unpaid. Women disappeared in the night and rioters were killed in the streets. It was only a matter of time, I reasoned, until the Deccans revolted again. And secretly, however traitorous the thought, I'd enjoy seeing them drive Aurangzeb from their land.

Dara, meanwhile, occupied himself with the courts. In what limited idle time he possessed, he occasionally brought his young son, Suleiman, to the Taj Mahal. Suleiman was a bright child and built forts of square blocks that Isa had given him. He could play so for an entire afternoon, always under the watchful eye of a trusted servant.

His father devoted more of himself to studying the two religions that divided our empire. While Aurangzeb sought to drive a wedge between our peoples, Dara tried to bring us together. During the monsoon season of that year, he wrote *The Mingling of the Two Oceans*. This book aimed to ease the animosity among Muslims and Hindus by proving that the religions possessed similar philosophic foundations. While scholars praised the work, the more militant Muslims, especially Aurangzeb, hated Dara for the comparison.

Soon after, I finally found myself to be pregnant. My monthly curse of womanhood stopped and I often became ill. How I longed to have Mother with me then, for she'd borne fourteen children and would have been a comfort. Father, needless to say, was elated by my whispers on the matter. And Isa, my sweet Isa, went to his home earlier than usual, so that he might follow the progress of my belly. Khondamir prayed to Allah each morning for a son, and I found myself praying ferociously for a daughter. A son would grow up in his father's company, whereas a daughter would blossom in mine.

As the months passed my womb filled. My back started to ache and I spent less time on my feet at the Taj Mahal. Instead, I lay in Mother's room and examined Isa's designs. Occasionally I solved a problem that he'd no time to pursue. Once I even found a mistake in his calculations. While most men would be mortified at such a mishap, Isa delighted in my comprehension.

His delight swelled when we soon felt flutters within my belly, and later when we smiled at sharp kicks and pondered names. One night, as a fever wracked me, and nothing afforded me solace, he handed me a letter he had crafted for our child. He had intended to refine it further, to share it with me at some distant time. Yet due to my misery, I read it by candlelight. And my suffering eased.

On back of a sketch, a fresh rendering of a minaret, he had written:

Our child,

As I sit and stare at the Yamuna, you grow slowly in your mother's womb. As barges and clouds drift before me, I ponder you. I want to share this moment with you, want you to hear the words that I now think.

I wish I could handle words as I do stones, for then I could truly speak to you as I desire. I could aptly explain how I long to meet you more with each finished day. I could express my love for you, which, like you, is already alive.

Though I do not yet know you, my understanding of your mother flows strong, and I am certain you will be quite extraordinary, as, indeed, is she. Of the dimensions of your disposition, I can only wonder. Shall you wield her benevolence? Her loyalty? Shall you share her impatient spirit? Perhaps you will possess my eye for precious sights, as well as my oftentimes misplaced optimism.

Assuredly you will inherit some of our traits, just as we inherited those of our parents. Yet you shall also create your own qualities, and these characteristics we will find most endearing.

I eagerly await your discoveries, your pleasure in their revelation. What mysteries will you unfold each day? What will you see that I do not? I will learn from watching you, learn what I have forgotten, or what I never had a chance to know. I hope to teach you as much, for earning an elephant's trust, painting what is not present, and listening to strangers are more complex undertakings than some would have you think.

Know, our daughter, our son, that you are already beloved. You have blessed us, and I thank you for bringing such joy into our lives. I thank you for being who you are, and who you shall be.
                                                             —Your father

My pain dissipated as I rolled his thoughts over in my mind. His words, cast unlike my father's, but fashioned of the same passions, reminded me of the similarities between these men. They hailed from different origins, and often displayed contrary temperaments, but were less varied than a lion and a leopard. Like the great cats, they were majestic within their own skins. Unlike most men, they were at ease with themselves and secure in their sensitivities.

I saw Father frequently in those days, for he often visited me after his duties at the Peacock Throne. Without fail he asked of the baby and offered his thoughts on what methods Mother used to ease her discomforts. I posed him questions as well; my curiosity about the Empire's affairs increased as my confinement lengthened. Soon I knew the doings of each noble and the thrusts of the Persians. Their boldness was mounting, and Father had sent Aurangzeb north to deal with them.

When Father and Isa were occupied, and I had no tasks to entertain me, I often yearned to see Ladli. Yet an encounter presented too great a risk. Nizam did convey a note from her, begging forgiveness for the vividness of our altercation. I burned her words and made Nizam promise to meet her secretly and say that I still loved her like a sister. He also told her of my pregnancy, though nothing was spoken of the true father.

As Isa had suspected, our child was as restless as I, and arrived early. The royal physician was so feeble and blind that he had to be carried to my bed by his young apprentice. Nonetheless, I felt comforted to have the aged master beside me, to hear him give the same commands as he had with Mother. Father was also present, though such participation was so uncustomary that he asked it be kept secret. Khondamir, naturally, wouldn't be bothered by the birth. Still, a runner was to be sent to him immediately so that he could learn the sex of the child.

My labor was bittersweet. While excited about the prospect of becoming a mother, neither the man I loved, nor my mother or best friend held my hand. Isa's absence troubled me the most, as it seemed that a child should hear its parents' voices before any others. And so, as my moans intensified, I wavered between glee and sorrow.

My hips were slight and the pain raging between them made me writhe. I asked for something to bite on, and the young physician, whose hands trembled, placed a wooden spoon within my mouth. I thought then that I might split, like a pod tearing open as a pea burst forth. I tried to be robust before the men, but suddenly I was weeping. How it ached! How I longed to have Isa next to me!

Father knelt by my side and did his best to soothe me. He told me of Mother's first labor, wiping sweat from my face as he spoke. I heard the nervousness in his voice, and he often paused to look toward Mecca. My prayers mingled with his.

When the child finally dropped I felt as if my innards were tearing. An almost unbearable pressure overwhelmed me, and I shuddered as my womb emptied. The old man chided his apprentice relentlessly, telling him to describe my baby's condition, to make sure that it breathed. The nervous youth swatted the infant. He cleaned its mouth and face with a white cloth as I fell back against my cushions, inordinately weary.

I fainted, and when consciousness returned my child was on my chest.

"A girl, Jahanara," Father whispered blissfully. "A girl whose smile shall make flowers limp with jealousy."

Her face, so magically small, was tethered in place by dark locks and a chubby chin. "She's perfect," I said, shedding tears as I thanked Allah. Father praised the physicians, giving each a thin bar of silver. After they left, he shut the door. Turning to him, I impulsively asked, "Father, might you . . . could you bring Isa here?"

I waited for his response, wondering how I could ask the Emperor, even if he was my father, to walk down a dark corridor and return with a man who wasn't my husband. A part of me was humiliated; a part of me rejoiced that he shared our secret.

"You do me honor," he said, rising from his knees. Once he found the key, he bolted the door to my room. "Will you be fine, child?"

I nodded. "Be careful of the trap."

"I'm not so foolish as to deprive myself of my granddaughter."

He quietly opened the closet, grabbed a candle, and disappeared into Mother's robes. In his absence, I weakly raised my child. I was amazed that this astounding creation came from within me, and that she would, please Allah, grow into a mother herself.

My child let out a whimper. She raised a miniature fist in the air, as if to protest this harsh induction to our world. She's already strong, I thought, bending down to kiss her fingers. They were impossibly small, and again I found myself in awe of her. Does every mother, I wondered, stumble upon this moment in time and discover that her life, however arduous, has import?

Robes parted and Isa and Father entered the room. A cobweb hung from Father's jeweled turban, and I smiled at the sight. Father, always tactful, bade us good night.

"Thank you, Father," I said.

He moved to the door. "Isa, lock this behind me," he whispered. "Your mother, Jahanara, would be proud. In fact, I know she is."

Before I could respond, he shut the door. Isa secured the room and hurried to where I lay. His gaze paused on me, then rested on our child.

I motioned that he should take her and, dropping to his knees, he lifted her from my chest. Even wrapped in a silk blanket she seemed hardly bigger than his hand. "A miracle," he said in a voice so quiet I might have imagined it. "I see us in her. Not you or me, but us."

My delight increased when he kissed her cheek. How lucky she is to have him as a father, I said to myself. Perhaps not so in name, but certainly in blood and in spirit. One day, when she's old enough, I'll speak of her true father. We'll sip chai on the steps of the Taj Mahal and I'll whisper the truth. And as much as she may hate me then, she shall come to understand why I lied for so many years. She'll forgive me and soon share my love for him.

He kissed her again. "Thank you, Swallow," he whispered. I grimaced as a spasm of pain pulsed in my loins. "Are you well, my love?" he asked tightly.

I nodded, though I did feel weak. "What should we name her?"

"So many to choose from," he said, smiling, "but surely there can be only one."

"Arjumand," I offered, immensely pleased to name her after Mother.

He set her down beside me, then lay so that she was between us. "Our precious Arjumand."

"Father shall be happy."

"As am I, love. As am I."

CHAPTER XII

Friends for Trade

Arjumand's first year was one of the finest of my life. Many nights I put her in a sling tight against my chest and carried her to Isa's home. There we simply held her, our lips often against her cheeks, our fingers forever tracing the curves of her calves and feet. We delighted in her eyes, which opened farther each day and sometimes seemed to follow our movements. She spoke to us as best she could, her coos reminding me of doves calling to each other. No matter how tired I was, these sounds made me smile, almost as if invisible strings tethered her voice to the corners of my mouth. Isa, not surprisingly, needed no such strings. His love for Arjumand so overwhelmed him that occasionally I felt a twinge of envy. Yet such moments were insignificant compared against the rapture I experienced when the three of us were together.

After her nighttime feeding, a beautiful ritual that I almost always found myself looking forward to, we put her to rest. She slept and fussed in a crib of my lover's making, padded thickly with cotton and lined with silk. Though the nearest house sat twenty paces away, I initially worried that a neighbor might hear her cries. Isa, however, reassured me that sound scarcely escaped his home. When I expressed skepticism, he quickly went outside and yelled as fiercely as his lungs permitted. Passersby must have thought him quite mad, but his point was well taken, for I hardly heard his voice.

As dawns unraveled, I returned with Arjumand to Mother's room. We spent each morning together and I marveled at how she grew, how she smiled at odd moments, how her chubby legs kicked in the bath. Sometimes we napped together, usually after she had fallen asleep against my chest. Before letting dreams overtake me, I'd whisper to her of Isa, describing her father in great detail. I told her what she'd not know until much later in life, about his delight in kissing her fingers, in humming as he soothed her to sleep.

I rarely took Arjumand to see Khondamir, for while he was pleased to have finally sown his seed, he would have traded her for a silver button. Rot his soul, he viewed Arjumand, I think, as simply another expense. And because I clearly loved her, and not him, he punished me by never showing her any semblance of affection.

After lunch I usually left Arjumand with a nursemaid in Mother's quarters or within the royal harem. An abundance of work needed attending at the Taj Mahal, and I knew Isa still counted on me. Besides, even though I'd become much more adept at hiding my feelings for him, sharing his company remained joyous.

As the months passed, thousands of slabs of marble were inlaid with semiprecious stones, set against structural bricks, and plastered into place. Elephants died, men succumbed to fever, and barges laden with supplies sank in storms. Despite these tragedies the mausoleum continued to rise. By now it was about half its intended height, and tales of its beauty spread throughout the Empire. Travelers—whether visiting nobles or pilgrims on their way to Mecca—always stopped to gaze at the Taj Mahal. Sometimes they even helped for a few days. In such cases, men left strangely content, as if awash in the knowledge that their hands had contributed, however slightly, to the creation of a legend.

Aurangzeb's return, alas, spoiled this year of progress and serenity. As usual, he had been campaigning against the Persians, though the fighting was fiercer than ever. He conquered and commandeered their fortifications, then was besieged in turn as enemy reinforcements arrived. His army dwindled until he was finally forced to flee south, arriving in Agra with tattered and starving troops.

Aurangzeb had never tasted defeat, and while the Red Fort teemed with stories of his forces vanquishing Persians thrice their number, the retreat home was humiliating for my brother, no matter that he was badly outnumbered. To worsen the situation, the Deccans, knowing that we were weakened, rebelled once again, declaring their independence. Our garrison to the south was overrun and thousands of our men died dreadfully.

Thus my brother was in a foul mood when he returned home. At his first appearance in the Diwan-i Am, he blamed his retreat on the Hindus in his army, claiming they fought without the same fever as Muslims. Father might have believed him but was certainly wise enough to guard his tongue, for he had gone to significant efforts to cultivate powerful Hindu friends, many of whom were present. Dara, who I think had finally started to loathe our brother, disagreed vehemently with Aurangzeb's complaints, and my siblings, to Father's somewhat hidden horror, argued openly. Soon the court was in an uproar, with Muslims and Hindus exchanging insults.

Although the Hindu population was the majority, Muslims had ruled for generations. We had succeeded in doing so by treating Hindus, for the most part, as our equals. Yet now the Emperor's son was deriding those of the other faith. One might think Aurangzeb would fear offending Hindus, who comprised a small part of his forces, but he seemed unconcerned by such matters, perhaps because Muslims were fiercely loyal to him and held virtually all positions of rank within his troops.

I did nothing to intervene in these boisterous proceedings but watched closely. I wanted to see which nobles flocked to Aurangzeb and which stayed loyal to Father and Dara. As far as I could tell, the split was nearly even. Balkhi, Aurangzeb's bodyguard, stayed close to his master during the argument, eyes scanning for potential danger. At one point he turned toward me and we glared at each other. He licked his lips while I shuddered inwardly.

It's only a matter of time, I thought, until blood flows between us. When Father dies—please Allah let it be many years hence—Aurangzeb shall take the Peacock Throne by force. Dara might stand against him, but will he be strong enough?

While I ought to side with the brother I loved, I wondered if, for the sake of my daughter, I should betray Dara and flock to Aurangzeb's standard. Clearly it was the safer course of action, for Aurangzeb slew his enemies, whereas Dara tried to befriend them.

Later that night, what little doubt swirled in my mind was put forever to rest. A prominent Hindu temple was mysteriously set ablaze, and four monks died within. Though no evidence linked Aurangzeb or any of his underlings to the crime, I believed that he was the culprit. But why, I asked myself, would he aim to upset the delicate balance of the Empire? How might anarchy aid his cause?

The answer emerged when a mosque was burnt in retribution. Clashes erupted between our people, and scores, if not hundreds, died that night. More Muslims perished than Hindus, and the next day additional nobles backed Aurangzeb. It seemed that he strove to build loyalty through a common fear of the Hindu majority.

Father, however, was no fool. He ordered the army to commandeer the streets and quell any further rioting. Regardless of Aurangzeb's quick rise through the ranks, the Emperor was our supreme ruler and men would follow him through hellfire. No one questioned his commands. The troublemakers, at least those still fighting and murdering, were captured. To show his allegiance to both Muslims and Hindus, Father had these men executed. He then provided equal amounts of gold to rebuild the temple and the mosque. And he let it be known that anyone breaking the peace would die without appeal.

Father summoned Dara and Aurangzeb. I was also present. We met on Father's private balcony atop the Red Fort, essentially a courtyard over-looking the river that boasted miniature cypress trees in glazed pots, tu-bular cushions and a cashmere carpet depicting a riverside garden. Father and I already leaned against one cushion when my brothers entered. Both looked angry.

Since dawn had just unfolded, servants brought us fruit and chai. They had spent enough time around the royal court to know of the rift be-tween my brothers and hurriedly departed, pulling bronze doors shut be-hind them. Dara and Aurangzeb sat as far apart as the carpet allowed. Aurangzeb now wore a trim beard. Rumor claimed that he observed an ancient Islamic tradition and wouldn't shave off the beard until all his enemies were dead.

Father made no move to speak. Nor did I. Instead, I looked to the southeast, my gaze resting on the Taj Mahal. Though scaffolding ob-scured much of its face, white marble sparkled beneath the wood. Men scurried about the scaffolding like ants on their hill. Steel tools glistened in the early light as masons worked stone.

Somewhere amid the chaos was Isa.

"The idiocy of yesterday shall never happen again," Father said simply, his fists tightening on his knees. "Not while I live." His features, usually so loving, were quite severe this morning. "Why, Aurangzeb, why in the name of Allah, would you create such upheaval, especially as our enemies attack our northern and southern flanks?"

My younger brother stiffened. "I lied about nothing."

"I mentioned nothing of lies. But your mind must dwell on them to raise the matter."

"The Hindus are worthless as fighters. More worthless than dogs. Their lines broke and the cowards fled their positions."

"Then have the officers who commanded them demoted, or executed if you wish, but don't come into my court and insult men who fought for the Empire while you suckled at your nursemaid!"

"We need peace with the Hindus—"

"I'm not finished, Dara, so hold your tongue!" Father exclaimed. Aurangzeb relaxed at his brother's rebuke and Father turned on him. "Setting the temple aflame was a treasonous act!"

"I did nothing of the sort."

"You didn't?"

"No."

"Do I look like a camel? Because if I don't, stop treating me like one!" Father bit hard into an apple. I had never seen him so angry. "Do you think, Aurangzeb, that you're the only one with spies? Of course I know you ordered the temple burnt. But why you would act like a vindictive child is between you and Allah. I certainly can't comprehend it. Oh, I understand the favor you seek to curry, but the nobles you endear are far fewer than those you inflame! Now, my son, I fear many Hindu blades shall seek your back."

"My enemies are always dealt with," Aurangzeb replied quickly, perhaps too quickly. Ladli had once told me of his paranoia of being assassinated, and it seemed that Father had struck upon his most profound fear.

Father bit again into his apple. "I'll tell you something," he said, glaring at Aurangzeb. "Enemies breed like rats. You stomp them, poison them, burn them, but more still come! It makes no difference if you live in times of peace or war, feast or famine! Enemies shall always plot behind you."

"Yet you still live."

"Because I don't strive to insult the very people who give me power! Who cook my food, field my armies and pay my taxes!"

"Muslims field my—"

"You're a fine soldier, Aurangzeb, but a child in matters of the court! You would be a leashed cheetah in the hands of a skilled noble, and Jahanara's puppet were she to sit on the Peacock Throne."

Aurangzeb clenched his teeth, his jaw knotting. "You'd let a woman—"

"She'd rule brilliantly!" Father retorted. "Do you think your mother couldn't have led the Empire? Surely she wouldn't divide our people, or spend all day studying religions."

Dara, who had thus far been spared Father's wrath, grimaced. I understood then my father's situation. However much he loved Dara, clearly he feared that his oldest son was too weak to lead us against our foes. He was prodding him now, hoping he'd take his duties more seriously.

"I need you, Aurangzeb," Father pronounced. "But I cannot have you undermining the Empire! From this day forward you'll treat Hindus with respect. We must have their support! If I hear of another temple being desecrated or some other such nonsense, I'll have you scrubbing stables!"

Aurangzeb's hand twitched, and I thought he might reach for his sword. Surely he debated taking his blade to us then. With us gutted, he could claim the throne. Ladli had said he feared that by killing Father he'd incur the wrath of the nobles. And while I believed she was partially right, I suspected his religion had more to do with his hesitation than anything else. For in Islam, no greater sin exists than to kill one's father.

"Where do I march?" he asked finally, hate simmering in his gaze.

"Take fifty thousand men north to deal with the Persians. They're the more imminent threat. The Deccans can be subdued later. Scatter the

Persians before you. Raze their forts, poison their wells and burn their grain. Make it impossible for them to war against us."

Aurangzeb had never led so many men. Though Father had humiliated him, my sibling must have been pleased at the command. "How many heads would you like?" he asked, looking at the floor.

"Hurt them badly, Aurangzeb. We'll be the ones to dictate the terms of peace."

Aurangzeb gracelessly excused himself. After he left, Dara straightened. "Do you remember the battle of—"

"The point, Dara?" Father interjected.

My oldest brother winced, for he was accustomed to speaking circuitously. "Is it wise, Father, to leave Agra so defenseless?"

Father and I both knew Dara was more concerned about having fifty thousand of our finest warriors under Aurangzeb's command. "Agra," Father countered, "is more than capable of defending itself. We have an even larger army within a half-day's march of the city."

"So close?"

"So I said. Now perhaps you should attend to your duties. That is, if no books need attending."

Dara sought to smile. "My books, Father, will rest unopened."

In my brothers' absence the sun seemed much warmer. The Emperor and I sat facing it, nibbling on cubes of melon. Father was suddenly quiet, and I hesitated to interfere with his mood. Instead, I pondered how to best deal with Aurangzeb. Obviously, Father and Aurangzeb wielded ample networks of spies. I had only Ladli. And to be of any use to Dara, I'd need more information than she could garner. But whom could I trust to help me?

"Mosquitoes," Father said. "My sons are like mosquitoes."

Far below, a monkey sprang from one rooftop to the next. The Red Fort was inundated with these creatures, which we often kept as pets. "Forgive me for saying so," I whispered, "but I think you rely too heavily on Aurangzeb."

"But what am I to do, Jahanara? The throne was always intended for Dara, but is he a man who will strike fear into the black hearts of the

Persians? The Deccans? The Portuguese? Sadly, I think not. And Au-rangzeb, though I . . . bear him little love, can defeat our foes."

"Defeat them at what price? He'll never want peace with our neigh-bors or with the Hindus. He'll destroy everythi—"

Father held up his hand. "That is why we must help Dara become a ruler. He's wiser than Aurangzeb. Now we must teach him to be almost as ferocious."

I deemed it an impossible task but said nothing. My mind was weary of such conversations. I wanted to tell Father about my little Arjumand, of how fast she could crawl. Or speak to him of our mausoleum. Instead, we sat and worried.

I shall think of his world for this day, I thought. I'll plan and plot as Mother would wish. But come evening, only Isa and Arjumand will oc-cupy my mind.

I kissed Father good-bye and headed toward the Taj Mahal. I chose to make the lengthy walk rather than ride. As I navigated Agra's streets and then the wide avenues leading toward the mausoleum, my mind focused on how I could better understand Aurangzeb. A solution revealed itself, but I hesitated to pursue its intricacies. For the solution placed in danger the life of yet another I adored.

Deciding with reluctance, with vast reluctance, to leave the choice to my companion, I proceeded through the mausoleum's garden. Its fruit trees, planted several years before, had grown to the height of my head. Beneath their slight trunks ran tidy rows of tulips, crocuses and dahlias. Koi swam in the canals along the path, gobbling at insects that landed in the water.

It took little time to locate Nizam. Atop the neck of a bull elephant, he urged it to drag a bundle of bamboo to the platform's base. When the elephant obeyed his command, he treated it to a piece of sugarcane, which the beast grasped with its limber trunk. Nizam, who had always seemed so feminine in the confines of the harem, was now more a man than most I knew. Years of toiling on the Taj Mahal had given him the muscles of a wrestler. His chest and shoulders had broadened. He even seemed to stand straighter.

Nizam leapt from his elephant with the agility of a cheetah. Without my asking, he followed me toward the river, away from the thousands of workers. A trio of barges were moored at its shore. We walked past these brooding giants to a quiet place where women beat clothes against rocks. I shivered, recognizing it as the spot where I had almost drowned.

"My lady?" Nizam said as we rounded a bend and found no one near.

"How are you, Nizam?"

"I'm well, thank you."

"I mean, how are you really?"

He glanced at the Taj Mahal, seeming to soak up the sight. "Content."

I almost discarded my question then, for I didn't want his happiness to be fleeting. But I was always taught that duty should supersede all such emotions. And so I forced myself to speak. "Would you care to leave this place?"

"Leave? But why?"

I debated again if I could seek anyone else. Perhaps I could simply employ a soldier to do what I desired.

"Why, my lady?"

Pulling my veil farther back on my brow, I said, "Aurangzeb will soon head north to fight the Persians."

"I've heard as much."

"You understand, Nizam, better than anyone, of his . . . dislike for Dara and me." After making certain no one had crept closer, I continued. "Only a few people know this, but he tried to murder Dara not long ago. Your rotten meat saved him."

"How?"

"It doesn't matter. What does is that I've become intimate with his tactics. His military tactics, that is. He commands fifty thousand warriors, Nizam. Fifty thousand. But how does he wield them? How are his traps sprung and what do his enemies dread most? I must learn of his strengths and weaknesses, for I fear that someday, when Father dies, Aurangzeb and Dara shall meet on a battlefield. If that happens I plan on being at Dara's side. And I need to give him sound advice."

"I'm not trained in military matters, my lady."

"Nor is anyone at birth. But some can learn of these things, and you'd

learn them better than most. You learn, Nizam, by watching. You don't
ask questions as I do, but you miss nothing. You see the best way to dress
stones and soon you're dressing them. And you'll see how his army de-
ploys and thus anticipate that deployment."

"How would I join his force?"

"Aurangzeb will conscript men before he marches. It would be easy for
you to join his ranks."

"And how badly, may I ask, do you need this done?"

I had never lied to Nizam and I wouldn't start now. "I need it, my
friend. But not enough to sadden you. If working with your new brothers on the Taj Mahal is what you love, then I ask that you stay. Work until it's done and perhaps history will remember you. Surely I shall."

He rubbed dirt from his hands, which seemed unnaturally large, as
did the rest of his features. "I wonder if Persia's as beautiful as Hindustan. Could it be?"

"Not likely. And you'll be at war, Nizam. You may die in battle or Aurangzeb might discover you."

"Discover me?" He grunted. "Your brother never saw me, my lady.
Not when I served him dinner, nor when I let him swat me with a
wooden sword."

Unable to keep myself composed at these words, I sought his hand.
Intertwined with his my fingers looked like a child's. "You are undeserving of such memories. You should have been our friend, not our slave."

"Aren't we friends, Jahanara?"

He had never called me by my name, and my grip tightened. Though
I wanted to kiss his cheek, I knew he'd feel awkward if I did. "Yes," I
replied. "And we'll always be so."

"Then don't worry about the past. For it's truly old."

How noble you are, I thought. How noble and strong and rare.
"Thank you, Nizam," I said. "Thank you for being the man you are."

"Thank you for seeing me."

We returned to the Taj Mahal, pausing to gaze at the stately dome
which was almost halfway finished. Beneath it stretched graceful supporting arches, four main arches in total, one on each of the square's

faces. Two smaller arches, stacked above each other, bordered the larger arches. And at each cut corner of the square, where it yearned to become an octagon, dwelt another set of stacked arches. Isa had designed the arches to resemble the white gates of Paradise. Though men once laughed at his idea and deemed it wishful thinking, Isa was clearly right. For the arches could have been portals. And Paradise, I hoped, was half as beautiful.

"I'll miss it, my lady."

"I know. And how I shall miss you."

"I won't be long in his war," he said. "For I want to see it finished."

"Promise me?" When he nodded, I said, "Return safely or I'll never forgive myself."

"Good-bye, my lady."

I squeezed his hand and watched him walk away. He didn't leave the mausoleum but returned to his elephant, as if he wanted to place a few more stones before departing. Someday, I thought, I'll repay this man. I'll repay all those who have risked so much.

Trembling, I wandered back to my room in the Red Fort. Arjumand gave me a moment of joy, then my thoughts soured as I worried for my friends. Who was I to put Ladli and Nizam in jeopardy? How could I twist our friendships into this . . . obedience? Such thoughts troubled me all afternoon. They plagued me throughout dinner and dusk. Finally, I was able to carry Arjumand down the long corridor to Isa's home. He met me on the stairs. Yet tonight, as almost never before, his appearance didn't cheer me. I felt unwashed in his presence, as if my sins had soiled my skin.

"What troubles you?" he asked as I sat down tiredly and gave Arjumand my breast. I had little interest in conversation, but when he persisted, I told him of all that had transpired, of how I used Nizam. "You gave him a choice, Jahanara," Isa countered. "He didn't have to go."

"Did I?"

He took Arjumand, kissing her fleshy cheek. "Truthfully? No, you didn't. But to Nizam, duty's a sacred thing. He might love working on the Taj Mahal, but he couldn't live with himself if he failed in his duty to you."

"He has never failed me. But I've failed him."

Isa kissed our child again before placing her gently in the crib. Humming, he stroked her thigh until she settled. He then sat on our sleeping carpet and pushed another pillow behind my back. "I think, Swallow, that Nizam might not find the army so terrible. Remember how at the Ganges he'd ride all day, exploring new lands? He was like a boy on that trip. His eyes never paused. And now, he'll travel to Persia, journey with men who'll become his friends."

"I remember. But he wasn't at war."

"Someday, Jahanara, you'll make it right. Buy him a piece of land, and let him build his own home. Even help him build it. Nothing would make him happier."

Sighing, I unpinned my veil, worried I might never be able to compensate Nizam. "And what would make you happy?"

"Truly happy?"

"Yes."

"For you to see yourself as I do."

"As what?"

"As inspiration. As beauty and grace and wisdom all gathered up in one little frame."

I bit my lip, cherishing his words but disbelieving them. "Can we talk tomorrow?"

"You should love yourself. But alas I think that in order to love yourself, you need other people to love you. This is your only weakness, Jahanara. Because you live your life as you believe others deem you should. You live it for your father, your mother, for everyone but yourself."

"But I need—"

"To live as you wish."

"I don't know how."

"Yes, yes, you do. But you rarely let yourself." My eyes tingled. My nose grew moist. "Even now," he said, his hands caressing my face, "you fight your tears, as if afraid I might think of you as being weak." I knew of nothing to say. Isa's words were true, but I'd never admitted as much. "See yourself as I do, Swallow. Do this and you'll no longer fight your tears. Live as you want, and you shall be at peace."

CHAPTER XIII

Karma

~:·)~

Exactly two days after I spoke with Nizam, Allah gave me a choice. A wretched choice it was, but one, without question, that would alter my entire world.

It was an auspicious day, by all accounts, for we had finished dressing one of the four minarets with white marble. The minaret was shaped like a bamboo stalk, as tall as fifty men and segmented by three rings. Atop it, graceful arches supported a small dome.

We celebrated the achievement for the better part of the day. Aurangzeb's army hadn't departed yet, and so Nizam stood beside us when the last slab of marble was carefully plastered into place. Father had arranged for barrels of wine to be rolled to the site, and for eighty bulls to be slaughtered and put upon spits. Of course, Hindus ate no such meat, but Father accounted for their presence. Piled atop the merchants' stalls were endless platters of spiced rice, sweet potatoes, sherbets, yogurts, nuts and fruits.

Twenty-two thousand laborers drank and feasted. Contests of wrestling, running and lifting ensued. Scores of polo matches, though lacking horses, also sprang up around the site. Amazingly, Muslims and Hindus celebrated together, despite being so recently at one another's throats. But with Dara and Father present, each of whom had many Hindu friends, tensions quickly evaporated.

We bled the barrels dry.

Never did I fondly share Isa's company in public, but on this day, it seemed natural. I was his assistant, after all, and we had a right to celebrate together. We stood, along with Nizam and a group of our master builders, in a circle. The men joked about amusing mishaps, such as when Nizam's elephant, inflamed by its need to copulate, had charged into the river, rammed a barge and nearly drowned my friend.

Only when the men began to return to their homes, shortly before dusk, did I wave good-bye to Isa and start back to the Red Fort. I missed Arjumand and wanted to hold her. I needed to hold her. I'd consumed a fair portion of wine and my legs were heavier than usual. My thoughts, however, were made light by the wine, buoyed further by Nizam's apparent readiness to forgive my request. Earlier today I'd sought him out and given him a porcelain brooch bearing a portrait of Mother. He had loved her, I was certain, and my gift had rendered him mute.

My mood had much improved with Nizam's thankful smiles, and I now hurried forward, eager to see Arjumand. The closer I came to the Red Fort, the more the usual chaos reigned in the ever-tightening streets. Children chased a baby monkey. Teams of oxen and warriors towed newly cast cannons toward the citadel. Incessant haggling dominated the passageways, for servants bought live chickens, ladies eyed garlands of flowers, and masons asked exorbitant prices for sheets of stone lattice.

When I neared the Red Fort, homeless children gathered about me. I handed coins to youths and lepers until my pockets were unburdened. Still, children followed me, beseeching for more. They walked with me until I shuffled past the fort's main gates, at which point guards congealed behind me and kept the beggars from entering. Passing a stand of fresh papayas, and seeing how delicious they looked, I reached for some rupees. Only then did I realize I'd given all my money away!

Wine is a precious gift, I thought, for it lets one simply forget.

I strode through the serpentine corridors of the fort and climbed endless stairways. When I finally reached the floor of the royal chambers, I was breathing heavily. My room was the second to last, and I went to greet my nursemaid and child. The woman's daughter had died of the fever and she took to Arjumand like a mallard to water. I trusted her completely.

While passing in front of Aurangzeb's door, I heard a noise, which emerged as a whimper and was barely audible. The wine must be playing games with me, I decided, but then the whimper came again. That it emanated from Aurangzeb's room was unusual because he often slept with his family in a palace outside the fort. Normally, I'd have passed the room without hesitating, but the wine emboldened me and I dared to knock. A whisper answered, urging me to enter.

"But come slowly," the voice advised.

Confused, I carefully opened the door. To my astonishment Aurangzeb and his wife—a young, plump girl of high rank—cowered in a corner. A few paces in front of them lay an overturned basket. Among the tulips that had spilled from the wicker swayed an enormous cobra. The snake stood upright, its black hood spread wide, its tongue flickering at the air.

It took me only a heartbeat to see what had happened. Someone had tried to murder Aurangzeb, sending death to his room in a basket. My brother's face trembled, for the snake was less than a pace from him. If Aurangzeb were to move, surely he'd die, and die painfully. His wife, her tears dropping to the floor, was farther from the serpent.

I stood motionless, may Allah forgive me, pondering what to do. If I simply left, slamming the door behind me, the cobra would likely strike Aurangzeb. Thus my worries would cease. Dara would become emperor while my loved ones lived in peace. And Muslims and Hindus might act as they had this day, as brothers, not foes.

I closed my eyes, praying that Allah would give me a sign. What was I to do? Save one brother to let him kill the others? Allow Aurangzeb, even though my enemy, to die? I groaned, terribly unsure of any action. What if the Hindus were right and karma ruled? If I let Aurangzeb die, surely I'd be punished later. But if I let him live, my family could suffer sooner. How much easier, I thought, it would be just to leave. Hadn't he asked for this death by offending so many? His murderer, whoever he might be, was simply helping me. Surely I should go!

Aurangzeb's wife whimpered and the cobra hissed in response. A monstrous thing, the snake was as long as my outstretched arms and thicker than my ankle. My brother was shaking, and I realized, to my amazement, that the serpent terrified him. Here stood a man who feared no blade or cannon, no charge of war elephants. He fought unlike any general, on the front lines, certain that Allah protected him. Yet where was his Allah now? Why did he have so little faith when a cobra poised before him?

My brother sought to speak to me, but only a rasp escaped his twitching lips. His wife edged away from him and the cobra rose higher, tongue darting. It appeared unconcerned with her and had eyes only for Aurangzeb. I knew I should leave, but doing so was impossible. How does one let a brother die? Yes, he had once turned his back on me; but if I did the same, could I claim to be better than he? If I abandoned him, could I ever tell Arjumand, in truth, that I had lived my life as a good woman?

And so I crept toward a low table bearing Aurangzeb's sword. The cobra must have smelled me but made no turn in my direction. My legs shook as I eased across the thick carpets, and I feared that the serpent could somehow sense my trembles. I never took my gaze from the creature, for if it spun at me, I'd have little time to react.

The room was small. I soon reached the table. Aurangzeb's sword was sheathed. Slowly dropping to my knees, I placed one hand on its hilt and the other on its scabbard. With infinite care I pulled on the hilt. The weapon was well oiled and made little noise as it slid free. Almost all our warriors brandished one-handed swords, but the hilt of my brother's weapon was meant to be held with both fists.

The sword's weight was appalling, but the weapon felt oddly reassuring in my grasp. Again I crept forward. Was this power what men experienced on a battlefield? I briefly imagined what it might be like to run toward a Persian warlord with this blade in my hands. Do men think at such times? Or was there only rage? Or fear?

Soon I was but two paces from the cobra. Amazingly, it still had its hooded head turned from me. I raised the sword, despite its unwieldiness, above my right shoulder. I started to take another step, just one more, when the creature whirled about. It hissed as it spied me, rearing its head back as if to strike.

With a shriek I swung down the blade. It fell toward the floor, as all heavy things do, with remarkable speed. As the cobra darted forward, its coiled body springing at my thigh, steel met scale. My sword caught the serpent just below its hood, severing head from body. The head spun to the side, while the body's momentum continued to carry it into me. I screamed as the bloody, twitching body struck my leg. I lifted the sword again, far over my head, and slammed it with all my strength against the cobra's thrashing torso. The blade bit down through the snake, through the carpet, and into the stone floor. It shattered, breaking off at the hilt. Three parts of the cobra still twisted, and, dropping the ruined weapon, I stepped back.

Aurangzeb's wife squealed, throwing her arms about him. He thrust her aside and she shrieked again, sobbing uncontrollably. He trembled, and his face still twitched. "Leave us!" he roared at his wife, grabbing her by the hair and throwing her toward the door.

She stumbled past me, tripped on a cushion, and fled into the hall. I found myself shaking and dazed. The cobra's tongue flickered, as if seeking me. How close I'd come to death! I could still see its head twisting in my direction, its mouth agape, its fangs curved and white.

"Have a change of heart?" Aurangzeb yelled, skirting the cobra's parts to near me.

I failed to understand his words. "What?"

"Decide, sinner, that you'd rather not kill me?" His hands were suddenly upon my shoulders, his fingers pressing painfully into my flesh. "Lack the courage?"

"The courage?"

"To watch me die!"

A pain exploded within me. I hated him then, abhorred that he was of my blood. "You think it was I?" I cried, hardly believing that he'd blame me. Furious, I pushed him away.

"You, Father, Dara. What does it matter?"

The wine and my brush with death gave me the strength to turn on him, to actually advance, hitting his chest with my fist. "It matters, you ass!" I screeched. "And it was someone else! How many men consider you an enemy? A hundred? A thousand? Perhaps it was the father of a girl you raped, a Hindu whose temple you burnt, or a Persian you let escape. Do I know who tried to kill you, or care? Of course not!" I punched him again, and he didn't ward off my blow, but merely stepped back.

"You swear, on Muhammad's grave, that you had nothing to do with it?"

"Would I save you, fool, if I did?"

He considered my words, looking fearfully at the dead cobra. "Then

I owe you a life," he said regretfully. "A life I'll repay on one condition." I cared little for his conditions and told him so. But Aurangzeb, his fists clenching in anger, merely spat. "When the time is right, sister, you'll join me, help me grab the throne. Or I'll kill you, and enslave your child."

The words, even coming from Aurangzeb, assaulted me. "But I saved you—"

"And I've forgiven your sins!" he exclaimed, spittle flying. "Which are countless, may Allah be merciful upon you! Join me and I'll let you live in peace. But back the heretic and your death will be terrible!"

"My duty is to Dara!" I argued, my rage a living thing. "Why can't you let him have the throne? He'd rule in name while you ruled in power!"

Aurangzeb's lips curved into a horrible smile. "The heretic will never rule. The throne shall be mine. And I, I alone, will restore order to the Empire. Order, by God!"

"A coward, Aurangzeb. A coward is all you'll ever be."

His slap caught me flush on the cheek and I fell to my knees. "Do you know, thief, what happens after a battle?" he asked. He stood over me, his tunic brushing my face. "It's a beautiful sight, let me assure you. I loosen my warriors, who are crazed with bloodlust, upon the infidels. The old ones we butcher with dull blades. The boys we castrate and take as slaves. But the girls and the women, their fate is much less pleasant." Aurangzeb leaned closer, spittle dropping, face twitching. He grabbed my sash and yanked me to my feet. "How long would you last, sinner, in the arms of my men?"

Sickened by his words, I pushed him away. "Cowards are good at rape. But how they do fear serpents!" With my bare foot I kicked the head of the cobra, which sailed between us, slapping against Aurangzeb's shin. He shrieked.

Hurrying from his fury, I ran into my room and locked the door. My nursemaid yelped at my sudden appearance, withdrawing Arjumand from a swollen nipple. I took my child and, kissing her brow, cursed myself for letting him live. For now there would never be peace between us.

PART 3

*Truly, indeed, when the living
soul leaves it,
this body dies; the living soul
does not die.
That which is the subtle essence
this whole world has for its soul.*

THE UPANISHADS

*B*ut why, Jaha, why didn't you let the cobra kill him?" asks Gulbadan.

How often have I pondered this question? A thousand times? Possibly more? "I couldn't kill my brother," I say sadly. "I wanted, Allah forgive me, to watch that cobra strike him down. But could you watch your brother die?"

"Never!" Rurayya exclaims.

"Of course not. After all, Aurangzeb came from the same womb as I. And he wasn't always cruel."

"But why did he change?"

I had once asked Father the same question. And now, I offer his response. "Why does the sun flee before the night? Because even the sun has fear in its heart. And Aurangzeb, who feared so many things, could only quiet his fear by giving it to others."

"He still does," Gulbadan adds.

"Yes, child. But others have love and thus can endure such fright. Whereas he has none and thus cannot."

My granddaughters contemplate my words. Looking at them, I own surprisingly little envy. Oh, I might long for their perfect skin and boundless energy, but they'll be lucky indeed to house similar memories. For I have known what it's like to love a man worth loving. He gave me everything, and though Allah has drawn us apart, and I miss him fiercely, I'm comforted by my belief that I'll join him soon, and that our building is unfinished.

I'm still thinking of Isa when Nizam opens a cotton bag at his feet, withdrawing combs of honey. As he hands these treats to Arjumand's girls, I notice a long, ugly scar on his forearm, left from some wicked blade. The scar spurs memories within me, for I can still see Nizam, bloodied sword in hand, fighting above me. How he howled that day! How his rage made him invulnerable. If only we had wielded a hundred Nizams. The poets would have immortalized our victory and Dara—

I force the thought away. Allah should remain deaf to such thoughts. He's done much for me, and I should honor Him by thinking only of the good. "Where was I?" I ask feebly, pretending to have an ancient mind when my thoughts are still as sharp as scythes.

"You just saved your brother," Gulbadan replies, shielding her eyes from the midday sun. "But what happened next?"

I wonder where to start. The years following Arjumand's birth were filled with joy and suffering. They were the best and the worst years of the Empire. "At first there was magic," I say simply. "And then came war."

CHAPTER XIV

A Tear on the Cheek of Time

Other than my deepening love for Isa and Arjumand, nothing vital to my story happened during her early childhood. Certainly events and troubles unfolded—which I'll briefly describe now—but nothing akin to what followed.

Aurangzeb soon departed the Red Fort with his army and marched north to attack the Persians. For his skill on horseback, Nizam was assigned to the cavalry. He was given a bow, quiver of arrows, sword, dagger and shield. I bought him a fine mount. So as not to arouse suspicions, I gave Nizam only a tattered hemp blanket and a battered saddle. Nobles lined their saddles with silk and held pearl-studded reins. Though his mount would be priceless in battle, Nizam looked like a common horseman.

Thereafter, I heard nothing from my friend for more than a year. When Nizam finally revisited Agra, I hardly recognized him. We met secretly far downstream. His face, which still warmed to me, seemed further blackened by the desert sun. He had grown a beard and, as all soldiers did, wore the jewelry of those he'd killed. His body was even stouter than when he had left, and his leather armor was cracked and scarred.

At the river, after I'd gripped his hardened hands and we'd exchanged pleasantries, Nizam told me of Aurangzeb's sacking of Persian strongholds. My brother, he said, was a ferocious leader, whose men loved him because he fought at their sides and let them pillage after victories. Though I thought Nizam would share my disdain for this practice, he said Aurangzeb acted prudently, for the Persians were equally ruthless.

Bidding farewell to Nizam once more was vexing, but there was no other choice. One thing Isa had taught me—rather painfully, I must confess—was that loved ones and friends are sometimes taken from us, either by death or circumstances outside our control. Yes, we should lament their departure, and yes, we should pray for them often. But we shouldn't dwell so deeply upon such vacancies that life itself becomes empty.

In but a week, Aurangzeb regrouped, conscripted additional men, and marched south to deal with the troublesome Deccans. Alas, their rebellion had spread like a prairie fire. Warlords joined the cause, and all along our southern frontier, forts were attacked and razed. The success of the rebellion was a tremendous drain on the Empire, and Father told Aurangzeb to stamp it out at all costs. Thus I didn't see Nizam again for some time.

In his absence the Taj Mahal continued to bloom, as did my love for Isa. Unfortunately, we spent fewer nights together, for soon Arjumand was too old to witness our affection in Isa's home. Though she had her own room in the Red Fort, I was reluctant to leave my quarters in case she needed me. Only when she slept soundly, and was free of any illness or nightmare, did I venture down the corridor to the embrace of my lover. For a short time we laughed, played games of chance, or talked about the Taj Mahal.

My emotions waxed and waned in those days, for Isa was near, yet he was at my side far less than I'd have liked. I worried that Allah might take him from me, perhaps by an accident or a fever. I couldn't imagine my existence without him, and prayed each night that we would somehow find a way to live together as man and wife.

I saw blessed little of Khondamir. His trading took him to the far corners of the Empire, where sometimes he conducted important business on Father's behalf. By now Father despised Khondamir almost as much as I did, but he still used my husband to promote trade with our neighbors. Given the immense profits in these undertakings, even a dullard like Khondamir was successful.

I half expected that my husband might not return from one such trip. He always did, alas, and once he'd tired of his girls, and wanted to humiliate me, he summoned me and I endured his cumbersome gyrations. How I loathed those nights! How I wanted to curse and scream and die! It felt so heinous to be in the grasp of that man. Afterward, I bathed in hot water until I was so weary that I could hardly stand. My encounters with Khondamir were the only thing, ever, that I kept from Isa. He asked little and I revealed less.

Allah graced me with one beautiful child, so I shall not complain; yet I was saddened when my womb never blossomed again. I had assumed that I'd bear many children, but Arjumand was to be our only creation. Though she was to my life as breath was to my lungs, I longed to give her a sibling.

I had four constant loves during those years: Arjumand, Isa and Father, of course, as well as the Taj Mahal. Our precious Arjumand was a clever girl but took her cleverness lightheartedly. I didn't overly encourage her studies, for many years lay ahead when she'd have to act much older than her age. No, to run and explore as a child was a healthier existence than to fall asleep memorizing texts. And so I let her play, and when my mood was light, I played with her. I taught her to swim and to paint with her fingers. We combed each other's hair on summer nights. We danced in the rain.

When she was five, I began taking her to the Taj Mahal so that Isa might see her more often. After all, it ailed him that she had no inkling he was her father. I saw it in his face when he gazed at her, in the way he sometimes started to reach out to her but then stopped. Occasionally I pretended to be busy and asked that he, or another worker, look after her. When Isa's turn arose, he placed her on his shoulders and climbed about the site, chasing butterflies or letting her pet elephants. I hid my tears then, for these moments were too rare and fleeting to make her love him. He was simply another playful worker.

Barely a week after Arjumand's seventh birthday, there came one of the most spectacular days in our lives, and in the history of the Empire. After eleven long years, the Taj Mahal was finally finished. To celebrate the completion of Mother's mausoleum, Father sent messengers to the far reaches of Hindustan, and even past our borders. They carried flags of truce, for we would war against no one during an entire month of celebration. Father even invited a few of our enemies to Agra to see the Taj Mahal.

On the morning that the last slab of marble was fitted into place, Father, Isa, and I stood in the mausoleum's garden. A full moon would rise the next night, and I knew Father itched to see his creation bask in the sun, then moonlight. Alas, this seemed impossible, for an almost impenetrable forest of scaffolding covered the entire structure. The latticework was comprised of a tremendous number of bamboo poles and teak logs tied together with enough rope and chains to encircle Agra.

"How long," Father asked, barely able to contain his joy, "until the scaffolding comes down?"

Isa hesitated, aware his answer would be unwelcome. "A full month, my lord. Most of it's been standing for years."

"By Allah, so long?"

"If we work through the nights maybe less, but I've only so many men. And as you know, we didn't have enough wood for the scaffolding, so we plastered bricks into place. It will take time to chisel them away, time to—"

Father, usually so patient, waved him to silence. "I'll not wait," he said stubbornly. "I've waited eleven years."

"But, my lord, we—"

"Jahanara," Father interrupted, "Aurangzeb's army is camped a half-day's ride from here. See that it is recalled at once." He paused to remove his spectacles, pocketing them with what seemed a sudden exuberance. His bloodshot eyes darted about like a pair of hungry fish. "I want every messenger fit for travel to spread the word that at dawn tomorrow, every man, woman, child, noble, slave, friend or foe may come here and take whatever lumber and bricks they may carry."

"Truly?" I asked, for Father was speaking so hurriedly that I could barely follow him.

"Tell them to bring their mules, barges and elephants. Let them take the wood, all the wood, and build new homes with it! And Isa, you lion among cubs, gather your tools and make certain that tomorrow our people can cut down that rubbish. But ensure they don't damage the structure!"

And so the word spread, slowly at first, but then sweeping across and beyond Agra like a joyous typhoon. For our country wasn't a realm of endless trees. Most homes were comprised of clay and mud with a few crooked branches for support. People cooked with cow dung and made boats of aged planks. Yet here was Father, giving away a mountain of lumber! Enough wood and bricks so that commoners could build new homes and nobles could raise new palaces.

By dawn our city had swollen to twice its size. Farmers from the countryside slept in the streets with their teams of oxen. Fishermen from the north and south filled our river with their boats. People who had never seen Father spoke of him with immense adoration, for surely such a benevolent leader was a man worthy of our throne.

At Father's command, our people—leading elephants, horses and camels—hurried to the mausoleum, swarming about it like ants on a drop of honey. Isa's master builders saw to it that each of the twenty-two thousand laborers was assigned to a group of peasants, nobles, monks or merchants. After the groups were allocated to particular sections of the scaffolding, work began in earnest. Knives attacked ropes and wood fell into eager hands. Some of our people had traveled to the site alone, and left bent under the weight of bamboo poles. Others, from poor villages, banded together and formed long lines of men, women and even children. Logs were passed down these lines, gleeful chanting accompanying the work.

The army soon arrived, and Father, much to Aurangzeb's dismay, ordered his men to help with the task. Warriors used swords to hack at ropes and horses to drag away heavy timber. Nizam, disguised as a worker, somehow found me, and was so caught up with emotion that he actually patted my back. I squeezed his hands tightly enough that he grimaced, or at least pretended to. Nearby, Arjumand sat on Isa's shoulders as he hurried about, somehow trying to supervise what had clearly turned into chaos. Even Father was busy working and had taken off his rich tunic and turban. Shirtless, a sight I'd never seen, he stood high on the scaffolding and cut at ropes with a jeweled dagger. The men around him cheered as he dislodged bamboo poles, tossing them to the masses below.

I never again encountered such fervor as I did that day. Innumerable men of all shades and stations labored until their hands bled. Women—whether aged, youthful or pregnant—carried away slighter pieces of wood, filling nearby carts and baskets. A strange excitement, almost an intoxication, gripped us all. The temporary road to the mausoleum became clogged with beasts, lumber and mayhem. Even the river was jammed. Several boats, overloaded with timber, toppled and sank. Most crew members were saved, but a few men disappeared, not to be seen again.

Despite our crazed work, we could only gradually undress the Taj Mahal. Layer by agonizing layer, the scaffolding came down; all the while workers prayed, sang and struggled. Few of our people stopped to rest, for too much was at stake to pause to fill hungry bellies or bandage bloodied hands. To my amazement, I saw several Persians laboring beside their ancient enemies. The men wore black robes, and massive scimitars hugged their hips. The Persian women were like shadows, for they dressed in shapeless gowns and veils hid their faces. Even if the foreigners could never carry much back to their homeland, they worked diligently, selecting only the finest pieces of bamboo.

The day lumbered past and soon the sun eased from its zenith, brilliantly illuminating the now uncovered dome of the Taj Mahal. Thousands of workers continued arriving at the site. Agra's streets swelled beyond capacity. When they proved impenetrable, cunning men built huge rafts of lumber, which they then sailed down the river. They beached the rafts, then ran back to the mausoleum to begin working on others.

Meanwhile, teams of fishermen lashed their boats together and ferried lumber to the other side of the river, soon returning to replenish their holds. Noblemen purchased Father's barges and piled them high with wood. He made them pay in chests of coin, for he planned to give this coin to our workers as a bonus. The nobles grumbled but paid quickly. The barges filled.

Seeing that their lords were getting so much of the scaffolding, the hordes of commoners worked even harder. Muslims and Hindus banded together and hauled down stout timbers of teak that they divided for their temples and mosques. None of us, save Aurangzeb, ceased for a moment that day, and we worked with the unity of friends.

As the Taj Mahal was slowly revealed, we each seemed to relish its extraordinary presence with an awe surpassing even our love for Allah, or the Hindu gods. For this presence was tangible. We gasped, reached out, and touched its sweeping sides. We looked skyward and shook our heads in astonishment at the sculpted mountain above. So many of our people dressed in rags and slept in filth. To look at such beauty was beyond anything they expected to experience in their lifetimes. Hindustanis cried openly at being alive this day.

When the last of the wood was carried from the mausoleum, we might as well have looked at the entrance to Paradise. Bloodstained and dusty, we sat on the rutted ground or on broken carts. Somehow, amid the hundreds of thousands, I discovered Father. Where Isa and Arjumand were, I had no inkling, but I was pleased they could share this moment together. Father, whose shoulders were cut and bruised, wept when he spied me.

"Thank you, Allah," he whispered, as his royal guards kept the crowds respectfully distant. "Thank you for granting me this wish."

His blistered hands drew me close and he kissed me. Yet his gaze didn't linger on me. Instead, he gazed with countless others at the Taj Mahal. The mausoleum possessed, as Isa had planned so long ago, the grace of a woman. Its heavenly arches were her eyes and its domes her upturned breasts. The minarets might be her jeweled fingers, while the white marble was surely the perfection of her face.

My mind was strangely lucid. Questions arose of their own accord. How could we have created this monument, which seemed almost too beautiful for this world? And why should we, mere mortals, even be allowed to stare at such majesty? Surely this creation was fit only for God. He should walk within its walls and He alone should contemplate its rapture. For weren't we but animals, and did swine and steers roam about our finest palaces?

Night fell and the celebrations began in earnest. Scant time was available to prepare a feast and most people went without food and drink. However, we lit the sky with Chinese rockets and our musicians played sitars until their fingers were numb. Men danced in unruly hordes, while Persian warlords and their women smiled or even clapped. Those of us fortunate enough to have wine drank until our flasks were dry.

At last Isa found me. Arjumand was still on his shoulders, and he handed her to Father, who again wore his tunic. Though I wanted to leap into Isa's arms, I could only give him a congratulatory nod. He winked and we laughed as one.

The rockets ceased when the moon, ripe and glowing, rose. The night was clear, and moonlight slanted down to illuminate the Taj Mahal. The vast structure seemed to attract and magnify the light. Thousands of torches were extinguished and laughter dwindled. A few elephants trumpeted wearily, but tranquility otherwise prevailed. Elation turned to awe and awe to reverence. People sat in the mud and watched, transfixed, as the Taj Mahal brightened, so smooth and seamless that it might have been carved from a single piece of ivory.

Father, acting as if he'd discovered a new world, walked toward the main archway. Our people parted like curtains to let him pass. I followed him, holding Arjumand's hand. Behind us trod Isa and Dara. Those inside must have sensed that Father wished to be alone with his wife, for as we entered the mausoleum, they left its gleaming interior. The tomb chamber was the centerpiece of the Taj Mahal and a sight to chill one's flesh. It was shaped as an octagon, with eight arched doorways offering access. A dozen men standing atop each other couldn't have touched the domed ceiling. Blackness should have prevailed here, yet the marble shone as if possessed of a magical transparency, as if each arch and wall were luminous from within. We seemed to stand beneath a white marble sky.

The eye of the room was Mother's tomb, though it remained empty. She was buried within a vault far below. Her tomb, a rectangular block of white marble, boasted the most splendid arrangements of jeweled flowers that I'd seen. Garlands of tulips and fuchsias, incredibly rich with detail, would blossom eternally here.

Father knelt before the tomb, kissed it, then began to pray. The room was a place of echoes, and Allah's name drifted eerily among us. Though Arjumand was tiring quickly, she honored us all by bowing to the tomb and, facing Mecca, adding her prayers to our own. We stood thus for some time.

Finally, Father turned to us and asked kindly if we'd leave. Dara smiled at me before disappearing into the crowds. Isa, Arjumand and I squeezed through the thousands of dusty and disheveled people surrounding the site. We walked to the trampled gardens, passing beneath palm and cypress trees. The songs of crickets mingled with the cry of an owl. Isa found a secluded patch of grass and we sat down tiredly. Arjumand stretched out, placing her head on my lap.

"Good night, Mother," she mumbled.

"Will you dream of us?" I asked.

"I'll try."

I ran my hands through her hair, loving her enormously. Though I wanted Isa to hold her, we weren't so hidden that I thought it safe. He sat respectfully apart from me and I had to kiss him with my eyes. Most men would have bent under such duress, but Isa smiled. We stared at each other, then looked to the Taj Mahal.

When Arjumand was asleep, I gently lowered her head to the grass. I then stepped a few paces away from her. "What shall you do," I asked Isa softly, "now that it's built?"

"There's still much work, years of work, to be done." He shrugged, as if he cared little to discuss such matters. When he next spoke his voice was hooded, like the call of the owl. "Do you remember, Swallow, our first night here together?"

"You were so excited."

"Yes. But even then . . . even then I somehow loved you." He reached for a rose that lay severed beneath its bush. "I'd give it all up," he whispered, glancing at the Taj Mahal, "for you."

A pair of boisterous Europeans passed and we quieted. Though I wanted to reach out to him, I dropped this coal of desire into cool water. "How is it, Isa, that we found each other?"

"Allah was kind."

"But was it Allah, or simple luck?"

He twirled the rose as he thought, inhaling its sweetness. "It was more than luck," he answered. "Luck might aid one in a game of chance, but

something much more . . . infinitely more unfaltering brought us together."

"What?"

"Truth, I think."

"Truth?"

"Aren't we true to ourselves, true to each other, when we're together?"

More rockets exploded above. Our people were celebrating, for burning floats started to come down the river. Thousands of floats were
visible, and soon the Yamuna was a vast shimmering torch. The floats
drifted south, spreading apart with the current.

"Are you saddened, Isa, that I've never borne you a son?"

He was surprised by the question. "Arjumand's priceless. She and you
are all I'll ever need."

"But does it hurt, to never hold her as your own?"

A shadow crossed his face and I knew his pain was real. "It does," he
muttered. "I bleed because I can't hold her. Nor you."

I stared at our daughter and saw how her face was narrow, like Isa's, and
how her eyes were round, like mine. "Perhaps we should just leave. We've
enough rupees and jewels to last a lifetime. Just leave and never return."

He reached out and, despite the risk, touched my lips. His fingers were
rough and rigid, yet reassuring and warm. "Someday, Jahanara, we shall.
We'll travel to the corners of the Empire. Perhaps we'll even visit Europe,
where I hear they build beautiful cathedrals. Then, when our hair is gray
and our bones are weary, we'll buy a simple house near the sea. We'll fish
and paint and grow old together."

My eyes watered at the thought, and I kissed his fingers. "Promise me,
Isa. Promise me that it will happen."

"I do, my Swallow, I do," he said, as dawn emerged from its cradle.
"All will be fine."

But in the years that followed, little would be fine.

And much would be horrible.

CHAPTER XV

The Hands of Isa

We had less than a year to enjoy the Taj Mahal.

During the next monsoon season, Father became ill. A fever struck him down and his flesh dwindled away until he was hardly more than a skeleton. He grew too weak to stand. He muttered, madly, for days on end. We summoned the Empire's best physicians and paid heavy gold for European doctors. Our physicians gave him herbs and tried to cleanse him with enemas. The Portuguese doctors bled him regularly. Still he weakened.

At the time, Aurangzeb was to the north, fighting a renewed war against the Persians. He had joined forces with my other brothers, Shah and Murad, whom I hadn't seen in many years. Between them, they commanded seventy-five thousand warriors and were scattering our enemy into the mountains rimming our northern frontier.

But when word of Father's illness spread across the Empire, the Persians were allowed to escape. We learned from one of Shah's officers, who had ridden south for days without rest, that Aurangzeb, after hearing the news, launched an attack on his brothers' armies. Greed, as well as a fanatical desire to place the anti-Hindu prince on the throne, motivated Aurangzeb's warriors, almost all of whom were Muslims. Aurangzeb surprised his brothers' much lesser forces at night, overwhelming them. In the end, the heads of ten thousand of our own men were taken.

Shah managed to escape, though no one could swear that he still lived. Murad was executed. According to Shah's man, who had lost a hand to swordplay and would likely die, Aurangzeb was marching south, hoping to attack us before tales of his treachery arrived. By the officer's account, we had less than two days to prepare for the assault.

And so we gathered at Father's bed. His face was the color of beeswax
and tendrils of his slate-gray hair, which had started to fall out, lay on his
cushions. He wore a fresh tunic but had often fouled himself and the room
stank of disease. Rods of incense did little to diminish the evil odors. Father was barely lucid, and the physicians advised rest. Yet we desperately
needed his counsel. I knelt by his side, while Dara and Nizam stood before
him. Nizam had fled south as soon as Aurangzeb's plans became apparent,
arriving shortly after the officer. Though a slave normally would have never
been present in such a situation, Father knew Nizam had become a warrior
to alert us of Aurangzeb's tactics. And my friend had done well in Aurangzeb's army, quietly making a name for himself as a man to be reckoned
with. After five long years of fighting, he owned a modest rank.

"How many men . . . have we?" Father asked weakly, his eyes closed.

Dara shifted from foot to foot. "Fewer than necessary."

"Not what I asked you."

"Aurangzeb has our best troops, Father, more than sixty-five thousand
strong. We can muster only sixty thousand. But here in the fort, we
should be able to—"

Father cut him off with a feeble wave of his hand. "Impossible . . . for
us to win here. Isn't that true, Nizam?"

My friend stepped forward noisily, for chain mail covered his torso.
Nizam also wore a dented helmet, a curved sword at his side and carried
a shield on his back. A quiver of arrows was attached to his belt, and a
bow lay draped across his shoulder. How, I thought, could the gentle boy
I grew up with in the harem have become such a warrior?

"Yes, my lord," Nizam said softly, his words slow to unfold. "If Aurangzeb traps us here, we'll never escape. His force will increase in size,
while ours weakens."

"How many elephants has he?"

"We think he wields some fifteen hundred," Dara replied uneasily, for
the number was vast.

"May Allah grant us strength," Father muttered.

"He has more men, cannons and elephants than we," Dara added.
"And his men are battle hardened."

I wiped beads of sweat from Father's creased brow. Over the past day I'd thought of a counter that might offer us victory. But it came with a price. Deciding to finally voice my idea, I said, "What would happen, Father, if we enlisted the aid of the Deccans?"

"The Deccans?" he echoed, strength momentarily returning to his voice. "Why would they flock to our banner?"

"If they fought for us, and we won, we could offer them independence."

A coughing spell wracked him. When it finally receded, he hacked into a rag I held. "A fine . . . fine idea, child. But there's no time. Such a treaty would take weeks to arrange."

"But couldn't we survive in the Red Fort for that long? Let's resist his siege, then when the Deccans arrive, we could attack him from both sides."

"And Aurangzeb, may Allah forgive his . . ." Father paused, and I thought he might cry. "Aurangzeb shall lay waste to Agra . . . if we remain here. He'll destroy all we've built. Starting with the Taj Mahal."

I shuddered at the thought. But I realized Father was right. "Then what can be done?"

"Attack, my lady," Nizam offered.

Dara grunted. "How and where?"

"Beyond Agra, my lord. In a place of our choosing." Nizam rubbed his large hands together. His face was beaded in sweat and his anxiety was palpable. "Aurangzeb knows our numbers," he said finally. "So it will be hard to deceive him. But perhaps we can use my lady's idea, after all."

"The Deccans?" Father asked.

Nizam's armor creaked as he shifted his weight. "Might I speak freely, my lord?" When Father nodded, Nizam still hesitated. "Say, my lord," he offered quietly, "we spread the word that we'd gone for their help. And if, in truth, we did so, would you send a few men into their land?"

"No."

"You'd send a strong force, my lord, one that would return safely. They'd be our fastest warriors. Our cavalry." Nizam paused again, waiting for some kind of approval.

"Go on."

"If we sent our cavalry, my lord, perhaps twenty thousand strong,

southward tomorrow, they could ride hard, then veer northwest and circle behind Aurangzeb's approaching force. The bulk of our army could
wait for him at a place of our choosing—perhaps a high hill. We could
defend it with our cannons and our thousand war elephants. Aurangzeb,
who craves the quick kill, will think we don't have cavalry and will attack
our lines. His rear—"

"Shall be unprotected," Father concluded, rising from his cushions.

"Yes, my lord. Our cavalry, when they hear the cannon fire, could
sweep down from the north and attack his rear flank. They'd destroy his
forward-facing cannons and much of his infantry."

"A dangerous plan," Dara interjected. "For if Aurangzeb should attack
our forces separately they'd face annihilation."

"Certainly a risk, my lord."

"A risk worth taking," Father concluded. He clenched his teeth and
weakly pointed at my friend. "You'll . . . you lead our cavalry."

"Me?" Nizam said in wonder, for surely he had never dreamed such an
honor possible.

Father grimaced. "I could give the task to someone more experienced.
But too many traitors . . . lurk within these walls. Do I know who among
my officers is my cheetah . . . and who is Aurangzeb's scorpion?" When
no one answered, Father continued haltingly, "Come to me tonight with
your plans. What hill will . . . Dara defend? And how will . . ." Father's
voice trailed off, and he seemed to sleep for an instant. "Come tonight,
both . . . of you."

Nizam bowed deeply to the Emperor. Though he always stood tall,
when he followed Dara from the room his height appeared to have increased. I knew that Father wanted me at his side and so I dipped clean
linen in water and wiped his brow again.

"You were clever, Jahanara, to send him . . . into Aurangzeb's army."

"Nizam's the clever one, not I." I offered him a sip of water, which he
declined. "When it's over," I said, "and if we win, will you grant him a
piece of land by the river?"

"More than that, my child." After I thanked him, he motioned that I
take his hand. When I did, he asked, "And what . . . what would you like?"

"For you to recover," I said, stroking his jeweled fingers.

"Dream larger," he whispered. "Do you think Allah could create such wonder by dreaming small?"

"You know what I want, Father."

A series of coughs wracked him. I held his arm as he shuddered, wishing I could somehow ease his pain. "Perhaps," he stammered, "if we should . . . be granted victory, I'll send you far away. I need a skilled politician in Varanasi. If you were to go there, with Arjumand, your shadow . . . your shadow might follow."

"My shadow?"

"Isn't he your shadow? Don't you live as one?"

"Sometimes."

"Your mother and I . . . would speak without talking, love without touching." He grunted, and I wiped more sweat from his brow. "She was my . . . no, I was her shadow."

Despite my fear for him and the looming battle, I tried to smile. "Yes, you were, Father. It was never the opposite."

"Never?"

"Get well, Father," I said, rising. "For we've much to talk about."

"Truly . . . never?"

I smiled and kissed his brow, bidding him farewell. The midday meal was approaching and I headed for the royal kitchen. Years had passed since Ladli labored within its walls, yet out of habit I looked for her. As I entered the warm room, spice-covered servants offered me delicacies. I filled a basket with food, for I wanted to visit the harem and have lunch with Arjumand, who was now old enough to study. About to leave the kitchen, I paused as a woman I'd known since childhood placed a burnt serving of naan in my basket. I started to ask why she'd give me ruined bread when I noticed a piece of folded paper pressed against it.

Heart sputtering, I thanked her and walked outside. When certain no one could see me, I opened the paper. "I rest with your mother," it said. Realizing that Ladli must have news, I found a horse and hurried toward the Taj Mahal. For once, the mausoleum didn't charm me to stillness. I resisted its majesty as I dismounted and, hoping to avoid Isa, strode to the underground passageway. Soon this corridor would be sealed off forever, but today it still offered a recessed door. I always carried keys I might need, and thus opened it swiftly. I left it slightly ajar before stepping inside. Soon a veiled woman, clad like a Persian, entered. Many women in Agra enjoyed anonymity by dressing this way, and thus Ladli could protect her identity without attracting too much attention. I shut and bolted the door behind her. Wordlessly we walked down the corridor, came to another room, entered and secured it.

Ladli pulled off her veil and hugged me tightly. "He plans to kill you!" she said frantically. "He's going to do it soon and—"

"Slow down, my friend," I replied, even as my chest tightened and my lungs struggled to draw air. "Is Aurangzeb—"

"He's sent someone, the half-wit, I think, to violate then kill you!"

"My death . . . it isn't enough?"

She squeezed my arm. "May Shiva geld him before I—he wants you to suffer. He wants your ears as proof!"

I covered my ears instinctively. My legs shook, and I swayed unsteadily, collapsing against a dusty wall. "But I saved him," I said weakly.

"That fornicator of lies denies it! He says you placed the cobra in his room!"

Pinching my thighs, I tried to clear my reeling mind. "But when, Ladli? When will it happen?"

"Soon! I think tonight. You must take Arjumand and—"

"Arjumand?"

"Do you think anyone's safe, my sister?"

"I must go for her. I must protect her."

"Then go."

I forced myself to stand, taking in Ladli's face with my gaze. "How blessed I am to have you!"

"Go, Jahanara!"

My instincts screamed at me to run, but I resisted. "But why aren't you with him?"

"He sent many of us ahead to spy! He's not a day behind!"

My thoughts were still scattered and I pinched myself again. "But then you must give him something. Tell him . . . no, send a messenger to him with a note saying . . . a note that says we won't defend the Red Fort but will attack him to the north. Say there's talk of our cavalry heading south to enlist the aid of the Deccans."

"Is it true?"

"No. But Aurangzeb's spies will think it is. And he'll deem us weaker than we are."

She hugged me fiercely. "Don't let him find you, Jahanara. He hates you. He hates you so much."

Suddenly I wanted to cry on her shoulder, for I wished that we were young again, whispering of boys and love instead of battle and hate. "I know," I said sadly. "He has for a long time. But he hates Hindus no less. So be careful, Ladli. He could turn against you."

"I've never seen a piglet turn against a tiger."

Her words were bold, but her face said otherwise. "May Krishna protect you," I said, for Ladli adored the Hindu god of war and love. "Pray to him, my friend, for we'll surely need his help."

We parted, and as I hurried to my horse I wondered if I'd see her again. Only if Aurangzeb were slain would we be together. Alas, how much of a coward I was! For surely I should have let that cobra wet its fangs with his blood!

As I stepped into the harem I tried to appear calm. But when I couldn't find Arjumand, my worry turned into something much worse, a fear that stabbed deeply into my gut. I stumbled outside, and, kicking off my sandals, ran toward her room in the royal chambers. Staircases fled beneath me. Hallways twisted backward. When I threw open her door, her room was empty.

"Arjumand!" I cried, hurrying to my quarters, frantic with urgency. I fumbled at the doorknob and flung open the heavy teak door. Arjumand whirled when I entered. She had my secret closet open and wore my nicest robe. Slamming the door shut, I rushed to grab her.

"I'm sorry, Mother. I only wanted to—"

"Sssh!" I said, sweeping her up in my arms. I couldn't contain my tears and my child looked at me with confusion. "I could never lose you," I muttered. "Please, Allah, please let it never happen."

"Why are you crying?" she asked.

How I wanted that innocence to remain on her face forever. "We must go," I said. Nearby, a jeweled dagger used for unsealing letters rested on my desk. Snatching it, I headed back to the hallway. "Follow me closely, Arjumand," I said, opening the door and then screaming with fright when I saw Balkhi before me. He grinned wickedly, reaching for me. Without hesitating, without a thought, I brought the dagger up and across, slashing at his face. I was quick, and my blade opened up the skin of his cheek, cutting so deeply that it struck bone. He howled in pain. As he threw up his arms I managed to slam the door shut, bolting it in place.

"The closet, Arjumand!" I shouted. "Run through the closet!"

My priceless daughter rarely disobeyed me, and she didn't now. I grabbed a candle, but realizing the darkness would trouble him more than me, I threw the candle against a wall. Arjumand was already within the robes.

"Where do I go?" she wailed.

"Ahead! Ahead and down the stairs! It will be dark, child, but go forward! Go!" We hurried through the garments and came to the stairs. Behind us, I heard Balkhi hurl himself against the door, which groaned and splintered beneath his onslaught. "Hurry, Arjumand!"

The stairs were dimly lit at first, then we entered a tomb of total blackness. We twisted downward, stumbling on our long robes. A distant crash reverberated, and Balkhi roared as he broke into the room. He'd soon be upon us. I stumbled going down the last few stairs and fell hard on my shoulder. Wind was knocked from my chest and I struggled to breathe. "Run . . . forward," I stammered. "But when you come to a stone . . . don't touch it. Step over it." I felt for my dagger but, to my dismay, couldn't find it.

"Come, Mother! Take my hand! Please take my hand!"

Balkhi was on the steps above me. Groaning, I rose unsteadily to my feet. The passageway was unmercifully black, and I reached out blindly until I found her grasp. "Follow me," I said, feeling the walls with my free hand. "And be silent." We did our best to hurry, even wading through the impenetrable darkness. We'd taken less than thirty stumbling paces when a shout erupted behind us.

"Know what I'll do to you?" he bellowed.

"Hurry," I whispered, dragging her. She stepped on my robe and we fell as one.

"I'll cut your—"

"Run!" I yelled, hating his words, wanting to save her from them.

"And you'll watch as I—"

"Run, Arjumand!"

"—your daughter."

His voice was stronger now, and I sensed him right behind me. If I still had the dagger, I'd have thrown myself against him. But I had no such weapon and all I could think to do was scream for Isa. I screamed his name again and again, screamed until pain exploded within my knees as I ran headlong into the stone block. My instinct was to double over, but then, magically, my mind cleared. Wailing in effort, I reached behind me, grabbed Arjumand, and with Nizam's strength heaved her over the stone. She cried out, but I had no ears for her, because I felt him then, right behind me.

His fingers clutched at my robe.

I threw myself over the block, and Balkhi grunted as he smashed into it. My legs hurt too much to stand and so I dragged myself away from him. Arjumand sobbed, pulling me forward. "Leave me!" I cried, yet she continued to pull.

"Who should I cut first, woman?" Balkhi hissed. "You or my plaything?"

I saw a strike of flint, a spark, a flicker of light, then a flaming cloth. He burned his shirt, holding it alight with a curved dagger. "Close your eyes, Arjumand," I warned, for surely she shouldn't see this devil. He was monstrous, and his face, cleaved open by my blade, was a mask of blood and fury. He stood on the opposite side of the stone, no more than ten paces away. "Pray, my child," I whispered.

"For what?" he mocked, moving forward, his shoulders brushing the walls. "A quick death, a—"

"Pray that it works," I said, as he stepped on the stone.

Balkhi paused, looking down. His eyes bulged. His mouth opened. But time existed for nothing else. The block of granite, with him perched atop it, dropped through the floor like a needle through silk. The corridor buckled. It groaned. Balkhi shrieked from somewhere below as the floor and ceiling cascaded upon him.

I dragged Arjumand away from the howling rock. The corridor, black again, was a tempest of noise, so violent that I thought my ears might burst. Dust poured into my throat and lungs. We were both choking, dying perhaps. I felt only pain and horror.

Then appeared a light, or perhaps a halo that the Christians spoke of. For a turbaned head materialized between my blinks. The apparition beneath this halo threw itself above us, protecting us. And a hand, a fierce hand that might have been stone, grabbed my robe and pulled me back. It was the same hand that had shaped the Taj Mahal, the same hand that had so loved my body.

For Isa, finally, had arrived.

"THERE, JAHANARA," he whispered, wiping the blood from my knees with a wet rag. I winced at the sting, squeezing Arjumand tighter. Our daughter, still shuddering and crying, sat beside me. Praise Allah, she was physically unhurt, though I feared that memories of Balkhi would haunt her forever.

"He's gone, Arjumand," I said softly, "and shall never return."

"He was going to do those things," she sobbed.

I saw Isa's face tighten, and felt his silent rage. "Yes, my child," I replied. "But that wasn't our fate. Nor will it ever be."

"Why not?"

"I'm proud of you," I said, pulling her closer. "You were quite a brave young woman."

"No, no, no."

"But it's true. He might have been stronger, but we were braver." Our daughter shook her head, sobbing. It pained me to see her so upset. Her distress was unjust, for life was long and ample time lay ahead for woe.

I had always tried to protect her from the pains that I'd endured. But how utterly I had failed. Desperate to ease her suffering, I hugged her tightly. My body trembled no less than hers. I cried with her.

Isa's eyes also glistened as he held us. His scalp still bled from where a stone had cut him, bandaged crudely beneath his turban. He seemed to feel no pain, gripping us for so long that my arms tingled. There was warmth and security and love in his embrace.

As the night ebbed, we did our best to soothe Arjumand. We whispered reassurances. We spoke of her future. And finally, praise Allah, her tears subsided. While watching her emotions settle, I noticed how she reacted to Isa's embrace. She studied his hand as he stroked her arm. She eased closer to him. And she realized, I think, that his tears were on her behalf. It occurred to me then that our daughter had never been so comforted by a man. Certainly, Father had hugged her. But his affections, as important and heartfelt as they were, lacked the paternal connection that Isa now displayed. Somehow, it seemed, she sensed his love.

I edged from his grip until only he held her. Should we tell her the truth? I wondered. Is now the time? Though such knowledge might add to her confusion, she appeared so much in need of him that I was tempted to whisper of her lineage. Indeed, she was of age to be trusted with this secret. And I believed that after tonight's horror she deserved to know everything.

When Isa slowly nodded to me, whatever doubt I possessed yielded at that moment. "Arjumand," I said earnestly, "there is something you should be told. Something I've kept secret for far too long, something you must tell no one."

"Kept secret?" she asked, her voice strained from earlier sobbing.

I kissed her forehead, smelling dust and lavender oil. "I was asked to marry your . . . asked to marry Khondamir because of politics. I didn't love him, nor did I ever learn to love him."

"But I know this."

"But what you don't know, my child, is that I fell in love with another man. With a wonderful man who is truly—"

"Your father," Isa finished.

"My father?"

"Look at his face, Arjumand. Do you see yourself in him?" My daughter, I knew, wanted to believe these words, for Khondamir had always treated her with indifference. And so she stared. "Isa's your father," I said. "And he loves you as much as I."

"How couldn't I?" he asked, holding her tighter, and crying freely.

"Truly?"

"I love you, Arjumand. You don't know how long I've waited to say that. How painfully long."

To me, the smallness of his home seemed more apparent than ever, for at that moment, the outside world vanished. There only existed my lover and our daughter, the warmth of their flesh against my hands. To my delight, Arjumand wrapped her arms about his neck. She started to weep again, but these were different tears, for she no longer shuddered and trembled but pressed herself against him. He held her as if she were still an infant, cradling her head against his shoulder, kissing her brow gently.

My eyes stayed upon them as candles burnt themselves out. Only when exhaustion had overcome her and she'd drifted to sleep, did Isa lay her on his bed. Moving to the other side of the room, we whispered of our daughter. Then I told him what had happened in the tunnel. I spoke of the coming war and of Nizam's strategy. Isa listened without rest, never questioning me. Only when I was finished did he kiss me.

"Had he hurt either of you, I'd have died," he said quietly.

"I know."

He stroked my hair. "We'll leave in the morning. I have a cousin to the south in Allahabad, a good man who owns a stable. He'll—"

"I can't go," I interrupted sadly, remembering my promise to Mother, made so long ago.

"What?"

"You must flee with Arjumand. But I—"

He stepped back, his face wrinkling in consternation. "Are you mad?"

"I must stay."

"Stay here and you'll die!"

"I have to help Father."

"By Allah, he's the Emperor! He's man enough to help himself!"

"He's sick, Isa. And I can't leave him."

"Then take him with us!"

"And give the throne to Aurangzeb, who'll destroy the Empire?"

"Better it than us!"

"Better neither!" I said fiercely. "I can't leave him, Isa. And we have a good plan, one that will work. Once Aurangzeb is defeated, I'll find you. Father has promised to send us to Varanasi, where we can live forever in peace."

"He can promise nothing!"

"Listen!" I demanded, poking a finger into his chest. "If you love me, if you truly, truly love me, you'll do this. Because if I left with you, and Father died at Aurangzeb's hands, then my heart would die as well. I'd become a stranger to you and our love would never—"

"Survive? Then it's a shallower love than I thought."

I started forward as if to slap him but stilled my arm. "Don't say that! You know it's not true!"

"But how can you leave us?"

"Would you, Isa, let your father and brother die?" When he didn't answer, I continued, "You think that I feel differently because I'm a woman, or that I might offer them less?"

"I've never treated you differently than any man," he replied, his hawklike face gleaming in sweat. "Not once."

"And I love you for that. More, it seems, than you think. But if you love me, you won't ask me to abandon my family."

"We are your family!"

"Don't you think that I'm torn?" I pleaded.

"Your father—"

"Has given you everything, Isa. Everything! He let you build the Taj Mahal. He brought us together when our love could have destroyed him! Would you have me abandon him now, when he needs me most?"

"Then I'll stay with you."

"No! You must flee with Arjumand. She's seen enough horror. More than enough."

Isa cursed, which I had never heard him do. He pounded his fist against his hip. "Is there no other way?"

"None." Isa started to shake his head, but I placed my hands on his cheeks, steadying him. "I'm sorry. I truly am."

"As am I."

"I know."

He looked at Arjumand, avoiding my eyes. "If the fighting . . . goes badly, will you escape south to find us?"

"Of course. But it won't."

We stood still for a time. When he next spoke his voice was distant, as if he had already left me. "Why, Swallow, why must you save everyone?"

"Because I love them. I love them too much to let go."

CHAPTER XVI

Consequences

The next morning, we exchanged tearful good-byes. Though our separation distressed her, Arjumand wasn't overly upset, for I promised to see her in a week. Isa and I, however, were hard pressed to subdue our emotions. Our farewell brimmed with as much torment as love, as much fear as hope.

Parting from them was a death of sorts. As I walked through the Red Fort's corridors toward my room, I was consumed by doubt. Perhaps Isa was right, and I should have left in their keep, alongside the thousands of our people fleeing south. Despite my confidence in the coming battle, Aurangzeb could prevail. If he did, a swift boat would take Father, Dara and me southward. Unfortunately, Aurangzeb might anticipate such a flight and seal off our escape route. Capture would likely mean execution.

Missing them acutely, I entered my room and inspected the secret passageway. Apparently, Balkhi had shut the closet's door after pursuing us through it, and as far as I could determine, no one had any inkling as to what kind of mayhem transpired in my room yesterday. Nor with Aurangzeb's army approaching did anyone care.

Satisfied with the passageway, I stepped into Father's sprawling chambers, where the stench of illness still hung. Curtains were drawn over his latticed windows and wind tugged at the fabric. I offered greetings to the young physician who had delivered Arjumand, and asked that we be left alone. Father smiled weakly as I knelt beside him. He lay on pashmina blankets and rested his head on plush cushions.

"You stayed."

"My duty is here," I said with little conviction.

"Are you sure, my child? For the Empire may perish but will always be reborn. It shall live long after you're gone."

"But you won't. Nor will Dara."

He coughed, gritted his teeth, then muttered, "I'm uncertain, Jahanara, that life is . . . worth living without your mother. Some days it is, but most, I'd rather be eating grapes with her in Paradise." Father coughed again. He clutched at his chest. "You might be wise . . . to escape south. At least then you could live in peace, with those you hold dearest."

I ran a hand through my hair, which today bore no veil or jewels. "Please, Father! Do not make this harder than it is. Dara needs me. He's—"

"A tiger with no teeth?"

"Not a man of war."

"Nor are you."

"But I may be of some use. And how can I leave when that possibility remains?"

Father nodded reluctantly. He fought back a cough, then said, "Tell me, my child, of what happens."

As I straightened his bedding, trying to make him comfortable, I passed along what I'd been told. Nizam and twenty thousand horsemen had thundered south in the day's first light. I added that Dara gathered his forces and would soon march his army north, later positioning it atop a nearby, but vacant, knob of land. It had been raining incessantly since last night, and Nizam expected the storm to cloak his movements. Our scouts reported Aurangzeb's force to be a half-day's march from Agra. If my brother fell for our ruse, he'd likely attack our army late in the afternoon.

"Dara should leave now . . . give himself time to set his cannons," Father said.

"He soon shall."

I finished arranging his cushions and knelt again at his side. As much as I tried to ponder all that needed doing, wrenching my mind from Arjumand and Isa was impossible. Where were they? Had they made it to safety or had Allah abandoned me?

"You don't think of marching with Dara?"

"No," I replied hastily, perhaps too hastily. "I'd be of little use in such a battle."

"That's truer . . . than you realize," he muttered, as harshly as his feeble voice permitted. "I want you here with me. Dara and his officers are better off alone."

I had never disobeyed Father, but as I sat in that foul room, I heard few of his words. How could I remain here, when the fate of the Empire was to be decided outside Agra? Would Mother have stayed? She never had, and though only Father's authority had allowed her to accompany him to battlefields, where women would never be welcome, he'd told me on several occasions that her advice had saved lives.

Though I am no military genius, I had recognized this morning that one element of Nizam's scheme required my presence at the battle. If I wasn't there to ensure a fight, Aurangzeb might simply march to Agra and conquer an unprotected Red Fort. Of course, I hadn't told Isa of my plan to visit the battlefield, for he'd have thrown me over his shoulder and carried me to Allahabad.

"I shall return," I said softly.

"Don't stray far, child. I might need your counsel."

"As you wish."

But I lied then, for the sun had barely climbed halfway up the sky when I found myself on the best stallion in Father's stables. In a nearby courtyard I quickly located the clothing of a soldier. After Dara marched, hundreds of his warriors must have extracted themselves from hiding places and joined the exodus south, for their discarded weapons and uniforms littered the square like leaves after a storm.

Normally, the courtyard brimmed with humanity. Today, only a bare-chested Hindu priest moved amid the rain. I jumped from my mount and slipped the yellow tunic of an officer about me. The garment was far too large and fit me more like a dress; but once atop my horse, with the tunic gathered about my waist, no one would be the wiser. Like all warriors, I'd attached a shield, quiver, bow and sword to my saddle. I couldn't use these weapons, needless to say, but after my hair was swallowed up in a black turban, at least I looked the part of a soldier.

Beyond Agra's cobbled streets the road north turned into an endless bog of mud. Following the tracks of forty thousand men and a thousand war elephants was hardly difficult, even if visibility diminished as the rain strengthened and drove itself against the land. An unwavering wind pummeled me. It had arisen swiftly from the southeast, giving me alarm as the worst typhoons often surged from Bengal.

My mount, so stout and strong, quickly caught Dara's army. I smelled it before I saw it—the odors of dung, hay and unwashed men lingered even in the storm. I stayed at the army's rear, trying not to think of my loved ones and watching foot soldiers struggle through ankle-deep mud. Deerskin drums beat morosely as we marched. Officers yelled at men as elephants pulled scores of cannons. Other elephants bore wooden platforms draped in bright fabrics and usually holding one or two musket-wielding officers.

Fortunately, the journey to the knoll that would serve as our battle-ground was brief. It was only a slight rise, perhaps as long as the Red Fort, albeit not nearly so high. Almost devoid of trees, the mound boasted a few clusters of rock and sad-looking shrubs. Though my eye was un-trained, shelter appeared scant.

Our army briskly prepared its defenses. I watched from afar as our men, with the rain thrashing them, cut down the few trees present and used elephants to arrange the trees between boulders. Smaller branches and shrubs were shoved into gaps. This barrier, even if incomplete, would protect some of our men. Our cannons, numbering perhaps fifty, were then placed behind the wooden wall. Thus we created a vast circle of men, beasts and cannons surrounding the base of our knoll.

It took some time for me to find Dara, who looked like a stranger in his helmet and chain mail painted with diagonal red and black stripes. He rode a magnificent elephant and was ordering the construction of ad-ditional barricades. His elephant wore armor over its skull, and its tusks were encased within silver casts ending in wicked points.

Few horses were present, for most of our cavalry had secreted itself away to the north. And so after my mount neighed, Dara turned to me, expecting an officer of some rank. When I pulled off my tur-ban, he froze in surprise, as did dozens of men about him. I spurred my horse toward his war elephant, which was clad in purple tapestries.

"Why, why in Allah's name are you here?" Dara demanded from his perch.

I pulled on my reins, stopping a spear's length from his elephant. "How soon," I asked, "until Aurangzeb arrives?"

"But why are you here?"

Suddenly I was tired of being treated like a child, or a dog that might be kicked about. Just because Allah had made me a woman, could I contribute nothing to this cause? "Because it is my wish!" I countered.

"Your wish? Does Father know of this wish?"

Dara wasn't above having me tied to a horse and returned in shame to Agra. And so I lied. "I am to leave once the fighting starts and tell him how it began."

"I have messengers for that!"

"But can you spare them?" He started to nod, but I cut him off, finally voicing the real reason I had come. "Did you ever think, Dara, what might happen if Aurangzeb simply decided to march around your little hill and capture an unprotected Agra? Why should he attack you here, where you're fortified, when he can grab the Peacock Throne and deal with you later?"

"His honor dictates—"

"You think that rat has any honor?" I interrupted. Though as women we were taught to subdue our emotions, I was too aggravated to quiet myself. In some ways, Dara's naïveté vexed me more than Aurangzeb's treachery. "Are the heads of your officers so deep in this mud that they can't guess what he'll do?" I asked scornfully. "Surely he'll avoid attacking you here! I would, and I know nothing of war."

"And yet you propose?"

"He hates me the most, Dara. He always has. And when he comes to us with his terms for our surrender, I'll ensure he attacks." I spurred my horse closer to him. It took immense will, but when I next spoke my voice was much lower. "I love you, Dara, but are you so blind as to not see that neither good, nor honor, dwells in him?"

My brother grimaced, as if he'd just been wounded. Then he asked, "Do you think, Jahanara, that I walk an easy road? That only you have sacrificed?" When I offered no answer, he absently fingered the hilt of his sword. He pursed his lips. "I have been blind, yes. And I've made mistakes that . . . mistakes men will die for, mistakes that keep me from sleep, night after night."

"But if you knew of this blindness, why didn't you open your eyes? Why didn't we talk about it?"

"I thought we would. But time moved too quickly."

"Yes, yes, it did," I admitted. "But you didn't have to wait. I would have helped you."

"I sought above all . . . to bring our people together," he lamented. Between the pauses in his words the rain roared, assaulting the fixed umbrella above him and falling onto his elephant. "I wanted Hindus and Muslims to live as one. I learned of religion instead of war because I thought understanding and respect would bring us together. I lived my life, dedicated my life, to achieving that union. Yet how I failed. For now I must fight my brother. And if brothers can't respect each other, how can strangers?"

"Aurangzeb's doings, not yours, brought us here today."

My brother nodded wearily. He looked lost on his enormous war elephant with all its dressings. "I wish, Jahanara, that we were far from here. You should be with . . . your man and daughter. And I should be beside my son."

I hadn't been sure whether Dara knew of Isa, but now I was. "If we win—"

"Winning matters little," he said sadly. "If we win, tens of thousands, perhaps a hundred thousand Hindustanis will die here today. The Empire will never recover. Never. And if Aurangzeb wins, it will be worse, for Hindus will be persecuted and we'll step centuries back into time. He'll war against anyone not of Islam, and the Empire will crumble about him."

I lacked the insight to respond, recognizing only then that Dara understood these matters far better than I had believed. "I wish it could be as it was when we were young."

"Those days seem so distant, almost as if they were dreams," he replied. "I wanted children of all religions to play as brothers and sisters. I wanted them to live in peace."

"Perhaps ours shall."

Dara absently licked rain from his lips. "A fine fate that would be. But I fear we'll never see it." A distant moan of horns rose and Dara immediately straightened. "If Aurangzeb comes forward with a flag of truce, seek me out. But if he attacks straight away, flee for Agra."

I wanted to tell him that I loved him, that I was proud to be his sister, but he ordered his mahout to turn his elephant northward. When I looked up from my horse, my heart shuddered in fear, for a sprawling, seemingly infinite, army approached. Aurangzeb had only five thousand men and five hundred elephants more than we did in our total force, but his army somehow looked thrice the size of our assemblage on the knoll. He did brandish thirty thousand horsemen, and these warriors wheeled like the growing wind about his formations. The traitor's cavalry was what our officers feared most, for it was a force of speed and strength, one we couldn't match until Nizam attacked.

"Let him come in time," I whispered toward Mecca. "Without him, we're lost."

As Aurangzeb's army approached it began to uncurl into a long and menacing line. His elephants trumpeted as they pulled cannons into place. The enemy was still out of range and I heard our officers yelling at men to hold their fire. Our elephants, temporarily behind our guns, stomped their feet in trepidation, causing bronze bells about their necks to ring discordantly. A boy carrying a banner walked too close to one giant, and I shrieked when it gored him with its tusks. He died slowly, but no soldier neared the nervous beast to aid him. I suddenly felt sick. I had never seen war this close. Nor did I want to.

When a cluster of enemy horsemen approached under a flag of truce, I spurred my mount in their direction. Dara, atop his vast elephant, headed down the hill toward them. The rain was strengthening and I had to wipe my eyes often. I quickly caught up with Dara and the officers surrounding him on their fine mounts. These men were loyal to Father, good men who would gladly die this day. In my ill-fitting tunic I must have invited laughter. Yet the officers nodded in respect as I approached.

The two groups gathered at the base of our hill. Aurangzeb rode a beautiful white stallion but wore a gouged helmet and a battered coat of armor. My brother laughed when he saw me, though I knew him well enough to recognize rage flash across his face.

"Hiding behind the skirts of women?" Aurangzeb taunted Dara.

"I'd prefer her skirt to your shield."

Our men chuckled at Dara's reply and the mood of our enemies darkened. Aurangzeb withdrew an onion and began to bite chunks from it. "My terms, heretic, for your surrender," he began, spitting its outer shell at Dara, "are simple. I want your head. Then I want your whelp's head."

"By what right," Dara replied, his voice shaking with sudden fury, "do you have to ask for anything more than a whipping? For a whipping is all you'll receive."

Aurangzeb shrugged. "Perhaps I'll march on and spare you the trouble. If you like, attack me on the road to Agra."

When my brother started to turn his stallion away, I kicked my horse, so that he bumped against Aurangzeb's. "Afraid of us, little brother?" I asked contemptuously. "Of course, a man who sends someone as foul as Balkhi to kill his sister could only be a coward. For surely a real man would have killed me himself." I paused to spit in his direction. "But if Balkhi couldn't do the deed, it seems unlikely that a man who cries at the sight of a snake would have the nerve."

Aurangzeb's hand darted to his sword and steel slid forth. Officers on both sides withdrew their weapons, leveling muskets and notching arrows. Aurangzeb understood that he'd be the first to die and hence slammed his blade back into its scabbard. "My men will enjoy you, sinner," he hissed at me. "And you, heretic, will make a fine target on that overblown beast."

Dara glanced skyward. "I shall pray for your soul."

"I want no lover of Hindus praying for me." Aurangzeb finished the remainder of his onion. I could smell his rank breath from three paces away. "The noble Qur'an says of infidels, 'If only disbelievers knew of the time when they cannot ward off the fire from their faces or from their backs. No, it will come upon them unawares, and confound them, so they cannot avert it, and no respite will they have.' "

My older brother stared at his sibling. "The Qur'an also says, 'Anyone who does kill, through enmity and oppression, shall be exposed to fire, for that is easy for God.' "

We turned then and climbed our hill. Dara positioned himself behind our guns, directly across from Aurangzeb's force. I waved good-bye to him, and was about to spur my mount toward Agra, when Aurangzeb's horsemen began to fan out around our position. We'd expected Aurangzeb to concentrate his attack on a weak point of defense, but instead it seemed he would harass us on all sides.

"Go to the highest part of the hill!" Dara yelled when he saw my predicament. "Go!"

I did as he said, suddenly fearful. Not far below, Aurangzeb's elephants pulled his guns into place. As they neared, Dara commanded our men to fire. Our cannons were primed and leapt upward as they hurtled their balls of steel. I covered my ears at this deafening eruption. Though it now rained so furiously that discerning the enemy was difficult, I caught glimpses of elephants reeling drunkenly, of groups of men lifeless on the ground.

"Hurry, Nizam," I pleaded, looking northward, beyond our foe.

Our men efficiently reloaded their cannons and fired at will. Below, the enemy advanced, spearheaded by murderous lines of cavalry and foot soldiers that charged our ranks. We were now within range of their cannons and I cringed as the world churned beneath me. I saw an elephant lose its leg, topple to the ground, and crush its riders and a slew of other men. Several of our cannons exploded as they were struck, and gunners died screaming.

The horror intensified as the enemy approached. Some of our warriors fired muskets while those lacking guns launched arrows. Aurangzeb's men did likewise and suddenly the air thickened with thousands of projectiles. These flew through the howling rain and wrought destruction. Men died instantly or clutched deliriously at their wounds. Some warriors left the safety of our barricade and charged unmolested at our foe, whereas others cowered in fear and were struck by numerous arrows. Nothing made sense.

Thunder boomed in tandem to the cannons, and the storm, already a full typhoon, intensified. I was nearly thrown from my saddle by a burst of wind. The rain assaulted me, stinging my face, my hands. I shielded my eyes and tried to find Dara, finally spotting him at the base of our hill atop his elephant. A beast near him rolled down the slope as my brother gestured wildly to the men about him, pointing below.

Then I saw the enemy. They carried green shields and rushed us like a swollen river bursting through a dike, charging up our hill, curved swords held high. There seemed to be an impossible number of them; screaming, crazed men whose fury frightened me more than the booming cannons. Our warriors fired their muskets and bows until the last instant, then drew their swords. A sudden clashing of steel rang out amid the curses, screams and explosions. Our men held their lines briefly, but then Dara's banners began to fall.

I wheeled my horse about, looking for a means to escape. But everywhere, it seemed, our positions were attacked. I could try to break through the fighting but would more likely than not be killed in the process.

"Isa," I muttered, frantic that I'd see neither him nor Arjumand again.

Where was Nizam? If he didn't arrive soon, all would be lost. Our men were putting up a brave defense, but we were outnumbered and our enemies seemed crazed. Aurangzeb's warriors had been killing Persians for years, while our men were either past their prime fighting age or were witnessing their first battle. Dara tried to rally our ranks, his huge elephant trampling the enemy. Though he had always seemed powerless, I realized again that he wasn't so, only naïve. For now he fought as a leader might. He fired his gun and shouted at his men to go forward and die. They listened to him, chanting his name as they battled.

Yet the enemy still surged up the hill. They flooded our ranks, pausing only to kill our wounded. I was within range now, and a few warriors, perhaps thinking me an officer, fired arrows upward. The bolts thudded into the soil about me as I pulled the heavy shield from the side of my saddle, and then cowered behind it. More arrows fell, accompanied now by bullets. To stay here, I knew, was to die. But what choice did I have?

Suddenly my horse, my beautiful mount, stumbled. He cried out in agony and toppled forward, throwing me from the saddle. Shrieking, I turned in the air, landing in the deep mud on my back. My body throbbed, but I rolled over and drew to my knees. I trembled uncontrollably now, for this horror was too overwhelming. Unsheathing my sword, I crawled to my mount, intent on ending his misery. But I needn't have bothered. His neck was ripped open and his eyes had already glazed over.

When the horns finally sounded, I barely heard them. But our men cheered abruptly and I knew Nizam had at last arrived. The enemy must be ripe for slaughter, I thought, for they had thrown all their foot soldiers and cavalry into us. Surely their gunners were unprotected.

The avenging screams of twenty thousand strong rose to obscure even the storm. Through the driving rain I caught glimpses of our horsemen decimating the surprised enemy, for suddenly Aurangzeb's force was caught between two deadly groups of men. Our cavalry below, and our foot soldiers above, rained bullets and arrows into their masses. The enemy began to fall in vast numbers and I stood, praying that Nizam's plan would work. It did for a time, and our forces howled in triumph.

Allah, however, deserted us then. One heartbeat Dara was atop his elephant urging his men forward, and the next, cannon fire ripped into the monstrous beast and the battle thus changed. The elephant wailed horribly before tumbling into our barricade of logs. Dara was thrown from his platform, thrown fast and hard. Several logs appeared to fall on him, as did the elephant.

I was already running toward him when the first shout of panic burst out. "The Prince is dead!" a young standard bearer yelled. "Dead!"

Panic rippled through our men like fire atop oil. Believing their leader slain, they suddenly retreated from the fighting, thinking of themselves rather than of the Empire. If Dara was lost, so was our cause, for he was the future emperor and a man worth fighting for. Officers yelled at those fleeing to face our foe, but all discipline had perished with Dara's disappearance. Frantic, I stumbled down the hill toward where he had fallen. The long tunic restricted my movements and I toppled awkwardly, sliding down the mud. Dara's elephant had a hole in its side the size of my head, yet it still lived. It tried to stand, managed to for an instant, and then toppled forward, crushing a trio of Aurangzeb's men. Amid the scattered wreckage of the barricade, I quickly found Dara. His head was bloodied beneath his dented helmet, but

I felt his breath against my hand. "He lives!" I shouted. "The Prince lives!"

Though a few warriors paused to look at me, I was far too late to save us from slaughter. Cradling Dara's head on my lap, I watched as our men tried to escape the encroaching hordes. Some did, but hundreds of our warriors were shot in the back as they fled about the hill. Others, finding no escape, turned to face their foes. These men fought like demons but were outnumbered and inundated. Their throats were slit and their pockets emptied with appalling efficiency.

I withdrew Dara's helmet, ripped off a piece of my tunic and tied it about his head to stop the bleeding. About to tighten it further, I paused as a horse galloped toward me. I was nearly beneath its hooves when a hand reached down and pulled me violently from the ground. The rider, with amazing strength, threw me behind him. My nails had started to claw at his face by the time I recognized Nizam.

"But Dara!" I cried.

He spurred his mount toward a break in the lines. A stout warrior stepped before us, leveling a musket. His weapon misfired and Nizam's curved blade fell swiftly as we passed, opening the man's shoulder. An arrow appeared simultaneously in Nizam's thigh. I'd no idea how it had arrived there. He roared in fury and spurred his horse as two more soldiers ran in front of us, grinning when they saw my long hair. Nizam thrust aside the spear of one, skewering the man with his sword. The other warrior shouted for help and men ran forward to surround us. They tried to pull me from the horse and Nizam beat them aside, howling like an animal. It seemed as if Allah had blessed him that day, for bullets missed him and swords rebounded from his armor. His vengeful blade rose and fell in never-ending arcs, most sweeps maiming an enemy.

Our mount jumped over a ruined cannon and suddenly I was falling. I struck the ground brutally, crosses of light dancing in my vision. Though I expected my clothes to be torn off immediately, I realized that an officer had reached me first. His sword was bright with the blood of our men, but his eyes weren't cruel and I hoped he would protect me.

Nizam turned his horse around and tried to fight his way back to me. Dozens of men surged between us, however, and many were busy notching arrows. "Leave me!" I screamed. "You'll do me no good dead!" He killed a balding warrior and winced as a blade glanced off his saddle. "Flee!" I shouted. "By the love of Allah, flee!"

His rage seemed to boil over and he snarled, spurring his steed into a thicket of men. They scattered before him and he was free, galloping toward a gap in the lines. Two more warriors died in his wake before he vaulted over a pile of bodies. Then the rain swallowed him whole, and I didn't know whether he lived or died.

The officer bent down, offering me a hand. "Princess Jahanara," he said, bowing slightly. Though men still fought around us, the battle ebbed and to him it appeared nonexistent.

I recognized him, recalling dimly that our fathers were acquaintances. I nodded, then remembered my brother. "Dara," I cried, trying to stand, my legs trembling and unresponsive.

"Alamgir has him, my lady. He lives."

"Who? Who has him?"

"Your brother, Alamgir. For that's what he now calls himself."

Alamgir meant "Conqueror of the World" and I shuddered at what the name portended. "He shall," I replied weakly, "always be Aurangzeb to me."

"That he might. But if I were you, I'd call him Alamgir. For I heard what you said to him, and his wrath will be terrible."

I closed my eyes, thinking of what he would do to me. Aurangzeb would be maddened by bloodlust and I knew that if I met him now, he would feed me to his warriors. "Are you, Humayun, a man of honor?"

He seemed surprised that I remembered his name. "Yes, my lady."

"Then strike me unconscious and take me thus to Alamgir. For if he finds me awake, I'll . . ." I paused, biting my lip, fighting sudden tears, "I'll die horribly."

Humayun nodded. "I will, my lady, always counsel him against your death."

"Thank you."

He bowed again before lifting the hilt of his blade. I had only time to turn toward Mecca before it smote my head. There was a blinding, consuming pain. And then there was nothing.

CHAPTER XVII

Death and Dishonor

The Red Fort surrendered in a single day. With tens of thousands of troops massed against it, and only a few thousand warriors within its walls, no other choice existed. Though still feverish, Father was imprisoned in the Musamman Burj, the Octagonal Tower. Father had built this two-story tower atop the Red Fort's eastern wall so ladies could see far beyond Agra's boundaries. Aurangzeb imprisoned him within it quite deliberately, for the Musamman Burj provided an unobstructed view of the Taj Mahal, offering Father sight of what he cherished above all but might not touch again.

The day of Father's imprisonment was the darkest of my life. Not because we had lost, but because of what was to happen. For Aurangzeb, now supreme ruler of the Empire, had accused and condemned Dara of heresy.

My brother, may Allah forgive us all, was to be beheaded.

Upon awakening I found myself naked, but, aside from a bloody scalp, otherwise unharmed. I lay in a gloomy cell. The place reeked of urine and it took me a moment to realize that I wasn't alone, for pacing about the cage was a pair of hunting cheetahs. I cried out instinctively but then stilled. The cheetahs growled and circled me as they might a wounded gazelle. No weapon was present in the cell but for a gnawed bone the size of my arm, which I grabbed as I crawled into a corner.

Little time passed before Aurangzeb called upon me. A handful of his men accompanied him, and each laughed at my nakedness and fear. "They haven't been fed for days," Aurangzeb announced, nodding at the cats. "Mustn't like the smell of infidels. But then, who does?" My brother eyed me, his gaze sweeping up and down my body. "Give them time, let their hunger grow, and they'll try you."

"I'll try her," one of his men said, as I sought to cover myself.

Aurangzeb ignored him. "You might like to know, sinner, that Dara was convicted of heresy. He'll lose his head tomorrow."

"No!" I yelled, disbelieving my ears. "No, please, no! He's an advocate of Islam! He—"

"Deserves to die!"

"For what? What has he done?"

"Must you always debate me?" Aurangzeb roared, spittle flying from his lips. "Would an advocate of Islam call Hinduism an equal faith? Equal, by God! He weakened the Empire with his treasonous book!"

"He only tried to bring us together, to show that we could live as one! Where's the treason in that?"

"It's everywhere! On every foul, infected page! And he'll die for those pages. For his blasphemy!"

"But please, Aur . . . Alamgir, he's your brother."

"Brothers lose heads like any others! As do sisters."

As he started to turn, I cried, "What does Allah say of murder?"

He wheeled around on me, grabbing the cell's iron bars. "Heretics are executed, not murdered!"

"He's no heretic! Imprison him if you must, but let him live."

"You'll watch him die tomorrow," he hissed, "unless my cheetahs grow hungry."

"It's murder! Murder!"

The men laughed as they left, making gestures that made me ill. In my haste to protect Dara I'd forgotten my nakedness and stood openly. "What's happening?" I mumbled to myself, barely able to brave my sorrow. If I had been alone in this world, with no father, lover or daughter, I might well have let the cheetahs devour me. Better to endure the gnashing of their teeth than to harbor thoughts of what tomorrow would bring. How, by all that was good, had it come to this?

When night arrived, my cell cooled considerably. In the darkness the cheetahs' eyes glowed like yellow moons, orbs that stared at me constantly, vanishing only when the great cats blinked. I urinated near my corner, as if marking my territory. My scent gave them pause, but their growls persisted and I became fearful. I could, maybe, tolerate the notion of their teeth on my flesh, but the idea of never again seeing Isa and Arjumand caused me to tremble in anguish. I tried to imagine what they were doing at this very moment. Did they sleep in the same room? Did he tell her a story, or show her how to design a fountain? Perhaps they thought of me. Perhaps our thoughts could meet, even if we could not.

Much later, after exhaustion had rendered me unconscious, I sensed a wetness against my head. The rank smell of decay pervaded my lungs. I gagged, screaming when I realized that the larger of the two cheetahs was licking my bloodied scalp. The beast bared its fangs and I swung my club, striking the animal hard in the backside. Yelping, it ran to the other corner.

Soon both cheetahs growled. They paced tirelessly about the cage, nearing me with each circle. I swung my bone when they approached too closely. I cursed them loudly and tried to appear bigger than was true. One of the beasts darted forward, sinking its teeth into my club. The cheetah yanked it from my grasp and suddenly I was defenseless. When they neared again, I didn't dare strike out, for they might grab hold of my leg or arm as they had my bone.

I'll try for their eyes, I thought frantically. If they attack me, I'll claw out their eyes!

Suddenly a shaft of light fell on my cage. Someone had opened the door to this place and now walked quietly down the corridor. The cheetahs retreated as my visitor approached. Whoever came calling wore a black robe and no sandals, apparently desiring to arrive in secrecy. I didn't know if an assassin had been sent to cut my throat, or if someone planned on liberating me.

Delicate hands rose to pull back a black hood, and to my joy I saw that the apparition was Ladli. My friend reached into a bag, producing a pair of bloody steaks. With a grunt she heaved the steaks toward the cheetahs, which growled before sniffing at the meat. I hurried toward her and our hands met outside the bars. Though I remained caged, my emotions were freed and I wept silently. She stroked my arm, leaning forward to kiss my cheek. "I've no time, my sister," she whispered.

"Have you news of—"

"Isa?"

"You know?"

Despite her nervousness, she smiled. "I can see, Jahanara," she replied, her fingers gripping my hand.

"I should have told you, but—"

She shrugged. Her eyes, with their long lashes, darted about. She glanced at my nakedness, and her face contorted. "I should bury a knife in his back for this." When I kept silent, she asked, "What do you need?"

Make the pain leave me, I thought. Wake me from this nightmare. "Can you pass a message to Isa?" I begged, longing to hold him, to kiss Arjumand. "He's in Allahabad with Arjumand, staying in some stable. Please tell him that I love him, that I'll see them soon."

"I'll try," she said, folding up her bag. "I don't think the pox-ridden coward will kill you. He knows the people hold you too dear and wouldn't stand for it. But there could be an accident, or he might imprison you for forever and a day."

"Does he truly mean to behead . . ." I couldn't finish the sentence. Ladli had once loved my brother, and her tears, abrupt and unguarded, were as real as mine. "Be strong," I whispered, though my words were a farce, for I felt like collapsing. "Be strong and be careful."

"And you."

"I love you, Ladli."

She kissed my forehead and departed. I prayed that Ladli returned unseen to her quarters and thanked Allah for giving her to me as a friend. This one woman, this daughter of a commoner, had proven herself more loyal, cunning and caring than Father's most powerful nobles. I beseeched Allah someday to free her from Aurangzeb and see to it that we were reunited.

The cheetahs slept after their meal and, despite being frightfully cold, I closed my eyes and endured the night. When morning finally arrived, I was amazed to see that the giant cats had crawled to less than a pace from me. They lay curled against each other, living pieces of art, though surely no man but Isa could create such beauty. I watched the beasts for some time, thinking that if I ever escaped my brother I'd return to free them.

They hadn't wanted to eat me last night, but animals lean with starvation had little choice in such matters. Like all beneath Aurangzeb's yoke, the cheetahs were forced to do his bidding.

Not long after dawn a warrior appeared and threw me a worn robe. I put it on hastily and asked him what was to happen. He grunted, and a moment later Aurangzeb, still wearing his armor, appeared with four bodyguards. My brother opened the cage, shook his head at the resting cheetahs, and kicked one hard. "Worthless beasts," he snarled, motioning for me to be brought out.

I started forward willingly, but his men nonetheless grabbed me. One squeezed my buttocks and I forced myself to still my tongue. I remained silent as the men followed Aurangzeb to the royal stables. There, they lifted me onto a horse. My brother leapt on his white stallion before leaning toward me. "You shall watch his death, sinner. And if your black eyes stray from him, stray just once, I'll make you carve off his head."

"He's never hurt you. Ne—"

Aurangzeb backhanded me across the face, almost knocking me from my saddle. Blood trickled from my lip. "He's a traitor and a heretic!" he retorted. "And our disgraceful brother will be dealt with as such!"

I didn't wipe the blood from my chin, as my beating would anger the people. Instead, I bit the wound, tore at it with my teeth until more blood oozed forth. Aurangzeb spurred his horse ahead and one of his brutes led my mare by her reins. We left the Red Fort and soon were on Agra's broadest street. A commotion raged ahead. As we neared, I saw that hundreds of people argued along the street. Though troops sought to keep the peace, sporadic fighting broke out in pockets. Men fell and did not rise. Hindus shouted about injustice and Muslims chanted fervently for Aurangzeb.

In the center of the uproar, at an immense intersection, was Dara. He sat with his son, Suleiman, atop a scarred war elephant. Both prisoners were naked but for loincloths, had their arms bound behind them, and were covered in filth. I watched in horror as dozens of onlookers hurled vegetables at them, onions and potatoes leaving welts upon their torsos.

Only this finite number of people, however, tossed vegetables and chanted for Dara's death. Most of those present were Hindus and stood before the drawn swords of Aurangzeb's men begging for my brother's life. Other Hindus struggled against whichever Muslims were most intent on humiliating and harming Dara. My brother pleaded with those defending him to refrain from violence. He beseeched them to stand still, saying that his death would be much worse if his last sight was of his people killing each other.

His vision of peace, even with his violent death at hand, made me frantic with the fear of losing him. "Dara!" I shrieked above the clamor. He turned to me and I saw that his face was bruised and swollen. He tried to respond, but a melon rose toward Suleiman, and Dara threw himself in front of it. His son wailed, maddening me, as he was only thirteen and guilty of nothing.

"Free the child!" I screamed.

Aurangzeb spun in his saddle and motioned to a man riding beside me. The warrior laughed and used the side of his hand to strike my throat. Suddenly I couldn't breathe. My neck burned and I gasped, finally managing to draw air through my nose. As I did, he slapped me.

Despite my brother's dream of harmony between our people, and even though I also abhorred the idea of Hindus fighting Muslims, at that moment, may Allah forgive me, I wanted the multitudes of Hindus to rise up and overwhelm Aurangzeb and his men. I wanted our captors dead and their corpses dragged through offal.

The elephant bearing Dara and Suleiman was guided down the street. Thousands of people followed us, jeering Aurangzeb or proudly waving his banners. We soon came to a square where a bloodstained block of wood lay on a raised platform. A muscle-bound slave stood on this stage, a massive sword in his hands. Dara was knocked from the elephant and carried toward the executioner. My brother nodded to me, tears in his eyes, and yelled good-bye to his son.

My world began to spin.

"My brother, Prince Dara," Aurangzeb shouted, "is guilty of heresy! And in accordance to our laws, he shall be put to death!"

I leapt from my horse and ran through Aurangzeb's warriors until

I reached Dara. He whispered my name as I threw my arms around him. "Go to God," I said before being torn from him. Aurangzeb's men tossed me to the ground and one kicked my thigh. At this sight, even Muslims grew restless, for nobles and commoners alike knew me and didn't appreciate seeing me mistreated. Angry threats ensued, as did calls to release me. Aurangzeb sensed the changing mood and came down from his horse to pull me up.

"Please, please, show him mercy," I cried, but he twisted from me and nodded to his men. They dragged Dara to the executioner's block, placing his head on the wood. Dara turned toward Mecca and I saw his lips quiver. I prayed with him, prayed so hard and fiercely that I trembled. I sobbed as I prayed, pleading with Allah to bring Dara swiftly through the gates of Paradise.

I didn't see the blade as it rose, but saw instead images of us as children. We rode a pony together. I dressed him in Mother's clothing, draping jewels about his neck. I swam with him, laughed with him, caught fireflies with him. Always he was kind to me. And always did he love me.

I closed my eyes as the sword fell, holding these images in my mind. A heavy thud of steel upon wood boomed and the crowd wept and roared.

The thud came again and I knew Dara's son was dead also.

I fell to my knees, crying as I'd never cried as a child, weeping as only an adult could. For I had seen the light of my brother, and now, in his absence, the world was cloaked in darkness.

THE DARKNESS FOLLOWED me like a shadow.

Later that day I was shoved into Father's room, where he lay feverish on a horse blanket with his tunic tightly drawn about him. How he still lived was astounding but not miraculous, for I believed in no miracles that afternoon. He was asleep and I stumbled to him, dropping to the stone floor. I edged toward him until our bodies touched. He mumbled incoherently, his face very old.

Through my tears I gazed at our octagonal cell, perhaps twelve paces across. Nothing resided in the room save Father's blanket and a chamber pot. Seven of its eight windows had been covered in wooden planks.

Between bars freshly set within the eighth window could be seen the Taj Mahal, serene and brilliant in the sun.

The view reminded me of Isa, and I wondered again what he and Arjumand were doing. How incomplete I felt in their absence, as if the best parts of me had been stolen away and buried deeply within the Earth. I didn't even need to talk to them, but simply to hear her laugh and hold his hand. I'd gladly have been beaten senseless for that instant of pleasure, though my lip still throbbed and my thigh ached. How long, I asked Allah, until I see them? A week? A year? Never?

My tears seemed infinite as I sniffed and hugged Father. I held him. I gave him warmth and he gave me strength. At last he opened his eyes, his face tightening with consternation when he recognized my mood. "What, my child, has happened?" he asked feebly. My voice in tatters, I told him all that had befallen us, starting with the battle and ceasing with the execution. I think he was too numbed to cry, for he simply closed his eyes and held me closer. "How I have failed," he said. "I sought to create peace, and now . . . and now my son has killed his brother."

"He felt no pain," I mumbled.

Father nodded, and the lines on his face seemed to deepen. "Such a loss. For us. And for Hindustan. Only Dara could have truly brought our people together."

"He wanted nothing more."

Father grimaced, coughed and then whispered, "What of Isa and Arjumand?"

"They fled south, to Allahabad."

A silence dawned and wouldn't go. At length, Father lamented, "I'd like . . . to see your mother in Paradise."

"She waits for you. With Dara."

"Should I go to them now?"

I knew he wanted to but shook my head. "Mother would disapprove. She'd say that the Empire needs you more than you need her."

"But what, my child, can a monkey do in its cage?"

I swatted away a fly that had landed on his bare head. He looked odd without his turban. What scant locks he possessed were the same iron-gray shade as his beard. I studied the signs of age on his face. My thoughts seemed distant, though, as if strangers in a crowd. "He can help," I finally replied, "his daughter become a better woman."

"She needs no help in that."

I hugged him and we rested. I must have slept, for when I next opened my eyes, Aurangzeb, Ladli, Khondamir and a young woman stood in our cell. Aurangzeb was dressed in orange, while Ladli, oddly enough, wore a yellow robe instead of a sari. Khondamir's belly stretched a leather jerkin, and his silk shirt and pants were equally filled. He was in the midst of devouring an oily drumstick. His companion, a girl of maybe fourteen, and as pretty as a butterfly, was clad in a transparent robe and shirt.

"A gift," Aurangzeb said, setting Dara's head on the floor. My older brother's eyes were open and his face was frozen in horror. I retched at the sight and might have fainted if not for my aching body.

Father tried to rise but could hardly move. "Why? Why, Aurangzeb?" he wailed. "You could have banished him, imprisoned him, let him flee to Persia!"

"A fool, like you, would let an enemy flee. But I'm no fool."

"You . . . you cannot be my son. For you are a coward and a villain . . . and no such blood flowed in your mother's veins."

Aurangzeb appeared to tremble. "Understand, fool," he said, avoiding Father's eyes, "that you'll never leave this cell. I won't kill you, for Islam forbids a son to kill a father. But you'll die here. Die looking at her grave, die wishing you were with her."

As much as Father must have quailed at such words, he sat taller. "Better to die here than to watch you destroy the Empire."

My brother shrugged, as if Father's opinion was now mere dust upon him. His gaze swung to me. "Did you know, sinner, that your old friend converted to the True Faith?"

I looked to Ladli in wonder, for though I realized she had done this deed only to further grace herself with Aurangzeb, I found her sacrifice surprising. She had always so loved her gods. "A mistake," I finally replied, staring at her, avoiding Dara's face. Impossible to think of my brother now. To think of him would break me.

"You," Ladli retorted, "aren't worth the pot Alamgir pisses in."

Khondamir dropped his bone and laughed. "Once perhaps. But you do wither quickly. There'd be little pleasure in bedding you now."

Though already thirty-one, I believed I was still modestly attractive. But his words stung nonetheless. And I was tired of pain. Father started to reply, but my voice rose above his. "What does your plaything think, Khondamir, of that twig you call your manhood? Or has your belly always hidden it from her?"

Khondamir started forward to hit me, but Aurangzeb shouted at him to stop. "Strike her later," he ordered. "Nobles, certain powerful nobles, will come calling here. And I don't want them thinking that our guests were mistreated."

"But, my lord, as her husband—"

"Have your way with her in time," Aurangzeb countered. "In a month, sell the sinner to a brothel. Or leave her naked in the desert. But for now, she'll remain as such."

"A brothel?" Khondamir repeated elatedly, wiping his greasy hands on his jerkin. "But she'd sell for so little."

It had been years since I saw Aurangzeb laugh, but laugh is what he did now. And so I stood and took a step toward him, my sorrow turning quickly to rage. "I'll always pray for you," I said, "for you killed your brother, and you'll never, never enter the gates of Paradise, as he has already."

"Better to pray for yourself, sinner. You won't last long in this world."

I moved closer, until a hand's breadth separated us. Looking up at him, I retorted, "If I should die, Aurangzeb, or if Father should die, know that a cobra will be placed in your bed. Know that it will strike you, and that you'll die horribly."

He stepped back. "A cobra? You lie."

"Do you think that I have no friends? No spies among your men who would delight in slaying you? You child! You simple, witless child! I've always known this day might come, and yet you think I took no precautions. Am I such a fool?" His face twitched, and he glanced about, almost as if he was looking for cobras. I remembered only then that a gardener had once been bitten by one and, as children, we watched as the man, crazed with pain and terror, hacked off his poisoned foot. "If you wish to test my words, kill me tonight," I dared. "But know that tomorrow, or the next day, a cobra will draw your blood."

"Kill the bitch now," Khondamir said, edging toward me.

"Silence!" Aurangzeb roared. His chest rose and fell as he massaged his temples. He seemed to be in sudden agony, as if my words were hornets in his head. "If it's true, why not kill me tomorrow?" he asked suddenly. "Kill me and all your problems are naught!"

"Because, Aurangzeb, unlike you, I am no murderer! But if I should die it won't be my hands that take your life. No, I'll be drinking wine in Paradise with Dara and Mother when you soil yourself."

Khondamir edged forward. "Let me sell her. Let me carve out her tongue."

I could see the fear in my brother's eyes and felt myself reeling in this unexpected power. How I hated these men! How they would destroy all that was noble to satiate their pathetic desires. "Did you know, Khondamir," I hissed, "that Arjumand isn't of your blood?" His face whitened and I continued relentlessly. "You think that twig of yours could ever lay but dead seeds? Do you—"

He screamed, his blow coming so fast that I had no time to react. It further split my lip and I fell. Aurangzeb cursed, throwing Khondamir from me. Yet I was unfinished. "How I laughed when you were upon me," I raged, spitting blood. "I imagined you as a goat and found the image quite pleasing!"

"Silence, woman! Be silent or I'll—"

"What?" I shrieked at my brother. "You'll murder me, in front of our people, as you did Dara? You'll create a thousand more enemies? A thousand more men who'd like to stick a blade through that stone you call a heart? No, Aurangzeb, you will do nothing! Because if we're hurt, then my cobra will strike. And we'll hear your pitiful wailing from our perches in Paradise!"

His fist caught me in the stomach and I doubled over, gasping for breath. The agony was so enormous that I couldn't speak. My anger ebbed quickly, replaced by pain. Aurangzeb spat on me, pushed his companions from the room, and locked the door behind him. Father moaned, crawling toward me. He collapsed, and we lay together, with aching bodies and minds.

I wondered if I were in hell.

"Rest, my child," Father said weakly.

The Qur'an is wrong, I thought dimly, for It says that hell is for the dead and yet I, still breathing, am surely in its bowels.

CHAPTER XVIII

Curse of the Living

Time spent caged ceases to feel like time. It's more akin to a long bout of illness, debilitating and wretched.

My first days in the Musamman Burj were dominated by an overwhelming sense of doom. As the dawns passed, I grew increasingly despondent, sleeping as much as possible, often rising only when lunch was served. I made no effort to comb my hair or bathe every day. Instead, I stood by the window and gazed at the Taj Mahal, thinking of Isa and Arjumand. I mused over each memory I possessed, each conversation I could reproduce. Constantly I lamented lost opportunities, moments when I'd been too busy to see my daughter, or too tired to secretly walk to Isa's home. I cursed myself mercilessly for these failings.

I had always been an active woman, but my imprisonment stole my energy as a hot day might. To be truthful, I was a feeble woman then, and if not for Father's health I might have simply shriveled up and blown away. But he was ill, and he needed my help. And so with what little resolve I maintained, I focused on him. I fed him soup, I bathed him each night and I cleaned up his mishaps. And gradually, so gradually that I could hardly discern it, he improved. I doubted he would ever be the man he once was, but some of his strength returned and his body went from gaunt to merely thin.

Two weeks into our imprisonment, perhaps a little more, Aurangzeb revisited our cell. He was upset, his mouth twitching with apprehension as he opened a sack and let a dead cobra fall to the floor. Shuddering, he kicked it toward me. Between his shouts, he hissed that it had been placed alive in his bed. The serpent's fangs had been removed and it couldn't bite him, but when Ladli's screams awoke him, he bellowed for his men to kill it. Though shocked by this revelation, I pretended to be pleased, as if the scare had been my doing. I quickly deduced that Ladli, quite incredibly, had set the serpent within her bed so that Aurangzeb would believe my warning and leave me in peace.

Aurangzeb threatened me with his blade that day, but he was clearly afraid to kill me. In his paranoia over the snake, he had all his body-guards executed and he replaced these men with others he trusted. Yet he trusted no one enough to murder me, for he believed that if I were to die, he would follow.

Perhaps to protect himself from me, perhaps to quench his insatiable thirst for war, Aurangzeb left Agra and marched northwest to attack the Rajputs. These warriors inhabited the Thar Desert, a wasteland far re-moved from Agra that had long been home to clans of Hindu warriors comprising the Rajput kingdoms.

Like the Deccans, the Rajputs warred against us for independence and were some of the fiercest fighters in Hindustan. They never fled an en-gagement and fought to the death wearing crimson-colored robes—they believed red was the color of holiness. If defeat was imminent, Rajput warriors swallowed opium and charged their enemies. Their wives and children subsequently performed the rite of jauhar, burning themselves alive rather than being captured and dishonored by their foes.

Aurangzeb marched into the Thar Desert with twenty thousand men, leaving the bulk of his forces to deal with the rising threat of the Per-sians. After the moon waned and waxed, we heard stories of my brother's victories. Though he lost a quarter of his troops, Aurangzeb razed several Rajput strongholds. The heads of their men were piled together to form grisly mountains. The ashes of their women and children coated sand dunes black.

Often I felt like sharing the fate of the Rajput women. How much easier death would have been, even a fiery death such as theirs, than liv-ing in my cage. But death wouldn't bring me Isa or Arjumand. And so I lived.

Father did his best to buoy my spirits, engaging me whenever my mood became too despondent. Fortunately, his mind was still keen and we whispered of all things. His secrets became mine, and mine his. I even told him of Ladli.

One afternoon, as I stared unmoving through our barred window toward the Taj Mahal, he said, "At first, I feared that Aurangzeb would destroy it. But not now. Our people would turn against him."

I continued to gaze at Mother's mausoleum. We were still in the monsoon season and a storm raged. Though I had made curtains for the window, I'd pulled them aside, as the driving rain against my face reminded me of better times. I eased my robe down and let the water splatter against my neck and shoulders.

"Jahanara?"

I turned toward his voice, my gaze swinging across our cell, which bore little resemblance to its former decrepitude. Now we had carpets, mirrors, racks of clothes, cushions, a washbasin, candles and plates of fresh food. I had hung tapestries and paintings upon the walls, and even nailed a portrait of Mother to the wooden door.

All these goods were gifts from influential nobles. Aurangzeb was wise enough to understand that he shouldn't deny us certain comforts, for we had visitors most days, and such men might be angered if our imprisonment was too harsh. After all, Father had many friends—nobles capable of understanding a son overthrowing his father, but not a son tormenting the man who had given him life.

"Can you hear me, Jahanara?"

"Yes?" I mumbled, blinking repeatedly.

"You left me, child. But where did you go?"

Nowhere, I thought. There's nowhere but here. "How strong," I asked to avoid his question, and the desperation of my thoughts, "is the Empire?"

He coughed, then replied, "As mighty as a two-legged dog. From what I hear, Dara lost twenty thousand men and Aurangzeb twenty-five when they met." He shook his head sadly. "Forty-five thousand warriors dead and not a single Persian slain."

"Will they attack us?"

"Would jackals assail a fawn?"

I nodded slowly, strangely indifferent to what fate would befall the Empire. The weight of its woes was a burden I no longer wished to carry. "Father?"

"Yes, my child?"

"Did you ever tire of ruling? Tire of duty?"

He tried to rise to a sitting position, and I placed a cushion behind his back. His turban was loosening and I rewound the indigo silk about his head. "Not when your mother was alive," he replied as I gathered a blanket about him, for dampness dominated the room. "But after she left me for Paradise, I found the court dramas suddenly trite. At any rate, as you told me not long ago, she was always the real ruler. She'd have been a better emperor than I, as you would have."

I absently pulled a loose thread from my robe, watching the garment unravel. "Hardly."

"But why not?"

"Because a true leader, one placing her people above all else, would have killed Aurangzeb long ago."

"But you're no killer, Jahanara. Killing him might have saved the Empire, but it wouldn't have saved you."

I poured him some Chinese tea, which he had always liked. "What shall he do with us?"

"Nothing, I expect. I'll die here. But not before I help you escape. You'll be reunited with—"

"But I don't know where they are, or even if they live." My voice cracked at these words, and I felt the familiar sense of dread swelling in my bones. "And I can't live without them."

He motioned for me to kneel beside him, and so I did, feeling the warmth of his body. "They live, my child. And when you're free, you should take them far from here. Go to Varanasi. Go there and build yourself a new life."

"I'll never escape him."

Father coughed. He then smiled. "How, my child, can a soup bowl contain an ocean?"

"I don't feel like an ocean. I feel as if I'm slipping toward madness."

"Hush, child." Father stroked my brow, reassuring me with the strength of his touch. "We'll think of something, Jahanara. Allah's given us ample time to plan."

AND SO THE MONTHS wore by. Though my mood remained dark, I tried to be strong for Father's sake, just as he sought to raise my spirits. Thinking flowers might do him good, I asked a visiting noble if he could bring us seeds and a box of soil. He did better than promised, returning with porcelain vases and bulbs of irises and tulips. We planted these and watched as they eased upward into the sun.

Shortly thereafter came another gift. A mysterious messenger delivered a young peregrine falcon housed in a silver cage. At the bottom of the cage, amid fresh leaves, nestled a tiny piece of paper. On it was written, "Remember to practice your curses."

I laughed then, truly laughed for the first time since Dara's death. "Sweet Ladli," I whispered, tearing up the note. "How I do miss your tongue."

We named the falcon Akbar, after Father's grandfather, the first ruler to treat Hindus and Muslims as equals. I stitched a glove of leather so we could hold the bird. Akbar came to trust us and seemed to even understand our words.

The Red Fort was beset with mice, and our room was no exception. Akbar hunted these irritants with boundless relish. Our guards weren't cruel men and sometimes entered our cell and cheered Akbar as he pursued mice or an occasional rat. He soon outgrew the cage, which we smashed, dropping the broken pieces of silver to the poor, who gathered far below outside the Red Fort's monstrous wall. At night our feathered friend roosted on a rafter.

We marked the passage of time by the blooming of our flowers, the changing of season from wet to dry, and by the size of Akbar. More of Father's strength returned, and he took short walks about the room. Sometimes we stood before the window and stared at the Taj Mahal. We studied its many faces, for the mausoleum was as expressive as a child. At dawn it looked to have been dyed a pale blue. In the early afternoon it was whiter than ivory. The mausoleum thus gleamed until the sun fell, at which point the marble teardrop began to glow, appearing to be gilded at dusk's onset, and to bleed as the sun dropped from sight.

While wondrous, these sights were often painful, for the Taj Mahal evoked memories of our loved ones, and the longing that accompanied our separation was absolute. I often cried, dried my tears, and cried again. Father rarely wept, yet he fell into profound trances, almost as if meditating. He stood before the window and looked unblinking at Mother's tomb. Though flies might land on his face, or muezzins might call for prayer, he was transfixed.

One day, when we were particularly distraught over our imprisonment, we decided to set Akbar free. After all, how could we keep him confined when our confinement caused us such pain? And so, as Akbar perched atop his gloved hand, Father reached through the bars. Suddenly Akbar was outside. We said good-bye to him and Father shook his fist. Our falcon soared then, drifting over the river, circling higher and higher. He rose into the clouds, so elevated that we wondered if he carried a message to Mother.

Despite our attempt to say farewell, Akbar had found a home. The next morning I awoke with a smile, for he rested again on his rafter. I put on the glove, held up my hand, and he roosted contentedly, roosted until I could no longer support my arm. Later I called to the guards, asking if they might catch us a mouse. When they brought back a rat, the four of us watched Akbar kill swiftly.

I often thought of Ladli when Akbar impressed us with his feats. My friend had done so much for me through the years, and what had I given her? What had her gods given her? She'd borne no child and she traveled with a man she despised. What must it be like, accompanying him while he campaigned against the Deccans and Persians? How did she endure her life beyond Agra, existing for moon after moon in a drafty tent?

We heard many stories of the fighting, because it raged fiercely during our imprisonment. Sometimes we watched our armies voyage southward on barges, accompanied by sounding horns and chanting men. Months later, these same men returned, usually far fewer in number, and with no fanfare announcing their presence.

Visiting nobles told us of unrest in Agra. Even though Aurangzeb had last set foot in our city many months ago, his disruptive presence continued to be felt. We learned, for instance, that he had increased taxes to pay for his military campaigns. Not surprisingly, frequent demonstrations were staged against the fighting, for widows begged at every corner, and grain was taken from rich and poor alike to fatten thousands of war elephants. Despite the unpopular taxes, the treasury's coffers shrank to dangerous levels.

Furthermore, because Aurangzeb had always derided the arts and now suppressed them with his policies, many courtiers and artists left Agra for more receptive environs. While my sibling was untroubled by these departures, nobles grumbled. Agra's intellectual aura—which Father and Dara had so diligently fostered, and which had given our city fame— soon dwindled to nothing.

I must confess that as the months, then years, passed, fewer of my thoughts were spent on the Empire's mounting ailments. Instead, I obsessed over my loved ones, wondering incessantly what kind of woman Arjumand was becoming. I never thought of her as dead, for I couldn't have survived such images. I barely survived being unable to see her mature. There were so many questions we might ask each other, so many conversations that might rise between us.

And Isa.

How I longed for Isa. It seemed a lifetime ago that he held my face. Though I tried to relive our conversations, each and every one, it became difficult for me to recall the exact tenor of his voice, and this failing kept me awake many a night. I didn't even possess a painting of him, and I began to fear that I'd forget the sharpness of his jaw, or the warmth of his crooked smile. These were some of my most terrifying thoughts.

I once heard of a man who, when deprived of opium after years of use, drowned himself rather than endure its absence. And in some capacities I was like this man, for my longing was so vast that I often doubted I could last another day. My failings as a mother and a lover haunted me. I never looked into a mirror, because I was ashamed of who I'd see.

Ultimately, my love saved me, for my love gave me strength. At night, when sleep was unwilling to rescue me, I gritted my teeth and devoured my fondest memories. In daylight, when I could no longer muster the will to pursue anything save thoughts of Isa, I imagined all that we'd do together, once we were reunited. I wrote him endless letters, which I whispered to myself, then destroyed. I even tried to craft him poems, though my hand lacked the grace of my heart.

In the end, I was just strong enough to find solace in my loved ones, the future and God. After all, I prayed to Him constantly during my imprisonment. And finally, in the middle of my fifth hot season within the cell, my prayers were heeded. One afternoon a knock sounded against our door and, expecting a noble, I answered it unhurriedly. When our guard swung it wide and Nizam stood in its center, I blinked, certain my eyes betrayed me. But the visitor was he! Though patches of gray inhabited his beard, and a scar bisected his cheek, he looked as he had when I last saw him as a soldier. He was dressed in iron-studded leather armor with a long blade hanging at his side.

"Nizam!" I shouted, leaping toward him. Above us, Akbar shrieked, ill at ease with my hysteria.

"My lady," he replied fondly. "It's been too long."

I shut the door behind him, then pulled him by the hand into our room. "I thought you were dead!"

"Almost," he said, touching his cheek.

Again, forgetting any semblance of etiquette, I reached over and felt his face. The scar was young, and I cringed at how close he must have come to death. "Thank Allah, you live," I said.

"I shall indeed," Father added, bowing slightly. Nizam fidgeted at the bow, for emperors never yielded to servants.

"What happened?" I asked, drumming my fingers against my hips.

Nizam started to speak, then stilled. "At Dara's battlefield," he muttered, "I was knocked from my horse. They shackled me, and later made me fight."

"And then?"

He avoided my eyes. Nor did he look at Father. "These past years I've
been in the Deccan, warring for Alamgir." He paused, and I recognized
sadness in his movements. "I'm sorry, my lady, for I failed you. I tried to
escape . . . but . . . but they chained us each night and our guards were
many."

"You've yet to fail me, my friend! Not once! We could live a hundred
lifetimes together and still you wouldn't. But how did you escape?"

"A moon ago, my lady, we fought a terrible battle." Nizam spoke
slowly, so slowly that I wanted to set a coal beneath his bottom. "I killed
many that day, and when we were routed, I feigned death. I was covered
in blood, for I'd a scalp wound that . . ." Nizam paused, looking about
uncertainly, as if he spoke too much.

"Go on."

"Leave him in peace, Jahanara," Father chided.

Nizam fingered the hilt of his sword. "The Deccans left me for dead.
I waited two days before finding a horse and heading north."

"How goes the fighting? Is it—"

I interrupted Father with a dismissive wave. "What of Isa? Have you
heard of him?"

"There's a rumor, my lady."

"What?"

"When Dara fought Alamgir, and our people fled south, many were
captured by the Deccans." He scratched his scar absently, as if unaccustomed to its presence. "The rumor says that in Bijapur, the proudest of
Deccan cities, a mosque is being built by the same man who created the
Taj Mahal. They say he's chained, and that as long as he builds, his
daughter and he shall live."

"His daughter?"

"I think, my lady, that it's Isa, for I've seen the site from a distance,
and it reminds me of him."

My mind, dulled by years of captivity, raced ahead. "So they live!"

"I pray," Nizam replied, raising his massive hands. "I saw the mosque
a year ago, but not him. Some say he's . . . some believe he's dead."

Suddenly my cell felt like a tomb. I couldn't breathe. A tightness exploded within my chest and beads of sweat broke out upon my brow. "I must go. I must—"

"Escape," Father whispered. "Escape and be reunited."

FATHER SUGGESTED THAT we bribe our jailers. Though it might have been less risky to have Nizam and a few warriors return and kill them, over the years we had grown to like these men. Around Aurangzeb, of course, they treated us harshly, but in his absence they were decent.

As I was coming to learn, Father was a man of many secrets. After recommending bribery as a course of action, he informed us about caches of weapons and gold throughout Agra. In case the Red Fort fell, as indeed it had, such resources would be invaluable to retake the throne. With rekindled passion Father told Nizam which of his strongholds held rupees and which contained other supplies we would need. Shortly thereafter, Father bribed our two evening guards, offering them enough coin to last a lifetime. They would let me out of the fort, then disappear forever with their families.

As dusk fell two days later, when all the arrangements had been made, I bade farewell to Father. I hated abandoning him and questioned the soundness of my judgment. Was I betraying my promise to my mother? Would anyone care for him once I was gone? I couldn't answer these questions, but knew that the last time this choice presented itself I had let my love and my child go without me. I couldn't bear to pass up this second chance. Furthermore, Father demanded that I take it. When he spoke about my escape his face glowed with animation. I knew that at least he was pleased to be plotting once again. These past few days had given him more strength and joy than he'd possessed since our imprisonment.

After hugging him and giving Akbar a piece of dried beef, I waited impatiently for the changing of the guard. When our conspirators finally arrived, I donned a nearly transparent robe and shirt, and covered myself in thick makeup and gaudy jewels. I splashed wine on my face and foul perfume on my body. It was common for courtesans to visit lords or soldiers in the fort. Now I only needed to convince the sentries at the main gates that I was a woman of the night.

Nizam came quickly. He was dressed as a lord—with an amber tunic, two necklaces of pearls, and a ruby-studded sword and scabbard. He had shaved his beard and wore only a mustache. At his arrival our guards unlocked my cell. Nizam paid them while I asked Father again if he might join me.

"I'm too weak," he insisted, as he had so many times already.

"Please."

"I'd endanger you. And my escape would only bring more chaos to the Empire, something it can ill afford." He silenced my protest with a raised hand. "Allah has granted me little time, my child. It's better to rest than run for that time. Besides, I like my view, and Akbar would miss me."

I looked into his bloodshot eyes, searching. "Thank you, Father, thank you for your love."

"It's eternal."

"As is mine." I kissed him, squeezing his weathered hands, my vision blurring as tears swelled between my lashes. "If Allah . . . should take you, please, please hold Mother for me." While he nodded I prayed that we Muslims were right, and that upon entering Paradise we would once again be in the company of friends and loved ones. Please let it be so, I thought.

"Before you leave, may I ask one thing?" he inquired. My grip on his hands tightened and he continued, "See to it that I lay out there." He nodded toward the Taj Mahal, "at her side."

"You shall," I answered, hugging him. "Good-bye, Father."

"Farewell, child. You are my reminder of all that is good in this world."

The guards bowed as I passed. Though I desperately yearned to run forth and find Isa and Arjumand, leaving Father was torture. How can one leave such a man, when one might never see him again? Suddenly I felt weak, as if my will would betray him, but my legs would not.

"Can you carry me?" I asked Nizam humbly.

He said nothing, but I was swiftly in his arms. As Nizam ushered me through a labyrinth of hallways and stairwells within the Red Fort, I flooded Allah with my prayers. I prayed that we found my loved ones and that we secretly returned to Agra to discover Father still alive. I couldn't conceive of him dying alone in that cold cell. Not when he had given me so much.

Prayer is for the strong and the weak, I reflected, but when my feet are next on the ground, I shall become one of the strong. I'll continue to pray, but my path will be of my choosing, and I'll never look back. Because until I again embrace Isa and Arjumand, I can't be complete.

When we approached sentries stationed at the citadel's main gate, I clenched my fists, and forced my thoughts to focus. I didn't think of Father, or even Isa, but the task before me. As the guards stepped closer, I pretended to swim in wine, and threw my arms about Nizam. I flirted with the gawking men, arching my back so that they might glimpse my breasts. In all regards, I became a courtesan—drunkenly tracing my lips with my tongue, stroking Nizam's face with my hands. He did his best to smile at my advances, but was a warrior, not an actor.

As one guard started to ask him something, I cleared my throat. "My younger sister," I slurred, "isn't far behind. Will you . . . won't you escort her through the gates? She's alone and but a child."

The men might as well have been dogs about to go on a hunt. Their eyes widened and all save one hurriedly left their posts. I muttered goodbye to him, smiling wickedly. Beyond the thick gates, among the mayhem of Agra's cobbled and darkening streets, our horses were tethered to an iron rail. I giggled as Nizam lifted me atop his mount. I draped my arms about his neck and he spurred the beast forward.

When far from the Red Fort, I stuffed my jewels into a pocket within Nizam's tunic. Normally, I'd have tossed the unshapely pearls to the poor, but I realized the pearls might be useful if we had cause to bribe someone. Though I reviled the thin robe adorning me, I could do little but pull myself against Nizam as we rode toward the river.

Nizam didn't speak but spurred his horse harder. On the way to the Yamuna, we passed the Taj Mahal. Five years had vanished since I had last seen it so close, and I felt a momentary urge to touch its precious walls. Yet there was no time for such indulgences. At any moment my absence could be discovered, though by now Father had arranged pillows under my blanket to resemble my body. With luck our ruse would remain undiscovered until long after the next change of guards.

We headed directly for a fishing boat beached beside a score of its brethren. Unlike them, it carried no nets and flopping carp, but several wooden chests. A warrior stood guard over the craft. Nizam gave him a coin and helped him push the boat into the water's embrace as I stepped within it. About us, fishermen paused in their chores, staring. I disliked so many eyes on us, for surely rumors would ensue. But we'd be far down the river by the time Aurangzeb's men traced our trail here.

Nizam leapt into the boat, followed by a fisherman. He must have owned the craft, for he scurried to the tiller and expertly guided us down the river. It was the dry season, and the Yamuna was low, moving lazily. Still, the shore drifted past as we headed south. I splashed water against my face, washing off the wine, perfume and makeup. As the night thickened, I wondered how our captain could safely steer us through such blackness. The lap of water against our hull and the pinpricks of light above made me think of that night so long ago, when Isa and I sat atop the barge as we returned from Delhi.

"Thank you, Nizam," I said softly, "for freeing me."

"Happily done, my lady." He moved toward me from the bow, sitting with his back against the mast. "You played your part well."

"Too well, you think?"

"I'm many things, my lady. But not a man who'd judge you."

I took a drink of sweetened lemon juice from a goatskin bag. "A slave, once. Then a builder. Then a warrior. What's next, my old friend?"

He shrugged his powerful shoulders. "I go with you." The wind freshened and, as I shivered, Nizam handed me a heavier garment. "We'll close our eyes," he said.

I changed quickly, pleased that he had brought me a simple desert tunic made to fit a boy. I also found a turban, which I wrapped tightly about my head. "Does this part suit me better?"

"Ask me after a few days on horseback." I offered him the juice, and he drank thirstily. "It won't be an easy journey," Nizam predicted. "We'll travel fast for many days, through deserts with no ends, across rivers and mountains."

"How long will it take?"

"Two weeks. Less if Allah smiles upon us. More, maybe never, if we come across the Deccans or Alamgir's forces."

"I'll not slow you, Nizam."

His eyes settled on mine. "You never have."

After so many nights within my cell, the vastness of this night overwhelmed me. I saw an infinite space above, and the river seemed eternal. Is this why Akbar returned to us every night? Did he feel so very small? And are we fools to think Allah might actually care for our struggles?

Though I believed Allah heard my prayers, upon this night I felt so insignificant that I found it hard to imagine that my life would matter to Him. Surely I was like a grain of sand to a sea. I might tumble against those around me, but currents, tides and time would cast me about until I was light enough for the wind to carry away.

"Nizam?"

"Yes, my lady?"

"Might you sing, as you did so long ago?"

He had a magnificent voice, and it surged and ebbed as we drifted. His words soothed me, and in truth, I needed soothing. I was afraid of this night, afraid of where the wind might carry me. I couldn't live without Isa and Arjumand. Already I'd lost my brothers, my mother, and soon I would lose my father. I was gaining strength with age, I knew that much, but how strong could I be when no color remained in the world?

I hummed with Nizam. Our voices blended—how good to dwell in those sounds. For a time I felt less alone, but then silence came, though it wasn't truly silence, as I could hear my own tortured thoughts.

"Please, Allah," I whispered. "Please let them live."

I looked for a sign that He had heard—a dropping star, a leopard's roar, perhaps. But no sign dawned. And I bit my nails until I bled.

CHAPTER XIX

Journeys

~·)

After arriving in Allahabad two days later, we purchased four stallions with Father's gold. They were fine Persian mounts, not large, but fleet of foot. What few supplies we possessed were packed behind our saddles. I hardly gave Allahabad a second glance, as I was preoccupied with thoughts of my loved ones. It seemed a dull place, with far fewer palaces and mosques than Agra.

We left Allahabad at dawn, following a beaten trail to the southwest. Nizam had changed into the clothing of a warrior and clearly looked the part. Strapped to his saddle were a musket, bow, quiver, shield, scimitar and two spears. His tunic and turban were light brown, so that he might blend into the landscape. I was clad similarly, though my only weapon was a dagger. The spare horses, also the color of sand, were tied to ours. Nizam said prudence required bringing extra mounts on such a journey. We could never hope to outfight any bandits we might stumble upon, but could outrun most.

Allahabad disappeared behind us. At the city's periphery, we encountered colossal fields of rice. Hundreds, if not thousands, of frogs lived within the fields, and as we trotted west the moans of these creatures obscured all other sounds. Much life stemmed from the paddies, for butterflies, grasshoppers and mosquitoes drifted above the verdant, ankle-high rice stalks. Amid the tidy rows, farmers had placed stuffed falcons atop bamboo poles. Such falcons, I had heard, kept troublesome crows and rats at bay. So did the slingshots I knew the half-dozen farmers in the fields brandished. The bare-chested men patrolled their crops vigilantly.

Not far from the paddies and the Yamuna that fed them, the land changed drastically. It became a flat realm, bereft of tall trees or whispering

brooks. Patches of tough grass and sickly-looking bushes led to the horizon. The trail, ample enough for us to ride abreast of each other, cut like
a scar into the barren earth. Dust rising from our horses' hooves painted
us brown.

We rode determinedly and the sun rose. No breeze drifted here, only
the air's kiss as our horses trotted. In Agra, with the coolness of the river
and the rich gardens, the hot season was endurable. Here it seemed overpowering. Even my light tunic felt thick and became heavier as sweat
trickled, then ran down my skin. The sensation was unfamiliar, sticky
and tiring.

My turban shielded my face from the furious sun but felt unwieldy. I
asked Nizam if I could remove it, but he made me promise not to do so.
I made many such vows. For instance, I wanted to splash water against
my skin, but we carried barely enough for the horses and ourselves.

So this is the life of a soldier, I thought, to march through deserts and
die in strange places.

We passed few travelers that morning. We did encounter a camel-
driven convoy of merchants and their wagons, as well as a group of pilgrims on their way to Mecca. We wished them well, for it is every
Muslim's duty to visit the holy shrine once in his life. The pilgrimage
represents that religion is a journey, and also unites travelers by their
mutual suffering. Most Muslims trek to Mecca, yet those in power—
including Father, alas—often can never set time aside for the long trip.

When it became too scorching to continue, we left the trail, traveled
southerly, and stopped near some boulders. No shade dwelt here, so
Nizam took his two spears and stuck them in the ground. He tied a sheet
of silk to the spears and the rocks. We stripped as far as decency permitted and rested on a thin carpet under the silk canopy. Nizam, however,
never truly relaxed. He kept his long musket near him and constantly
scanned the horizon.

"Is it always so hot?" I asked, oiling his sword as he had earlier shown me.

He glanced about us. "No, my lady. When the rains come, they fall
very hard." He had stripped to the waist and the muscles of his torso rippled as he moved. I noticed that he had fashioned the brooch I gave him

into a necklace. Mother's face hung upon his chest. "You can drown in those rains," he added.

Wiping sweat and grime from my brow, I tried to imagine him as a young boy in the harem. The day I had first seen him, Mother was attending to wounds on his feet, where shackles once bound him. "How was it, Nizam, serving my mother?"

He began to clean his gun, breaking it apart and wiping traces of dust and sand from its workings. "At first, I thought she was like all the others," he replied. "But soon I saw she was different."

"How so?"

"She was kind." His hands slowed on the musket. He stopped cleaning it, his forefinger absently scratching at a gouge on the barrel. "She wanted me to be happy."

"Do you miss her?"

He nodded and reassembled his musket. "Do you know, my lady, what we called you?"

Confused, I stopped working on his sword. "Called me?"

"So many questions you ask," he said fondly. "Even as a young girl. And so the servants nicknamed you Little Squirrel, for such animals are always chattering to each other."

"I was a rodent?"

Nizam chuckled. "It seems so."

"Couldn't you have called me something else? After all, tigers constantly growl at each other."

"You were always Little Squirrel, my lady. It suited you well."

I feigned displeasure with him, though he knew I jested. As he grinned, I recalled my childhood. Yes, I probably had acted like a rodent, but I was a child who forever sought to please her parents. And to do so, I had to be as interested in their worlds as they were in mine. "But, Nizam, do you miss her?"

"Much. Though I see her in you."

"Her or a squirrel?"

"Both, I think."

I grunted, then lay on my back. He checked the readiness of his bow, plucking its cord as if it were a sitar. Next he inspected his sword to ensure that I'd oiled it properly. "Nizam, would you answer a personal question?"

"Perhaps."

"Have you ever loved a woman?" I asked, voicing what I had wondered for so many years.

As I might have expected, he didn't respond immediately. Instead, he removed his sandals and sat beside me on the carpet. I knew he had brought this small luxury only for me and that he would sleep on the ground. "It's not easy, my lady, for a man such as myself to love."

At first, perhaps because he seemed so much a man to me, I misunderstood him. Then, sadly, I realized that he spoke of his maiming. I bit my lip at the thought. What could it be like for him, to know that he would never make love, nor be a father? "I don't pretend to comprehend how difficult it must be for you," I said. "But isn't there a woman who's stolen your heart?"

"There's such a woman."

I bolted upright, thrilled to have heard so. "But who? Who is she and how can I help?"

He smiled at my reaction. "I won't tell you, for surely you'll enjoy discovering her name."

"Why, Nizam, how you toy with me! Just whisper her—"

He moved away from me and stretched out on a cotton blanket. "Rest, my lady. It will be a long night."

I lay against the carpet, my mind spinning. I was wonderfully excited for him and hoped that I could somehow bring them together. As Father had helped me with Isa, I'd help Nizam with . . .

When I couldn't guess the object of his endearment, I finally tried to sleep. Fitful dreams of Arjumand entertained me, and when I awoke, Nizam was boiling rice while the sun painted the horizon with its receding brushstrokes. We soon ate his rice, along with some dried fish. Then we broke camp and were again on our horses.

In the darkness I found it hard to discern the trail and hence dropped behind my friend, letting my horse follow his. The night was neither cool, nor hot. I could see why Nizam wanted to travel at such a time, for the blackness felt soothing and secretive. The trail was strangely comforting, and I felt more at ease here than I had on the boat. Perhaps my lack of disquiet was because I believed I drew nearer to Isa and Arjumand. Though unable to sense them, I was calmed by a growing conviction that they lived. Nizam thought they did and had repeatedly reinforced this notion the previous day. Each time I had asked him of them, he replied that I'd meet them soon enough.

A half-moon hung above us and we traveled under its stare. At one point we saw a group of burning torches approach from the south, and Nizam quickly led us off the trail. He pulled our mounts to the ground and we spied the distant silhouettes of twenty men on warhorses pass. Nizam didn't know if they were Aurangzeb's men or the Deccans. Neither group, however, was one we wanted to encounter.

After their torches had vanished we were again on the trail. We moved at a steady pace, pausing only twice during the night to change horses. I thought we'd sleep once the sun rose, but Nizam said not a word and continued onward. My thighs had long ago been chafed raw by the saddle and my buttocks were equally aflame. Yet I asked for no pause, though I desired a reprieve desperately, as each step of my mount sent a spasm of pain whipping through me. I tried to reposition myself on the saddle but found that every adjustment only served to assault another portion of flesh.

The merciless sun had almost reached its zenith when Nizam finally left the trail, heading for a trio of dead palm trees to the east. When we reached them he stepped off his horse and I stumbled from mine. My body throbbed and I shuffled toward the trees, where he tied our sheet. He attached it low on the trunks, perhaps making it harder to spot from the distant trail. I cared little for what he did or why he did it. I was too tired and scorched to think, and could only stare dumbly as he cut bushes with my dagger and piled them between the trail and us. After tethering the horses, he collapsed beside me. I said quick prayers for Isa, Arjumand and Father, then let sleep bear me away.

For the next ten days we traveled in such a manner—sleeping all afternoon and riding all night and morning. We talked infrequently. Nizam felt exposed on that trail and wanted to get into the southern mountains as quickly as possible. His fears were well-founded, for on five more occasions we came across war bands. Though they never carried torches, as they had that first night, Nizam always heard them approaching and led us off the trail before they passed.

We also skirted villages of mud-brick homes and decrepit inns, settlements that served as way stations for traders, nomads, scouts and bandits. Several dozen tethered camels usually surrounded the weather-beaten outposts, as did flocks of desert birds, which plucked ticks from the beasts' coarse hides. Just beyond the settlements, villagers inevitably labored in dust-choked fields—driving thin oxen, reaping stunted crops. While men tilled soil, women cooked, worked looms and collected camel dung. Much dung was needed, for each village had a stone tower where dung was burned at night to beckon lost and distant travelers.

One morning we discovered the legacy of a battle. Strewn across the blood-soaked plains were hundreds of rotting corpses. The day was windless, and the stench of the dead was so thick that I thought it might rise up and knock me from my saddle. The decaying flesh reeked like the maggot-ridden, bloated carcass of a water buffalo. I couldn't help but gag.

Most of the warriors were Deccans, though some of our men dotted the landscape. It was an odd place for a battle, as no fort stood nearby. Nizam guessed that the two forces had simply stumbled into each other during the night. Most of the men died from swordplay, further indicating that they met by surprise.

The carnage sickened me as much as it did when Aurangzeb's army overran us. Birds of prey devoured the faces of men, while a smattering of Deccans, mostly old and young, stripped the corpses of anything valuable. They paid us little heed as we passed, for all were intent on looting friend and foe alike. They were a tired-looking people. Most went barefoot, and all were emaciated and clad in tattered clothes. Aurangzeb must be burning their food, I thought, with a surprising amount of guilt. Even if these people were our enemies, I didn't see why children and grandparents had to starve.

We left the reeking death in our wake. Images of the mutilated bodies lingered in my mind, however. "Do you believe, Nizam," I asked, spurring my horse until it trotted next to his, "that all the world is as violent as Hindustan?"

He kept his eyes on the trail, gazing for fresh hoofprints. "Impossible, my lady."

I turned about in my saddle, and watched birds circle the dead. I was weary of such sights. "I don't want to kill anyone to free Isa and Arjumand."

"I know. But we may have to."

"Have to what? Discover their whereabouts and liberate them with your blade?"

"I'll free them in the night. By the time they're missed we'll be—"

"They might have a dozen guards, Nizam. What would happen if you killed a handful and then you died? Or if you were wounded?" He started to speak, but I cut him off. "No, there's a better option, though also risky."

He swatted at an immense fly. "What do you propose?"

"It's simple. We'll go to the Sultan of Bijapur and tell him who we are."

"And he'll slash our throats!"

"No, no, he won't. For I'll give him something in exchange for their freedom."

"But we have nothing, my lady."

"We have," I corrected, "everything. For I can give him Aurangzeb, whom he must hate above all men."

Nizam hacked, then spat out the dust that seemed to breed in our throats. "You'd betray your brother?"

"He is only a brother in blood. In all else he's a foe. And I have never moved to hurt him. I could have killed him long ago, or watched him die."

"But you will in Bijapur?"

"I've no choice," I said, licking my cracked lips.

"Quiet," Nizam hissed, staring behind us. Beneath the birds rose a cloud of dust, drawing swiftly in our direction. "Switch horses!" he shouted, leaping off his saddle.

I struggled to climb the fresher of our steeds. Nizam grabbed our most precious supplies, then struck the backsides of the riderless stallions, so that they ran toward the approaching force. "What are you—"

"With luck they'll pursue the mounts," he snapped, leaping onto his stallion. "Now ride! Ride hard!"

I charged ahead, holding my reins desperately. In a few heartbeats we galloped with frightening speed. The wind snatched my turban, and my hair streamed behind me. My saddle beat against my buttocks with the clap of a deerskin drum. Someone fired a musket.

"Faster!" Nizam roared.

Though fearful of being thrown from the horse, I spurred him harder. He neighed, accelerating. I glanced around and, to my awe, saw Nizam draw his bow and twist in his saddle. He launched an arrow, which disappeared into the cloud of men and horses behind. The other riders fired more muskets, the air cracking with their discharges. Puffs of soil kicked up around us, but we weren't hit. The men must have been unable to reload their guns while charging, for they began to release arrows. Nizam shot another bolt, then realized that I'd turned toward him.

"Ride!" he screamed, and I looked ahead once more. The trail, seemingly always straight at a slower pace, twisted now, the landscape flying past until it was but a blur of brown. I shrieked at my mount to go faster, my heels relentless. He neighed again, redoubling his efforts. An arrow churned into the soil before me and I glanced behind in time to see a pursuer fall screaming from his mount. Nizam notched another arrow, and a second man fell. "They gain on us!" Nizam yelled, and he was right, for the trail was becoming rocky. If my horse was to stumble, we'd surely die.

But then, quite magically, my fear turned to instinct and my mind emptied of all thoughts except those that could save our lives. "The gold!" I shouted. "Throw them the gold!"

Nizam didn't hesitate. He dropped his bow and reached into his saddlebag, pulling out handfuls of gold coins. He threw the coins high, so that the sun sparkled off their faces. They tumbled into the dust behind us, hundreds of them. I thought Nizam might stop at one bag, but he quickly emptied the other. Soon enough gold rolled on the ground to last a hundred men a lifetime.

The warriors approached the coins and I prayed they would stop. Allah must have been bored that day, for upon coming to the glittering gold, they dismounted, shouting triumphantly. Most men dove into the dirt and dug like mongooses, while some drew their blades and attacked each other.

"Don't slow!" Nizam yelled.

I maintained our pace, and soon the men were gone. We galloped long thereafter, until at last I began to fear for our horses. The heat was blistering, and white froth dropped from my mount's mouth. I gradually reined him in, only then realizing how my heart throbbed. Nizam slowed beside me. He dripped sweat and was covered in dust.

"Have we lost them?" I asked breathlessly.

"Perhaps. But we'd best keep moving." He let his horse trot down the trail, though he often twisted about in his saddle to look behind. "That was a fine idea, my lady."

Shielding my eyes from the relentless sun, I replied, "It was odd, Nizam. Suddenly everything became clear to me. I was fearful, yet my mind remained sharp."

"In battle, some men have such clarity. They see things that the rest of us don't. They might not be the strongest, but by Allah, they can lead. Your brother, alas, is—"

"Such a man," I interjected. "But I'll betray him all the same."

"As you should. But how?"

I was tired from the chase and still formulating my plan. "Might we rest, Nizam?" I asked, looking ahead. On the horizon rose a range of mountains. I knew we were close to the Deccans' stronghold, for my companion had said this morning that we would cross a river and mountains, and that Bijapur wasn't far beyond the peaks.

Midday approached, and Nizam, I think, was also ready to sleep. He left the trail and proceeded down a dry streambed. We followed it for some time, then rode on a vast expanse of sandstone, passing the sun-bleached bones of a camel. Nizam circled back to the stream and, to my delight, found a sizable pool of water, a hollow place in the earth, shaded by bushes and an overhang of rock. We tethered our mounts and made camp.

Nizam gazed northward. "By now they've killed each other, or are drunk in the nearest settlement."

"Were they Deccans?"

He nodded as he unraveled his sweat-soaked turban. "Your brother's men are more disciplined. They wouldn't have chased us."

"Why not?"

"Because we might have lured them into a trap."

We replenished our waterbags before leading the horses to the pool. Nizam pulled them away before they drank too much. "If you'd like, my lady, you can bathe. I'll wash in a moment."

I was so spent that all I wanted was sleep. Yet the thought of that cool water against me was tempting. Once Nizam had tied up our sheet and lay down, I stripped quickly. Squatting on a rock, I rinsed my dirty clothes and draped them across a bush to dry. I then carefully stepped into the water, groaned, and sat on the streambed. I hadn't taken a bath in two weeks and used sand to rub the grime from my body. It gave me scant surprise to see that since my escape from the Red Fort I'd shed what little fat I carried. Yet I disliked how my skin was starting to age. It didn't appear as ripe as before and seemed looser on my bones. I had seen thirty-six years, after all, and I knew that a woman's beauty was considered a fleeting thing. Perhaps mine was already gone.

I scrubbed myself angrily, then put on my damp tunic. As I sat beside Nizam, his eyes fluttered open. "How was it?" he asked.

I shrugged, combing my hair with my fingers. "My mind was elsewhere." Nizam was polite enough not to ask its whereabouts, and so I said, "May I ask you a question? A rather childish question?"

"It depends—"

"Do you think . . ." I sighed, feeling foolish and quite young. Why could I be so sure of myself in battle, where I had no business being, but at times so unsure when it came to love? "Do you think I'm still attractive?" I asked weakly. Nizam seemed startled and before he could respond, my words spilled out. "It's been five years since I saw him. Perhaps he's found someone younger and prettier. Most men do. And why should he be any different, especially in my absence?"

"Most men are fools," Nizam replied, his face serious.

"But why? They get younger women, whose bodies haven't started to sag and whose—"

"Minds send them to sleep."

"But do men truly care about minds? My husband doesn't. And most nobles have mistresses half their age. These girls must give them something we can't. Perhaps their beauty makes men feel young. Or maybe they're jewels that men like to be seen with."

Nizam sat up, glancing around our camp's perimeter. "I don't know the thinking of other men. But I know myself. And I know Isa. He loves you and he'll never tire of you."

"But he loves beautiful things, Nizam. Think of the Taj Mahal, think of what he creates. Why would such a man care for old things, when he can have something new?"

"You aren't a thing," he replied. "And perhaps that's the difference between us and other men. For most think of women as things, while we think of you as . . ." He paused, embarrassed. "I'm not a man of many words, my lady, nor am I a poet. But it seems to me that we think of you as . . . as white elephants. We search a lifetime for you, and when we finally find you, we'll not toss you away."

In all the years I had known Nizam, I'd never heard him speak so. Was he becoming more secure with himself, or was I finally treating him as an equal? Hoping it was the former, I reached out to take his hand, thinking that my feelings, no, my love for him, would be no more complete if he were my brother. "Thank you, my old friend," I said. "I'm undeserving of you. Truly." Nizam shook his head, though I paid the gesture little heed. "Who," I asked, "my warrior-poet, is your white elephant?"

He laughed, which was rare indeed for Nizam. "She's purple perhaps. For surely no such other woman exists."

I saw her then, and I clapped my hands. "Ladli!" I exclaimed. "It's Ladli you love!"

He froze. "But how . . . how do you know?"

"How was I so blind as to have not seen it sooner?" I bit my lip as my mind trod in memories. It had been ages since I saw them together, but when we were younger, and she was smitten with Dara, how many times had I noticed him staring at her? "How long have you loved her?" I asked excitedly.

"I'd better prepare lunch."

I swatted him on the arm. "How long?"

"Too long," he muttered, looking away.

"Does she know?"

"Why would she care?" he replied, with a trace of bitterness. "I'm a man beneath her and always will be." He rose and began to gather firewood.

"Rubbish! Total and complete rubbish!"

"We should eat, then rest, my lady."

I ignored his words, for I was already scheming about how I could steal Ladli from Aurangzeb and reintroduce her to Nizam. I knew what my friend thought of men, but hoped that she might see Nizam as I did, as one who would love her unconditionally. Surely I might bring them together, the way Father brought Isa to me so long ago!

"Oh, Ladli," I whispered mischievously, just loud enough for Nizam to hear, "how very happy you shall be."

CHAPTER XX

Shivaji

We slept all afternoon and through the night, leaving just before dawn. Nizam said the mountains were cooler and thus traveling in darkness was unnecessary. In fact, the path would soon grow treacherous, and even our sure-footed horses would need light. And so in plain view we crossed the river, then eased into the foothills. Peaks towered majestically above us, and I found myself often gazing toward Paradise. The mountains made me think of green waves. They rose from the earth, shrouded in mist, to lap at the underbellies of clouds.

I couldn't fathom why, but as we neared the range, the arid land of Hindustan grew fertile. A sweetness permeated the sky, as if it yielded water. Where once only bushes bordered the trail, now there rose lush trees. I had never seen so much foliage. Certainly, I'd heard of jungles where rain fell each day, but to study a true forest was mesmerizing. More shades of green flourished here, it seemed, than all other colors combined. Monkeys hung from moss-covered limbs and red parrots mingled within leaves the size of shields. Sometimes the birds took flight together, and the sky turned scarlet as thousands of the creatures sought new perches.

For three days we journeyed through the mountains on a narrow and rocky trail. Nizam was quite nervous, for the trees were so thick that a score of enemies might surprise us at any moment. My companion kept his sword resting on his lap. He also showed me how to fire the musket and tied it to my saddle so I'd have it nearby. The gun was long and heavy, but I thought I could aim it straight if needed.

Several times we passed small groups of Deccans, who were always on foot and never paused to give us trouble. Occasionally we saw women picking berries and men hunting wild boar with spears. I gave some dried fish to a girl in exchange for a pouch of cherries. Thus we ate fruit for the first time in weeks.

As we neared Bijapur, signs of war increased. Soon many forts straddled the mountains. These structures were made of stone blocks and were hardly more than walls set on each side of a ridge, often flanked by towers. Warriors stood behind the fortifications, silently watching all below.

We also came across Deccan war bands. Such parties were unavoidable and ranged from hundreds of foot soldiers to scatterings of horsemen. The Deccans, surprisingly, caused us no woe. Sometimes they asked where we hailed from, and our lies rose smoothly. We looked and spoke in their manner and hence were believed. The warriors appeared worn, and, in fact, many were wounded and all held their weapons uneasily. At one point, Nizam was bold enough to ask of Alamgir's raiders. He was told that they rode through the valley only a week ago. They sought to capture the high forts but were beaten back at a terrible cost. Some believed they'd retreated northward to their cities, whereas others swore they were raiding farther to the south. Nizam and I digested this news with churned emotions. While we were saddened to hear of the battles, at least Aurangzeb's forces appeared to be far from Bijapur.

It took us another day to reach the Deccan stronghold. Bijapur was a city like any other, with cobbled streets, bazaars and palaces. Yet Bijapur was a city at war. There was ample evidence of recent fighting: scorched homes and crops, toppled fortifications, rows of ravaged bodies awaiting burial or cremation. At the center of Bijapur stood its fort—a stout, circular edifice of stone and mortar. Cannons topped its palisades, which were inundated by helmeted warriors. Scores of rooftops rose from behind the fort's towering walls.

We tethered our horses at a nearby stable and walked toward the fort. It was built into a hill of rocky snags, and men watched us from above as we climbed. At a ramp leading to the main gate, guards didn't question us as we passed but scrutinized our movements. They were dressed in full armor and held long spears. Along the wall above the gate stood a dozen more men, their muskets pointed downward.

"Is this wise?" Nizam whispered after we were beyond the gate.

Now that we were so close to Isa and Arjumand, I refused to waste time fabricating a different strategy. Not when they drew nearer with each passing moment. Not when I wanted to kick off my sandals and run to them, throw my arms about them and never let go. Therefore, though harboring doubts, I tried to appear confident. "It shall work."

"It must."

My plan depended on reaching the Sultan without incident. I expected him to be on his throne, with his advisors gathered close. The problem, however, was that numerous buildings surrounded us. Most had spires and looked little different from their neighbors. The Sultan could be in any one of them.

A soldier stepped from a doorway and I walked toward him. Initially he frowned at my approach, but when I smiled and bowed slightly, his scowl vanished. "Excuse me, sir," I asked, "but where might I call upon the Sultan?"

He thrust a handless arm toward a structure with its own balcony. "But he'll see no woman. He's entertaining Shivaji." The warrior grunted, then moved away.

It took me a moment to follow his words. On several occasions Father had spoken of Shivaji, the military leader of the Hindu Marathas, another sworn enemy of the Empire. The Marathas hailed from the mountainous region surrounding Bijapur. Drawn from the lowest caste of Hindus, they had become a fierce military force under the command of Shivaji, a charismatic young man.

Suspecting that Shivaji and the Sultan of Bijapur were now allies, I headed directly for the spired building. Surprisingly, only two guards manned its entrance. They started to bar our entrance, but I produced the misshapen pearls, depositing them in rough hands. Without further pause we were allowed inside, where coolness prevailed. The marble floors and tapestry-covered walls radiated comfort. Scattered about were men dressed in fine tunics—a sight which rendered me self-conscious in my tattered and dust-stained garments. Servants clad in white linen served fresh fruit, goat cheese and venison. My mouth watered at the smell of roasted stag, but I resisted giving the trays a third glance. Instead, I walked up granite steps that I supposed led to the balcony, where I hoped to find the Sultan and Shivaji. Lining the curved stairway were several warriors. These men asked nothing of our business but their hands never strayed from the hilts of their swords.

The next floor bore an elaborate bedroom. Its style was the same as ours, replete with carpets, blankets and thick cushions. Down the corridor, beyond the bedroom, was a balcony which contained potted plants, tables, and a raised dais that supported two men. Other figures, including nobles and warriors, mingled below. No women were present.

"We can still free them with my blade," Nizam whispered as we approached the balcony. "The Deccans are treacherous."

I slowed, thinking that perhaps he was right. Would Mother have marched, defenseless, straight into the lair of an enemy? Undoubtedly, she'd have concocted a better plan. Yet here I was, wholly unprepared for what could happen, proceeding against the wishes of a friend who knew the enemy well.

My knees trembling, I started to turn around. But a man on the balcony spied us, saw the fear in my eyes, and motioned that we come closer. I hesitated, and he gestured again. I tried to read his face, to see if he could be friend or foe. He was an old man, however, wise enough to give no such indications. As I stepped onto the balcony, a hush fell over those assembled. Heads turned in my direction, and I again wished I wore more suitable clothes. Mercifully, Nizam was right behind me, and I sensed that these men, many of whom were warriors, regarded him the way leopards might watch a tiger.

The two men on the dais gazed at us curiously. One was a barrel-chested warrior with a face seemingly chiseled from stone. He dressed in studded leather armor and a curved blade hung at his side. The other man was much smaller, almost feminine, in fact. He wore a russet shirt and leggings. On his back hung a longbow. His face was delicate, and a strange, upturned hat perched on his brow. The larger of the men hacked, spitting off the balcony. He appeared to have eyes only for me. "The servants' quarters are outside," he said harshly. "If you beg a position, clean yourself and go."

I bowed to him slightly, guessing that he was the Sultan, since he would employ the servants. "I'm not a servant, my lord," I said, bowing again.

Conversation wavered about us. "Do I care if you're a slave or a whore?" the Sultan retorted. "Leave!" He started to turn, but I stood still. When he realized that I hadn't moved, his jaw dropped in outrage. "If you're a whore, you'd better bathe and rid yourself of that ridiculous tunic! Return later and I'll inspect your wares."

Men chuckled, though I noticed that the figure I presumed to be Shivaji studied me intently. "I've come a long way, my lord," I replied, hoping my voice didn't quail too much. "All the way from Agra."

At these words the Sultan frowned. Nobles muttered among themselves and warriors glanced beyond the mountains to the north. "Do Mughal whores travel so far?"

"No," I said, growing angry with this fool. "But Mughal princesses do."

"The only such whore is in prison with her bastard father. There they fornicate and breed new bastards."

At this insult Nizam drew his blade, stepping in front of me. "No!" I shouted, grabbing his sword arm. "I said, no!" I watched fearfully as other swords leapt forth. Warriors growled yet did not attack. If we further insulted the Sultan, or if he commanded them to kill us, we'd die quickly. Nizam might be a tiger, but even he couldn't fight twenty men. "Forgive us, my lord," I beseeched him, guiding Nizam's blade back into its scabbard. "But we're tired and our manners aren't what they should be."

"Are you truly Princess Jahanara?" the diminutive man asked, his voice belying his stature.

"Yes, Shivaji."

If surprised that I knew his name, he didn't show it. "But why come to this den?"

"Can we speak alone?" I queried, impatient with these proceedings and desperate to see Isa and Arjumand. "My words aren't for everyone."

The two leaders conferred for a moment, whispering. "If your dog leaves as well," the Sultan said.

"Nizam shall stay," I countered evenly, "but will give his weapons to your men."

The Sultan grunted, motioning for Nizam to set his sword and dagger on the ground. A one-eyed warrior picked up his weapons, then the balcony emptied save us four. The Sultan and Shivaji stepped down from the dais and we stood face-to-face.

"Why foul my land with your presence?" the Sultan asked. "And why shouldn't I have you strung from the nearest tree?"

"We come in peace."

"Fools seek peace."

"Fools?" I repeated, giving myself time to decipher this man, praying that some sense lived within him. "Did you know, my lord, that my brother, Alamgir, tried to kill me? And that he murdered our brothers?"

Shivaji nodded. "We have heard rumors."

"Have you heard that my oldest brother, Dara, died because he supported our Hindus and was against the war here?"

"The weak always die," the Sultan spat.

An image of Dara's execution flashed before me and I washed it away. "Alamgir's as weak as granite," I said. "And you can't fight him forever."

"Perhaps we can," Shivaji remarked, for he commanded a formidable force, as did the Sultan.

"Perhaps." I took a slow breath, aware that this moment was my only chance. "But say he was assassinated. Wouldn't you prefer that to spending precious gold and the lives of your men in this endless war? I could give you that ending, and with his death you'd finally be free."

"We've already tried to assassinate him," Shivaji countered. "A dozen times by a dozen methods. It's impossible."

"Not if you knew what I do. Then it would be easy."

"Easy!" the Sultan exclaimed. "You think we're fools?"

Shivaji silenced him with a disgusted wave. "Better to hear her out, Ahmed."

The Sultan opened his rotting mouth, but I said hurriedly, "There's a secret passageway into the Red Fort—"

"She lies—"

"—leading directly to the royal chambers. An assassin could enter it and kill Alamgir. No one would ever know who did it, or how they did it."

"You'd believe her?" the Sultan asked incredulously. "The whore sister of our enemy?"

"Better a whore sister than a halfwit," I stammered, no longer able to restrain myself. I was drained from my journey, both physically and mentally. And now that I stood in the same city as Isa and Arjumand, I could hardly breathe. "I come, bearing the greatest gift your worthless kingdom has ever been offered, and all you can do is insult me! Do you think I'd betray Alamgir unless I wanted something in return? Something only you can give!"

Shivaji laughed at this outburst—a deep belching of his lungs that surprised us all. "And what would that be?"

"For him to free my man and my daughter, who were captured five years ago, and now, as his slaves, build a mosque somewhere in this putrid city. Give me them, and I'll give you Alamgir!"

Continuing to chuckle, Shivaji looked at the Sultan. "It seems, Ahmed, that she's got more tongue than you're accustomed to."

"She needs a good whipping."

"Nonsense, man," Shivaji advised. "A bath and new clothes, yes, but a whipping, most definitely not. I suspect she'd throttle you someday with that same whip."

The Sultan ignored his words, looking directly at me. When he spoke next his voice was rough, but less threatening. "The man you speak of lives, as does the girl."

My knees weakened at the news, and Nizam reached out to steady me. "Thank you, thank you, Allah," I whispered.

"You should thank me," the Sultan declared.

I tried to compose myself, though I was consumed with such joy that I didn't know what to say. I wanted to run to them, run as I never had before. "I am sorry, my lord, for my . . . earlier words. And I do thank you. Thank you so very much."

"I don't despise this man," he said, somewhat reluctantly, "for he's honorable and does what I ask. And his skills are God-given."

"Will you free him, my lord, if I tell you of the passageway?"

"Perhaps."

"The war might end if Alamgir died," Shivaji interjected.

The Sultan glared at his smaller companion, who seemed completely unintimidated. "He could go free," the Sultan said, "once my mosque is complete. But it is to be the finest mosque in all the Deccan and I'll not part with him, by Allah, until the last stone's set in place."

"But how long, my lord, might that be?" I asked fearfully.

"A short time. Five years. Maybe three."

"Five years? I can't—"

"Would you rather," he interrupted, "I sold him to the highest bidder? For he's a slave and the fate of slaves is such."

"Then I shall stay with them."

Shivaji stepped forward. "Impossible. Too many of us saw you and heard who you are. If you stayed, you'd be in grave danger, as would your man and child."

"But what am I to do?"

"My friend," Shivaji said, "isn't as unreasonable as he seems. But I fear his mind is set. I've seen this mosque and know what it means to him. It means almost as much to his people, who've lost so many in the fighting. Everyone wants to see it finished." Shivaji looked at me carefully, as if judging my mettle. "Why not give them a few days, Ahmed? Send them somewhere quiet, under guard, and when they return she'll leave for . . ." he paused, shrugging, "for wherever the gods might take her."

"What of my daughter?"

"She stays," the Sultan replied. "She knows more of building than anyone but her father."

How confused I was then. A part of me rejoiced at finding them alive and bartering for their freedom, whereas another part lamented our inevitable separation. How could I endure another five years in their absence? "What do you think?" I asked Nizam, knowing that he had missed nothing.

"I think that time is fleeting. Far better to have them in a few years than not at all."

"Would you, my old friend, be so patient?"

"I have, my lady. I always have."

I thanked him before turning to the Sultan and Shivaji. "I'll tell you of the passageway," I said, "but its end shall remain locked until my loved ones return. And its entrance will remain hidden as well."

"But you promised me his head!" the Sultan exclaimed.

"And you'll have it. But if I am to wait, then so will you. Or else give them to me now."

Again Shivaji laughed. "A fair demand, Ahmed."

"The mosque must be finished! It's the only decent thing to come from this war."

"The fighting might stop if—"

"They'll stay!"

"And so will your war," I said, wondering if Nizam had been right all along. Perhaps we should have simply killed their guards and escaped with Isa and Arjumand. Then I wouldn't be here, wasting words with a stubborn fool, wasting moments with my loved ones so nearby. "The passageway," I said, "begins at a house near an old cypress tree. But you won't know which house until my loved ones return. When they do, I'll mark the house for you by arranging for a black stallion to be tethered to the tree." I proceeded to tell the Sultan how an assassin might enter the passageway, and how he would need help to circumvent the ruined trap. The Sultan's questions were offered eagerly and my responses driven by desire.

"Two days," the Sultan said. "Spend two days with them. Then you'll leave. And when they're finished, they'll be sent to you. And when your brother's gutted, consider our truce a thing of the past."

"So be it."

The Sultan walked away. Though I had feared him a moment ago, I knew he wouldn't harm me, or Isa or Arjumand. He had too little to gain and too much to lose by doing so.

Shivaji chuckled, shaking his head. "Are all Mughal women such as you?"

"If Allah had wanted me useless he wouldn't have given me a brain."

"I'm glad we fight your men. A battle with such women would surely break us."

"I'm only obstinate because I have to be," I said. "Do you think I want to deal with imps like him? That it gives me joy?" I shook my head, thinking that joy was something I found with those I loved. "Aren't many of your gods female? I've heard of Parvati, Saraswati and Lakshmi. How can one believe so profoundly in these wonderful goddesses, but be surprised when a woman speaks her mind?"

Shivaji listened carefully. "It would please me," he finally said, "to one day see you again. Perhaps when this foolishness is over."

"You'll always be welcome in Agra. Come and let us show you the Taj Mahal—a sight that will never leave you."

"Perhaps in my next life."

"Please let it be this one."

He bowed to me and then, quite surprisingly, bowed to Nizam. "Let's find your loved ones," he said. "I'd like nothing more than to see you reunited."

At these words I smiled. I had found a friend among enemies, and I was again to touch Isa.

CHAPTER XXI

Rebirth

⟶∴

I had to force myself not to run as Nizam and I followed Shivaji through Bijapur's narrow streets. I cared nothing for the city's sights, only for the tempest of my feelings. After five dreadful years of separation from my loved ones, my emotions, so long repressed, were overwhelming. My heart quickened with each step. My feet seemed to barely touch ground. I could have sprouted wings and flown to them, as Akbar might, and still not have arrived fast enough!

"Where's this mosque?" I asked hungrily.

Shivaji chuckled. "I'm not taking you there, but to my quarters."

"But why?"

"So no one will see your reunion." When I started to protest he quickly added, "I'll bring them to you soon enough." The Hindu warlord turned down an alley, walking briskly toward a sandstone block of a house, which bore four stone lattice windows but little else. Its interior was rich with furnishings, however, and looked comfortable. "I'll return with them," Shivaji promised.

I had barely slept the past few nights but couldn't rest against a cushion alongside Nizam. "I wouldn't have made it here without you," I said, pacing.

"That's not true. But I'm glad I helped."

I clapped like a girl. Running to the nearest window, I peered outside. Dusk was approaching and soldiers traversed the streets. Women, seeming to far outnumber the city's men, returned from unseen bazaars carrying goods or pushing carts. Their clothes were tattered and I saw few jewels. "Will they never get here?" I asked, attacking my hair with an ivory comb I discovered on the windowsill.

"Patience, my lady, was never your gift."

"I've no time for patience!"

He laughed gently. "Perhaps when you're old."

"No, because I'll have less time left and just as much to do."

We shared a grin and I leaned down impulsively to kiss his forehead. My companion stiffened, and I wondered if he had ever felt a woman's lips. I hoped so. "Someday, Nizam, I shall repay you. I know I always say that, and I never do, but as Allah's my witness, I'll reward—"

"You have repaid me."

"No, not yet."

"You gave me the Taj Mahal, my lady. You let me advise the Emperor. I need nothing more."

I warmed at these words, for they were gifts. "Thank you, my friend."

"But it's I, my lady, who thanks you."

Outside came the pulse of a blacksmith's hammer. The blows were relentless, an unnerving sound of iron against iron. "Oh, Nizam, are their feet made of stone?"

"It might be far."

I was about to respond when someone knocked. Without hesitating, I yanked open the door. Shivaji quickly entered, followed, praise Allah, by Isa and Arjumand. When Isa saw me, he stopped in wonder. He tried to speak, but no sound escaped his lips.

"Mother?" Arjumand stuttered, equally surprised. "Is it truly you?"

I ran to them, throwing an arm around each and hugging them together. I kissed their faces from all angles, my tears unfettered. Isa yelped in glee and, leaning backward, lifted both his women off the ground. "I feared you were dead!" he cried in joyous disbelief.

"No, no, no! Only imprisoned!"

Isa finally dropped us, yet still we embraced. Everything felt so unreal. Here I was, reunited with Arjumand and Isa! Recent memories were suddenly insignificant; what mattered was that we were together. We had survived so much and seemed no worse for it.

"How I love you both!" I shouted, pulling them even closer.

Isa whooped again. He'd always been a merry man, and now it appeared that his bliss might overwhelm him. It was a contagious bliss, for Shivaji and Nizam laughed as we danced about, still clinging to each other.

"Let me look at you!" I finally stammered, pulling away. I put my hands on Isa's face and gazed at him ferociously. His hair and beard, once as black as my locks, were streaked with strands of silver. His face was as finely sculpted as ever, though wrinkles bordered his eyes and the corners of his mouth.

Arjumand truly mesmerized me, for when I saw her last she was but a girl. Now she stood as a young woman—taller than me, and with more striking features. She had lost the baby fat in her cheeks, and her face was sleek and narrow like Isa's. Her lips, however, had the fullness of mine. As did her eyes.

"So beautiful," I stammered. "My girl is so beautiful!"

She laughed, and I noticed that even her voice had changed, become more confident. "But how did you find us?" she asked, squeezing my hands.

"Later. For now I want to just look at you."

Isa could no longer restrain himself and picked me up again. The room twirled about us. "What a woman you are!"

"Indeed," Shivaji concurred, clearing his throat. "I'll have food and drink brought to you. May I ask that you stay within these walls?" After I thanked him, he bowed politely to Arjumand. "Good night, ladies." He started for the door, then paused. "Nizam, if you'd like to join me tonight, you may. I'll return in the morning."

"I'd be honored, my lord."

I bade good night to Nizam, and he smiled and shut the door. I was still too animated to sit, and so we spoke while standing. They listened intently as I told of all that had befallen me during the past five years. Arjumand and Isa hadn't known Dara well, but my mention of his death caused their smiles to vanish temporarily. Their grins reappeared when I spoke of my escape.

Isa, in turn, described their capture. Their fates would have been infinitely worse if Isa hadn't convinced his jailers that the Sultan would find his skills useful. At first, Arjumand was to be sold to the highest bidder, but Isa swore to build no mosque unless she was his apprentice. They had lived thus ever since, sharing a home always locked from the outside. The mosque, which Isa took little pride in, rose slowly because the Sultan gave him only old men and boys as workers. Great domes and courtyards were expected, but since Isa had limited supplies, the mosque was forever in disarray.

"It would be a sorrier thing," Isa said fondly, "if our daughter lacked a keen eye. I design the walls and ceilings, but she ensures that plans are followed. And better yet, she now comes to me with drawings of her own, bold creations that surprise us all."

"But when we make models of them, they always fall," Arjumand added sheepishly. She obviously basked in her father's attention, and I was pleased that they had become so close.

"Someday, Arjumand, perhaps you can design your father and me a house," I suggested.

"Certainly, though you'd pray whenever it stormed."

Isa winked at her and we laughed. How lucky I felt then to have found her thus. Many girls, it seemed, would be saddened by imprisonment. But Arjumand appeared almost happier than she had as a child. Perhaps because she was learning skills that no other girl would. Or perhaps she had simply blossomed in Isa's presence, as had I.

Whatever the cause, I offered a quick prayer of thanks to Allah, adding another when our food arrived. A pair of servants—each bearing a silver tray—brought us a feast of roasted duck, pickled vegetables and rice wine. We asked them to tell Shivaji of our appreciation, and then Isa locked the door. The duck was the first fresh meat I'd tasted in weeks and I forced myself to eat slowly. Isa didn't eat at all but sipped his wine and stared at me. I think he was still in shock at finding me here.

"You made the right choice, Jahanara," he said finally.

"To stay in Agra?"

"You were right to stay. I know that now."

I made no reply, and my silence caused Isa's face to wrinkle. He realized then that I held something back. "Perhaps," I said hesitantly. "But I couldn't save Dara and . . . and I'll have to leave you both again."

"What?" Arjumand exclaimed, setting down her goblet of wine.

I told them of my bargain with the Sultan and Isa groaned. "I had no other choice," I said. "He'd never just let you go, and I had to give him something."

"I don't care of your brother's fate, but of ours," Isa replied. "And it will take—"

"Build it faster," I interrupted. "Build it not to last ten centuries but one."

"But you can't leave."

"Surely you can hurry the process. The Sultan says it could take three years, but you could finish it in two."

"Why not stay here?"

"How many Deccans, Isa, would like to kill Alamgir's sister?"

A stillness ensued between us. I knew how painful these words must have been for them and regretted telling them the truth so soon. Perhaps I should have waited until our last day together. Perhaps—

Arjumand sat upright, scattering my thoughts. "We're forever waiting for marble, Father," she said determinedly, and my pride for her swelled. "We shouldn't throw away the marred pieces but should use them for ceilings and other places where the eye won't see their imperfections. And we could use more timber and less sandstone. We could—"

"Do much," Isa added, trying to smile. "And yes, we might finish in two years. But is there no other choice?"

I shook my head. "None better. Even if we escaped here, we'd never make it to Agra. He'd hunt us down and . . ." I paused before reaching out to grasp their hands. "We've lasted five years. Another two will pass and then we'll never be separated again."

"Promise?" Arjumand asked.

"I do, my child, I truly do."

Isa tugged at his beard, an old habit I'd forgotten about. "Then his beloved mosque shall be but a mirror, beautiful to behold, but easy to break."

"The Sultan knows nothing of architecture," Arjumand added. "It would be harder to fool a bullock."

We laughed, and despite our looming separation, our mood brightened.

Wanting to let the subject die, I said, "I think, Arjumand, that Shivaji took a liking to you."

"He did?"

Her perplexed look made me sigh, for while she might have been an expert on building, she obviously knew little of men. "We've much to talk about," I replied.

Isa refilled our goblets and we drank together. Our bellies were warmed by the wine; we ate more, laughed, and cared little how late it became. We conversed as only the closest of families might—listening carefully, offering praise or compassion when needed. As dawn readied to unravel the night, Arjumand kissed us good night and went upstairs to a second bedroom. Isa and I, having restrained ourselves so long, stood and held each other. It had been necessary that I act strong in front of Arjumand, but now, as he sheltered me, I no longer held back my tears. Nor did he.

"How I've missed you," I whispered. "It was almost . . . too much."

"The same for us."

"Is Arjumand well? Truly well?"

"She's fine, Swallow. The first year was terrible, of course. But even though I thought you were dead, I promised her that you lived. She made me repeat my promise each night. I promised and promised and promised. And, in time, she believed me. She grew happier, and I taught her how to build, watched her become a woman."

"And you? How did you manage?"

He stroked my cheek with a callused thumb. "I didn't," he said softly. "On the outside, perhaps. But if you ever see this mosque, you'll know that a part of me left when you did. For the mosque doesn't inspire. I couldn't see you when I built it, and thus its walls appear tired. There's no grace to them, no love."

"From our cell in the Red Fort," I replied, feeling his warmth, "I could eye the Taj Mahal. I stared at it until my legs trembled. I think Aurangzeb gave us that view so that we'd go mad. But he misjudged us. It gave Father more fulfillment than pain, and it made me smile, and sometimes laugh. Because it reminded me of all that was good in my life, of all that I had to be thankful for." Isa's lips touched mine. His was a gentle kiss, a kiss of rediscovery. He started toward me again, but I took a slight step back. "Have I grown old?"

"What?"

"Men seem . . . to tire of old things."

"We grow together, my Swallow. Not grow old, but simply grow."

"But my beauty shall not last."

"Your beauty? Beauty is a feeling, and feelings last forever."

"How so?"

Isa's dark eyes, so piercing, locked on mine. "There's a range of mountains, my love, far from here. Some of the leaves in the tallest of these mountains change with the seasons. It's an astounding evolution. They turn from green to gold to crimson, and I tell you that the leaves of fall are even more beautiful than those of spring." He leaned forward, kissing me again. "Your beauty, Jahanara, is like those leaves. It will only become richer."

"This is why I missed you," I whispered thickly, "for you see things when everyone else is blind."

He smiled, his hands working on my tunic, which fell to the floor. We didn't rush into our love as the young might but explored each other's bodies as if for the first time. And Isa was right—they were still things of beauty.

When at last we finished, we simply held each other. "You must show me these leaves," I said.

"We'll climb a mountain together," he promised. "But you should see them alone, my love, for only alone will you come to understand their true nature."

THE NEXT MORNING ensued with a surprise.

"There are four horses," Shivaji pronounced cheerfully as Arjumand and I finished the remnants of a late breakfast, while Isa and Nizam spoke upstairs. "Split into pairs and ride separately from town," he continued, "then come together and head directly west. Goa is on the coast. It's full of Jesuits but not without charm. Still, you'll wish to ride north when you near Goa. Beyond the city, bungalows sit near the sea and you can rent these for a pittance."

"The sea?" I asked.

"It's just a two-day ride," he replied, handing me some coins.

"But the Sultan said I was to only have a few days here."

The little Hindu shrugged. "Ahmed isn't always a good man, but neither is he as bad as he seems. I asked him to give you a week together, and he said no. And so we drank a flask of wine, and he said yes." Shivaji laughed. "Perhaps it was two flasks."

"But why do you help us?" Arjumand wondered.

"Because I'd like to think of you as friends, not foes."

I pocketed his coins. "What's to stop us from fleeing?"

"Because, good wine or not, Ahmed will have my head if you escape."

"You'd take that risk?"

Shivaji bowed slightly. "I'm a fool when beautiful . . . no, when wise women are near. Nevertheless, the horses are tethered outside. When you return, perhaps you'll do me the honor of saying good-bye." The warlord glanced quickly at Arjumand before turning to leave.

I reached out to touch his arm. "I pray that we can be friends."

"Kingdoms war, my lady. But we mustn't."

We exchanged farewells and I hurried upstairs to tell Isa and Nizam the joyful news. Scant time was needed to pack our few possessions and leave Bijapur. Nizam and I departed first, pausing just beyond the city. Waiting for my family was wrenching and, overtaken by restlessness, I was about to return for them when they finally appeared. Neither had spent much time on a horse, and I was unsure who looked more ill at ease on the saddle. Both, however, shouted gleefully when they spied us, and soon we trotted in single file to the west.

It took us the better part of the morning to leave the foothills around Bijapur. I was sad to see them vanish but also felt giddy at the prospect of the ocean. None of us had ever seen the sea, and we were eager to reach Goa. Nizam led us, setting a swift pace, his eyes constantly scanning our environs, even as he spoke with Isa. Arjumand and I talked incessantly. It had been years since I'd gossiped so, and as much as I'd thought myself above such chatter, I confess I enjoyed telling her the many stories visitors had conveyed to me about Agra's citizens.

By evening we could faintly smell the sea. It was a foreign scent—almost as if an infinite kitchen were nearby and something sweet baked on its stove. At first I thought myself to be imagining things, but my companions confirmed that salt-laden air teased their lungs. The sea's taste invigorated us, and though Isa and Arjumand grimaced in their saddles, we rode harder.

Long after the sun hid itself, we made camp. Dinner consisted of kichri, a simple stew of lentils and rice. Talk was short, as we were weary and faced another full day of riding. Isa and I lay close on our sleeping carpet, sharing the gift of each other's warmth.

The following morning we left early, pushing our mounts. The land flattened, the trail broadened. A breeze carried the ocean to us, and we inhaled its wonders like an exotic perfume. The Deccans we met didn't trouble us. They seemed a more contented people than their brethren to the east, and I wondered if Aurangzeb's war parties had spared this land.

We ate lunch as we rode. While Nizam asked Isa about building, Arjumand and I whispered of men. The more I was reacquainted with my daughter, the prouder I became. Somehow, despite all her hardships, she had remained happy in her outlook. She joked and laughed often, and was much less serious than her scheming mother. I felt younger in her presence and wondered if all parents experienced this same slippage of time.

The trail unspooled. By late afternoon we could see the faint outskirts of Goa, a city nestled in gentle hills and thus somewhat discrete. Yet I could discern enough to determine it to be a place unlike any I'd witnessed before. Several minarets rose above the verdant hills from unseen mosques, but so did the steeple of what Nizam said was a Christian church. More distantly, the masts of Portuguese trading ships reached skyward. Eagerly I looked between these towering pillars for the sea, wondering what shade of blue it might be. Alas, I saw only the horizon.

As Shivaji had foretold, the trail forked northward. We veered right and, inspired by the knowledge that our goal was so close, soon rushed ahead. We galloped until even my thighs burned, and I knew that Isa and Arjumand must hurt terribly. Yet they asked for no respite. We thundered forward, passing immense dunes of sand, coconut trees, and men building racks to dry fish. We then crossed a shallow river.

White birds wheeled overhead. Nizam called them gulls and I thought them an auspicious sight. They were vocal creatures, chattering like women in the harem. The trail, now completely sand, turned again to the west, rising over a series of dunes.

And there sprawled the sea!

It stretched out like a sheet of indigo silk, impossibly grand in its dimensions. Not even the endless deserts of Hindustan appeared so infinite. The sea merged somewhere distant with the sky, but where water and air met I couldn't discern. There was simply a gradual lightening of blue.

As we drew nearer I could see waves, capped with froth, lumbering toward the coast. Boats drifted out on that blue vastness, minuscule swathes of brown with white sail. How deep the water must be beneath them! What denizens must thrive below their vessels! I'd heard of sharks and whales, but to think of them swimming out there made me shiver with dread and awe.

Nizam led us down a sandy slope. A stone's toss to our right ran a slew of thatched huts that looked empty. But I disregarded these dwellings. My horse had made it to the beach and even he seemed excited. He snorted more loudly than usual, his neighs mingling with our shouts. Nizam's mount charged along the water's edge and we followed his deep tracks. Wind-whipped spray flew against me. I tasted salt on my lips. I felt like a child then, for surely the sea was one of Allah's most wondrous creations.

We dashed along this border of sea and land, long and curved like a crescent moon and just as gleaming. My troubles washed away in the cleansing water and I felt free. For the moment, the outside world was unborn. Only this slice of sand in all its majesty existed. Nizam left the water, galloping a short way up the bank toward a palm tree. He dismounted as a warrior might, launching himself up and out of his saddle. After tying his horse to the tree, he helped Arjumand off her mare.

I had lived all my life under the conservative, stifling rules of others.

Today I did not. And so I kicked off my sandals and pulled up my trousers. I hadn't run, truly run, in years. But I ran now, and it was glorious! Isa dashed beside me—his strides long and his laughter priceless. He begged me to catch him as he hurried into the water. I tried, shrieking as it rose above my ankles, then calves, then thighs. A wave slapped at me and I was suddenly underwater. Springing to the surface, I licked the salty foam from my lips, disbelieving the strength of its taste.

Arjumand and Nizam caught us, and the two women in Isa's life splashed him until he begged us to stop. Next, we assailed each other. The sea was up to my chest, and when waves rose about me, I experienced an unfamiliar sensation of weightlessness. I could almost float and felt like a toy that the sea merrily tossed about. I let it lift and drop me, grinning in amazement as each swell rolled forth to carry me skyward.

I wondered then why children played so in the river, but adults ceased to see it with the same eyes. Why couldn't we embrace such simple joys? Yes, pondering the problems before us was fine and noble, as was gaining wisdom, but must our physical sensations, our joy, wither in the process?

A bigger wave, a mountain among these hills, came at us then. It swept us up, and suddenly I was driven toward shore. I shrieked as the wave collapsed and I dropped heavily on the sand. Though the blow stung my hands and I coughed up seawater, I found myself laughing.

"Behind you!" Isa yelled, and I turned in time to see another wave rolling toward me. It struck me down hard. I tumbled underwater, not knowing up from down from sideways. When I thought my lungs might burst, I was finally able to kneel on the sand. Despite being a strong swimmer, I was suddenly unsure of myself, so unaccustomed to these waves. Where should one stand or swim?

"Come here!" Isa shouted from deeper water.

I waded through the receding sea until I reached him. Not bothering to ask, I jumped on his back and he held me somewhat out of the wetness. "They're strong!" I exclaimed, as Isa leapt up when another wave arrived.

"You have to jump," he replied, his crooked smile quite boyish.

"Easy for you to say! Your legs are as tall as trees!"

Arjumand crept behind her old mother, and when a wave lifted us, climbed up my back. The wave dropped and suddenly Isa stood with two women atop him. He staggered for a heartbeat, then we toppled backward.

"Issssssssssa!"

The sea engulfed my voice, and another wave threw me closer to shore. My tunic felt increasingly heavy, and though still euphoric, I was prudent enough to wade to shallower water. When it only lapped at my knees I sat down, watching contentedly as Isa tossed Arjumand into the waves and Nizam swam far out in the blue. I asked Allah if such seas existed in Paradise, and when He offered no answer, I concluded that they must. For how could Paradise be complete without them?

History books claimed that Europeans crossed boundless seas to reach Hindustan, and I shook my head in disbelief, impressed by such deeds. If Ladli were right, I thought, and we do lead many lives, perhaps in my next life I'll be an explorer. I could name islands after my loved ones and maybe even a speck of land after myself. And why shouldn't I? After all, the finest explorers always honored themselves.

But such adventures could wait, I decided gladly, for I had many more years to live in this body. I had a daughter for whom I must find a man, and a man I must hoard for myself. "Stop!" I muttered, for already I was plotting anew.

"Come in, Mother!" Arjumand shouted.

I shook my head but was warmed by her words. Any man would be lucky to have her. And though my mother was nearly perfect, and above criticism, unlike her, I'd ensure that my daughter married a loving man. It didn't matter if he resembled a slug or a gold coin. As long as he treated her with decency, I'd help her catch him.

"I cherish you, my child," I whispered.

The day was mostly done when we finally left the sea. As Nizam and Arjumand gathered our horses, Isa and I shuffled to the bungalows. We must have made an odd sight, but the owner seemed a kind man and welcomed us. We rented three rooms, and he asked that we share his supper. Naturally, we accepted.

His wife, a homely woman stooped over from a lifetime of mending nets, cooked us the strangest meal I'd ever encountered. She served thick soup brimming with curved creatures called shrimp and many-armed things known as squid. I half-expected them to start swimming in my broth!

We had brought some wine from Bijapur, which we shared with our hosts. Though the Qur'an was our Holy Book, and Its words were my guides, the forbiddance of wine was something I couldn't condone. For how it loosened tongues and enlivened conversation. Soon we were laughing and talking with these strangers as if they were childhood companions.

When all the strange little creatures were safely in our stomachs and the night and sea were black, we parted company and drifted to our rooms. In bed, I held Isa close. And his touch, which I'd dreamed about for so long, was achingly real.

THE NEXT THREE DAYS were spent thus. We rode or took long walks on the beach. We laughed, chatted, even argued. One afternoon we saw monstrous leaping fish our host called dolphins. We sprang into the sea to chase them, and they didn't flee but swam about us in dizzying circles.

We made many such discoveries while collecting spiral shells, chasing crabs and building cities in the sand. At one point, Nizam, who we thought had been napping, showed us a replica of the Taj Mahal that he'd crafted. Even if his minarets kept falling, the mausoleum itself was well proportioned and to our liking. Nizam was an easy man to read, and I was pleased for his pride. I knew that working on the Taj Mahal was his life's grandest chapter. Anyone could fight or serve, but to shape stone into such beauty was an accomplishment worth remembering.

Our host carried us out each afternoon on his fishing boat, and we learned to set traps and throw nets. Isa took a surprising liking to this process. Though he couldn't cast the nets as far as Nizam, his throws were better placed, falling on schools of fish that devoured bread we had discarded. The fish he hauled in were long or fat, brown or spotted with color. Some we ate for dinner. Others we threw back.

After returning from the sea, we swam at dusk, for dusk was when the waters receded and lessened in ferocity. Arjumand and I shed our robes, and wearing shirts and breeches intended for boys, we frolicked like sisters. As we swam, she told me of her building, in which she found great joy, and I spoke of Agra and her grandfather.

It amazed me to see what a convergence she was between Isa and me. Not only did her looks reflect our merging, but so did her temperament. She had a clever mind, which I believed she inherited from us both. Moreover, she was feisty like me, and she also possessed Isa's youthful enthusiasm. This relentless good nature bound them strongly, and I knew, without remorse, that they'd forever be closer than she and I.

None of us spoke about our looming departure. Only the present moment mattered, and we endeavored to enjoy it to the fullest. We lived fiercely—laughing until our stomachs hurt, swimming until our arms were leaden weights.

Naturally, our last night was different. After drinking the remainder of our wine, the four of us made a fire on the beach. We spoke little and stared listlessly into the flames. Though we couldn't see the waves, their crashing seemed louder than hitherto, and I found myself realizing how much I'd miss them.

"We'll have to return to the sea," I said. No one answered, and so I added, "Two years isn't so long. Build it hard and build it safely. When my brother is dead we'll meet in Delhi."

Arjumand flicked a stick into the fire. "You make it sound so easy," she said harshly. "But what if your precious plan doesn't work? What if the Sultan betrays us?"

"He won't, my child."

"But what if he does? Will you abandon us for Grandfather again?"

I paused at these words, for I hadn't known Arjumand harbored such resentment, though I could hardly blame her. Hating to see her so upset, I asked her to see the situation from my point of view. "What would you do, Arjumand, if your father were dying? Would you leave him and flee, or stay and make him well?" I stared at her, but she avoided my gaze. "Do you believe a single night passed in that awful cell when I didn't think about you?"

Isa cleared his throat. "It was hard, Arjumand, for all of us. But what your mother did was right. You'll understand that someday."

"And now that I'm a child, I can't?"

"You're no child."

"Yet you treat me as such!"

"Quite the contrary," I interjected. "Your strength allowed me to stay behind. If you were a weak girl, I'd have been forced to leave my father and brother. And though my leaving might have served you, it would have been at their expense. Dara died less terrified because I was at his side. And Father I nursed back to health because I hadn't fled south. So your strength, Arjumand, was a gift to me, and to them."

"Do the strong . . . cry every night for a month?" she asked softly.

"When they need to," I countered, clasping her hand. "Women, Arjumand, women are taught that there's no strength in our tears. But why are tears powerless, if those tears lead to insight, or a sense of peace?"

"But I don't want you to go, Mother. What if—"

"Your father kept his promise to you, didn't he? The promise that I lived. And so I shall keep this promise, the promise that we'll be together within two years."

"We must be."

"I know, my child," I replied, stroking her arm. Nizam carefully placed a log in the fire, and I wondered where his thoughts lay. "I'm proud of you, Arjumand, for you're strong. And yet, you're also free." I saw her eyes flicker away and I squeezed her elbow. "People, both foes and friends, will try to take this freedom. But never, ever, let them have it."

"I'll miss you," Arjumand said, hugging me. "Be careful in Agra. Your brother won't be happy that you escaped."

I did my best to seem unruffled. "Aurangzeb's like a wasp with no stinger."

"Perhaps he may find it."

"I've been stung before. And I suspect your old mother will be stung again." I kissed her forehead. "It's late, my child, and we have a long, long day of riding tomorrow. Will you rest?"

Arjumand said good night and Nizam accompanied her to the huts.

Isa moved next to me, kissing my ear. "Your brother, Swallow, is far more dangerous than any insect. And he hasn't lost his stinger."

"But he won't find me."

"But why, why must you even return to Agra?" he asked. "It would be safer to live in Delhi or Lahore. Visit your sisters in Delhi. Surely you'd enjoy their company."

"I would."

"Then go to them."

I thought of my little sisters, wishing life hadn't thrust us so far apart. "Our last word of them was that both were recently wed. Thus I can't intrude upon their lives with their new families. Not now, at least."

"I know your guilt about leaving him is overwhelming, but—"

"I shall be safe. And Father needs me . . . he needs me as much as he did when he was first imprisoned."

"He needs you, yes, but would he want you to take such a risk?" When I offered no answer, Isa asked, "Then why do you take it?"

"Why? Because he gave me you. And without that gift I'd be loveless and childless. And what have I given him? I left him alone in a miserable cell, abandoned him when I should have demanded that he escape with me."

"Jahanara, the worst pain you could ever cause him would be to get hurt. You should go—"

"I'd stay with you," I interrupted, "if it were possible. But without you and Arjumand beside me, I must go to him."

Isa's frame loosened at these words. "You think you're the sole owner of guilt?" he asked, his voice overshadowed by the breaking surf. "My father's last wish was that I become an architect. And so I studied. I studied as he quietly fought his agony, studied as he died."

"But how you've made him happy."

"I've tried." Isa's gaze left the fire and found me. "But you've also brought happiness to your father's heart. You need prove nothing more. Not to him. Not to anyone."

"I can't let him die alone in that cell, Isa. And I'll be careful, quite careful, visiting him rarely, and only in disguise."

"But why take the risk?"

I shifted atop my blanket. "I once made a promise, a promise to my mother as she died."

"What promise?"

"That I'd care for Father in her absence."

"And you have. You gave him five years of your life. Five years, Jahanara. Give the rest to yourself."

A star plunged from the sky. I sat straighter, not wanting our last night here to be spent talking of duty and death. "Why do they fall?" I asked.

His eyes remained on me. "We're not all clay in your hands."

"But why, Isa, why should we obsess further about tomorrow? Will it do us any good? Will it give us solace? Believe me, my mind is consumed enough by such thoughts. And if I sit here and discuss them with you, then soon, when I'm alone, I'll regret the time we lost."

He sighed, glancing upward. Despite the sky's shimmering brilliance, I watched only his face. "Perhaps they simply tire," he finally replied. "It's said that the same stars have been above us for centuries. And it seems to me, at least, that after so very long they simply go out, like a fire or a candle."

"But fires never fall. Nor candles."

"Maybe the sky is but Allah's black robe and the stars are diamonds sewn onto it. When He moves, the diamonds sparkle. And sometimes, when He runs, they fall from their moorings."

"And where do they fall?"

"Into the sea," he replied, draping his arm about my shoulders. "It's so full of diamonds that fish use them to build homes and palaces."

"Allah doesn't mind?"

"Allah, I think, has enough diamonds to last Him forever." We edged closer to the fire, as the air was cooling. A breeze carried the water to us and we breathed deeply. "I'd like," Isa said, "for us to return to the sea someday."

"Shall we grow old on a beach together?"

"Very old."

I picked up an unusual piece of coral, offering it to him. "What do you dream of, Isa, when night falls and you're alone?"

"The future. Of what it will be like when you return."

"Do you think of me often?"

He pointed at another dropping star. It flickered and was gone. "Sometimes, Jahanara, I draw your face with charcoal. I draw you while walking through a memory. Your face is pensive when I think of our first meeting. It's joyful when Arjumand is born." He pushed the finger-shaped piece of coral along the sand, creating curved lines within its grainy tapestry. A rough image of myself appeared. "I've drawn your face so many times. Because then, in some small way, I've felt as if you were with me."

I kissed him, biting my lip so tears wouldn't descend. "Isa?"

"Yes, love?"

"Would you draw your face, so that I might carry you to Agra?" Before he could respond, I continued. "I'd like it to be a happy face, for it's your joy that endears me to you most."

"I don't know—"

"Draw yourself with Arjumand. One sketch is all I ask."

He ran his hand through my hair, which that night bore no veil. "I've a price."

"What?"

"That you keep your promise to her." After I earnestly agreed, he nodded. "Then our faces shall accompany you to Agra."

The fire dwindled. No more wood was at hand to offer it, so we watched the flames recede. Although I had no choice, the thought of leaving my family was worse than any physical pain I'd ever experienced. I had tried to hide that pain from everyone, including myself, save Isa. As he held me, I cried. "Build it quickly," I said through my tears, "for there's still so much to see together and I'm weary of the years slipping by."

"As am I," he whispered. "When the moon's full, Jahanara, sit against the Taj Mahal and look skyward. As you do, know that I gaze at the same sky." He kissed me lightly. "And when Allah sheds one of His diamonds and it falls to the sea, we'll each see its flight and our thoughts shall mingle."

PART 4

*Know that the names of God,
the Most High,
are numberless
and beyond comprehension.*

THE MINGLING
OF THE TWO OCEANS

t is late in the afternoon and the boats about us are alive with flopping fish. My eyes, not being quite what they once were, can't distinguish the varieties of fish, only that they're brown things that die with little grace. I think of all the beautiful creatures we hauled from the sea and conclude that Allah must have been much more inspired when He seeded its waters than when He created the Yamuna River.

"And so you just left?" Rurayya asks incredulously.

Before I can reply, Gulbadan responds, "She had to, Rurayya. Haven't you been listening?"

I love these girls dearly, for I can see Arjumand in their faces. A trace of myself also exists, as does the narrow slant of Isa's cheekbones. "No, Rurayya is right. I didn't have to leave, and what I did was foolish."

Gulbadan tugs at her veil. "Then why did you go?"

I lean forward to adjust her crooked covering, as Mother often did to me so many years ago. "Isa recognized how much I sought my father's approval. But what he didn't recognize is why I truly sought it. Nor did I, until recently."

"Why did you?"

"Because as a young girl, I knew that I could . . . I couldn't ever match my brothers. In the eyes of nobles and warriors and artists I'd always be a weak girl. I'd never be treated as they were, never be as cherished and encouraged the way a boy would. And so I tried, always tried, to show my father that I was truly worthy of his love. And he did love me tremendously and valued my thoughts as much as anyone's. He praised me night and day. But sometimes I wondered if I truly merited such praise. That's why I went back to him, to prove to myself that his love and praise weren't misplaced, that he'd been right about me when my brother, my husband and so many others had been wrong."

My granddaughters don't respond. I see the sudden anguish in their eyes, and I grasp their hands. "You needn't prove anything to anyone, including yourselves. If you take one message from my story, take that."

Gulbadan slowly nods. Rurayya's fingers work their way deeper into mine. "But what happened then, Jaha?" she asks.

"We returned to Bijapur. And Nizam and I left for Agra."

"Did you meet Aurangzeb?" Gulbadan wonders.

"Doesn't a cat finally meet its fleas?" I answer, thinking of Ladli. "Many terrible things happened upon my return to Agra." I force away a memory that I wish didn't exist. "You see, my children, I imprisoned myself, and I set Nizam free."

CHAPTER XXII

Allah's Desertion

It took us a full month to ride back to Agra. Though it felt disheartening to return, I was comforted by knowing that my loved ones were safe and that I would see them again. After renting a room far from the Red Fort, I used the few gold coins remaining in Nizam's saddlebags to buy an expensive, oversized robe and a long necklace of pearls. I carefully used makeup to age myself, going so far as to dye my hair silver. Then I went to the Red Fort as a noblewoman might—rudely ignoring beggars and walking silently past inquiring guards. Though quite uneasy about returning to Father's cell, my fears were softened by rumors placing Aurangzeb to the north, warring against the Persians.

I proceeded directly toward the octagonal room that had housed me for so long. After entering the corridor leading to it, I was surprised to see that the number of guards had tripled. They asked me of my business, and, my heart quickening, I pretended to be a noblewoman from Lahore visiting the dethroned Emperor. The guards, perhaps accustomed to bullying women about, refused me passage. Only when I handed their captain a silver coin did he finally swing open the big door.

I stepped inside and shut it behind me. Expecting nothing to have changed, my hands leapt to cover a shriek when I witnessed the state of the cell. Though I'd only been gone for two moons, the room looked to have aged many years. Cobwebs hung from the rafters and a layer of dust covered the furniture. I sought Father out amid the chaos, moaning when I spied him near the window, clad in a filthy tunic. He seemed dead, for he didn't turn toward me. His white beard was untrimmed while his face was pale and his flesh withered.

"No!" I cried, hurrying toward him. Terrified, I swept through the clutter of the room, my robe whispering as I rushed to him. "Father!"

He groaned and his eyes fluttered open. For a moment he seemed not to recognize me. "You're safe," he mumbled weakly. "Thank Allah, you're safe."

I eased my hands beneath his head, lifting it upon my lap. His skin was damp with perspiration. "What happened?"

He tried valiantly to smile. "The sickness . . . came again. But—"

"No one was here to help you."

"Akbar tried."

I glanced up and saw the falcon on his roost. The sight normally would have cheered me, but I felt exhausted. My head throbbed and my limbs might as well have been logs. "Forgive me," I whispered.

"No reason for sorrow, Jahanara," he replied. "Would Akbar have reason to forgive the wind?" Father coughed violently. I used the hem of my robe to wipe grime from his brow. "You should leave, child. Dangerous . . . to be here."

"I know."

"What of Isa and Arjumand?"

"Imprisoned. But they'll soon be free." I briefly told him of their story, ending with the Sultan's promise to let them go. I made no mention of my bargain with him.

Father winked at me. "I hope you didn't give him too much." He nodded toward the window. "I always sleep here. Sometimes, when I'm strong . . . I look out and see her. And I watch Akbar come and go." He coughed again, harder this time. He groaned loudly enough that I knew his pain was terrible.

"What does the physician say?" I asked.

"Nothing. He says—" A series of coughs wracked him. Father shuddered in their aftermath, his body damp and rigid. "He says nothing, because he's forbidden to visit me."

"Forbidden? But you're the Emperor!"

"Be silent, child."

"You, you who gave them so much," I said, my voice rising with my anger.

He tried to reply but instead battled an urge to cough. Seeing him in such misery sparked a flame of rage within me, a rage I hadn't known since Dara's murder. Though aware I should remain calm, my anger swelled unchecked. It swelled until any semblance of reason had fled my mind. I left Father at his window and hurried to the door. When it opened I advanced on a jailer swiftly, startling him. "Why isn't a physician present?" I demanded, disgusted by his lack of concern.

The captain of the guards came forward. He was as thin as a post and his eyes were quite hard. "The prisoner looks well enough to me."

"As would a pile of dung! But anyone other than a maggot would know he needs help!"

I thought the man would quail, but seeing his soldiers gather about him, he rallied. "Hold your tongue, woman!"

"I'll hold nothing!"

"No?"

"Your name?" I commanded, trying my best to intimidate him.

"I ask the questions here!"

"By what right?"

"By the Emperor's right!" I glimpsed an iron tooth as the man shouted. Something about his relentless stare and iron grin seemed familiar. "Forget me?" he asked, reaching out to touch my arm.

I stepped back. "We haven't met."

"The rich always forget the poor," he hissed, coming closer. "We're nothing to you."

"I don't know what you mean."

"You don't? Well, you should, for I also worked on the mausoleum. And I could never forget you. Not even now, as you stand here with your gray hair and your tired body. You see, I watched you every day. And I told Alamgir everything you did."

My stomach dropped. "You . . . you mistake me for another. I came here only to see the Emperor."

The guard spat at my feet. "Lies!"

"No, you must be confused."

"I'm not confused, Princess. The swine in that sty is your father. Alamgir let the old man sicken to draw you out. Only his daughter would act so concerned."

"His daughters are in Delhi," I said, trying frantically to think of how I could escape.

"You tire me, woman, though you could warm me well enough."

His men laughed as they encircled me. My heart began to race and my legs shook. The captain fingered my robe. I recoiled from his touch, but he moved closer. "Be careful, sir," I whispered, my voice trembling. "Aurangzeb might hate me, but he'll kill the man who steals his revenge."

"True," he said, pushing me violently into the cell, throwing me to my knees. The door slammed shut behind me, momentarily obscuring the laughter that rose from the corridor. I bit my lip, and fought to contain the panic surging up from within me. Emotions of dread and self-contempt overwhelmed me. How could I have behaved so recklessly? And how could I have been so naïve as not to have seen the trap? I'd betrayed Isa and Arjumand with my unfounded arrogance and rashness. If only I had listened to them!

"What have I done?" I cried out aloud. "No! Please, please no."

"Jahanara?"

I opened my eyes in time to see Father raise his head. "Yes?"

"What happened?" he asked feebly.

I thought of Isa awaiting me, and suddenly I was brushing away tears. "They recognized me," I said helplessly.

"Your temper—" A cough tore at him. He moaned, abruptly slumping, his head dropping to his pillow.

For an awful instant as I hurried to him I feared that he'd succumbed to his fever. His face was fiery in my hands. His jaw quivered. "You can't die, Father. Please, please don't die."

He tried to respond, but his suffering was too great. A cry of protest escaped his lips as he voided his bowels. Though the stench was overpowering, it served to focus my shattered mind. Still shaking, I dug through a pile of clothes on the floor and found a scarf to thrust into the cool water of the washbasin. I placed the wet cloth on his brow. Father tried to object as I stripped him, but few of his words were coherent. His tunic, I saw to my dismay, was infested with lice. I pushed the garment through our window's bars and let it drop far below. Then I steadied myself before the window, drawing strength from the Taj Mahal. Needing to concentrate on Father, I gripped the iron bars and forced all other considerations aside. I stood until my trembling ceased.

I did my best to clean him. After raiding piles of goods left by nobles, I filled a copper pitcher with water and held it above candles until my arm ached and the water was warm. Then I gently emptied it over him, using a hemp cloth to scrub his lice-infested and festering skin. I washed his hair and beard with soap, rinsed him, cut his nails and sprinkled perfume about him.

After I dressed Father in the cleanest clothes I could find, I tended to the corner where he slept. The lice-covered carpets and blankets went out the window. Fortunately, I discovered a mound of fresh bedding and made a bed for him directly beneath the window. The air might do him some good, I reasoned.

Father uttered no further words as I worked. He held his eyes closed and coughed occasionally. He grimaced. He clutched at his sides. It grieved me to see him in so much pain, and even though I was disgusted with myself for getting caught, I was glad I could help him. Not long after he rested on his new bed, the door opened and a surly guard left a tray bearing a thin broth of rice and corn, a pair of blackened bananas and a piece of naan.

By the time I'd fed Father, watched him fall asleep, and forced the fruit and bread down my own throat, dusk was nearing. Akbar screeched and, spreading his wings, flew to the window. He settled on the sill for a moment before squeezing through the bars and soaring into the dying light. I watched him disappear and then crawled to my bed.

I, too, was tired, though not from exhaustion born of physical strain, but of mental anguish. I had expected to find Father in good spirits, and in better health than when I left him. My plan had been to make his life as comfortable as possible in the cell, without placing myself in too much danger. Yet here I was, imprisoned again, and without question my promise to Arjumand was in peril.

As our cell darkened I thought of Isa and Arjumand. The sketch of them was in the room I had rented, along with the rest of my belongings. Nizam, once he realized that I'd been captured, would destroy it to protect them, and then no doubt would try to plan my second escape. But I wouldn't let him face such danger alone, for the men he would have to fight were far too numerous.

My bedding seemed empty and I pulled a cushion close, wrapping my body about it, my tears blurring my vision. I thought of my loved ones. I felt as alone as I had that day when I'd almost drowned in the river. My grip tightening on the pillow, I tried to sleep. But Allah gave me no such reprieve. He must have already granted me enough wishes, for He ignored my prayers. And the night would worsen.

Much later, as I still wrestled with sleep, the door to our cell opened. I heard the padding of feet and saw a figure approach in the darkness. At first I thought Nizam had arrived to rescue me, but then I realized that this man was wider than my friend and didn't move with his stealth. To my horror, the apparition materialized into Khondamir. More than five years had passed since I had suffered his presence, and time hadn't treated him kindly. His girth had nearly doubled, and the flesh of his swollen face drooped like an elephant's backside.

I started to rise. "My lord—"

His sandaled foot leapt into my gut and I doubled over in pain. Grabbing my neck, he yanked me upward. "So, it's true," he hissed. "My man was right."

I managed to breathe. "Aurangzeb . . . Aurangzeb will—"

He slapped me violently. "Silence, woman!" he rasped murderously. "Speak again and I'll cut out your forked tongue." I tried to nod to him, but his grip on my neck only tightened. "Your brother, whore, fights the Persians in a distant land. And I don't fear your threats. I think you bluff about the cobra and have told him so. But he believes your lie, for lying is what you do best." His next slap stung fiercely and I whimpered. "No one will save you tonight," he promised. "The guards drink with my coin and no one else knows you're here."

He looked at Father and at that instant I reached up and clawed at his eyes. My nails snapped against his cheeks as they peeled skin from his face. He yelped like a kicked dog. Then his fist descended, striking me so hard that my world spun in frenzied arcs. I groaned and weakly spat blood.

Khondamir hit me again. "Resist another time, and I'll wet my dagger in the old man's heart."

Please grant me strength, I prayed, as Khondamir tore off my clothes. Please let this night end with me alive.

"Remember, whore, your last words to me?" I nodded as his hands fell to my breasts. He pinched my nipples until I couldn't help but cry out. I wept now. "You told me of your lover, whom I'll surely kill, and you mocked my manhood. Do you mock me now?" he asked, exposing himself. I shook my head, but it mattered little. His rage was insatiable. "You should have never returned, but how glad I am that you did! Because tonight I'll have my revenge." His breath, fouled with liquor, cascaded over me. "Now stand like a bitch in heat, for that's what you surely are."

Though I wanted to fight him, he would kill Father if I did. And so I moved to my hands and knees. This is no different than all the other nights, I thought through my tears. But, Allah help me, it was, for Khondamir forced himself inside a place not meant for his passage.

The pain was instant and terrible, a thunderous, suffocating kind of agony, and I shuddered with each thrust. I ground my teeth, striving to stay silent, even as he moved harder and faster. He tried to hurt me. And hurt me he did. He was drunk, I think, and didn't finish quickly. When at last he convulsed, he threw himself on me and I fell to the bed. He remained atop me, and I lay gasping beneath his vast weight. I tried to subdue my sobs, as I couldn't bear for Father to wake to such a sight.

Khondamir grunted and finally rose. "Mention this to your brother," he whispered, "and I'll visit you again." My shame was so dreadful that I was unable to look at him. I closed my eyes and sought to withdraw myself to a distant place. But a fire raged within me, and the horrible pain kept me locked within this moment. "Know that your lover's a dead man," he said. "I'll tell him, while I carve him into pieces, of what I just did to you." A moan escaped my lips and Khondamir leaned closer. "Who is he, Jahanara? Give me his name and I'll see you freed from this place."

"He's dead," I whispered.

"You lie. But it doesn't matter. For I also have spies, and his name won't escape me forever. Nor will the whereabouts of his daughter, whom I'll violate a hundred times, then sell to a brothel. I'm certain she'll fetch a fair amount of coin. Much more than you."

Despite my agony and humiliation, I turned to him. "You'll never find them," I promised weakly. "And when you die . . . when you soon die, I'll rejoice, for your seed will be forever gone from this Earth."

He kicked me once more, then clothed himself and disappeared. Mustering all my will, I wrapped myself in fresh clothes and tidied the bed. Overwhelmed with pain and misery, I leaned against a wall and wept. Though my insides were still aflame, I knew, in truth, that my spirit had been raped more violently than my body. The physical pain would soon leave, but I would never forget tonight.

I stood until I had no more tears to cleanse my face. In the amber light of dawn I crept toward Father, and lay down beside him. I edged to him until our bodies met. His breaths were shallow, yet he was still asleep.

That morning I didn't pray. For the first time in my life I felt that Allah had truly abandoned me. He no longer resided in my world. Instead, where He had once dwelt, I found only darkness. In this place of nothingness I felt neither the warmth of Father nor the pain within me.

In this place not even my love existed.

CHAPTER XXIII

Retribution

In the following year, my world went from black to gray.

I did my best to deny what had happened, instead concentrating on helping Father recover. His fever departed begrudgingly, like heat from coals. Though he never regained even close to his full strength, a time came when he could stand unaided by the window. His mind, mercifully, again grew sharp, and he asked probing questions about the outside world. If he ever guessed what had happened to me, he kept this knowledge to himself. Sometimes he asked about the sadness that had befallen me, but I always replied that it was my longing for Isa and Arjumand that made me so cheerless.

I whispered only to myself of what had happened. If anyone ever suspected that something heinous had occurred, it was Nizam. My old friend visited on occasion, and even if he said little, I sensed in the silences between his words that he understood my pain. As the days passed, I became increasingly convinced that Nizam had discovered the nature of my grief. Perhaps a guard had talked. Perhaps Khondamir had boasted to the wrong man. Either way, Nizam aimed to hide his knowledge from me, but wore his emotions so openly that I knew what troubled him.

I debated asking Nizam to kill Khondamir, but before I could gather the nerve, my husband traveled north to Persia. Khondamir was rumored to be meeting Aurangzeb in the north, but our informants were uncertain why. If I had been concerned about his threats to my loved ones, I'd have asked Nizam to follow my husband on his long journey, and to seek his death. But to be truthful, I didn't worry that he might discover their whereabouts. Khondamir knew surprisingly little of the Deccan. And,

more important, Nizam used Father's caches of gold to give Khondamir's spies—whose names Father had unearthed long ago—twice the
coin that my husband paid them. These men were promised more gold
at the end of the year if they continued to provide Khondamir with false
information.

It goes without saying that Nizam wanted to free me. But freedom
represented a risk that I wasn't ready to take. If I left, Father would
surely suffer, and perhaps even be punished by Aurangzeb for my escape.
Beyond that, I was still tormented with guilt that my last escape had re-
duced him to the state I found him in. I knew that if I abandoned him
again he'd deteriorate quickly, dying alone and without dignity. And so I
told Nizam that instead of worrying about me he should focus his energy
and attention on the Taj Mahal. For while Father was right about Aurangzeb's fear of destroying it, stories of the mausoleum's untidiness
abounded. My brother had always despised Father's creation and thus
spent nothing on its upkeep. The structure itself remained in good order,
but the gardens were in disarray. Nobles spoke of algae-infested waterways, devastated flower beds and dead trees.

The gardens symbolized the Empire's health, for by all accounts Hindustan was gravely ill. Aurangzeb had so depleted the treasury warring
against our neighbors that few rupees remained for basic needs. Roads
and bridges were in disrepair. The poor starved to death by the thousands. And our armies continued to weaken—our weapons growing
older, our warriors much younger.

Aurangzeb blamed everyone but himself for the plight of our land. He
disparaged Hindus with increasing belligerence. Muslims he held to impossible standards. My brother scorned the advice of the brightest minds
in Agra, deriding their overtures for peace. He mocked the advocates of
such plans, though they increased in number with each battlefield defeat.
Nobles who once flocked to Aurangzeb's standard now conspired against
him. There were treasonous whispers. There were betrayals.

The Empire's fate, I must admit, meant less to me than it once had,
though Father and I were saddened to hear of these tidings. The thought
of our people suffering was a crushing reminder of our failures. So many

Hindustanis had depended on us, and by our shortcomings many of these brave citizens were dead.

We lamented but could do little else. How can I explain our enfeeblement other than to say that prison sapped our strength and resolve? I wallowed in guilt, anger and sorrow. Father, meanwhile, readied himself for death and sometimes was troubled that I kept him from it. After all, he had spent almost seven years in that cell. With each passing year, he told me, he felt further removed from Mother.

I kept him from death partly for selfish reasons. Quite simply, I loved him far too much to let him go. Though visiting nobles begged me to nurture him back to health for the Empire's sake, I cared for him mainly because he had always cared for me. Besides, the nobles were right. The Empire might need him one day soon. Mother wouldn't have wanted him to die, not when there was a chance, no matter how small, that Aurangzeb might be overthrown. If Father could rule again, he could bring peace to Hindustan. He could feed our poor, mend our mistakes.

"I want to be with her," he whispered late one night as we stood next to the window.

The moon was ripe, and as I did at this time each month, I stared at its face. My eyes always watered when I thought of Isa looking out, over the mountains, at this same moon. Tonight was no different. "I know, Father."

"I'd like to visit her tomb once more before I die."

"Look at it," I whispered. "Do you think in all the world another such thing exists?"

Under a full moon the Taj Mahal's brilliance was staggering. "No. But neither does another version of your mother." Father tried to smile. "You're close, my child, but even pearls stolen from the same oyster have differences."

"Is enough of her in me?" I asked quietly. I'd sought this answer for as long as I could remember.

"Aren't such pearls made of the same sand?"

A star fell from the sky, and I thought of Isa seeing it in the Deccan. "He shall think of me now."

"He'll be finished in another year," he said. "And then you'll be re-united."

I wondered if Father was right. When word came that Isa and Arju-mand were free, would Aurangzeb be assassinated shortly afterward? Or would the Sultan somehow fail to get his men into the Red Fort? If he failed, could I escape with Father, even if he didn't want to flee with me? Or would I have to go alone? Such questions troubled me often, for though I was determined to keep my promise to Isa and Arjumand, the thought of leaving Father behind made me lose sleep almost every night.

The next morning, to my surprise, Aurangzeb, Ladli and Khondamir entered our cell. I'd last seen my friend and my brother many years pre-vious and my eyes widened in shock. Ladli appeared little different: even if her hips and belly had thickened, age hadn't tempered her beauty. Her face was still youthful and her hair remained black. She wore a cream-colored robe painted with Chinese dragons, and her neck was draped with a golden chain.

Aurangzeb, meanwhile, looked as if time had sucked the vigor from him. He was much thinner than I remembered. His face was deeply lined, though not with wrinkles of laughter but of vexation. His beard was gray and his hair had receded. He limped as he came forward, and I wondered in what manner he had been wounded.

Father stood as the group approached, while I remained on the floor. "It's good to see you, my son," Father said, for in his heart of hearts he wanted to forgive Aurangzeb.

Aurangzeb's face twitched, and to me he seemed a nervous man. "I'm no son of yours, remember?" he replied, his right hand wrapped about the hilt of his sword.

An uncomfortable silence followed. Then Khondamir smiled at me. "You look old, woman. What ails you?"

"Your stench."

Aurangzeb grunted. I sought his eyes, which seemed lifeless. "A mis-take to have returned," he said.

"So it seems," I replied. Behind Aurangzeb, Ladli blinked rapidly. She was telling me of danger.

"Did you know, sinner, that last week there was another attempt on my life?" Before I could comment, he added, "Poison this time. A poison arrow shot into my tent that struck my best bodyguard instead of me."

"I'm sorry to hear—"

"That it failed?" he finished, his ire palpable.

Father weakly shuffled forward. "We had no idea, my son, of where you were a week ago. Surely you don't think Jahanara was responsible?"

"She's threatened me with her cobra, with her assassin!" he shouted, his voice like a clap of thunder. "Now that she's been caught again, she wants me dead!"

"But Aurangzeb—"

"Call me Alamgir, by God!"

"It wasn't her doing!" Father argued, the effort making him cough.

Aurangzeb disregarded him. He stepped closer to me, and I rose to face him. "You told me about your snake. You boasted that your assassin would place it in my bed. You threatened me! Your brother! And because of your threat I've killed more traitors than I can count."

"They were only traitors to Dara."

"Even now, you confront me. You foolish, useless woman. Without your assassin you'd be nothing to me. But because of him, I'm here, away from where I'm needed. Because I believe he still lives."

"He does. You've murdered the wrong men."

"Well, what would happen if I discovered his name? What if you told me his name and I killed him? Then where would we stand? What power would you hold over me with him dead?"

"I'll never tell you."

"Won't you?" he asked sarcastically, his face twitching again. "Guards!" Four jailers hurried into the room, which was now crammed with people. "Hold the old man," he said to two men, who moved to grab Father. "And you two, give the sinner a drink."

"Please, my son, she's innocent," Father pleaded.

At a nod from Aurangzeb one of the guards cuffed Father. A pair of my brother's underlings grabbed me roughly and dragged me to the washbasin, a porcelain tub filled with water.

"I've done nothing!"

"Drink up!" he roared.

The men forced me to my knees and dunked my head beneath the water. I struggled against them but might as well have fought the tide. Still I thrashed, banging my head several times against the basin. When at last I could hold my breath no longer, I was abruptly yanked from the water. I gasped, retched and gasped again.

"Who is he?" Aurangzeb demanded, pulling my hair, raising me up.

"Leave her be!" Father begged.

"Take him from here!"

I looked to Ladli for help as Father was dragged from the room. However much she tried to hide her emotions, I could plainly see her terror. Surprisingly, Khondamir also appeared fearful. Perhaps he had underestimated Aurangzeb's wrath.

"Tell me!"

I said nothing and was again thrown beneath the water. I struggled less this time, but when I began to black out, I kicked with my legs and clawed with my nails. I saw Isa and Arjumand in my mind's eye and begged Allah to give me an answer.

The jailers pulled me out, tossing me to the ground. I whimpered pathetically, forcing myself to look around the room. Ladli bit her lip. Khondamir sweated. Though I'd ignored prayer since the night I was raped, I asked Allah again for guidance. I was unafraid of death but couldn't imagine dying without seeing my loved ones again.

This time they held me longer, gripping my hair, forcing me to the tub's bottom. I hardly fought them but opened my eyes and saw the light around me. My lungs finally expanded and I inhaled a mouthful of water. Convulsing, I threw myself against my tormentors, managing to knock the basin over. I was unaware of it falling—only of myself coughing up water and dropping to the stone floor.

Slowly the world gathered into focus. Aurangzeb had unsheathed his

sword and stood above me. "Give me the answer I seek, Jahanara, or lose a hand." His voice possessed less of an edge, as if he now tried to speak to me as a brother.

I nodded weakly, praying as I never had. Though I was numb with pain and horror, my mind was strangely lucid. I saw Isa and Arjumand working on their mosque. I saw Mother. And then I saw the answer that would save me.

"Please, brother," I begged, my voice cracking and strained. "I love him." My tears were real as I thought of Isa, longing for his comfort even now. "Our love's a secret. Please, please don't hurt him."

The blade dropped to my hand. Its tip traced the contours of a knuckle, and though I felt nothing, I saw blood seep from my skin. Aurangzeb's face twitched again. He seemed unable to control it. "His name. Give me his name and you'll live."

"But I love him!"

"Hold her arm!"

"Wait! Wait!" I sobbed. I tried to rise, but my legs were as strong as strings.

"His name!"

I gulped for breath, and Aurangzeb lifted his sword. "I'll tell you!" I shrieked as the blade began its descent. My brother stopped in midswing, but again placed the steel against my flesh.

"Tell me now," he stammered, "or lose the hand."

I moaned in abject sorrow, then looked over to where Khondamir stood. "I'm sorry, my love."

For a moment, confusion reigned. No one seemed to understand what I had said. Khondamir, unexpectedly, was the first to recover from the shock of my words. "She's mad!" he muttered.

"Please, my husband, please forgive me!" I wailed.

"You lying whore! She speaks nonsense, Alamgir. The bitch hates me and you know it!"

I pretended to be wounded by him. "What? How can . . . why would you say that?"

"You treacherous whore!"

"Please don't say such things!" I wept mightily, my sobs true and unyielding. "Not now. Not after we've been through so much."

Khondamir started to speak, but my brother angrily motioned him to silence. "Been through what? Tell me! Tell me now, by God!"

"Do you remember . . . the golden ring?" When he nodded, I continued reluctantly, "It was my lord's idea that I pretend to steal it."

"What?"

"It was right after I discovered that Ladli had betrayed me by becoming your companion."

"She lies!" Khondamir screamed.

"Please, my husband. I've no choice."

"Don't listen to her!"

Aurangzeb strode to Khondamir quickly and, without a word, smashed the hilt of his sword into that ponderous stomach. My husband lost his breath, falling to his knees. He retched. He began to weep.

"Please don't hurt him. Please!" I cried, reaching out toward Khondamir.

"What of Ladli?"

"It was my husband's idea that I tell Ladli I stole his ring. He thought she might tell you. And he knew you hated me."

"So?"

"So, just as my lord guessed, Ladli told you, and you told him of the theft. He pretended to beat me because he knew you'd relish my suffering. And thus he might earn your favor and trust."

"You used me!" Ladli screeched, so loud that Akbar took flight, slipping through the window. "You deceitful dog!"

I allowed myself a thin smile. "I wish it had been my idea."

"But what did he gain by my favor?" Aurangzeb challenged.

"What did he gain?" I repeated, and I knew then that Khondamir was dead, since my next words were true. "Didn't you grant him special trading privileges with the army? Didn't he grow richer because of you? Because of your hate for me, and your joy in my beating? And that first day, when I told you of the cobra, he was here. Who but he could have arranged for the snake to be placed in your bed?"

"But he wanted to sell you to a brothel. And you said your child wasn't of his seed."

"All an act!"

"For what reason?"

"Because he loves me!" I shrieked, sobbing. "And he understood that only if you feared my revenge would I be safe from you. And so he had the snake placed in your bed, all the while pretending to be your friend and advisor. And all the while he told me of your doings! He told me everything!"

"No!"

"He wanted to assassinate you! Shoot you in the chaos of a hunt! But I never let him! I made him promise—"

Aurangzeb screamed then, a terrible cry of rage that seemed to shake the Red Fort itself. He moved so quickly that I hardly had time to react. "Stop!" I cried as he rushed Khondamir, with his sword held high.

My husband's eyes bulged and he held up his arms as if to ward off the blow. He tried to speak, but only a moan escaped his lips. Aurangzeb's blade hissed as it swept down, lopping off Khondamir's thick left arm as if it were made of butter. The blade continued without pause. It tore into his neck, cleaving through flesh and bone. Two thumps sounded as his body and head fell to the floor.

Aurangzeb spun toward me. I made no move to resist his blade. Twisting toward Mecca, I prayed for an easy road to Paradise. I felt the touch of iron at my chest, and I closed my eyes.

"I should slay you now!" Aurangzeb roared, his blade pressing harder against me.

"Please do."

"No!" he raged.

"Please," I begged, praying that he would do the opposite of what I asked, as he always had.

"No, a better punishment for you is life! And how can you live, knowing that you betrayed not only me, but also your husband?" He spat on me. His blade rose to touch my chin.

"Send me to Paradise," I pleaded.

"You're no woman, sinner, but a thing that crawls into men's hearts and eats away at our flesh. Such a thing doesn't deserve death, but life!" He knocked me from my knees and I fell backward. The guards then dragged Khondamir's remains away, and Aurangzeb stormed out of the cell with Ladli behind him.

Revenge was unlike what I had imagined. It didn't satisfy, nor did it please.

I felt only emptiness.

"WHAT YOU DID was right," Father said the next day, after he had returned to the cell and I told him the story.

"Right?"

"It kept you alive, my child. Would you rather that Arjumand be motherless? And that Khondamir, who was like the mud beneath your feet, still live?"

"He—"

"Deserved to die slower," Father voiced. "And you should think of him no more. He's gone and you're better for it, as are your loved ones." Father pulled on his leather glove and held up a scrap of breakfast for Akbar, who alighted on his wrist and gulped down the fatty meat. "I wonder how long our friend shall live," Father mused. "When I'm gone, will you free him?"

"He is free," I muttered, wondering if freedom truly existed.

Father raised the falcon higher, so that he might see outside. "He won't like living here alone. Board up the window and let him find a mate."

I nodded, watching Akbar, as he in turn studied me. The falcon alerted me to someone's approach. His head spun toward the door and he flew up to the rafter as our cell opened. I expected Aurangzeb, or one of our jailers, and let out a gasp when I spied Ladli. She was dressed in black like a Persian, with a thick veil covering all but her eyes.

After the door was shut and locked behind her, she hurried toward me. It had been infinitely too long since I held her, and I wept as she hugged me tight. We didn't speak but clung to each other as only best friends could. The bond that held us was different than that which tethered Isa and me, but no less strong.

I pulled down her veil to kiss her cheek. Only then did I notice that one of her eyes was bruised and that her lips were swollen. "He hurt you," I whispered, motioning at Father to guard the door.

"He flew into such a rage, Jahanara." She pulled the veil back over her face. "The brainless coward blamed me for being duped by Khondamir's plan."

"He was the one duped!"

"I'm leaving him, leaving Agra forever. I can't tolerate him any longer. He's . . . he's changed me into a different woman, one who's fearful and weak." A tear tumbled from her eye. "I'm sorry."

"Sorry for what?"

"That I'm deserting you."

"How many times have you saved me, Ladli? Twice? Three times? You aren't deserting me, and I'd die if he hurt you more."

A sudden commotion rang from the hallway, and Ladli flinched. "I shouldn't be here. He'd kill us all if he found out." She turned to and from the door. "Since he was bested by Shivaji, he seems to have lost any trace of reason."

I leaned closer to my friend. "Bested by Shivaji?"

"Your flea-infested brother fell into a trap, chasing Shivaji into a valley, a valley whose peaks were laced with explosives. They say the mountains themselves fell on our men. We lost four thousand of our best troops and Aurangzeb limped home in shame."

"Did Shivaji escape?"

"Yes, though the Sultan of Bijapur was less fortunate."

It took me a breath to digest her words. "The Sultan's dead?"

"A cannon knocked his head clean off."

I clapped my hands together excitedly, for this was the most welcome news I'd heard in some time. Ladli looked at me in confusion and I quickly told her the story of Isa and Arjumand's imprisonment. "His death changes everything," I whispered, tapping my foot in sudden glee.

"But who would let them go? The Deccans despise us."

"Not Shivaji!" I countered, then explained my dealings with him. "He's Hindu, Ladli. And a good man! He'll free them because only then can he use the tunnel to assassinate Aurangzeb."

"Somehow you'll have to escape and ride south again."

I shook my head vigorously, for everything was finally as it should be. I'd send Ladli south, with Nizam. "No, my friend. It has to be you. For one thing, you're Hindu, and so Shivaji will trust you more than me."

"But what would I say to him?"

"Say that the tunnel shall be unlocked. You'll unlock it before you leave Agra. Tell Shivaji of how the tunnel begins at Isa's home. Tell him everything he needs to know. And then, after he has honored our agreement, come north with Isa and Arjumand!"

"But I can't travel to Bijapur alone! Has your mind turned to mud?"

"You won't go alone. I know someone, the stoutest of all warriors and the kindest of men. He's been there many times. He'll guide you safely." She started to protest, and I held up my hand. "You were going to leave anyway, Ladli. You may as well go south. There are mountains and rivers—and the sea, if you're lucky enough to swim in it, is something you'll never forget."

"But I . . ."

"Find yourself on the trail, Ladli. You said that you've grown fearful and weak. What better place to rediscover your strength than in the desert? Go there, and return north as your old self." I glanced at Father, who tried his best to ignore us, leaning against the door. "I can't leave him again," I whispered.

"I know."

"Please, please do it for me."

"But what of the rest of the plan? Once I reveal the secret and have Isa and Arjumand safely with me, what will you do?"

"Once Shivaji's assassin has done his work, I'll be free."

A hint of slyness returned to her face. "And where, my conniving little friend, will we meet?"

I searched for a solution, my excitement so overwhelming I thought my heart might burst. Though we had planned to meet in Delhi, suddenly it felt too close to Agra. Allah only knew what chaos would befall both cities once Aurangzeb was dead. "The best course, I think, would be for you to travel east from Bijapur, across to the other coast. I've heard that Calcutta's a fine city. We could meet there, then go wherever we wish."

"Where in Calcutta?"

I bit my nails as I pondered where to meet. "At its largest mosque. Send Isa to pray there every eve at dusk. I'll find him."

"It's a half-baked plan at best."

"Can you think of anything better?"

"No, but be careful, Jahanara," she whispered. "Aurangzeb's not right in the head. He's lashing out at everyone."

"He always has."

"True. But not like these days. He's as paranoid as a virgin in a brothel."

"But with Khondamir dead and the threat of my assassin gone, he shouldn't be."

"The fool created a new tax upon anyone not of his faith, Jahanara. For any infidel, as he calls us. Those he can't force into Islam he punishes by taking half their crops. Half! He feeds his war elephants our grain while our people starve. And when our people riot, he sends those same elephants against them. Dozens are trampled each week. And if the tax isn't insult enough, he forbids Hindus to build new temples; we're not even allowed to repair those that age. For every one that we secretly mend, his followers desecrate a dozen more."

I wondered silently how my brother could be so imprudent. The tax Ladli mentioned was in fact quite old, though it had been abolished for many decades. It was known as the jizya. "How many attempts have there been on his life?" I asked.

"The man has more enemies than leprosy, despite the disappearance of anyone he deems a threat. You only live because he thinks you're bested. He's vanquished you, he's killed your husband, and he lets you breathe just to remind him of his victory."

"What should I do?"

"The worm takes joy in your misery, my sister. So continue to give him that joy. Let him think you'd prefer to die, and you'll live. Pretend to lose all spirit, and when his guards tell him that you're a defeated woman, he'll trumpet like a copulating elephant."

"Really, Ladli!" I replied, happy to see that our scheming had fueled her old fire.

"I don't jest, Jahanara. Only if he thinks you're defeated, will you live to defeat him."

I nodded. As we hugged again, I whispered to her of where and when to meet Nizam. Naturally, I made no mention of his name, for I wanted my friends to be surprised. I'd tell Nizam tonight of my plan, and he'd rejoice tomorrow upon discovering that Ladli was to be his traveling companion.

I carefully repositioned Ladli's veil so that only her dark eyes showed. "Thank you, my friend."

"Thank me in Calcutta, you little fox." She playfully pinched my cheek, as she had so many times as a child. "Better pray that I don't steal your man on the return journey."

"Never," I said, stifling a laugh.

"And why not?"

"Because you'll steal another."

She pretended to spit. "I'd sooner steal sand."

"I love you," I said, kissing her brow. She was about to answer, but I continued, "So be careful in the Deccan. And when we meet next in Calcutta, we'll be young again together."

CHAPTER XXIV

Passages

~)

I followed Ladli's advice and let myself drop into disrepair, fasting for a week after her departure, drinking only juice and water. Flesh dwindled from my body until I lacked the strength to stand. I ignored my hair, my face. I wore unwashed clothes and went barefoot. In all such matters, I pretended to be vanquished and in mourning.

I didn't let myself venture too far into delirium, yet dreams often visited when I was awake. Visions of my childhood, the building of the mausoleum and my nights with Isa entertained me. As time passed, I began to relish these sights. They transported me from my cell and I lived again in less troubled days.

Father and I deteriorated together. He didn't want me tending to him in my weakened state, for surely such nurturing would betray my act to our jailers. After all, how could I care for him when I couldn't care for myself? Normally, I might have fought Father over his decision, but nursing him was impossible when simply rising from the floor made my head spin. Moreover, we both knew he'd rather be with Mother in Paradise than with me in this cell. And so he wasted away.

Aurangzeb came to our room a month after Ladli had fled. He smirked at the sight of me, called my feebleness pathetic and asked Allah to forgive my sins. I ignored my brother's words, acting as though unaware of him. But my ears were keen that day, as were my eyes. And I saw how his face twitched, how he seemed ill at ease with himself. Clearly, in some strange way he had loved Ladli, and her betrayal wounded him grievously.

Had I been defiant, he'd have killed me. Had I smiled, he'd have struck me down. But my friend was right. And he left our cell a slightly less morose man than when he had entered. Though he had gripped his sword hilt apprehensively, as if assassins might attack him at any moment, I think Father and I made him feel victorious. Here we were—his two keenest adversaries—broken and near death.

As the moons successively waxed and waned, I waited anxiously for news of my brother's assassination. No such word came forth. The silence tormented me, and I worried that my plan had gone awry. Did my friends fail to reach Bijapur? Had I misjudged Shivaji? My desperation rapidly mounted as the days passed, for I possessed no answers. In my darkest moments I prayed for Aurangzeb's death, believing that the end of his life would be the only thing that would restore my own.

My time in prison gave me one invaluable gift, however. It gave me Father. Though Father and I had always shared a bond, during those long years in confinement this bond grew one hundredfold its original strength. When I fasted and was too weak to play games or even stare out the window, all we did was whisper. He told me every story he could recall about Mother. I entertained him with tales of Isa and Arjumand; what I imagined they were doing, what we did when last I saw them. Father and I taught each other many things. I learned of forgiveness, faith and poetry. He learned of women's woes in Hindustan, and of the sea.

On our last night together we spoke of Mother. By then his pain was such that he must have known he was about to leave me, for he had me ask for wine, which we'd last wetted our lips upon a full change of seasons ago. The wine was sweet, as were the figs we sucked.

"How do you think she shall appear, Jahanara?" he asked feebly. "As she did when we first met, or when she left me?"

I raised his damp head higher on his pillow, so that he might look out the window and see the stars. "Perhaps," I said, "she'll come to you as she did when you were first married."

He sipped from the goblet I held to his lips. "I'd like that. But then, I think the glow . . . I think the glow of motherhood made her beauty brighten." Pain swept through him and he gripped his side. When it finally passed, he asked for more wine. "Don't weep for me," he whispered, though his own eyes swelled with water. "I've always been lucky, as lucky as a boat on your sea."

My tears came suddenly. I didn't fight them. "But I'll miss you."

"Yes, but you'll have Isa, and your beautiful daughter."

I traced the contours of his weathered hand. "Please, tell Mother that I love her, that I tried to live my life as she'd want. I tried to honor her memory."

"And you did, Jahanara. You did. But she's no memory, child, for she lives in you. I see her now. She touches me as I speak."

"She loves you, Father. She loves . . ." I paused, wondering what he might like to hear. "She loves you as words love a poet."

The corners of his mouth rose. "Perhaps I live in you also."

"You do."

He tasted wine again. "I don't know . . . how a father could cherish a daughter more. I'm ready to go in all regards, but for leaving you."

I whimpered then and he held my hand. Somehow, even as he died, it was he who soothed me. "Is there anything you'd like, Father, before you go?" I asked, my voice beneath even the wind.

"Grant me one promise," he said, "so that I might die in peace."

"Anything, Father."

"I want you to be happy. Go to your sea and . . . and live there as a child might. Swim and eat and drink and love and dream. Do all these things for me, and I shall be content in Paradise."

He moaned again and asked for more wine. He didn't sip now, as he always had, but took a deep gulp. "Set Akbar free," he muttered, nodding toward our silent companion. "He's a good friend."

"As are you."

His face brightened. I saw joy and sorrow in his smile. Something else lingered within him. Something he hadn't felt for many years. I think it was hope.

"How I love you, my child," he whispered.

I responded in kind and pulled myself closer to him. I found warmth in his arms and was taken back to a time when I was but a girl and he was the man of all men. He comforted me then and he comforted me now.

We spoke, cried, grinned once or twice, and much later watched a diamond fall from the sky.

He traveled with it, for when I again turned to him, he was gone.

* * *

I learned later that news of Father's death spread throughout Agra like fire amid thatch. The city's inhabitants—be they Hindu or Muslim; man, woman or child—wore colors of mourning the following day. No task was undertaken, no squabbles pursued. Indeed, Agra itself appeared to grieve. The city teemed only with silence, not the elephants, horses and merchants that usually inundated its streets.

Aurangzeb decided to hold an immense funeral at the Taj Mahal. Nobles of every rank were welcome to attend the ceremony, which was to ensue at dusk. After a public viewing, Father would be laid to rest beside Mother. They'd then be left forever in peace.

Initially I was puzzled by my brother's magnanimous gesture, for I knew he would rather bury Father in a pauper's grave, as he had Dara. But the more I pondered his path, the more obvious it became that Aurangzeb had no choice but to honor his father. If he spurned the former emperor—who was suddenly revered again in light of Hindustan's recent woes—what little support Aurangzeb retained would vanish.

My vile guards told me that I was to attend the event, that Aurangzeb wanted me at his side, smiling and looking my best. Evidently he thought my presence would ease any tensions regarding Father's imprisonment and death. I cursed my jailers as they relayed this message. And I cursed my brother until a guard's cool blade pressed against my throat. Since I was too weak to walk properly, Aurangzeb's men placed me on a litter and carried me to the royal harem. At its gates they ordered the harem's keepers to ensure that I was presentable by mid-afternoon. I was to be bathed, my hair and nails cut, my body dressed in the finest clothes.

Four female servants carried me toward the harem's innermost reaches. Deep within this labyrinth, I was left alone in a communal bathing room, which sparkled like an immense jewel. Thousands of miniature mirrors adorned its walls and ceiling. No windows were present, and with the door tightly shut, light from a solitary lamp was reflected and magnified by each mirror. A marble channel carried fresh river water into the room, and in my dazed state I lay on a granite bench and watched starlike images flutter atop diminutive waves.

The door opened and a number of seasoned women gathered about me, women I had not seen for many years. They were artists who once entertained my parents but were presumably ignored by Aurangzeb. The oldest and most powerful concubines remembered me well. Though I never thought they had liked me, they now fawned over me as if I were a child of their loins. They trembled at my appearance, for I was gaunt, filthy and aged.

These women asked of Father and I told them that he had died peacefully. Then came queries regarding my wishes, and with freedom seemingly so near, I wept, knowing Aurangzeb would send me back to prison after the funeral. The thought of a solitary life in that cell was almost more than I could shoulder.

What happened next, as my clothes were removed, caught me unaware. These women, whom I never gave much acclaim, started planning on how to free me. While they scrubbed my body with soap and hemp, they spoke of bribes and unwalked passages, of boats and horses and men. Their tongues were so quick that I could barely follow the exchanges.

My eyes sought their faces as they dressed me in simple but clean garments. Each woman, I recalled from my childhood, had rarely left the harem. They never spoke of politics and power, but laughed, lounged and refined their crafts. I had once believed them weak and now begged their forgiveness. How wrong, how foolish I'd been. To my surprise, the concubines told me to still my words. They cackled as old women do— each chatting, none listening. I asked why they were willing to risk so much to free me.

"Many of us within these walls, my lady, were saved in some manner by your mother," said the most outspoken woman of the group. Her face was horribly disfigured, as if it were a wax mask that had started to melt.

"She saved you?" I asked weakly.

"My mother once stitched your robes," she replied, tenderly combing my locks. "Stitched them for your brothers as well."

"Did I know her?"

"You were but a girl. I was hardly older when fire swept through our home, stealing my parents from me. I'd have died on the streets if your mother hadn't brought me here. She paid for me to learn music. And learn I did. Of course, with my face I could never play for most lords, but in time, I taught younger girls my art. And I performed for your family on occasion."

"I remember," I said, recalling nights by the Yamuna, wonderful nights when a scarred girl played her sitar beautifully. As I slipped deeper into the past, two eunuchs entered the room, quickly stripping off their fine robes. One of the women smeared grease on their faces as the diminutive men stepped into filthy clothes.

"We all have such stories," a younger concubine added.

"But you risk too much," I said. "My brother will—"

"He doesn't frighten us, my lady, for he knows nothing of our world," the musician interrupted. "And freeing you will make your mother happy. It will do honor to her memory."

Before I could think what to say, the eunuchs placed me again on the litter and carried me from the room. I cried out my thanks as the concubines disappeared from sight. An ancient eunuch then appeared, draping a thin blanket over my body and face. He set a reeking, bloody sack of what must have been decaying flesh between my feet before covering me with a foul carpet.

In this newfound darkness I heard only footsteps. Though the stench made me gag, I purged it from my mind. Breathing through my mouth, I prayed fiercely to Allah to protect my saviors, who had spoken of spreading dozens of rumors about the harem, each tale offering a different version of my escape. Some stories had me faking my frailty and darting outside the cloistered walls. In others, a fictitious servant or concubine rescued me. If the women created enough confusion, as I suspected they would, Aurangzeb might never learn the truth. He'd be enraged, certainly, but without proof, I didn't believe he would punish those responsible for my escape. His hold on power was far too precarious to upset nobles who patronized these women.

I was carried for some distance. At one point we must have come upon the Red Fort's sentries, for my bearers abruptly halted as voices rang out.

"What's your load?" a guard demanded.

No response was given, and my pulse quickened. Someone coughed.

I tensed at this outburst, my body twitching. Certain that someone must have seen me move, I felt a wave of fear wash over me. I wanted to tumble from my litter, and somehow to outrun my pursuers. Resisting the powerful urge, I remained still. Aurangzeb would kill me for trying to escape, for he would understand that I wasn't broken but, in fact, had tricked him once again.

"Your load, boy? Have dirt in your ears? I asked—"

"A leper, sir. Dead . . . dead and full of boils and ready to burn."

The guard grunted and I heard him step forward. Light invaded my cocoon as the carpet above my feet was lifted. I shut my eyes, unable to look upon the man who would send me to death.

I'm sorry, Arjumand, I thought desperately, as a mailed arm brushed against my leg. Please forgive—

"The stench!" the guard roared. "You ought to burn yourselves with him! You're paid to keep the fort free of such filth!"

"We only found him today, sir."

"Ten days too late by the smell of it! Now leave before you infect us all!"

The litter bounced beneath me and we were under way again. The eunuchs didn't speak as they walked. My heart slowed only when the sounds of the guards behind us faded completely away. When all was quiet, I cried, wracked by relief and sorrow. I whispered to my bearers, explaining where they could find a large cache of Father's gold. I told them to share it with the concubines, to spend it on whomever needed bribing. So much gold would make it harder for my brother to discover what happened.

Soon I heard sandals against wood, then felt myself being settled on the ground. A series of splashes came next, followed by a sense of wind. "Safe to rise," a hoarse voice finally advised. I struggled upright, pushing aside the carpet and blanket, my lungs drawing in sweet, unspoiled air. The broad deck of a trading boat sprawled beneath me. "Nothing to fear here," said a man beset with wrinkles.

I blinked at the sunlight. "Where are we headed?"

"South."

"To Calcutta?"

"If you like."

I glanced at the distant Taj Mahal, which faded slowly as the current gathered us up. Already groups of nobles assembled atop the mausoleum's gleaming platform. Soon the ceremony would begin. "Farewell, Father," I said gently.

I waited to hear his voice. But nothing came.

IT WAS A LONG, albeit uneventful journey. The boat's captain seemed a decent man and tried his best to ensure that I recovered my strength. He brought me a dozen varieties of fish soup, and while he claimed that each was different, they all tasted as one to me. After not eating properly for almost a year, my appetite was as fickle as the wind.

Over the next ten days we drifted southeast. The land along the Yamuna was mostly devoid of man's presence. One morning I saw a tiger amid a bamboo grove, stalking something I failed to detect. We also came upon a massive banyan tree—a relic of a forgotten age. Its branches, falling straight to the shore, were thicker than its original trunk. Hundreds, if not thousands, of bats slept in these branches. The bats screeched eerily, and their droppings coated the ground white. Indeed, much life thrived on that river. Life seeking to kill, such as the alligator we spied one afternoon. And life seeking to blossom, such as the fields of lotus flowers gracing the water.

I watched all Allah's creatures, including the few people inhabiting the muddy banks, with fleeting interest. Certainly, I was thankful for these sights. Yet how could I truly appreciate the cunning of the alligator, as impressive as it might be, when the fate of my family was uncertain?

I passed much of the time praying. My mind was otherwise occupied by my parents, Aurangzeb and visions of my family's reunion. It seemed so long since I'd embraced Isa and Arjumand. My questions regarding them were infinite. Had our daughter fallen in love? Was Isa still a joyous man? Had Ladli found them and relayed my message?

When at last the river bore us to Calcutta, I was strong enough to stand and walk unaided. I could again taste the sea as I shuffled through the city, which was much more compact than Agra. Its buildings, so chaotically ordered, seemed stacked against each other. I saw fewer palaces and gardens than in the north, and those I did stumble past looked neglected. Brown lichen covered most structures, as did hordes of monkeys.

A bazaar occupied the street I followed. After asking directions to Calcutta's greatest mosque, I hurried ahead, hardly noticing the piles of fish, fruit and meat dressing the endless tables. Merchants shoved wares before me, but I paid these men no heed. I forced myself to continue on, even as my legs trembled with fatigue.

When I found the mosque—a narrow building supported by four identical arches—dusk was still distant. Seating myself under a cypress tree, I watched Muslims come and go from the holy place. Though I stayed outside the site, I did pray, begging for the safe return of my family. I prayed and beseeched all afternoon. Moments before the sun set, my prayers were answered.

Isa appeared in front of me, his face aflame and his body clad in white. Despite conventions against such interaction, I couldn't resist leaping up to hug him. Nor did he seek to curb my excitement. Instead, he held me tightly, and I felt the hard muscles of his arms contract about my shoulders. My joy eclipsed all conscious thought. I was uncertain what to say to him. Only a poet might aptly describe the feelings shuddering within me. Enough people were about that I refrained from kissing him, though I did press my lips against the back of his hand. "Take me from here," I said, wanting to be alone with him.

He grinned, and I followed him through the cluttered streets of Calcutta. We came to a stable and found his horse. He helped me onto the saddle before gathering the reins and leading his mount toward the setting sun. I asked of Arjumand, and he replied that she, as well as Nizam and Ladli, were living by the sea, less than a quarter day's ride from here.

"Are they lovers?" I asked eagerly.

"As if they'd been forever."

I clapped, immensely pleased that I had finally done my friends some good. "And what of Arjumand? Is she still well?"

"She's fine, Jahanara. Put your worries to rest."

"Can worries rest?" I asked happily. "I hope mine learn how."

It took scant time to reach the outskirts of the city. Once free of its confines, and far from the stares of its inhabitants, Isa leapt on his horse, moving forward until his chest pressed against my back. I turned around to kiss him, passionately enough that I tasted salt on his lips. Our stallion trotted slowly, and I held his reins with a firm hand, so that he wouldn't quicken his pace.

I told Isa things then, whispered to him of my love and my longing. He echoed my words and I thanked Allah again for delivering him to me. As Isa spoke, his hands sought to renew their friendship with my flesh. He caressed my face, then wrapped his arms about my stomach.

"You're thinner, my Swallow," he said quietly.

I nodded, staring at the sea, which stretched eastward like a mirror image of the sky. "Father died," I whispered, thinking that there were many things Isa would never discover. What good would it serve to tell him of Khondamir? Or of how Aurangzeb had nearly killed me?

"I'm sorry, my love," he said forlornly. "He was the rarest of men."

"The night he died, he made me promise him something." Isa kissed my neck and I continued, "He asked me to live as a child might. Do you think . . ." I paused, wondering if eyes that had seen so much could ever appreciate simple sights again. "Do you think I can grant his wish?"

"I don't know," he said, tightening his grip upon me. "But hold those reins, Jahanara. Spur him forward and let's discover if a child still dwells in you."

I nodded, and kicked the stallion hard in his belly. He neighed loudly, put his head down, and began to thunder down the path.

"Harder, Jahanara! Harder!" Isa yelled.

I slapped our mount's shoulder with my free hand and shouted for more speed. The magnificent steed responded, earth churning from his hooves, bushes blurring around us.

"Harder!"

I tasted freedom then. I was laughing and shouting, and my worries weren't asleep but simply gone!

"Faster!"

Isa's bellows mingled with the hammering of hooves. I screamed with him, for suddenly I didn't wield the reins to this horse, but those to my life.

Finally I was free.

CHAPTER XXV

The Clarity of Twilight

The years that followed were the finest of my life.

We settled in a village just south of Calcutta. Isa had always been careful with rupees and had more than enough money to buy seaside cottages for Nizam and Ladli, as well as Arjumand and ourselves. Our homes were within eyesight of each other and we spent our days together as friends. We told our neighbors nothing of our past and they asked nothing of it.

Isa and Nizam tried their hand at fishing, but upon discovering that they were skilled with stone, villagers suggested they leave the sea to exploit their true talents. While Ladli and I mended nets with the other women, Isa, Nizam and Arjumand repaired tired homes until they defied the elements once again. My loved ones never worked for coin, but every night we were brought fresh fish, vegetables, fruit and bread.

Our daughter soon fell in love. Though he was only a fisherman, I made no effort to steer her toward a man of higher rank. Ibrahim was a good-natured youth and adored Arjumand. They were wed near the ruins of an old mosque. Little did he know that he was marrying the granddaughter of the former emperor. Later she would tell him the truth, but on that glorious day it seemed wonderfully irrelevant. As the years passed, Arjumand and Ibrahim had two daughters. A son died before he reached his first year of life, yet the daughters grew strong. A second son was born much later, and quickly became the object of his sisters' endless attention.

Watching Arjumand become a mother was a source of boundless joy. I had abandoned her once, and I'd have never forgiven myself if she had turned into an unhappy person. I loved her so very much, perhaps because she was able to forgive me. When I saw her with Gulbadan and Rurayya, laughing and running across the sand, I thanked Allah.

Ladli and Nizam needed no children. Theirs wasn't a love of poets, but rather of friends. Ladli ruled their home, forever ordering Nizam about. Every instance his tongue moved, hers waggled ten times in response. It often seemed to me that she talked to herself as I watched them. He nodded or laughed occasionally, while she continued to rant. Old age loosened what few inhibitions she possessed. She cared even less for convention than I, and her language, always so coarse, deteriorated into downright vulgarity. Nizam, who had spent much of his life in the gentle confines of the harem, sporadically chided her. But, as Father might say, how could an eagle ask a magpie to stop its chatterings?

Isa and I, finally able to live and act as lovers, found to our surprise and delight that our adoration for each other became more profound with age. His irrepressible happiness was a catharsis to my painful past. Naturally, unwelcome memories surfaced, but in his company I was strong enough to accept such recollections as a part of me. Though they still ached, I understood that they shouldn't be denied, but simply accepted. Yes, Khondamir and Aurangzeb had wounded me. But how could such wounds, regardless of their depth, compare with the rapture I felt as I played with my grandson, or walked along the beach with Isa? My loved ones were my triumphs, and my triumphs far outshone my tragedies.

Gulbadan was ten when we resolved to build our village a mosque and a temple. Our friends were Muslims and Hindus, but neither group had a true place of worship in which to usher their prayers upward. And they needed prayer, for the sea was an unforgiving realm and we often lost men to storms.

We decided that the mosque and temple should share the same courtyard. Both would be small structures, cut of sandstone and lacking decoration. Those who didn't fish helped us lay the foundations and raise the walls.

Temples and mosques are magical things. When you build them, there is a sense of peace that seeps from the rocks. All creation, in my opinion, is thus. I felt the same peace when Arjumand slipped from my womb. I swam in such peace at the Taj Mahal. And even our little shrines at the sea caused more than one tear to dampen my face.

Perhaps this peace stems from the knowledge that you're leaving something upon this Earth. For though I know that Paradise will shepherd me, it's comforting to recognize that as a woman born in Agra, I'll leave some sign of my passage. My blood will journey forward in Arjumand and her children. And the rock I caressed shall stand proud in the sun and be touched by people who will inhabit a far different world. Did I earn all the gifts that Allah bestowed upon me? Perhaps yes, perhaps no. But in leaving signs of my struggle, I feel that I've tried.

The temple and mosque were completed in my fifty-fifth year. Our village celebrated the achievement with an afternoon of prayer. Of course, Muslims didn't pray in the temple, nor did Hindus enter the mosque, but we were respectful of each other's worlds, and we met in the common courtyard and watered flowers together. As I tidied stones beneath rosebushes, I thought of Dara, and hoped that he could see us. No one would have loved this moment more than he.

That night Hindus and Muslims celebrated as one. We sat in our boats and watched as men lit Chinese rockets that surged into the sky. The rockets exploded, casting their magic light on the domed roofs of our making. Nizam, Ladli, Isa and I rejoiced in one boat. We sipped wine and clapped at the bursts of fire. As I watched the rockets detonate, I recalled that eve, endless seasons ago, when we celebrated the Taj Mahal's creation. What a sight that had been!

How many moments, I wondered, existed in any life when everything came together in such perfection? Perhaps no more than a handful? For me, there were but three. The night on the Ganges when Isa and I first made love. The celebration of the Taj Mahal. And this very moment of being with my friends and loved ones, my life utterly complete.

"A good night," I whispered, dipping my hand in the sea.

"Aren't they all?" Isa asked.

I nodded. "But not like this."

A wave slapped our bow and spray dampened us. Nizam, who gripped

the oars and hence steered the craft, propelled our boat into deeper water. "You've gone blind in your old age," Ladli muttered, chastising him
for the wave. When Nizam only chuckled in reply, Ladli turned to me.
"He's a good man, my cunning little friend. He lets me do the talking
and obeys me like a pet."

"He'll surprise you someday," I said, knowing that she loved him immensely, "for I've seen him in action."

"And what do you call action? He moves slower than a mule, though a
mule's much quicker with its mind."

"Ignore her tongue, my lady," Nizam said.

My old companion called me so because it vexed Ladli. "She has a
name, you beef-eating Muslim!" Ladli retorted. "Is it too long a name for
that melon you call a mind to remember?"

A wave struck the boat's stern, where Ladli sat. We all knew Nizam
had twisted the craft just so she'd be soaked. And soaked she was. As she
berated him, I leaned closer to Isa. His face was etched in a smile as he
laughed at their antics.

"A coupling made in Paradise," he said gaily.

A trio of rockets exploded and I grinned. "Are we so crafted?"

Instead of answering he kissed me, and in that kiss I found his answer.

NOT EVEN THE widest of banyan trees can grow forever. It has to die so
that a sapling may rise from its flesh.

And so it was with Ladli. She went for a swim one day, and when the
sea returned her she had traveled from this world to the next. We followed the Hindu tradition and burned her body, casting her ashes into
the water. We were all aged by then, and her death didn't surprise us.
Still, we missed her terribly and our world emptied somewhat with her
passing. Nizam was even quieter in her absence, though enough of her
stayed in him that he remained a content man.

I often thought that I should have died before Ladli. She sacrificed so
much for me, gave up such a large piece of her life to protect me. She
should have outlived me, should have kept Nizam chuckling until they

were too old to stand. In many ways, Ladli was more of a sibling to me than my brothers and sisters had ever been. After she died I awoke each day, as I had after Mother and Father departed, expecting to hear her voice. But I heard it only in my dreams, in my memories.

Arjumand and her family left several months later. They moved near Agra to a fishing village on the Yamuna. My daughter hadn't wanted to move but had almost seen her husband stolen by the sea. Most of the older women in our village were widows, and Arjumand couldn't imagine losing Ibrahim. And as much as I hated to see her leave, I encouraged her to do so, for her happiness was what I wanted most.

After her departure I felt, as any mother might, that time was moving swifter. Still, I had Isa. And our love didn't dwindle with age. It flourished, even if growing old together wasn't always easy. A time came when Isa couldn't lift the heavy stones that he built with. He often hurt himself, and I spent long nights tending to his crushed fingers and toes. He also began to forget things. I slept more, walked less and rarely went swimming. But despite our aches and pains, we were happy. We had each other, and almost every day that blessing was more than good enough.

Our happiness lasted until one bright afternoon. We were standing on the shoreline when a horrifying pain burst into Isa's head. He cried out, falling to the sand. In the dawn that followed, his body, even his miraculous hands, went limp. He lingered for three days and I never left his side. On our last eve together, I slipped into bed with him and held him tightly. He couldn't return my embrace, but his eyes spoke of his love and our tears were many.

How do you say good-bye to someone you love so? Is there a word, a look, or a touch that can quell the pain in your hearts? I have known so many things in this life, but I'd read no books that taught me of such separation. I wanted to be strong, for the sniffling of a woman wasn't what he should hear as he began his journey. Yet my emotions were impossible to still.

"Stay," I muttered, "please stay."

"You'll find me," he whispered. "You've always . . . found me."

I felt the life slipping from him and I hugged him tightly, as if my hands might stop him from leaving. "Will you take me with you?" I asked, kissing his tears, tasting him. "Please, please take me with you."

"You are . . . with me. You always have been."

His voice was weakening and I leaned closer. "Are you cold, my love? Hot? What can I do for you?"

"Kiss me."

I did as he asked, wishing we could leap three decades back in time, wishing we were once again young. I stroked his hair, which was now white. "Thank you, my love, for making me feel so whole."

"You made yourself."

"Perhaps. But without you there is only me, and with you there is us," I whispered, my tears falling on his chin. His eyes fluttered and he mumbled something. "I shall find you," I said. "I'll find you covered in stone chippings and help you build in Paradise."

"Promise?"

"I do. And we'll live together again as one."

He fixed his gaze upon me. "I love you, Swallow."

And then he left me.

*t is dark by the time I finish my story. My granddaughters
cry and pose many questions. They ask of Shivaji, who perished in a landslide but two months after freeing my loved
ones. I suspect that our secret died with him, though I once heard a rumor of
assassins in the Red Fort. My granddaughters also wonder if I am fearful of
Aurangzeb discovering me.*

"Two days is enough here," I reply. "Tomorrow I'll return to the sea."

"So soon?" Rurayya asks, rubbing her tear-stained cheeks. When I
nod, she adds, "Can we come? Father misses it. And Mother misses you
terribly."

"Then you should join me."

Gulbadan stares at the Red Fort. "But why, Jaha, why not confront
your brother?"

"Because revenge is hollow," I say. "I won and he lost. His empire
crumbles, his people despise him and thoughts of assassins steal his sleep.
He's grown weak in his hate and I've grown strong in my love."

They offer more questions.

But my mind is elsewhere.

Perhaps the Hindus are partly right, for I do think we lead many lives.
Yet these lives aren't separate, as they believe, but one. My lives were simple. I learned as a child. I explored as a girl. And I bled and loved as a
woman.

Now that I am old, I see many lives in my life. They're as different as
stones, and yet they're connected. When I look back on them I wonder
sometimes if they were but dreams.

I kiss my granddaughters good night as Nizam rows us to shore, where their father awaits. I then bid my friend farewell, though he follows me as I shuffle toward the Taj Mahal. It is as I remember. I see Mother's grace in its arches and Isa's brilliance everywhere.

As a child I was taught that Muslims don't believe that the soul remains upon the land, but that after death we're carried to Paradise—where we walk among friends and feast upon our favorite foods, and where our happiness blooms eternally. But now, as I sit with my hands against the marble that Isa once held, I'm struck profoundly by the sense that a part of him lingers here. It's almost as if I can feel him.

Is it love I feel? Or a oneness surpassing even love? For love is a human emotion, and what I sense now is beyond anything of this Earth. It's too perfect to have been conjured by mortals. For Isa is with me, and as my face tightens and tears come forth, I see only him. He laughs. He cries. He holds me and we whisper, as candles burn low.

"How I miss you," I say to the rock. "Will you come to me, in my dreams?"

Even if no answer is offered, I know he shall. Allah might have taken Isa's body, but he isn't truly gone. We speak sometimes in the night; talk of our Taj Mahal, or our child. He still calls me Swallow.

My hands touch the marble and again I feel Isa. He is here. Mother sits with him, as do Dara and Father. I feel Ladli as well. Their mood is gay and they're as young as the seasons. Soon I will join them.

Many fear death. But I do not. For I've tasted this oneness we call love. Death cannot steal it. Nor temper it.

No, I'll take my love with me, wherever I travel.

And it shall endure.

You know, Shah Jahan, life and youth,
wealth and glory,
they all drift away in the current
of time.
You strove, therefore, to perpetuate only
the sorrow of your heart.
Let the splendor of diamond, pearl and
ruby vanish.
Only let this one teardrop, this
Taj Mahal,
glisten spotlessly bright on the cheek
of time,
forever and ever.

RABINDRANATH TAGORE

ACKNOWLEDGMENTS

About seven years ago, in the back of a lurching rickshaw in southern India, my youngest brother, Luke, told me of his idea for a novel based on the creation of the Taj Mahal. "It's never been done before," he said, "and couldn't be a better story." Shortly thereafter, Luke was kind enough to let me write the tale, and as the seasons passed, he offered his expertise on a land that he had grown to know intimately. Without Luke's generosity, his willingness to share a marvelous idea, my novel would not exist. I can only hope that I've created a tale worthy of his benevolence.

My other brothers, Tom and Matt, also deserve my gratitude. I could scour the Earth and not find a better pair of siblings. My parents, Patsy and John, have always given me unending support and asked for little in return. They introduced me to books, and it was mainly due to their advocacy of reading that I grew so enamored with storytelling. And the personal evolution that every traveler experiences wouldn't have been complete without my best friend, Carter, who crossed three continents with me.

Crafting this novel was made easier through the help and support of family, friends and colleagues. Mary and Doug Barakat, Hiroko Okita, Pete Kotz, Denise McNamee, Bill Day, Laura Love, Tracey Zeeck, Wendy Artman, Bruce McPherson, and my friends at GroundFloor Media—I owe you all in different ways. I've been quite blessed to have you in my life. I've also been fortunate to have a fantastic editor, Kara Cesare, at my side during this process. Kara is certainly going to leave her mark on this industry, as she's nothing short of spectacular.

Finally, I would like to thank my wife, Allison, who walked beside me within the Taj Mahal as we retraced the footsteps of those who built the mausoleum three-and-a-half centuries ago. Thank you, Allison, for sharing such a moment with me. From that day forward, you believed in *Beneath a Marble Sky*. Seven years of steadfast belief in a dream is a lot to ask of someone—even a spouse. And yet you never wavered. Thank you for this gift, and for being such a wonderful friend and mother.

Dear Reader,

In many ways, I am a fortunate man. I have a wonderful wife. We have two healthy, happy and astonishing children. A home comforts us. Food fills our bellies. Clothes keep us warm.

Another area that I have been extraordinarily blessed in is the realm of travel. I have treasured travel since childhood. During the years thereafter, I have gone to enormous lengths to ensure that I could continue to explore. In many cases, I risked a fair amount to set foot in new lands. For instance, I didn't pursue a career out of college, but headed across the Pacific with neither job nor money. While traveling, I didn't stay in swank hotels but rented mosquito-infested, cinder block rooms for a few dollars a night. I often stayed in slums so that I could stay longer. And to be honest, I was scared witless on more occasions than I care to remember.

But I was lucky, for I managed to see much of the world before I returned to America. I witnessed birth and beauty, misery and death. I realized that the world we live in isn't defined by a collection of countries at odds with one another, but by the striking commonalities of the individuals who compose those countries.

While traveling, I was constantly reminded of my blessings. Seeing homeless children asleep on soiled streets has a way of doing that—so do sights of beggars and leprosy and shanties.

I've experienced the good fortune to have my book, Beneath a Marble Sky, *published, and I'd like to share this blessing. Hence, I will donate a portion of what I earn through the sale of the book you hold in your hands to a fantastic organization called CISV (Children's International*

Summer Villages), which promotes cross-cultural understanding in children, youths and adults from around the world.

Speaking of support, I'd like to thank you for reading Beneath a Marble Sky. *I realize thousands of books are available, and I am indebted to you for taking the time to read mine. I sincerely appreciate the encouragement you've given me and hope* Beneath a Marble Sky *provided you with a pleasant escape from your computer, your house projects, your long layover at a crowded airport, or whatever other demands life might place on you.*

I'd like to further express my thanks to you for your support, and perhaps I can. As someone who grew up reading everything I could get my eyes on, I always found myself wishing I could talk to authors about elements of their books. Of course I never could, but I promised myself that someday, if a novel of mine was published, I'd make myself available to readers as best as I could. In short, I'd try to give readers the experience I had wanted but never enjoyed.

So, if you have a book club that plans on reading my novel, please let me know. I'd be delighted to call your group, and over a speakerphone, we can chat about Beneath a Marble Sky. *I'd like to hear what the members of your group think about it—such feedback is quite enjoyable to me. If you're not in a book club, but would just like to drop me a line, please do so. Either way, I can be reached via e-mail at shors@aol.com.*

I truly wish you the best in all of your endeavors.

Sincerely,

John Shors

Beneath a Marble Sky

JOHN SHORS

A CONVERSATION WITH
JOHN SHORS

Q. *What inspired you to write* Beneath a Marble Sky*?*

A. I've been lucky enough to spend a great deal of time in Asia and have been powerfully influenced by its history, as well as the sights, sounds, smells, and customs found today in that part of the world. For a decade I've wanted to write a novel set somewhere in Asia but waited to find the right story—or rather to have the right story find me.

In 1999, my wife and I were traveling in India and of course made it a point to visit the Taj Mahal. We arrived at the mausoleum as soon as it opened to the public and were the first people there that day. Walking within its chambers, hearing our voices echo in the same manner as voices did hundreds of years ago, and touching its sculpted walls was an overwhelming experience. Seeing the wonder of the Taj Mahal, and understanding that a man built it for his wife—a woman he cherished above all else in life—was uniquely inspiring. Indian poets have been writing about this love story for centuries. And yet not many people in the West know the tale. I realized that I had to tell it. Quite honestly, I was amazed and delighted to discover upon my return to America that no one in the West had ever fictionalized the story.

I should add that my youngest brother, Luke, who had been studying in India for some time, told me long ago that the story behind the Taj Mahal would make for a poignant novel. Luke brims with great ideas, and I'm glad that he let me run with this particular one.

Q. *What impressed you most about the Taj Mahal?*

A. People always think about the Taj Mahal from a macro level. That is, they envision it from afar and are moved by the image that arises. And while the Taj Mahal is certainly one of the world's most striking buildings from a distance, it is equally as remarkable up close. Most impressive is that millions of semiprecious stones adorn its walls. Lapis, jade, quartz, amber, emeralds, and onyx are set into the white marble in ways that defy reason. Marvelously detailed arrangements of these polished and shaped stones form garlands of flowers, timeless and impossibly exquisite. Such flowers are as beautiful as any that grace a garden, and they have thrived on the Taj Mahal for three and a half centuries.

Q. *What was the hardest thing about writing* Beneath a Marble Sky?

A. Let's just say that writing in the first person as a seventeenth-century Hindustani woman wasn't completely natural to me. Additionally, not only did I need to write convincingly as a woman from another place and another time, but I had to re-create the way in which Hindustanis spoke in general. Upon reading memoirs from that time, I quickly realized that the manner in which people spoke was much more formal than how people converse today. I wanted to capture some of this formality without getting carried away.

So a great deal of work went into Jahanara's voice, as well as the other voices within *Beneath a Marble Sky*. I edited my novel fifty-six times. This number did not always sit well with my wife, as I was forever editing at night or during a much needed vacation! However, I think that all of these edits allowed me to create consistent, unique voices within my novel.

Q. *How were you able to so effectively research your novel?*

A. I spent about a year researching *Beneath a Marble Sky*. A fair amount of this work revolved around reading religious texts, memoirs, and historical accounts of seventeenth-century Hindustan. Surprisingly, the written word was not my greatest aid in terms of research material. Instead, hundreds and hundreds of period paintings provided me with a rich sense of the time and place that my novel is set in. Mughal paintings are exquisite and offered glimpses of life within the harem, of how battles unfolded, of how people ate and celebrated and loved. I could not have written *Beneath a Marble Sky* without such visual aids.

Q. *Whom did you model your characters after?*

A. When possible, I based the characters in my novel on what is known about the people who were responsible for the creation of the Taj Mahal. Much of *Beneath a Marble Sky* is steeped in truth. Of course, elements of fiction also are present in my novel. I created several of the ancillary characters and took liberties with members of the royal family. At the core, though, the royal family was much as I depict: headed by a couple very much in love and sent toward destruction by a son bent on increasing his power.

Q. *What do you like most about writing?*

A. I'll be honest—most of the time writing is without question extremely hard work. Having said that, moments of clarity exist that are profoundly enjoyable. For me, during such moments, characters seem to speak of their own accord, and scenes unfold as if I've already lived them. When I am in such a groove, I type as fast as I can, not caring if words are spelled properly or if everything makes perfect sense. As I type, the outside world simply disappears. I don't think about what might be happening over the weekend or bills that need to be paid or house projects with my name on them. I'm simply consumed with writing as much as possible during this rare moment of clarity. What's best about these moments is that as I write I experience a remarkable sense of contentedness—likely because I know that I am creating something that most people will find enjoyable. When reality inevitably chases me away from the computer, I always depart with great regret.

Q. *Why did you decide to write within the historical fiction genre?*

A. I have always loved reading novels that both were page-turners and taught me something of the world. To me, novels set within an interesting era have provided escapes into new realms that I have always departed feeling a bit richer from the experience. Additionally, having encountered the wonder of the Taj Mahal made me want to share this experience with as many people as possible. *Beneath a Marble Sky* is my attempt at doing so.

Q. *Is there anything that you would like to share with your readers?*

A. I am grateful for their support, and I look forward to creating other novels that they may enjoy.

QUESTIONS
FOR DISCUSSION

1. The working title for the book was *Souls in Stone*. John Shors only thought of the name *Beneath a Marble Sky* after his novel was finished. Which title do you prefer and why?

2. Why do you think that John Shors chose Jahanara to tell his story? Was she the right character to narrate *Beneath a Marble Sky*?

3. Did you like the scenes on the river with Jahanara and her granddaughters, or would the book have been complete without them?

4. Jahanara's character is greatly influenced by her need to please her parents. Are such needs any less important today, especially as family members age and are increasingly drawn apart by geography?

5. If you were Jahanara, would you have let the cobra kill Aurangzeb? Did you like Jahanara more or less because of this decision?

6. Isa and Nizam both experienced tragedies at a young age. Are their positive dispositions believable? Which character did you enjoy most?

7. Did John Shors mishandle any emotions that a female author might have conveyed better? If not, why do you suspect that he was able to so effectively write from a woman's point of view?

8. What is the most memorable scene in the novel?

9. Did the book provide you with any insight into Islam that might offer you answers regarding issues at hand today?

10. What was the most important message that you gained from *Beneath a Marble Sky*? How is that message relevant to your own journey?

11. Is *Beneath a Marble Sky* a novel that will stand out in your mind for some time to come?

12. Is historical fiction a genre that greatly appeals to you?

John Shors traveled extensively throughout Asia after graduating from Colorado College in 1991, living for several years in Japan, where he taught English, and then trekking across the continent, visiting ten countries and climbing the Himalayas. More recently, Mr. Shors worked as a newspaper reporter in his hometown, Des Moines, Iowa, before entering public relations and moving to Boulder, Colorado. *Beneath a Marble Sky* is his first novel.